Previous Titles in the Desert Sailors Series

Note from the author: These books should be read sequentially from the beginning as main characters are not reintroduced.

Desert Sailors
Azure Tiger
Grecian Vendetta
Sea Duty

Non-fiction books by this author

Israel Basics: What Every Christian Should Know
Israel II: Beyond the Basics
Israel III: Finding Ancient Israel Among the Modern Nations

Praying for the Nations: A Guide for Short-term Missionaries

Desert Sailors Series
Book 5

Baghdad
Green Zone

by K. J. Frolander

Baghdad Green Zone
Copyright © 2018 by K. J. Frolander

All rights reserved. 3rd Printing May 2020. No part of this book may be reproduced or transmitted in any form or by any means without written permission from the author. Contact at Frolander.permissions@gmail.com

Cover art designed by Janis Teller. Contact at Chelsea2583@hotmail.com

Author photo by Melissa Wilson
Cover photos purchased at Shutterstock.com

ISBN 978-0-9977245-5-4

Dedication

With special thanks to my beta readers, Sue Frolander and Gia Downs who challenge me to better stories. Also, to fans of Rivers and Wakefield who keep asking "when's the next one coming out?" I hope this hefty sized book will hold you over for a little while.

Chapter One

Dust plumes. A dirt runway. A pile of crates. One lonely mail COD, parked haphazardly. A single Humvee also covered in dust and the tracks of at least three others were easily identifiable. Lieutenant Commander Judah Wakefield hung onto the doorway of her ride as she surveyed the landscape from the helo.

It was so much greener than she had expected, despite the dust that covered everything. About five clicks north, a city crowned with smoke pushed against the horizon. It was large. Much larger than she had pictured, even though she knew the population statistics by heart. Closer in her view, a bombed-out, and hopefully deserted, village of about a dozen-and-a-half stone buildings with foundations in an orderly double stripe about 600 yards away. The foundations were the only orderly part of the former village main street. Whether from neglect, general aging or a bomb that missed Baghdad proper, she couldn't tell from this distance.

"Commander?" A hesitant voice sounded behind her. "The pilot says he needs to turn around immediately because there is no gas station established here yet."

Since no one was on the ground to meet them, Wakefield tossed her seabag to the dirt and slid the rucksack from her shoulder, tossing it down as well. Then she squatted and hopped down the four feet from the open doorway to the ground, landing fairly flatfooted, but keeping her balance. The transition from ship to shore was jarring all around even with a quick stopover.

She slung her weapon around to rest on her back and after dragging her bags out of the way, she reached up and grabbed Lieutenant Marks' seabag as he took in his new environs. His face expressed the same surprise she felt. Marks and another man had boarded the plane with her on the ground in Germany. She had flown into Germany with retiring Captain MacSod at sunrise from the aircraft carrier USS *Theodore Roosevelt* which should now be making its way through the Strait of Hormuz without any further trouble to join the rest of the ships in the Carrier Strike Group, making way into the Persian Gulf, as safe and sound as a U.S. Navy battle group could be off the coast of Iraq and fairly near Iran.

LCDR Wakefield hadn't talked much on the five-hour flight. She tried to catch some shut eye after staying up way too late doing laundry and packing her life up for the transfer. She didn't even get to say goodbye to her roommate. But Navy life was like that sometimes.

Marks was a pinch-faced young lieutenant from Kentucky, and he reached back to hand down the bags of Barrow, a well-spoken petty officer first class from Utah who completed their trio.

Wakefield shrugged as she took a last empty glance around, rested her hand on the butt of the plain M-16 slung on a nylon military-black strap across her body, and the three walked toward the pile of crates as the COD engines spooled up for takeoff. One of the pilots slammed the door shut from the inside, but none of the trio even glanced back. Marks took right, Barrow took the left and Wakefield took middle and fell behind a few steps as if they had been a team for months instead of minutes.

The pallet-sized square crates were stamped PROPERTY OF THE U.S. ARMY in black ink. Wakefield frowned. That sign of ownership seemed positive, but where was everyone?

It was eerily quiet as the thrum of the COD's engines dissipated.

"Where is everyone, ma'am?" asked Marks.

She didn't answer right away, her eyes on the horizon. It was difficult to see anything from ground level. Even just four feet off the ground from the plane doorway afforded a better angle.

A sneeze sounded from behind the crates when they were about 10 yards off. Wakefield had never seen two people move their weapons to ready as fast as Marks and Barrow did at that moment. "Ahoy, Navy!" came a somewhat muffled voice. Wakefield recognized the sound, but she could not quite place it.

A thin arm waved over the crates from behind. It disappeared just as suddenly. A huge sneeze exploded behind the pile of crates. After the honk of a blowing nose, a head appeared. In the angle of the late afternoon sun it was only a black silhouette. "Welcome to Baghdad." The young man stiffened to attention and saluted the incoming party. The poor man's voice was raw and his sinuses were obviously full, but she could still distinguish a strong New Jersey accent that no one would purposefully imitate in a deception.

9

Wakefield relaxed her stance, and the other two followed her example. "Thanks. I think," she said as she popped off a stiff hand to her eyebrow so the private could relax his stance.

The three made their way around behind the crate pile, which was larger than she had first assessed. There were at least twenty crates and half of them were labeled WATER. She smiled gratefully in remembrance of the last time she had been dropped in the middle of a desert and they ran out of water reserves.

"Got a bit of a cold?" she asked.

"I don't think so, ma'am." The soldier's eyes were red-rimmed and peeked out, creamy tear tracks and all, above a black handkerchief he had knotted over his mouth and nose cowboy style. "Private First Class (PFC) Tom Bailey," he said. "I'm allergic to dust."

Marks let out a little chuckle. Wakefield wasn't sure if it was relief after the strain or at the soldier's expense. Maybe a little of both.

"Are you here on your own, PFC?" PO2 Barrow asked.

"Just for now. The Seabees are taking advantage of the break in afternoon bombardment to scout the area for fence building, and another group of them are seeing about the route into Baghdad." His nasal accent was even more pronounced just before Bailey broke into another pair of sneezes.

Wakefield smiled. He had not even bothered to cover his mouth he had been sneezing so often; he just kind of bowed his head and let it come.

Barrow offered to get their bags and add them to the heap while Wakefield looked around.

"Who is in charge out here?" she asked Bailey. She couldn't tear her eyes off the city in the distance. The smoke plumed over it like incense. The various colors of smoke showed fire consuming multiple things. The gasoline smoke she recognized easily. "What are those threads of super black smoke?" She pointed and broke her gaze back to Bailey with his tear-streaked upper cheek and his black nose guard that was doing exactly zero good.

"That's the tires, ma'am. They burn them day and night, and when you get in closer it stinks to high heaven."

"How long have you been out here?"

"Just a couple of days. And Admiral Graham is in charge, ma'am."

Wakefield closed one eye and tilted her head as she looked at the young soldier. "Yes, I know Graham is running the war. But who is on the ground at the FOB (forward operating base) here?"

"Oh. That would be Navy Chief Petty Officer Smitherman under orders from Army Major General Blount. The army Third Infantry Division is on its way, but until they get here, the Navy Seabees are in charge. And Chief S told me to watch for the brass. I mean other than you, ma'am. It is a bit of a turf war until then." Bailey sneezed again in his loud yet understated way. "Commander Grady should be here sometime tonight. He'll lead—"

"Commander Brady Grady?" Wakefield smirked.

Bailey shook his head slowly and his eyes rolled to the right as he studied the sky in thought and wiped at his leaking eyes again. "I don't think I know, ma'am."

Judah chuckled softly at the memory of Grady. "If it is him, this party is about to get a whole lot more fun. We went through OCS (Officer's Candidacy School) together." She nodded once. The only time she had been in serious trouble, besides the events of the last year and a half, was when she had gotten swept up in one of Brady Grady's practical jokes. She could feel her lips tighten to suppress the mirth of those 8-year-old memories. The chairs, the pool, all those tiles, and the effigy…oh and the look on their faces when the instructors showed up at sunrise for PT that day!

"What is it, ma'am?" Bailey's eyes looked like he was laughing at her trying not to laugh.

"Let's just say, fourteen days of extra duty pressure washing the entire base's teaching and administrative buildings was worth it."

"That must have been something." PO2 Barrow chimed in from behind her as he unloaded the two desert camouflage sea bags and rucksacks.

Wakefield turned, still smiling widely at the thought, "It was, Barrow. It was."

Marks kept his bags on his shoulders standing next to Barrow. He gestured with a strong jaw toward the cluster of buildings. "Did we do that?"

Bailey shrugged. "It was like that when we arrived, sir. It looks like it has been there a while, maybe months, but I can't really tell."

"Hmm." Marks pursed his lips. "When will the bombing runs start back up?"

"Any time, sir. Maybe five minutes, maybe an hour."

"Let's go check it out." Wakefield saw Marks eye her for reaction.

Bailey swiped at his eyes again. "It's all clear, ma'am, sir." He shrugged. "The mess tent is set up on the other side. The Seabees wanted to provide a little shelter from the airplane noise and wind. Chow line starts at 1730."

"The mess tent is already in place?" Wakefield felt her jaw slacken. "God bless the Seabees and their stomach priorities.

Thanks, Bailey. Let's head over." She picked up her bags and marched in the direction he had gestured. She could hear the other two follow her as she studied the ground in the golden light. As many regions as she had served in or visited, this was her first time in Iraq. The ground between the rivers Tigris and Euphrates was green. *Almost marshy in this area*, she re-assessed as she felt her boots push into the soft earth. She had always pictured Iraq as grey-brown and rocky like Afghanistan. But it really was part of the Fertile Crescent. However, all the bombing runs on the city's concrete and stone buildings of the last week, had filled the air with dust, soot and smoke.

As they came around the west side of the little bombed-out village, a mini-town of U.S. Army tents was revealed. Infrastructure was already in place for a main boulevard and side "streets." In the center of the FOB music from the 1970s was streaming out of the largest tent which appeared to even have a front porch of sorts, with limited outdoor seating.

The village they were passing by actually consisted of more than a dozen smaller homes, some still standing, though obviously deserted and dark.

"Why do I feel like we just walked into an empty set on *MASH*?" LT Marks asked.

A man stepped out of the shadows in front of them. His feet were planted in a wide stop-here stance, and he carried an Uzi rather than the regular M-16. Wakefield recognized that his rifle sat at a purposefully relaxed angle across his body. Both of his hands rested on his weapon with deceptive calm, one hand halfway between the stock and the trigger and the other curled around the barrel grip. He would not need a moment's notice to complete a shot. "I don't know, Lieutenant, because it is not empty," the blank-faced guard said.

13

The three of them stopped in their tracks. Wakefield had not heard even a breath of movement, but when the guard materialized in front of them, Wakefield instinctively reached for her weapon. After her heart recovered from the missed beat, it jumped to double time.

"I.D." he required of them. They each held up plastic encased military photo ID. He nodded them past his post, but gestured with his forehead to their battle helmets, each dangling off their ruck sacks. "You'll want to cover up. It'll be starting back up shortly."

Wakefield nodded and took a single step toward the tent-city before she felt the ground groan, and the sound of the evening bombing run followed less than a second later. Instead of waiting until they arrived at the mess hall, she dropped her bag, unfastened her helmet's strap from her bag and tightened the strap under her chin.

"Good call." She nodded to the guard and continued toward the sound of the music. The men followed her silently.

As they walked under the awning on the mess tent, Marks asked, "What's with the Uzi, do you think?"

"Israel must be here someplace too." Barrow remarked.

"That's quick. Really quick." Wakefield tossed her bag down again with some other things stacked around the edges of the "front porch" of the mess tent. "Britain should be here pretty soon too, but I suppose Israel lives pretty close." She shrugged.

"We sure do," came a female reply in Hebrew-accented English from the doorway, just feet from the trio. "I suppose it makes us want to keep a close eye on things over here." A young, dark short-curly haired beauty cocked a single thin eyebrow as she coolly assessed them from the mess tent doorway.

14

Chapter Two

Homer Asheed, fourteen-year veteran as Hussein's Chief Chemical Engineer in Iraq, pushed firmly on his knees to keep them from quaking under the table as King Hussein read what he had privately dubbed the "kill report."

He had never even heard of a weaponized chemical this deadly in his lifetime. But the reports didn't lie. Humanity kept finding more and more horrible ways to hurt one another. The quick time of expiration was the only mercy in this new chemical combination they had duplicated from one Arafeh Filasek, rumored to be the illegitimate offspring of bin Laden himself.

Asheed prayed to Allah every time he bowed his face that the Americans would find and destroy every last gram of this potent killer, before the king ordered Captain Mafias to send the atomized version into the rumored encampments being raised around the city. Still, Asheed had already sent his teenage children to Syria to visit their "aunt" before the final testing

15

phase had begun. His wife had a seat on a flight in the morning to "go get them and escort them home." Or so they had told the visa office upon applying for emergency papers to get seats on the over-full flights out of the country. He was still working on his own escape.

"This is very good!" Hussein dabbed his moustache with a white linen napkin, identical to the one absorbing the sweat from Asheed's palms under the tablecloth. "How did the three-percent failure rate among the northern Kurds manage to survive?"

Asheed felt like a bug being mounted on a science project board as Hussein's stare pierced him. Scientifically, Asheed knew the king could not read his thoughts, but he still did not allow his mind to criticize anything about the Hussein family while in their presence. *I've seen too many murders...oops, too many cleansings, in my tenure with this family.*

"Since I was not on the ground for the...test, I cannot be certain, your majesty." Homer Asheed lowered his gaze to the table, not just because palace protocol insisted, but because fear demanded it. "I would venture a guess that the survivors must have noticed what was happening to the people around them and happened to have gas masks ready to be used with them in the market where it was released."

"Not people. Rats!" Hussein's face tightened into a hate mask.

Asheed tried to swallow; it was impossible. He just nodded three times in quick succession.

He started shaking uncontrollably then. Several concussions sounded and they were getting closer. A young guard that Asheed recognized from the doorway to the dining room ran in. "The bombings have begun again!" He screeched.

16

"Everyone to the shelter." Captain Mafias rose first in response. By the elbow, Asheed was hustled out an opening behind a larger-than-life-sized painting of Saddam in the dining room wall, along with the other diners.

Twists and turns and several steep stairwells down later, the five men were brought into a large room, reinforced with thick pillars in a center square.

Opulent did not even begin to describe it. Thick drapes hung on the walls, fresh flowers decorated the pillars, and Persian rugs in deep reds, purples, and browns softened the floor. Gaming tables occupied the left side of the room while theater seating and a massive screen took up the right-hand wall. A dozen seating areas, both tables and chairs and floor cushion areas, complete with servers walking around with trays of drinks, took up the middle section around the pillars.

All Asheed could do was stare. His wife would be hunkered down in the lower floor of their home with an old bike helmet on her head now that their kids didn't need it, while he observed the party of royalty in their bomb shelter.

Qusay Hussein cuffed him on the shoulder, and Asheed stumbled forward a step. "Grab a drink, get to know some of the ladies." The crown prince reached with meaty hands for tall glasses being brought over. He pushed one into Asheed hands, which Asheed knew the man would notice were still trembling. Qusay had a keen eye for fear in others. To exploit it whenever possible. The liquid sloshed over the rim a bit, dampening Asheed's fingers. Qusay took the first gulp of his own drink through the little triangle between the lip of the glass and the fleshy part between his thumb and forefinger where he gripped the glass at the rim.

Asheed, rooted in place, gripped in one hand the report he had picked up from the table where the king dropped it and the slipping, quivering drink in the other. The elder and younger Hussein, along with Captain Mafais hustled away to a room just off the gaming tables side of the shelter.

Asheed noticed flashing boards of lights and dozens of CCTV monitors in the darkened space before the door was closed.

Forward Operating Base—Baghdad Outskirts
Monday, 23 March 2003
1735 hours

The young woman was dressed in olive green from head to mid-calf where clompy dull-black boots took over. Judah got the impression she could have as easily been minding kids on a playground as physically subduing someone. A deep confidence exuded from her being. But it was more than that. Wakefield looked her up and down trying to figure out what was off.

"Israeli Defense Force *Seren* Elisheva Dayan. *Seren* translates to captain, but the rank is about the same as your full commander." The woman held out her hand to Judah who grasped it, but was speechless for a moment. She was so young for her rank. "You sound like you've given that little speech before," Wakefield finally said.

"A few times." Her English was perfect with just a hint of the guttural Hebrew sounds in the Cs and Rs.

"Lieutenant Commander Judah Wakefield." She nodded and let go of the young woman's hand.

"Judah? Really? That's a man's name in its original Hebrew: *Yehudah*." The woman's face was a mask and Wakefield felt like she was being prodded a tiny bit.

"Well, it's a man's world we are part of over here." Wakefield responded. She stepped closer to the soldier, but the woman didn't move. "May we come in?"

"Of course."

The woman still didn't move. It was certainly a challenge now, but Judah wasn't sure why or over what, so she went with the most unexpected response she could think of. Wakefield turned her shoulder slightly and threaded her arm through the young woman elbow as if they were elementary school chums and said, "What's for dinner? You should come and eat with us, *Seren* Dayan."

When Elishava Dayan laughed it sounded like an alto opera singer crooning. "You can call me Ellie," she said, and Wakefield knew that whatever gauntlet had been thrown down was now back in Ellie's pocket.

Marks and Barrow skirted the women and were already picking up a hot meal to join the 15 or so other men scattered among four long tables on the far side of the tent.

As Ellie and Judah sat down in folding chairs, men began streaming through the flap of the tent door. They stopped at an open-pipe hand-washing station set up a few feet inside the doorway, washed up, shook dry, and lined up for chow. It was definitely a dirty-shirt dining room tonight. Several of the Seabees looked as though they had been digging ditches, or was it sewers?

While the din rose, the tent's thick canvas walls did little to absorb the chatter of the young soldiers. Wakefield observed their company as Ellie explained Israel's presence and numbers in Iraq on the joint task force. Judah was noticing how young the average age of the Seabees actually was. She heard a group of them arguing about the finer points of something she deduced to be a video game she'd never heard of, as she also heard Ellie saying that her mother's side of the family used to live in Baghdad before 1949 when they joined over 120,000 Jews who had lived in the region of former-Babylon since the days of Daniel and Esther. Wakefield was nodding before she realized the information she was absorbing.

"Wait, what?" Judah cut her eyes back to Ellie's dark brown ones. The Israeli's fork paused halfway to her mouth, and overly re-constituted mashed sweet potato splatted back onto her plate. The young soldier's thin right eyebrow arched high, while the other lowered in an obvious question. "With a name such as Judah, you must be Christian or Jewish, no? You know Daniel and Esther, yes?"

"Well, yes, Christian." Judah gestured with her fork in a forward circle as she chewed, "But the Jews were released back from Persia to Israel after 70 years. Nehemiah rebuilding the wall and all."

"Yes, of course. A whole 10% of the Jews of that day returned to the Promised Land and carried on life as recorded in the Tenakh, your Old Testament, and then into the New Covenant. But 90% of the Jews of the diaspora decided to remain in place. And so they did, for about 2800 years. If there is anything left of the old neighborhood, I hope to see it while we are here."

"Ninety percent?" Judah was processing aloud, a rarity for her as a profiler and interrogator for Naval Intelligence. "That's huge! How did I not know this? Why didn't they go back?"

"Pardon me, ladies." A deep voice cut through the noise over their table. "I was hoping to sit at the adults' table."

Wakefield looked up to see a hefty major with purple-ringed eyes whose uniform might never see clean again. He held a tray with both hands about waist high. The tiny carton of chocolate milk on the tray looked like kindergarten on a professional boxer.

"Of course, Major. Sit down before you fall down." Wakefield patted the table next to her.

He sighed as he slid the tray onto the table and dropped heavily into the folding chair on Wakefield's right.

He just sat for a moment staring into space, his eyes at half-mast. "Fulton?" Wakefield read his name from his uniform. She looked at Ellie who just shrugged and she tried again. "Major Fulton?"

"Ma'am?" He finally responded, though still didn't actually turn his head.

"The peas need salt." Wakefield replied and slid the pair of salt and pepper shakers to him. "How long have you been on duty?" Judah asked. A third, much-slighter shaking of the ground indicated that another jet had dropped its payload at least 7-8 kilometers away, or maybe the bombings were just easier to take when sitting down over dinner.

"Um, since yesterday morning. I think." The officer began shoveling food into his mouth between each sentence. "Maybe the day before. I'm not sure what day it is, ma'am. We've had some food breaks, but I just can't sleep. You know?" He did finally turn his head. "We've been clearing the camp area and road into Baghdad of IEDs and mines. Have to be ready for the troops to come in."

Wakefield nodded, but before she could even get a word in, Fulton began again.

"Hey, what's the U.S. Navy and the IDF doing cavorting around here in Army country anyway?" Apparently the chicken, sweet potatoes, and English peas had hit the officer's blood stream. He was waking up.

Wakefield chuckled out loud.

"Are you the only non-Seabee Navy person here?" He shoveled in another enormous bite. Somehow it didn't seem impolite. He seemed to swallow the bite whole, so he never missed a beat and never spoke with his mouth full. Wakefield stared; she'd never seen anything quite like it. "I'm supposed to check in with a Navy guy in intelligence to get some direction for the interrogation space we cleared out yesterday. I think it was yesterday. I've got his name written down here somewhere." He patted his pockets.

"There are a couple of us that came in on the COD an hour or so ago. I'm Lieutenant Commander Wakefield, Naval Intel. Does that ring any bells?"

"Oops. Yes, ma'am. I'm not used to having women out here in the combat zone. No offense. You look like you could handle yourself." The major's dark eyes cut over to Ellie. "And she certainly does. Of course I'm sure the uniform insignia adds to that idea." Fulton smiled disarmingly wide. "I've nothing but respect for the IDF, ma'am. My wife and I toured Israel back in '95 when I was stationed in Turkey. Changed our lives for good."

"Glad to hear it." Ellie smiled widely. Wakefield guessed that in her line of work, she didn't hear appreciation very often. At least not from outsiders. "There are about two dozen of us who will be on the ground by tomorrow evening serving in various specialties."

Fulton poured some chocolate milk on top of his cherry cobbler, brought the dessert dish to his chin, and spooned the whole bowlful into his mouth in three large scoops. "Sorry, ma'am. Did that gross you out?"

Fulton had caught her staring. "Not at all." Judah licked her lips. "I imagine it tasted a bit like chocolate covered cherries."

Fulton gave several tiny nods while wiping his mouth with a paper napkin. "So, ma'am, can I get you to inspect the interrogation center, so you can let me know what other specs might be of help to get you guys up and running?"

"You think this is the calm before the storm too, Major?" Wakefield asked.

"I don't think. I know. The current bombing runs are only every 10 minutes or so. Full-on bombing sorties start at 9 o'clock sharp. The leaflets and cell phone robo-calls are on-going between 6 and 9 PM." Fulton nodded toward Ellie. "That was her idea."

"Well, not mine originally." Ellie tilted her head to shrug off the praise. "I just suggested we try it here."

"What are leaflets and robo-calls?" Wakefield asked.

"You know like in World War Two when the allies dropped papers warning civilians to stay in their homes away from congested areas or military areas and such?" Fulton asked, and Judah nodded, remembering something like that from a war class she had taken as part of OCS.

Ellie explained further when Fulton left the conversation hanging. "We have had some success in the Palestinian Territories with warning the civilian populations to minimize casualties. We just recently started calling people's mobile phones with warnings too. It seems to be working. As long as people are not held hostage in the areas we have promised to bomb. You know we do our best to gather real-time data on civilian activity before taking out a target. I've heard about a few times we have

23

had to abort a mission on a strategic target because children have been brought into the house where a high-value target was staying." Ellie shrugged. "So sometimes it works for us, other times, it works against us."

"So that's what we are doing in Baghdad?" Wakefield looked back and forth between Fulton and Ellie. "Warning our targets when and where we will bomb."

Both of them nodded.

"And this is working?" Wakefield shook her head.

"As far as we can tell." Ellie said. "But I've only been here about 36 hours. The intel we are processing and the newscasts from imbedded journalists are as favorable as I've ever seen during wartime." Ellie cleared her throat and threw in a hint of sarcasm. "But I *am* from Israel, so..." her voice trailed off.

Fulton shook his head.

Wakefield didn't know how to respond to that, so she asked Fulton, "Which building do you want me to inspect?"

"It is the second on the right from here. It is the two story across from another two story."

"I'll go with you." Ellie said. "I'll be working with translation in interrogation of insurgents. Won't hurt to see what we have to work with."

Wakefield started putting her used napkins on the tray. "I won't have final authority on this, MAJ Fulton. But I seem to be the highest-ranking officer in the department here so far. So I'll get you started."

"Fair enough, ma'am. Thanks. I'll be up in a few minutes."

Wakefield rose, hooked her weapon over her shoulder like a long purse that grazed her knee, and walked her tray over to the washing up area where she left it.

"Do you still want to know why my people did not return to Jerusalem and the Promised Land?" Ellie asked as she cleared her dinner tray too. The roar of conversation still pulsated in the tent, so Judah just nodded.

Ellie didn't reply right away, which of course peaked Judah interest. She combed through every Sunday School lesson she had ever heard or taught to see if she could figure it out on her own. *I profile people for a living, surely I can understand why 90% of an oppressed population group would not return to their homeland of freedom.*

As the tent flap closed behind them, the din lifted and Judah's ears felt like they were actually expanding in peace as the quiet of the night opened in front of them. The sun had set while they ate.

Ellie pointed toward the silhouette of the building that MAJ Fulton had described and they slowly walked toward it. Judah left her bags at the mess tent area to pick up later.

"Like any good Jew I'll answer a question with a question." Ellie adjusted her Uzi to flatten a wrinkle that had bunched on her belly as they sat at dinner. Wakefield smirked at the self-depreciating humor. It didn't feel depreciating at all, merely observant about one's own culture. And that was good humor.

"If your family was offered a free pass today to return to Finland after three generations would you go?" Ellie asked.

Wakefield smiled for real this time. "Probably not." Everything clicked into clear sense. "First, my family is from Sweden, and second, we have been in America for four generations. We are Americans, but your point is well made and taken. I suppose the Jews in Babylon didn't return for the same reason. They had adjusted to their new culture and felt like they were Babylonian by then."

Ellie nodded. "They had homes, families, businesses or trades, and after the business with Haman and Esther many of them had accumulated wealth and knew who their friends were." She shrugged. "They had grown up assimilated—well, as well as Jews can assimilate—and Hebrew was a second or even third language rather than their primary language for most of them, so they felt no tug to go home even though God had invited them back."

The two of them walked along the beginnings of a path from the mess tent to the concrete-and-mud former village with the stars clearly shining above the forward operating basecamp, but the glow of the city reflected off the smoke hovering over multiple smoldering Baghdad fires.

"I wonder what would have happened if they had followed God's plan and invitation to return." Judah mumbled aloud.

She heard a stifled noise come from Ellie's throat and she looked over. A sadness reflected in eyes that seemed too damp. "My people have such trouble being obedient to the Covenant. I pray every day that I am in the right place in the right time to follow my God."

Wakefield looked over at her new friend. It seemed such a strong reaction to a simple musing.

"Another question to answer a question?" Ellie asked.

Judah nodded as they stepped up to the guard Judah had passed earlier, and showed him their IDs. They were let past into the semblance of what used to be a village road with buildings that used to face one another. "It's that closer two-story, right?" Judah checked her memory and Ellie pointed to the building that Wakefield had been headed toward already.

"What did the Jews who stayed behind miss out on when we stayed in Babylon?"

"Well, I suppose the whole history of Israel could have been different." Wakefield began to see the implications of having 90 percent more Jews living and fighting in the land when Rome had forced their way in. "Perhaps the Romans would not have been able to conquer Israel if the Jews had presented a more formidable force."

"Well, it was the Greeks, before the Hasmoneans, and *then* the Romans, but yes, any or all of those could have been different outcomes, but it is not the bigger picture I was getting at." Ellie prompted.

Bigger than the dynasties and empire that ruled the known world? Wakefield lifted her eyes up and again compared the smoky night sky over the city to the clear night sky directly above them as she looked for answers. Another wonder flited across her mind, *is this what the sky looked like to Abraham when God promised the old barren man descendants as numerous as the stars and the sand.* There was an ancientness to this land in which she currently plodded that she could feel, yet couldn't quite understand. She could feel God working and rearranging furniture in her heart even in this conversation with Ellie. *Everything was in order just fine*, she thought. *Until now.* And God started moving things.

"What my people missed through disobedience," Ellie started. Her voice, so melodic when laughing, hit depths of grief Judah didn't know a female voice was capable of carrying, "is our Messiah. When Yeshua was revealed in Jerusalem, in Galilee, and in Judea and Samaria most of my people never got to meet Him, to make up their own minds about Him. They only heard what the leading rabbis and other unbelieving leaders had to say about Him. Opinions that were darkly colored by those leaders' own political yearnings for power. My people, my family, who stayed behind in Babylon were in the wrong place at the wrong time."

27

Judah was silent. She didn't know what to say. The pair of them stood in the doorway of the dark interrogation center without entering. The military officer part of Wakefield was aware enough to realize that her wits were not as about her as they needed to be to enter the building, which was probably cleared, but they were in a war zone after all and she needed full concentration. While the person part of Judah was processing this new information on so many levels at once. Her spirit was grieved and a sadness enveloped her as she realized that millions and millions of people for whom Jesus died had rejected Him without having met Him for themselves, the Gospel would have gone out farther and faster.

Or would it?

Was it God's plan all along to have His chosen people still distributed among the nations so that the Gospel could go to the Gentiles? What was that scripture about the eyes being blinded until the time of the Gentiles was full? *What does that even mean in light of this new knowledge? Ninety percent. That is huge.* A flash of offense rose up in her heart. It was so unfair that so many people missed Jesus just because they made the choice to stay. *Only 10 percent of the Jews*—Judah arrested her thoughts and flagged where to pick back up later as she saw Ellie staring off over her shoulder.

Wakefield followed her gaze and saw nothing but a concrete wall with bullet-sized chunks torn out of it at heart height. "What is it?" Wakefield asked.

"What is what? I'm just waiting for you."

Judah felt a blush creep up her neck. "Oh." She turned her body toward the entrance and pulled her flashlight out. "How long was I in thought?" she asked a bit sheepishly.

"About seven to ten seconds maybe. Not too long."

"So you're a believer?"

Ellie's tinkling laugh had returned. "We are all believers. Even most of the atheists in Israel are believers. But I believe Israel's Messiah has already come, in the person of Yeshua, yes."

Before Wakefield could respond, the low growl of distant engines grew louder and louder.

"The sorties have begun." Ellie said. "I hope you were not planning on any sleep. Sources tell me the campaign is to begin in earnest tonight. The infrastructure is to come down over the next couple of days even as the troops are being deployed to this base camp and the other camps."

Wakefield scanned back and forth in the heavens and could see nothing but stars and dust even though she could hear untold numbers of aircraft. She tore her eyes from the sky to look at Ellie in her oddly fitting uniform. "How is it you know so much?"

Ellie was already heading into the two-story structure with her mag-light shining on low beam when the first lightning flashes reflected off the cloud over Baghdad. Then dozens more.

For the briefest of moments Wakefield thought it was a summer lightning storm building strength on the horizon. The percussion and ground trembles followed. There was no mistaking the drums of war.

Chapter Three

Forward Operating Base
5 km outside Baghdad
30 March 2003
0600 hrs

The third morning after the air war began, Wakefield had finally gotten some sleep despite the constant thrum of the war planes and dropping bombs, the explosions.

Outside the tent fabric, she could hear a buzz of movement and whispers. The U.S. Air Force and Navy had been flying nearly 1,000 missions per day over targets in Baghdad, launched from locations other than their little airstrip, which was now known as FOB Beta. Although the helicopter traffic had picked up there as well. The number of Black Hawks flying in and out nearly created the camp's own personal weather patterns.

There was a population explosion in their little tent city, the constant growl of generators buzzed in Judah's head. She was sharing a tent with the five other female officers in the camp, right next door to the female enlisted tent, which offered much more crowded conditions. Someone in her tent was always trying to get comfortable on the squeaky cots, but at least they were off the ground and didn't have to share day-space with the night-shift.

Judah pulled on her thick desert camo uniform. It had been much stiffer three days earlier when it was fresh, but now it was beginning to cling a bit like a protective second skin. She strapped her sidearm to her right leg at draw height, raked her hair back into the navy-regulation bun without a comb, and marveled at how different living in the suburbs of Washington was from living in the suburbs of Baghdad.

Pulling aside the tent flap Judah nearly plowed into Ellie. Her new friend was soaked through from an early run. "Want me to grab you a coffee?" Judah asked glancing at her watch. She and Ellie had planned to meet with the intelligence commander and other pairs of investigators/interrogators and interpreters from the night shift at 0630. It was 0615 already.

"Yes, please. As big a cup as you can find. Black. And some cheese from the chow line. I'll meet you in the room."

"The room" was the front half of the first floor of the new intelligence "headquarters" in FOB Beta where all the interrogators and interpreters compared notes each shift change. Detainees were housed on the second floor and interrogation rooms in the basement. The basement was an unexpected luxury which used to be the stockroom of the former general store. It allowed space for up to four detainees to be questioned at one time in separate rooms.

A central viewing room in the basement offered supervisors, camp commanders, or even visitors a chance to watch interviews through one-way glass windows at any time. Recording equipment lined two walls in the central viewing room, and each set of audio-visual equipment was synched to and labeled A, B, C, and D, corresponding to the rooms' labels.

A single laptop simultaneously backed up every interrogation. There was no live broadcasting capability from the basement, but each day during their early senior-staff meeting, the tech guy brought the laptop up, and the previous days' work was compressed into files that could be uploaded for further analysis at Naval Intel and Langley. And, Wakefield assumed, NSA also got, or took, a copy to be run through their supercomputer for anomalies or larger patterns that might be present and missed by the human element.

Captain George sat down in a folding metal chair at the head of the table which was formerly a wooden door, effectively calling the meeting to order in his quiet way of bringing authority. Wakefield sat with the nine others crowded around the table at haphazard angles. One of the broken metal hinges was directly in front of her, offering a bumpy writing space. Ellie smoothly slid next to Wakefield into the last empty chair, the one with the bent leg that had a tendency to dump an unsuspecting sitter on the concrete floor. She reached for the large coffee Judah brought for her and took an eager three swallows.

"What kind of progress are we making with the detainees we have in custody?" CAPT George asked. "How many have been processed?"

"A solid 40 percent" came a deep voice from the back of the room. It was Lieutenant (j.g.) Cade Marlow. He functioned in administration, case assignments, coffee supply, and general gofer for the more senior officers. "Some teams are able to more quickly assess detainees than others."

George cleared his throat. "We all need to pull our own weight around here." Wakefield felt like his gaze lingered on her longer than any of the others at the table. *I need thoroughness, but this is not a tea party where you get to know the entire family* history and religious background. That can come through the interrogators at Gitmo. We are triage here. George's gaze was back on her, so she nodded her understanding.

Maybe they could move a bit faster, but Judah didn't see how. When they hit an interrogation stall or anomaly, they returned a prisoner to the cells and began again with someone new, rotating people in and out until she felt confident in assigning an assessment, and when she and Ellie were in agreement.

Apparently Marlow noticed the captain's eyes resting on the women as well. "The ladies are performing disproportionally to the rest of the teams." He spoke up again.

Wakefield felt her face begin to heat, and every pair of eyes in the room found something else to look at in that moment. She forced herself to hone in on CAPT George's ruddy complexion and not look away.

"They have cleared," Marlow shuffled some papers around, "I'd say, thirty to thirty-three percent more detainees than any other team. And the bulk of actionable intelligence, corroborated and forwarded on to the commanders, has come from their reports."

Since Wakefield's eyes were glued to George's face, she didn't miss the micro-expression of shock, the bushy eyebrows that jumped into his freckled and lined forehead, the slight jaw slack, and the very fast change of opinion. "My apologies for misjudging you, ladies." There was no half-way about this senior officer. He quickly learned from mistakes, both his own and others', and he made amends. "What are you doing differently?"

Wakefield and Dayan exchanged glances. Wakefield shrugged. "What are the rest of you doing?"

Ellie Dayan spoke up then. "Well, the devout Muslim men certainly do not like being interrogated by women, and an American and Israeli to boot. That was readily apparent by the end of our first day."

Wakefield laughed at the memory. "We had had a man claiming religious asylum as a Christian for himself and his family. The family was still at their home. He was one of the walk-up surrenderers." More than two dozen men had claimed religious persecution this way in the first few days that the Seabees were working their way toward the city. They had to be interrogated as to their sincerity. "When her necklace—a Star of David—slipped out from her uniform neck." Judah went on. "The man saw it and bowed his head and began praying in Arabic."

"So he outted himself as a spy? What did you do with him?" LT John Miller asked excitedly from the opposite side of the door-table.

"Oh, he was no spy," Wakefield laughed. "He was thanking God for sending him a rescuer who was a daughter of Abraham, Isaac, and Jacob."

"You verified the translation?" CAPT George asked.

"No need to verify. I speak Arabic, Farsi, and a good bit of Kurdish. I heard his voice inflection with my own ears. We saw his body language." All of it together showed his genuine gratefulness to be out of the religious bondage of Islamic government. Even under the freedom to lie to their enemies offered by the Quran when jihad is being waged, a fanatical Muslim would have had trouble coordinating even his micro-facial expressions while blessing the God of Israel for salvation." A titter made its way around the table. "You can look at a copy of the tape we sent to Washington that day. Right, Marlow?"

"Sure," the young man shrugged. "Only take me a minute to cue it up."

George nodded at him. "Let us know when you're ready." The captain turned back to Wakefield and Dayan. "So that's your technique? Flash a Star of David and see how they react?"

Wakefield couldn't quite read the captain's face, he seemed conflicted.

Ellie jumped in before Judah had a chance to test the waters of confusion in her superior officer's mind. "No. We use that to confirm our decision now. I've had a chance to see a lot in the IDF. Body language under pressure can tell you so much more than the words people speak. And you all seem pretty familiar with most universally accepted body language identification. But there is so much more than that which seems to be missing from your toolbox."

The whole room was tuned into what the youngest member of the group was saying. Her being seemed to command that attention with her animated yet pleasant voice and large-movement gestures while she spoke, even from the chair with the bent leg. There was a freedom in her vocal nuances when speaking of unspeakable subjects that the Americans just couldn't conjure up. She presumed a great equality among them, despite rank differences.

Even the captain didn't seem to mind that she had hijacked his meeting. "God created our bodies in such a way," Ellie went on, "that they want to tell the truth especially about our emotions. Mankind was created from the beginning to be in God's image. God is truthful. Always." The room was silent enough to hear the upstairs guards' pacing as they passed the stairs. The underlying tempo of the far-away pounding of Baghdad continued as it did 24/7 these days.

Not even Anderson who Wakefield knew was an outspoken atheist seemed willing to argue with an Israeli Jew about whether there was a God or not. Dayan continued, "So the body and the face's first reaction is going to be the true reaction to information."

Ellie went on for about twenty minutes. Even Marlow had stopped taking notes in the back of the room and stared with rapt attention. Wakefield observed the men around the table trying out different expressions as Ellie modeled them for the interrogator and translator teams. "Any expression that is held for more than a second is a put-on for your benefit. He wants to make sure you see it. Surprise isn't—" Ellie broke to suck in her breath, shoot her eyebrows up and make a tiny O with her lips as she reached for her nearly empty coffee cup.

As she brought the cup to her mouth, instead she threw it to the ground and it shattered, splashing glass and cold coffee on pant legs and walls. "That is surprise! Did you feel what your face did? That little jerk of your jaw and your eyes widening?"

"Everything all right down there, Captain?" A guard was half-way down the 18-step staircase, with his gun at the ready in less than two seconds.

Capt George cleared his throat and seemed to shake himself. "All good, soldier. We are just learning from the Israelis what surprise is." He chuckled good-naturedly. The soldier took him at his word and disappeared noiselessly upstairs.

That seemed to loosen everyone's tongues, suddenly questions were flying faster than the young Israeli could answer them, even with Wakefield's help.

Ellie calmed them down with her hands patting the open air. "Yes, there can be some confusion between facial expression and body language, especially when your subject is faced with new information and they don't know how they feel about it at first. And if you detect a micro-expression of anger or distain, you don't know what that emotion is attached to. Your interrogation skills can then hone in and question related topics, or do the topic switch-a-roo and come back to a question or topic."

Wakefield saw a few smiles around the table. "What?" Dayan asked. "I got it right, didn't I? Kangaroo is the Aussie animal, switch-a-roo is the changing of question order."

"Yes," Anderson spoke up. "We just don't really use that word much."

Ellie Dayan looked at Wakefield for confirmation. Wakefield shrugged. "Not sure when it was ever in fashion. Though we all knew what you meant."

True to her teacher's heart, Dayan used it as a teaching moment. "It is exactly like that in translation. Sometimes a translator will hear something that just sounds off in a native language, and it is hard for a non-native speaker to pick up on it. Or, as in my case, even though it was my second language, I have heard Arabic every day of my life as far back as I can remember—well maybe not on Yom Kippur. But that translator is picking up on something intangible and needs to be expressing that feeling of something being off to the translator in real time. Not in a debrief after the fact."

Ellie had them reeled in again. Even Wakefield who had been working with the young, over-experienced Israeli for four days 14-18 hours a day as they had come up with their protocols, was captivated by this hands-on display. "Wakefield and I," Dayan gestured to Judah on her left, "came up with an English code word to use when there is something off about an interviewee's answer. Or in some cases his questions."

37

"So your translator is conducting your interview for you?" It was the translator who worked with Anderson. Wakefield could never remember his name.

"No." Wakefield spoke up then. "We work together as equals to investigate a detainee's story and motivations."

"Well, you have an unfair advantage over the rest of us." LT Miller said. "You both being women and speaking Arabic. Of course you will bring in better numbers."

"Hold it right there." The captain's fist actually fell onto the door-table shaking the whole surface and every coffee cup, spoon and paper on it. "As much as I preach about getting numbers up and doing your share, the bottom line is always the truth and keeping our troops and our country safe." He looked around the table until every eye met his. "This is not a competition folks. This is life or death. I don't care how long it takes to break someone. If your gut feels uneasy, you keep at it, or send him to someone else."

"Yes, sir." There were nods all around.

"Now, Goldberg, I'd like to ask you something." George said. Dov Goldburg was the other Israeli in the room. Judah had gotten to know him over breakfast as a first-generation Israeli whose parents were from New York and grandparents still lived there. He was helping with translation for LCDR Jason Meyer-Smith the newest interrogator to have arrived. He was fresh off a promotion ceremony in California.

"What do you think about all this God-talk, Goldberg?"

"In Israel we have learned that to live we must believe in miracles. It is an ordinary thing in Israel, sir, to believe in miracles, or in the unexplained. I am not religious, not at all." Goldberg shook his head as some secret sin must have crossed his mind. "But it is undeniable, sir, that I am a created being.

That you are a created being. Look at the sum of the intelligence represented among just us here in this room. Did that spring from primordial stew? That takes more faith than it does to believe in a God who created us." In that simple moment presented by a non-religious Jewish man in olive green, with guards and prisoners upstairs and a thousand sorties a day being flown over them into Baghdad, God made more sense than Darwin's theory of evolution. And the team of interrogators accepted both God and that He had created man to desire to tell the truth.

"Before we go to the video, if you don't mind?" Ellie asked permission.

"By all means." George's open-handed gesture gave the floor back to Ellie.

Ellie nodded and smiled. "There is a certain gesture that Americans all take wrong. No offense meant," she shrugged. "It is a cultural thing. When I hold up these two fingers, what do you see?" Dayan held up her first two fingers split into a peace sign with her other fingers curled down, facing her audience.

"Peace-out," said someone right off.

"Peace," said most of the others as she showed her signal around the table.

Wakefield heard someone say "rabbit ears."

Ellie flipped her wrist around so that the curled fingers were facing herself and the back of her hand faced outward. "Now what does it mean?" she asked.

"Peace?" Two or three voices said together, but they didn't sound as sure to Wakefield's ear.

"Nope!" said CAPT George. "I spent some time in England. I know what that one means."

Ellie Dayan smiled sweetly. "Why don't you enlighten your men, Captain."

"It's the same as shooting the bird." George grinned and shot the group the V.

Before the group began to experiment, Ellie said "That's right. It is totally different in the British culture than the 'peace' understood by the American culture." She flipped her wrist back around and flashed it at a quiet translator in the back who worked with Lieutenant Blackstone. "Hakim Bousaid, what does this mean in your culture?"

Hakim's turban tilted back as he lifted his head and spoke to the group for the first time. "Victory, ma'am. It means we *will* win or we *have* won. We have beaten you."

The group went silent again. Wakefield reassessed every time she thought she had been blessed with peace, but was actually being told in clear cultural language, "I beat you."

CAPT George broke the dense silence first. "You have that tape ready?" he asked Marlow. "It looks like we all have a lot to learn." He nodded once at Ellie.

Chapter Four

Lieutenant Commander David Rivers paced the back of the mammoth C-5 Galaxy aircraft. Courtesy of the U.S. Air Force, his enormous SEAL team had been divided between two aircraft already deployed to haul supplies to the Middle East. He had catnapped for the first two hours of the 19 hours they would be in the air. Now he stretched his legs while looking over his equipment.

Besides human resources and their gear, Rivers had convinced command that it would be prudent to go ahead and outfit some old dirty pickup trucks with back mounted guns and bring them along instead of wasting time on the ground commandeering those vehicles. He stopped next to a faded blue truck from the early 1990s. The dust around the wheel wells looked odd. Too even.

He swiped his fingers over the dust. It didn't move. He licked his first finger and rubbed again. It squeaked but nothing changed. The dust had been painted on.

Rivers shook his head. "Somebody back in Virginia is probably congratulating himself on his ingenuity."

"What's that, sir?"

Rivers looked up to see his partner, Chief Petty Officer Masterson (Mass), making his way around the equipment as well. "Hey." Rivers greeted him. "I was just commenting on our dirt here." He pointed. "It's painted on."

Mass squinted and shook his head. "Why didn't they just throw real dirt on it?"

Rivers shrugged. "Color matching the dust maybe? At least they were trying to be thorough."

"Speaking of thorough." Mass said slowly, seeming to fish for an invitation to speak freely.

"We are partners now, Mass. No matter your history." Rivers scrubbed his bristly hair with a flat palm.

"It's not *my* history," Mass emphasized. "If you're going to have Howard on your team, you'd better make peace with him before you hit the sand."

"I can't figure that guy out. What did I do to him?" Rivers blew out frustration in a huff.

"It started before the dressing down for not completing the mission and leaving men behind, so I don't know. But I wouldn't go parachuting with him if I were you. That's all I wanted to say." Mass moved his large girth past Rivers and disappeared around the corner of the lead vehicle chained in place in the cargo hold.

"Lord, I don't know what to do." Rivers whispered. He chipped at the paint with a jagged fingernail. "Surely Howard wouldn't sabotage such an important mission to get some kind of payback or something on me." Howard had been a problem from the beginning, but it was the first time Rivers had really

42

considered the ramifications of this behavior from what he considered petty aggravation. Maybe it wasn't as petty as he assumed.

Rivers walked around the edge of the line of trucks and other gear toward where all the members on this half of the team sat. Rivers recognized the seat where Mass had been sitting next to Howard on take-off. It was empty, so Rivers slid into it and pulled a buckle forward to secure himself.

Before he could even open his mouth, Howard popped his seatbelt and stood up. He made a slight pretense of shaking one leg and then the other while stretching his arms above his head. Then he walked off.

Rivers sighed.

Baghdad, Iraq
Republican Palace
1 April 2003
9:30 PM local time

Hussein released all his breath at once. He was tired of arguing with his sons. They thought they knew everything, but they were both just simpering young pups. Since Uday had returned from quelling the Kurdish noise in the north he had been intolerable. Constantly berating his older brother.

They neither one seemed to notice his displeasure and went on arguing across the table from one another. "We've always done it this way," Qusay stressed. "We must show our power in big demonstrations in the West, or the Great Satan will never take us seriously."

"But we could accomplish so much more, stir fear into the West like never before if we just tried this." Uday emphasized. "We could call for like-minded men on every continent to fight for us. We give them a name, such as 'solo raptor' or 'lone wolf', to appeal to their savage nature," he said. Hussein studied his younger son's face. Uday had always been his little experimenter. As a child, he drove his nurses to ask for new positions with his wild thinking indoors and out-of-doors. From his unusual choice in pets and their mysterious disappearances to very impractical jokes.

"Uday has always understood what brings terror into people's hearts." Hussein nodded to Qusay, the boy he had been grooming to take his place for decades. "I appreciate tradition like you, and the ways in which we have made a name for ourselves in the past. But surely we can do both?"

The younger son's triumphant smirk nearly undid all Hussein was trying to accomplish. Which was mainly peace and quiet for his dinner. The latest bombing runs by the Coalition Forces were destroying all the infrastructure in his city, even outside the city.

"Once the Americans are driven back to their own shores, we can implement a two-pronged attack. Each of you will head your own projects and we will see which has the most impact." Saddam frowned as he looked between the two of them, only moving his eyes, until he saw Qusay lean back slightly in his chair and Uday's jaw lose some of its tightness. A little family competition could work nicely. Maybe.

"On to the more pressing business," he said and pushed back his plate. Uday's jaw clenched again. "Imam Ali Zezchen will not be invited to accompany the family in the event of an evacuation." Saddam eyeballed his traditional son urging him silently not to press him on this. "His deputy, Nephtali something—strange as his name is for a good Muslim—will better suit our needs once the Americans retreat. Captain Mafias has deployed men in every direction to keep us informed of the roadways and bridges navigability.

"The body doubles have already been called in. Arriving throughout today."

"Why go to all this trouble?" Qusay huffed.

"Wake up, son!" Hussein fisted the table, shaking the glasses and silverware, "and do what I tell you. We must be ready to preserve our line for generations to come. Even if it means retreating for a few days or weeks while the Guard defends the city. I have every confidence in Mafias, but there is no point in putting ourselves at risk or enduring all this noise. You will arrange, you *both* will arrange," he emphasized with a pointed finger, "doubles to accompany mine in the motorcades through various routes out of the city, so that we can buy time for our departure."

When both of his sons nodded their ascent, he added, "You can go see to it now."

They left quietly for once, and Saddam brought his dessert plate back in front of him. He slurped his strong Turkish coffee and patted his moustache. Grabbing a fork, he sliced it sideways into the rich baklava with pistachio nuts. The honey drizzled on top dripped off the sides onto the tablecloth. Saddam smeared his finger through the drop and brought it to his lips.

> **FOB—Camp Liberty North**
> **North of Baghdad Airport**
> **30 March 2003**
> **1235 hours local time**

Rivers shoveled another forkful of mashed potatoes drenched in chicken gravy into his mouth.

"It's been nice having your team in camp, commander." CDR O'Reilly gave a firm nod.

Rivers swallowed quickly. "Thank you, sir. I appreciate the accommodations you have made for us in training."

"When is go-day?" The base C.O. asked.

We are waiting only for the airport to be commandeered. My men are sitting on pins and thumb tacks waiting for the word."

"I think it's 'pins and needles' Rivers." The man who was only slightly older than he was chuckled.

"Yeah. I hate clichés." Rivers stabbed a wimpy broccoli tree. "Always have." He shrugged. "Maybe that's why I like you. Well, besides arranging for my team to receive the most comfortable bedding in Iraq."

When the dark complected senior officer shot him a curious look, Rivers said. "I haven't met any Shawn O'Reillys with your coloring. You are far from the cliché of ruddy short-tempered Irishmen."

"That I am." The man chucked. My mother and father adopted me when I was two. My biological mother gave me the name Shawn and it stuck. Get to surprise a lot of people that way."

Rivers went back to his plate. The base commander had invited him to eat with him and Rivers was sure he would get around to whatever he wanted when he was ready.

Rivers drained his coffee cup and glanced at his empty plate and then looked expectantly at O'Reilly who leaned back in his metal folding chair in the quickly emptying dining hall.

"Is it true?" O'Reilly's mouth closed like a drawstring purse.

"Is what true?" Rivers asked.

46

"The rumors. That you got married and went on your honeymoon alone."

"Oh. That again." Rivers shrugged. "Yeah." He plunked his mug on the table. "My wife got shipped out early and left directly from the wedding. No sense wasting good diving time already paid for."

"SEALS and their water." O'Reilly rolled his eyes.

"That wasn't all you wanted to know when you invited me to eat was it?"

"Well, I had a feeling it was true, and I wanted to offer you the use of my computer and internet connection if you wanted to send her a note. Before you go out. Brides like that sort of thing."

"Thank you, sir. That's generous of you. I'll give it some thought."

"What's the hold up?"

Rivers hesitated as he assessed. "I'm not entirely comfortable ordering my men to go communications-dark and then sneaking off to send my new wife a love note."

O'Reilly just looked at him for a moment. "And the other thing?" He leaned forward slightly.

Rivers inclined his head automatically, even though there was no one left within ear shot, as long as O'Reilly didn't shout.

"One of my staffers overheard a LT Howard."

"Oh what does LT Howard have to say this time?"

"Well, he sounded none too happy with you. That's according to my yeoman. And he's not usually a snitch. I'd watch my back if I were you." O'Reilly backed up his chair with a screech against the floor.

Rivers followed suit. He guessed the base C.O. had said what he had come to say.

Walking back to his quarters across the new city that had sprung up north of the airport as the American troops had begun to prepare for the Baghdad invasion, Rivers began to pray.

"Lord, I can't sit him down on this mission. He is mission critical. What do I do?"

It was a pretty quiet walk to his barracks, despite the booming air campaign over the city just miles away. "I'm going to strain my ear if I listen any harder, Father."

"Do you trust Me?"

Rivers kept walking but paused in his heart. "I think I do, Lord. But if you're asking, I know you're not looking for information, but drawing information to the surface for my benefit. So, if there are areas of my heart that don't yet trust You, please, bring them into submission, or help *me* to, or however that works."

After the time Rivers had spent in Filasek's torture chamber in Greece last year, he found it freeing to admit his own need and brokenness before the Lord. All the Survival, Evasion, Resistance, Escape (SERE) School training that he had endured and even taught his SEAL teams, didn't prepare him for the inability to control his own environment and heart that he had experienced in that time in Greece. He had noticed that the time it took to get to the pliable state of relationship when confronted with his own humanity had exponentially shrunk since those dark few days where the Father had lightened his soul.

Chapter Five

"Wakefield and Dayan, I need you stay." CAPT George said after dismissing the others from the morning briefing around the door-table. Wakefield caught Ellie's eye as she replanted herself in her chair. Ellie shrugged.

Collecting papers, laptops, and coffee mugs, and shuffling out the doors, to outside for one team and to the basement for three other teams to wait for their first detainees of the day to be brought down to interrogation; everybody was moving a little slower that morning. The basement's Interrogation D was where she and Ellie had been headed.

"What is it, sir?" Ellie got the sentence out of her mouth first, not bothering to wait for Dov to close the door behind his exit. Her finger pads drummed lightly on the tabletop.

George waited for the door to close before meeting first Dayan's fixed gaze and then stopping his sharp eyes on Wakefield. "I know you're not happy about the word that came down last night, but it needs to be implemented a-sap."

"Orders are orders, Captain." Wakefield said. "Doesn't matter what we think of them."

"I am happy you think so. Because I am about to add to those orders from the brass. We need to clear up the questions surrounding Asam. You guys were the third team to question him yesterday. None of us are comfortable with him, but we can't shake his story."

"Part of it is that he is just so arrogant." Ellie offered shaking her head.

"That scar on his face doesn't help. I know, I know, I'm one to talk," Wakefield shrugged, fingering her own scarred cheek. "But the way his skin pulls down around his eye makes him look, well, a little scary. And he has to tilt his neck back to see decently, so that makes him appear arrogant. Well, besides his language."

Ellie snorted. Asam's Arabic was beyond arrogant and disdainful, especially toward women. "Our interview yesterday certainly didn't give us any good vibes concerning his view of Americans."

Wakefield sucked in her breath at the memory. "Why he would come here to an American FOB to seek asylum is beyond me, sir. But then he tears up when he talks about the persecution he's experienced under Saddam. He is still a bit of an enigma."

"I want you two to crack the enigma. Today." CAPT George frowned. The longer he stays here in triage—" George cut himself off. "I'm not comfortable sending him into a refugee camp. I'm definitely not sending him to the mainland. But I don't want to send him to Gitmo just because he's ugly and we don't like his personality. You understand?"

"Are we talking enhanced interrogation, sir?" Ellie raised a single eyebrow.

"Definitely not." George leaned forward to pierce her with his look.

Ellie shrugged, unperturbed. "Just clarifying." she said.

"We will figure it out for Asam." Wakefield put a hand on Ellie's shoulder. "And we will talk to Muhamad, uh Moe first thing."

"Very good. I knew I could count on my two best girls. Dismissed."

Wakefield kept her eye roll to herself until she was facing a concrete block wall that would not reflect her irritation at her C.O. Flattery was annoying. So was the way he referred to them as girls.

> Interrogation Room D
> FOB B outskirts of Baghdad
> 3 April 2003
> 0715 hours

"So here's the thing, Muhamad, we need more intelligence." Wakefield said in Arabic to the detainee who Wakefield was fairly certain had shared all he knew, which was not much.

"Please. Call me Moe. As I have told you before. I want no association with Allah, but if I change my name, I get trouble with everyone. You think I am spy; my family and neighbors think I am traitor."

"Yes, *Moe.*" Wakefield acted like she was remembering. Ellie's face gave a left-side-only smile that Wakefield could see in her peripheral vision. They went through this same routine at least once a day. But today would be the last day.

"What more can I say to you, Missy Judah?" Moe gave a deep shrug and lifted work-gnarled hands with oil-blackened nailbeds that looked like they belonged to a man at least three

51

decades older than his 55 years. They had confirmed his age through hacking into computerized hospital records. In fact, as much of his story as possible had been corroborated. Everything he had told them about himself, his family and even his arrest record was true. Nothing he had said in six days of questioning had ever been proven false. CAPT George labeled it highly unusual, but Ellie Dayan agreed with Wakefield. Moe's forthcoming information, while not very valuable as far as intelligence, showed him to be exactly what he claimed to be: a Christian man stuck in impossible and dangerous circumstances because of his faith who was seeking asylum for himself and his family.

"Unfortunately, it is not enough." Wakefield coughed as she put it to him. She hated this duty. She nearly choked on the words she had been ordered to tell him.

Moe's black-brown eyes fell at the corners. "What more is there?" He shrugged again, his hands imploring her. "I don't know any more."

"We believe you." Wakefield included Ellie as she gestured. "In fact, most everyone here believes you. There is always someone who is skeptical about everyone." Judah tried to smile encouragingly at this brother in the faith, but it fell short. "We trust you. That is why I've been instructed to make you this offer."

Moe's chest swelled and his sun-darkened skin brightened.

Wakefield felt horrible at the disappointment she knew she was about to set on him. "We need you to go back in, go back to life as it was." Wakefield watched as his eyes grew round under his heavy black brow while she spoke. "You have a unique position, and we need you to listen the Republican Guard, feed us information as you work on their vehicles. We will arrange to get your family out in the midst of an attack as cover. You can claim they all died or something. The bombings are continuous, so you'd just be one more man who has lost his family."

By now Moe was shaking his head and Wakefield had no trouble identifying terror on his features. "No, no, no, no, no!" he said. "This I cannot do. To my neighbors I am already dead." Moe's hands were shaking now as he implored Judah for another plan.

Something about him reminded Judah of her grandfather. Maybe it was the arthritic shape to his thick fingers or the heavy brows in need of a trim. She felt compassion for him, but also knew this decision had come from the top. The brass back in Washington had picked him from among all the detainees as someone who could help. There would be no change to his deal.

He was saying something about his plan with his wife had been to spread the word that he had been killed by one of the American's bombs, that his mother didn't even know he was still living, when Judah held up a hand to interrupt him. "We will get you out too, Moe. Eventually. And we can get your family out now. Well, day after tomorrow." She needed a distraction. His respiration had picked up and his face was expressing so many negative emotions he looked like he had a facial tic. He was not handling this well. "Where would you like for them to live while they wait for you? California, New York, a little Midwestern town? They won't have to go to the camps first." She was definitely outside the bounds of her authority. She knew it and Ellie knew it. They had been drinking their coffee yesterday afternoon, Turkish style with the grounds still in the bottom of the tiny demitasse cup, when the offer had come through CAPT George's boss, ADM Glicce.

But Ellie didn't say a word or even move a muscle.

"But they have probably already had my funeral. Maybe yesterday, maybe today. You see, I cannot go back." He gave that deep shrug again.

"I understand it will be hard, Moe. We will help you with the story."

"Yeshua will be with you, Moe. You can do this." Ellie's voice was low and comforting. When she spoke, Judah could believe it, but she wished her friend had not said it. What if Moe did end up hurt or imprisoned and tortured? It was not outside the realm of possibilities, or even probabilities. What would he believe then? Or dead. Moe could end up dead because she sent him back in, just for some lousy information, that probably wouldn't help in any measurable sense anyway.

It was quiet for a long while.

"Do you have children, Missy Judah?"

"No, Moe. I just got married, uh…" She had to stop and do the math. She had been working so much and been so focused on the job she had forgotten her new husband and their beautiful declaration of love on the White House lawn. So much had happened. So much had not happened. So much time together with David had already been lost. She had not even remembered to email him about her transfer off sea duty to an FOB before her departure from the *TR*. "Twenty-six days ago."

Judah heard a sharp intake of breath from Ellie, and Judah guessed that in all their conversation time, she had not mentioned her husband. How could that be?

"Congratulations, Missy Judah." He grinned widely at her for the first time that day. He couldn't realize what being married such a short time meant in the U.S. military. "When you do have your babies. You will understand Father God so much more. It is a beautiful thing that God sent his Son to die in our place. You will also understand laying your life down for your children at that moment when your child is in your arms for the first time." Moe looked far away. "Life makes sense all of a sudden with those soft tiny fingers wrapped around yours, nails as thin as tissue paper. And so white." Moe rubbed one gnarled hand over his fully-bearded jaw. "I never thought I could have a child so white," he chuckled, "but they all came out that way."

Wakefield watched courage fill Moe's eyes with liquid as his heart swelled with love for his children. He nodded at Ellie first then met Judah's eyes. "I will do this thing for you. It is my privilege to lay down my life for my children. Again."

"Thank you, Moe. We will keep a watch over you, and I will pray for your safety." Judah felt personally responsible for this man somehow.

Resigned now to his circumstances, Moe asked Judah, "Where do you think my family will be most accepted and find friends? That's where I want them to go. My mother, she is not Christian, but she doesn't like Islam either. Is there a place for her in your Christian nation? It might help her to believe in *Isa*, Jesus, if people are nice to her and will love her." Tears tracked down his cheeks, but purpose was firm in his eyes.

All the possibilities went through her mind, and she ticked one after the other out of the running: the Deep South, the northeast, western states, small towns, the Eastern Seaboard, large cities. All had their prejudices on full display after September 11th, and, in the year and a half since, nothing had really calmed down. "Maybe Kansas City would be good. It is in the middle of the country. They have people who pray there. It goes on twenty-four hours a day for years now. They might love unrestrained."

55

"God will put me in a place to feed information to my brothers." He sat up straighter and broke the seal on his bottle of water. "Send my family to this city in Kansas." He drank two big gulps of water, and set the bottle down, pushed it back to clear the table between them. "How can I send what God shows me back to you?" he asked.

As surprised as she was at the quick change, Wakefield drew a deep breath and said, "Here is what we were thinking."

Chapter Six

"Is there any other entry point we can use as plan B?" Rivers asked his crew. He poured over palace blueprints which had penciled additions drawn over the original palace layout.

Eleven of the twelve members of Echo Company-Al Faw Palace lay on a small piece of shade from a tattered desert-camo tarp. In various states of exhaustion, they sucked against 1-liter water bottles, with heads propped against 70-pound packs in a patch of what passed for grass at Camp Liberty North. Every one of them was soaked through their BDUs after five hours of running drills in the recreated layout of the underwater entry point to the catacomb labyrinth of the Al Faw Palace.

Bravo Company-Al Faw Palace was also assigned to Camp Liberty North. The buzz of the Black Hawks as they practiced their fast-rope descents kicked dirt into the air, but offered a nice breeze at this distance which helped cool Rivers' Echo Company down. Even in mid-spring, afternoon temperatures in Baghdad climbed toward the triple digits daily.

"I'm ready to just walk in the front door," one of the young petty officers groaned.

"You just going to blow the door and go in guns blazing?"

"Hey, Rambo! What are you going to do about the Republican Guards in front of it?"

"Overwhelming force, eh?"

"I was thinking more like Terminator."

The ribbing began in triplicate then. Each man trying to talk over his buddy. "Gentlemen." Rivers interrupted before it went off the rails. "How about if we keep that for plan C, and you guys find a place for a quieter plan B with me."

The dozen of them crowded around the map. Mass stood in the second tier and leaned over the others' shoulders.

A lot of mumbling and grunts of dissatisfaction were interrupted after a few minutes.

"Perhaps it is my upside-down perspective." Masterson began. "But tell me what you think of this. Excuse me." He reached over two men and put his pointer finger on the smaller satellite map next to the blue prints everyone had been studying. He pointed to the exact spot where plan A was to come across the Tigris underwater with rebreathers. The two men stepped back so Mass could reach better.

"We enter the water where we had planned from the tree cover there, swimming downstream with the current. Continuing on course we attempt underwater entry on plan A. If it doesn't work by the second waypoint, we deviate to plan B. We can abandon the metal cutting torches, but keep the C-4. That might save a minute."

"To the plan, Mass!" Howard scratched his ears and adjusted his collar.

"Hold your horses." Masterson countered without regard for Howard's rank. "We continue downstream. See how this little finger of water diverts and eddies around the edge of the property. We could stay completely under the cover of the water."

Rivers watched as his partner's eyes flited back and forth between the satellite photo of the whole property and the blue prints.

Mass reoriented the two papers to the same angle, fully upside down from his position. "We exit the water here. Doesn't that look like there is a little rise in the terrain?" Mass asked rubbing his finger on the map to point it out. "It would hide us as we unwrap our weapons from the waterproofing and get out of the rebreathers. Then we cut across here." He traced an invisible path across the palace's side yard on the satellite photo to the inverted corner where a recent addition to the palace layout adjoined the original structure.

"See how this section sticks out to the side and creates a little alcove? Can we get a night shot from the satellite to see if that back side is lit at night?" Mass looked up at Rivers.

"I don't see why not." Rivers shrugged. He could see where Mass was going with his idea now. It looked plausible.

"Okay. Good. See, if Howard can blow us a little hole here, in the new exterior wall," Mass shifted to the blue prints now, putting his finger at the same spot in the exterior wall. "We come in here, up this hallway," he traced it for them. "And we are in the main dining room."

"That's a lot of ifs."

"Howard, can we carry enough reserve C-4 for this as a back-up plan after we've used what we need in the primary initiative?"

59

"What makes you think the dining room is important?"

"Is that really a rise that will protect the view of the water exit?"

"We are sitting ducks all the way across that lawn. And if Howard doesn't get us through the exterior wall, what do we do then?"

"What if Howard and Allen went first?" Rivers saw that the whole team could be in immediate danger if someone didn't test the security first. "They wouldn't scurry or anything, but just walk as if they are on patrol. In the dark and from a distance, that shouldn't create suspicion if any guards see them. Wouldn't they just think they are the regular patrol coming by early?" Rivers asked.

"Works for me." Allen said.

At the same time Howard asked, "You trying to stick it to me?" Though the words were teasing, the sentiment behind it, coming from Howard to Rivers, made the team shift uneasily.

"Of course not! We will all cover you from the rise out of the river. I will have my sniper rifle, scope, and silencer with me, so if it is just one or two guys, we don't have to get the whole Republican Guard out with the noise of a full of attack."

"We could do it," Allen said. "There is even that one window there," he pointed a few yards away from the corner Mass had originally pointed out. "That makes it even easier than going straight through a reinforced palace wall." Allen had worked as an explosives expert in training Teams for about six months. He had covered one class of BUD/S candidates, and Rivers knew that between Allen and Howard, if it could be blown open with C-4 or shaped charges, the two of them could do it.

"What is all this?" Another work-worn finger with split nails circled around some regular dark spots in that alcove in the satellite photo.

"Pretty sure that's a garden."

"Will it have a fence?"

"Ugh. We really need a source that has been there or closer satellite images both day time and night time."

Rivers pulled out his SatFone. "Mass, good eye! I think this is a workable plan. We will do modifications in a walk-through after everybody has a good lunch. You guys head to the mess line, and I will work on some more research with intel services in the area." He glanced at his wrist quickly. "Meet at 1:30 at our mock Tigris River."

The men cut out quickly. Rivers dialed and smiled to himself as he considered that his request might hit the ship-board desk of a certain blond sailor in intelligence who now carried his last name.

Interrogation Room D
FOB B outskirts of Baghdad
3 April 2003
1209 hours

Judah shifted her eyes to assess Ellie one last time. She wasn't comfortable with the plan to get George's agenda for their day accomplished. Talking to Moe had already been an emotional drain, and trying to decipher Asam's mismatched expressions and words, while digging to his motivations didn't promise to go quickly.

After the chat with CAPT George that morning, she and Ellie had decided to give it one try before lunch and then dig in again after a break.

Judah sat at the metal table bolted to the floor in a metal chair, also bolted to the floor, just a tad too far away to make leaning forward comfortable for her. The Seabees had been called in to make some amendments to the underground room after one of the early surrenderers had lost his temper to rage at a question he evidently found impertinent. Wakefield and Dayan had been in the next room when the crash of the table against concrete resounded through the entire building.

Asam shuffled in handcuffs and leg irons to the far side of the table to another chair, also newly bolted to the floor.

Holding up his cuffs in a plea that actually reached his eyes this time. "You may uncuff him, Lance Corporal Hanson."

Ellie came in then, rushing. She set her metal chair down with a clatter and skootched it up closer with a scrape against the stone. "Sorry, ma'am." She sat slightly behind Judah, in deference to Judah's role as primary interrogator. She fluffed her hair slightly as Judah watched her. "Are you ready now?" She asked allowing a tinge of annoyance to bend her English.

Ellie gave two quick nods without looking her in the eye.

Judah turned back toward Hanson and Asam with the click of the handcuffs.

"I'll be right outside the door, ma'am." Hanson retreated outside.

The door bolt slammed in place and Judah began, "Tell me about your job again, Asam."

Ellie repeated what she said in Arabic.

"I told you yesterday. I have not been working in two years." Asam said in Arabic while looking at Wakefield. Ellie repeated Asam's statement in English to Judah.

Back and forth and all around the same story he had told them the day before. Word for word. He'd been fired from working at a Persian rug factory and showroom. His boss had been threatened and forced to fire him at gun point by the Republican Guard. He didn't know who the order had come from. A name he'd never heard and couldn't remember. Why would they do that? Religious differences. Why couldn't he get another job? Rumors had spread in the neighborhood that money had gone missing at the rug factory store and that was why he was fired. Why didn't he move? He couldn't afford to move. What was the name of the rug store? The address? What mosque did he attend? Who was the Imam there?

The question in English, then Arabic; the answer in Arabic and then English, exactly the same as the day before.

Except this time, Ellie made slight changes in the information as she translated his answers. At first it was just nuances, then she added some derogatory remarks. Finally she said he couldn't remember, when he had just given specific information.

Asam's face flashed tiny movements of displeasure and annoyance, but his voice was collected and shoulders relaxed.

It was obvious to Judah that the man spoke English, and well, but he didn't want to reveal that information to them.

Wakefield twisted in her seat to whisper to Ellie in English, "I've really got to run to the ladies' room. Will you be okay here on your own so we don't have to have the guard put him away and then wait for him to be brought back down?"

"Sure. Sure." Ellie nodded. Judah saw her shrink back in her chair with the slightest show of hesitation. "Hanson is right outside and armed. If I need anything."

Judah blew out her breath. "Thanks, I'll be right back." She double rapped on the door, and Hanson opened it for her to step out.

Wakefield did not race for the ladies' room however. She stepped around the corner into the central viewing room and stood at the observation window into room D.

Chapter Seven

The concussion shook the ground. Smoke and dust plumed upward. Half of Echo Company ended in a tangle of arms and legs on the hard earth even behind the protection offered by the alcove.

Quickly righting themselves with a few swallowed choice words that Rivers could see behind black smear-painted features.

The team rounded the corner in a crouched position two at a time with the rest facing outward, silently keeping watch for any movement that would need to be mowed down. As if they needed to be silent after that explosion.

What is taking so long? Rivers glanced at his watch. Twenty-five seconds behind the previous drill to this point. Then he got the tap.

Mass and Rivers went last. Around the corner at half-height, Rivers followed Mass. His head moved on swivel, checking every angle within his field of vision, especially his six. Mass threw up a tree-branch arm that nearly clotheslined Rivers as they were about to step into the shelter of the inside of the alcove.

Someone had set lasers at a three-and-a-half-foot height that appeared as a fence surrounding the garden. He had not been expecting that. Nice work, on someone's part. Must have been set up during lunch or when Allen and Howard were setting the charges. The red lines would not have been visible without their overkill on the smoke and dust in the air on this second attempt at a run through with live ordinance.

Allen and Howard stood like sentries on either side of a very large hole in a concrete wall. Allen's face looked murderously at Howard. He was whispering something Rivers couldn't quite hear as he stooped down to one knee and created a step for Mass to spring over the red fence.

When Mass had cleared it, even landing lightly, Rivers shrugged out of his weapon and handed it to his partner over the laser line. He motioned Mass to step out of the way, and he swung his right leg and arm back to start his momentum then as he swung his leg and arm forward, he pushed off the ground with his left to take a standing, twisting leap that lifted him four feet into the air. He lifted his legs sideways to use the full height of his jump to clear the fence. One hundred and sixty degrees later, Rivers managed to pull his feet back under himself and land almost facing the fence. He pulled back his left arm just before he broke the plane of the laser.

"Ooh-rah!" Mass smirked as he handed Rivers' weapon back to him. "Maybe a little less ballerina next time, sir?"

Rivers snorted lightly and tuned in to Allen and Howard.

"I told you it was too much." It was Allen's whisper accusing Howard. Rivers moved the last fifteen feet toward the giant hole in their concrete block wall. "Our wall is no longer sound. Look at that crack behind you!" Allen pointed.

Rivers' eye followed Allen's finger even as he came closer and the offending crack became clear.

"Better hurry through then." Rivers advised and jutted his chin forward for Allen to move through the opening.

Allen's assessment was correct, the whole wall was about to crumble. Rivers wanted to stop the drill but knew that this would be their last run through until the wall was rebuilt for them to practice blowing it up again. If they even had time to let the Quikcrete® dry before they got the green light from Washington.

Allen pivoted to rush through the opening. His sleeve brushed the surface and little pieces crumbled away to the ground. Howard moved through next. A groan loosened over their practice field.

Rivers could see the wall buckling and bulging. He shoved Mass through from behind and leapt forward himself as the bottom layer above their heads at the entry point let go. The concrete snapped in some places and crumbled in others, and in the areas where the blocks held together, they just went tumbling to the ground.

Rivers landed on Mass who had fallen forward not expecting to be shoved from behind. He grunted as Rivers' full weight crashed down on him. Neither man could move forward out of the way as the wall collapsed behind them.

It was a full four seconds before the wall stopped crumbling and another three seconds before the pieces stopped tumbling into their new arrangement. Rivers' right ankle screamed unhappy messages to his brain, demanding attention.

He tried to roll off Mass who wiggled under him. He could not move.

Rivers twisted back to look down his body. His legs were pinned under a section of masonry that had managed to stay mortared together.

The entire team rushed back from their forward progress inside the mock-palace corridor and rooms they were clearing on either side of the hallway.

Everything began to happen at once. The team began to remove the debris to dig him out and Mass's giant girth slithered forward, moving out from under him.

Rivers' commanded then. "Allen and Howard stay here. The rest of you back to plan B. We will catch up. We can't lose space we've already cleared."

The men jumped back into the live-fire drill, re-checking rooms as they moved through the corridor.

"Mass, keep moving if you can."

"Sure thing, boss."

With every movement, Mass jostled Rivers. He winced inwardly as the rough concrete dug into the bare skin of his ankle which was pressed into the large block of wall that had found its resting place on top of his leg up to mid-calf.

Allen and Howard were bent in half tossing blocks and pieces of block behind them as if they were twin steam shovels.

When Mass had slithered out completely, Rivers' body angle was able to shift. His torso fell to the ground with a grunt, but he was able to pull up at his knee and free himself from a small gap left by the blocks and pieces.

"I'm free." Rivers rolled over to hands and knees, his rifle dangled under his body. "Let's go. Let's go," he said. Howard and Allen straightened up, and swung their weapons back to the ready position.

In the bright afternoon Rivers' now saw the gash in his wetsuit and in his ankle. Bright blood flowed freely. It didn't feel broken now that the pressure of the wall was off, but he gingerly shifted his weight to it and pushed himself off of his hands to stand upright. Mass moved toward him to put a supporting arm under his armpit.

Rivers shifted his weight to test its strength and rolled his angle to check agility. "Everything moves," he assessed for Mass. "Move out."

The clock-work drill ended as Rivers jumped up to the platform that represented the helo exfiltration that would be offered by Bravo Company assigned to the Al Faw Palace rooftop. Both plan A and B ended there. If something went wrong with the helos, exfiltration plan 2 called for Echo Company to hoof it to the city square where they would hold position until the back-up ride could ferry everyone out.

Rivers depressed the stop button on his watch. "Two hours, forty-eight minutes, and thirty-two seconds." He nodded with a satisfied frown. "That'll do it for plan B. Back to the shade to debrief that explosion." He was looking at the back of Howard's head when he said it and didn't miss the cords in the man's thick neck muscles pop up and flatten out.

> **Al Faw Palace**
> **3 April 2003**
> **12:05 PM local time**

"Thank you for meeting us here." Saddam swept into the dining room of a palace he only occasionally had visited since it was built just over a decade ago. He nodded to Imam Ali Zuzchen who stood calmly with his hands resting on the bulk of his belly.

69

"I enjoy moments of our dining together, your majesty. I am curious that your invitation did not include Nephtali." Zuzchen said. The words chosen sounded like deference, but the arrogant tone, reinforced Saddam's decision to replace the man. Immediately.

Saddam did not indulge the man's curiosity but nodded to the servant standing by the sideboard where silver-lidded dishes kept warm over tiny candle lights. He didn't want to waste any more time than necessary in this location. He felt over-exposed here. Even with look-alikes shifting from palace to palace above ground to confuse any spies or traitors. Being stuck on an island with one bridge on and off in the middle of a city under the American barrage was not the odds to which he preferred to leave his survival.

"My boys will be down momentarily." Saddam said even as the soup was being placed in front of him.

"We won't wait for them? I don't mind." Zuzchen leaned back as soup was placed in front of him, and didn't remove his hands from his lap.

Saddam slurped his soup from a large spoon. "We won't wait."

"While they have yet to arrive, I wonder if I might take a moment to address my concerns about the U.N. threats again."

Saddam did not look up.

Unfortunately, the imam took it as an invitation to speak. "We must allow the inspectors to come in. We are being slaughtered in the streets, your majesty."

Saddam fixed the older man with a stare. "Is it not a blessing to give one's life for the Quran and its holy teachings?"

"The American bombings are not *that*." Zuzchen shook his head and his jowls jiggled.

"If you will not speak about the inspectors, perhaps we could discuss your sons." Zuzchen plunged right in. "I know you think I've gone soft and moderate in my old age. But the debauchery I am hearing about those two from my men, trusted holy men mind you, I cannot even repeat."

"Excellent." Saddam used the man's breath meant to emphasize his son's wrong-doing to interrupt. "Don't repeat it," he enunciated harshly. "We are in crisis mode and I will not hear of your criticism of the princes who seek small human comforts."

Saddam slurped another spoonful without looking up. But out of the corner of his eye he did see the fat old man blanch. Good. For today's plan to work, he needed a little fearful compliance from the old imam.

The silence stretched long, which normally would have been to Saddam's liking but he was feeling the pressure of being trapped in this easy target. Zuzchen sat with one hand in his lap, the other playing with his silver curled sideburn, staring at the bowlful of soup.

"Eat." Saddam commanded the imam.

The old man smoothed his silver beard as he picked up his spoon. Saddam saw him swallow hard as fear flashed in his eyes before taking the first bite. Maybe the old codger wasn't as stupid as he had thought if he was afraid to eat in the king's dining room.

"Don't worry," Saddam slurped again. "It was all taken from the same pot over there on the sideboard."

Uday and Qusay burst in just as planned. Saddam pulled nervously at his eyebrows. He had never attempted this before.

"Imam, can you come quickly? Please hurry." Qusay called from the doorway.

"Oh hurry, Imam." Uday's words tangled up in his brother's. The two exited the room hurriedly, leaving the door ajar.

The pleading sound caused Saddam's heartrate to increase. His son's clattering shoes against the marble floors echoed through the room. Saddam rose quickly, knocking back his dining chair to the floor. The unplanned crash was the perfect punctuation.

The imam rose. Saddam supposed it was quick for the man's age and girth.

The guards at the door were on high alert, but Saddam calmed them with a fast, "Stay!" on the way through with Imam Zuzchen's white robe billowing behind them.

Chapter Eight

Ellie still sat. Asam was saying something to her, but Wakefield couldn't read his lips.

Asam slid forward slowly and also to the far side of his chair. It was nearly imperceptive except that Wakefield was staring at him without his knowledge, and measuring his progress against a shadow on one of the dimples in the concrete block wall. He was still talking to Ellie, and slowly unfolding his hands where they had been resting with interlaced fingers on the tabletop. The man's large shoulders began to bunch up as he still talked away. His body tightened and tightened.

Then he sprang.

Up and over the table he pounced like a lithe jungle cat, kicking off the bolted-down chair for leverage and spring.

His body weight slammed into Ellie's shoulders in her seated position. She tipped backward. Asam's hands wrapped around her small neck and his fingertips whitened with the pressure he applied, except his right scared forefinger which remained useless.

When the metal chair clattered to the stone floor, Wakefield held a flat hand toward the lance corporal at the door and said, "Give it a second."

Ellie had ridden the chair to the floor, protecting her skull by bending her neck forward into Asam's strangle hold instead of trying to break it. She used the bounce and repositioned her legs as Asam's body dragged across the table to follow her down to the floor.

As Asam fell off the height of the table, she had maneuvered her booted feet so that when he landed, his pelvis struck her boots. She gave a mighty kick at the height of his flight which used Asam's own bodyweight against him.

Suddenly Asam was sailing over Ellie's head and had to break his grip on her neck to keep from face-planting on the hewn stone floor. He twisted in the air enough to cause his hip to graze the wall instead of hitting the wall full force as he fell out of an unintentional somersault. He also managed to avoid getting dumped directly on his head.

That the man had eight inches and at least 70 pounds on Ellie's slight frame didn't seem to discourage her at all.

At the same time Ellie used Asam's forward momentum to push him over her head and break his choke, instead of ripping at his fingers, she jabbed with stiff fingers into his exposed armpits, and then pinched the tender skin just under his arm as he moved away from her in a twisting motion.

It was as if he pinched himself. But she added to it by continuing her own backward motion, in the opposite direction from the way he twisted when crashing to the ground.

Wakefield saw that Ellie only released Asam as she bounced to her feet. Humiliation colored Asam's marked featured and fueled his rage. He unscrambled himself and his long robe as he jumped to his feet. His deep growl vibrated the one-way glass in front of Wakefield.

Hanson's key was turning in the lock and his body leaning into the slide bolt as his eyes locked with Wakefield's waiting for her signal to release him.

Wakefield kept watching through the glass. The IT guy who monitored all recordings, Wilson, had set aside his headphone monitors and froze halfway to standing as he stared into Interrogation D.

Asam charged Ellie again. His right arm drew back for a powerful roundhouse aimed at her jaw. Ellie threw her body around in the direction his fist was moving while snapping her head around in the same direction. His blow only glanced past the skin of her cheek. The burst of energy not coming into the expected contact carried him forward, and her move carried her into a full-circle wind up for a body blow to his unprotected kidneys.

Asam's head snapped back at the contact and Wakefield could see Ellie had stung the breath out of him.

If possible the guard stiffened more alert at the sudden quiet than the clatter. "Ma'am!"

"You might want to come watch this." Wakefield said, smoothing back her blond hair. She tore her eyes from the action only long enough to meet the lance corporal's wide cornflower eyes.

Ellie and Asam exchanged another set of blows as the guard fixed the lock, pocketed the key and took the three steps needed to see the action.

Ellie's back was to the window now and Asam's eyes narrowed just before he charged at Ellie like a bull, head down and everything, which put him at a disadvantage, again.

Just as Asam's now-bare head—he had lost his kufiyah near the door—went into Ellie's stomach, she leaned into him, slid to her left, grabbing Asam's arm in both hands, one hand on his shoulder and the other on his wrist. As she twisted out of his way, she again used his movement to her advantage. She twisted him hard, moving his arm behind his back as he bent forward. Now that she was beside him, he fell to his knees trying to relieve the pain of the shoulder hold practiced by police worldwide.

With a guttural yell, he threw Ellie's smaller frame right over to the floor with brute strength and rolled, flattening her like asphalt-laying equipment. His arm untwisted with that movement.

As he reared back for a punch, she aimed for his Adam's apple with the heel of her right palm. On his knees over her now, Asam shifted his weight off his left hand to rub the pain out of his throat while his right shot out like an adder and grabbed a fistful of Ellie's cropped hair.

Still on the stone floor she twisted one way and then the other, quickly, to try to break his hold. Asam rolled off his knees to a standing position, yanking her up by her hair as he went.

She continued twisting, as Wakefield observed her wincing. But Ellie's hair was just long enough for her to look like a little like a marionette as both hands lifted simultaneously, up, higher and higher.

Wakefield opened her mouth to send the guard in as Asam shifted Ellie's slight yet squirmy figure to the crook of his left elbow and reached down to his right. Suddenly Asam had a shiv pressed to her carotid artery. It had to have been hidden in the folds of his long caftan.

Wakefield could see Ellie's pulse as he pulled her head back to expose her neck to the window.

Before Wakefield could send in the marine, Wilson spoke. "She's baiting him, ma'am." He had replaced his headphones and was standing, hands on hips, corded to the equipment. Wilson's eyes bugged as he stared at the glass and listened to the action in his ears.

Both Asam and Ellie were facing the window too. Ellie went still for an eternal four seconds, according to Judah's internal clock. Wakefield opened her jaw again to send the guard to end the standoff, but Ellie winked at her. Well, at the window.

Wakefield watched soundlessly as Ellie inhaled and swung up with both hands and grabbed Asam's ears. One in each fist. She yanked him forward, ignoring the make-shift knife at her throat, and leaned down using her body as a fulcrum to move the large man toward the floor. Ellie's dominant right leg took his full weight and her left foot encouraged him off balance as she stomped on his left instep with her heavy boot.

Wakefield saw the reflection of her own wince as she remembered Asam was wearing sandals.

Ellie's left fist grasped her right fist and she shoved her elbow back with great force.

Bent nearly in half now, Asam's knife hand pedaled backward like a windmill, catching nothing but air, until Ellie grabbed his thumb on its next round and jerked his arm back at an impossible angle. Ellie stood over Asam as he leaned further and further forward to keep his shoulder from popping out of its socket. She pressed him to the floor.

She was saying something to him as she pressed her full body weight on her knee which was now in his upper back and his face was pressed into the rough-hewn floor, bleeding just a little on his non-scared side.

His legs went flat from under him all at once which must have been what Ellie was instructing him. She released his head for one moment and moved with precision quickness to pluck the shaved down plastic comb-knife from where he had dropped it next to his body. She tossed it over the table toward the door.

Asam pushed up against her release to gain the advantage back, but as he shifted, she came down harder, jerked his arm further up his back and gave three fast blows to his shoulder.

"Oh!" yelped Wilson. "She did warn him."

"What?" Wakefield felt the word drift out of her mouth.

"Pretty sure that pop was his shoulder either breaking or the bone coming out of the joint. But she told him not to move. It's his own fault for not listening." He chuckled deep in his throat.

Wakefield frowned at him in the reflection, but he just shrugged back at her.

"Why don't we join them, marine?" Wakefield nodded to Hanson.

"Shouldn't we call a medic?" He asked, even as he dug the key from his pocket to follow orders.

"If he asks nicely, I can pop it back in."

The guard's eye brows wrinkled his forehead into a music staff.

"He's not making enough noise for her to have broken the bone. I started out as a corpsman." Wakefield explained as she stepped around the corner to the door.

Hanson clicked open the lock and slid back the bolt, one with each hand. Entering first, he picked up the shiv from the floor, and stepped back to hold the door for Wakefield.

"Feel like answering a few more questions, Asam? Or do you need a rest?" Wakefield asked lightly as if they were still sitting across the table civilly.

Ellie translated to Arabic and then added in English, "As if you need an interpreter."

Asam remained silent a touch of arrogance still tinged his features as they were smashed into the floor.

Ellie feigned a stretch with a small sigh. She shifted her knee and her bodyweight ground into Asam's spine.

"I think, um." Asam panted to control his reaction. "I think, I'm done for the day."

"I think you owe *Seren* Dayan an apology for almost killing her, don't you?"

"*Trying* to kill me." Ellie corrected. "He was nowhere close to almost killing me."

"Trying to kill her." Wakefield repeated taking her eyes off Asam to observe that Ellie was hardly even breathing hard. "But that can wait for tomorrow." Judah added, "If you're still here tomorrow. Isn't there an early morning direct flight to Gitmo?"

"Every morning." Ellie responded.

They had ceased translating. As they suspected before, Asam's eyes showed he understood every word.

With a nod from Wakefield, Ellie stood up all at once, leaving Asam in a heap on the floor.

"You want some help with that shoulder?" Judah asked.

Asam just grunted as Hanson replaced the handcuffs, picked him up under the other arm, and helped him to his feet.

When the prisoner was out of earshot on the stairs, Wakefield said, "You ready for lunch? I think you've earned an extra helping."

"Sure." Ellie said as she straightened her hair again. She rubbed her scalp where Asam had pulled her hair." I might recommend that we shorten detainee leg irons from here on out."

Wakefield nodded slowly with pursed lips as they made their way upstairs to the front door. Restricted movement from shorter chains between ankle cuffs could help in the case of a similar performance by another prisoner. "I think you'll get some agreement on that when we review in the staff meeting in the morning. Where did you learn to fight like that? I mean I know you said you could hold your own, but…"

"It's Krav Maga." Ellie shrugged, "Israeli-style fighting. Mixed methods; hard, fast, and repeated movements; and using momentum to incapacitate the enemy."

The two women replaced their battle helmets for the walk to the mess hall. "Can you teach me?" Judah asked.

Al Faw Palace
3 April 2003
12:55 PM local time

Saddam reach back with a shudder to help Imam Zuzchen down the stairs into the tunnels below his boys' Al Faw Palace. They followed the sound of the princes of Iraq, but the younger men were always just out of sight.

The old man was out of breath and wheezing against more exercise than his heavy body had had in years. *Good thing he did not have to worry about going back up the stairs,* Saddam's lip curled in the flickering gas-lamp light.

At the bottom of the haphazardly hewn stairs the imam stopped with a hand to the damp wall. "Wait. Wait." He bent at

80

the waist and gave a weak cough. Saddam recognized that he was trying to catch his breath.

"We're almost there."

The old man looked up sharply. "How do you know?"

"I can't hear the boys moving anymore. They must be just around that bend." Saddam pointed to the corridor that bended around to the right. Saddam knew that it opened into a little ante-chamber as so many of these tunnels did. They had chosen this one because behind the ante-chamber lay a cell with bars for doors and obviously no windows, since they were deep underground, and under the river by now.

Saddam could have easily overpowered the old man, but he wanted him to walk into the cell all on his own.

"Hello?" Uday's voice eeked around the corner. "Imam, are you there?"

"We must hurry." Saddam adjusted his bandolier across his uniformed chest. The cool humidity of being under the Tigris River was seeping into his bones already. He knew it would be worse for the arthritic joints of the man at least fifteen years his senior who carried so much excess flab.

Saddam tugged on the man's arm. "The princes need your help."

He heard the unmistakable snort of his eldest son.

The imam must not have recognized it, for he lumbered forward as Saddam towed him by his elbow. "I didn't know all this was down here," he rasped.

They rounded the corner and the princes took the lead. Normally they would leave this sort of work to others, but taking out the head and face of the Islamic faith in Iraq would not be an assignment that could be kept silent. Naphtali was groomed to readiness now, and Zuzchen had become a liability with his knowledge of polarizing palace politics and weakening stances toward the fundamentalism that kept the populous in check.

From the main corridor, Saddam watched his boys working together perhaps for the first time since elementary school. Each of the princes took an elbow, and they practically picked up the obese man and carried him the final 12 feet to the barred cell.

"You'll wait here." Qusay laughed. "For a long time. We can't have traitors among us."

"Traitors? I'm no traitor!" Zuzchen coughed and the rattle reverberated off the cavern walls. His fat fingers curled around the iron bars.

Uday smiled cruelly. "Sure you are. You defected to the Americans today."

"What! No!"

Saddam watched his sons pry his fingers loose and seat the man on a chair in the cell. He smiled as he saw that he had gone just far enough in letting them in on the plan. They still held some respect for the man who had been the head of their faith since before their birth.

Uday pulled the door closed with a clang.

"Why?" the old man shook his head and leaned forward still trying to catch his breath. "Why would you do such a thing?"

"Let's go." Saddam shuffled his sons ahead of him and back up the stairs. The man's repeating question echoed around them.

"We should finish lunch and then get out of here. Even with the tunnels for escape, this place is not where you want to get trapped if the Americans attempt a ground invasion."

Saddam made up his mind. After lunch he would insist they pack their personal items and depart with the Royal Motorcade back to the Republican Palace. While they packed, he would make one last trip downstairs. This time with a knife.

The imam must not be allowed to speak of the things he had seen. And he most certainly would not be accompanying them out of the city.

Chapter Nine

The shade was nice, the sitting felt nicer. Rivers sank back against one of the thick wooden posts that anchored the ragged desert camouflage netting over their heads. He had recomposed his opening line of his speech a dozen times as Echo Company trudged back from the drill that had destroyed the alcove set for entry in case they had to move to plan B.

He had finally decided on "What happened at the wall?"

A dozen water bottles crackled as they sucked against the plastic. Gulping down the final swallow of his first liter, Rivers screwed the lid back in place and opened his mouth to begin the discussion.

But Howard beat him to the punch. "I'm not comfortable with the plan as it stands now. Nothing personal, commander," Howard rubbed a cloth, grey with use, against his face paint, "But I don't feel comfortable sprinting across the field first to set the charges with you covering my back from the ditch…which we still are not sure exists."

Rivers fixed him with his eyes, and Howard was confident enough to hold his gaze. Any phrase that began or ended with "nothing personal" usually was. Very personal.

Rivers stuffed it down. "What do you suggest?"

"Either someone else take point. Or someone else take the scope." Howard's head tilted matter of factly.

"Hold up." Allen interrupted with a raised arm and fingers spread wide. "Rivers has the best shot record. I want *him* covering me."

Ash Campbell, one of Howard's men when he had formerly commanded SEAL Team Two, spewed a mouthful of water like a fountain toward the dirt outside of their small shelter. "Listen, the L.T. shouldn't have to go first if he doesn't want to."

Rivers looked around the group. Three men from Howard's former Team sat with Howard. They seemed to be in agreement with him. Which was strange. Rivers was used to having to keep the peace with everyone vying for the front spot.

He turned his attention toward removing his dive bootie. Brown dried blood flaked off as he separated the black rubber and neoprene boot from his skin. The ankle gash had clotted, but gravel from the wall's crumble was embedded in the forming scab, so it would have to come off and be rinsed so infection didn't set it. The debrief swirled around him. He would let allegiances be shaken out by not interfering as the conversation deteriorated.

He listened for underlying complaints, fears, and sound ideas as he worked out the best way to lead Echo Company to a success.

Rivers leaned over to the cooler and grabbed another one-liter bottle. Pouring it over his ankle, the water pooled around his bare heel on a little tuft of grass. He grabbed some gauze from the abbreviated medical kit that Garcia had been carrying throughout their drills, and began to scrub the scab away, lightly at first to peel the gravel out of the wound, not grind it in further.

Out of the corner of his eye, Rivers saw Mass grimace as he watched, unable to look away. He too seemed to be ignoring the rising noise under the shelter.

Rivers ripped open a new sanitary gauze package and caught the blood below the wound which had begun to flow freely again. When the white square was saturated, Rivers set it aside and poured water slowly from the water bottle to make sure the laceration was rinsed well.

He opened and covered the sore with another gauze pad and applied pressure. When it soaked through, he tore open and applied a fourth pad. This one he taped in place with white medical tape around his lower leg. *Don't forget to grab the medical kit scissors*, he made a mental note for when he went to change out the bandage that night. *Ripping that tape off could sting like crazy.*

Rivers held up his water bottle and still had just under a half liter left, so he took another long slug, then cleared his throat to interrupt the clamor.

"Here's a solution. I'm sure you'll let us know if you disapprove." Rivers avoided looking toward Howard and his group. "We enact plan A and B simultaneously. Splitting our two explosives experts, Howard and Allen. Allen will stay with me on plan B at the alcove. Howard, you take the sharp shooter of your choice and lead plan A with half the team through the labyrinth entrance underwater and clear the tunnels, and I will lead plan B team through the palace, we flush the building from above ground and below decks simultaneously and meet in the western wing where the original plan called for us to come up and sweep east. We do the western wing of the palace together and exfil as normal."

Howard's little posse of men looked to see his reaction before they responded.

"You can pick your team from among us," Rivers offered. He pinched his inner thigh to keep himself from adding, *you're not a great follower, let's see how you lead.* But oh, it burned on the roof of his mouth.

"I'll take, Burns, Garcia, Campbell, Lettuce, and Bags." So Howard had finally found a plan of his agreeable. Rivers smiled, besides Mass, Howard had taken the top half of the performers in Echo Company-Al Faw Palace.

"Good man." Rivers said, not so much because he assessed Howard as being good at being a human being, but because Rivers found it good to have the man out from under his feet. He was sorry to lose Letz-Ellis, better known as Lettuce on the Teams. The man was a deep thinker whom he had just begun to get to know.

"Any disagreement?" Rivers asked.

He saw shoulders shrug and heads shake. "Very well. I'm happy to have the rest of you. If either way should fail, we join up the other half. Let's take an early dinner and run through again with our smaller teams as soon as the sun sets. We will have to coordinate our reintegration to clear that western wing."

Rivers felt antsy about cleaving the large team into teams of half a dozen men, but Howard's undermining attitude was not ironing out. So it was probably better this way.

"Are you happy now?" He overheard Garcia probe Howard. The man was probably getting more than he bargained for with that one. Rivers smiled. Garcia had held his own opinions every step of the way, but had never aired grievances in public, so Howard had not seen the way the man would challenge his authority. Rivers had never minded the checks and balances

Garcia offered, but he didn't think Howard was going to be as appreciative.

Rivers motioned Allen over, "Walk with me." And he began walking toward the chow tent. When Allen moved in at his elbow, he began to speak. "Let's figure out the proper volume, shape, and detonators for the C-4 charges you'll need. And you get first pick of who you want to accompany you."

"Aye, sir!" Allen said. "How's that leg?"

"Just fine. Thanks." Rivers nodded in appreciation.

Chapter Ten

"What happened to you?" Ellie's jaw dropped as she looked over Moe and then at Wakefield.

Judah gently touched the man's right arm in the white sling. The back of his hand was covered in tiny red hair-line slivers. His whole right eye socket was a yellow-green that looked more like it belonged in a newborn's diaper than on his face. "What happened?" Judah repeated. "We talked about a cast and a sling, but you look like someone got you in the hot room. And I don't mean *our* hot room."

Moe pulled up the hem of his traditional garment a few inches to show off more cuts and bruises. "It's great isn't it?" he said with a grin.

He rubbed the yellow eye and held up his finger. "It doesn't rub off, or sweat off apparently. They said it goes away in about five to seven days. And whatever chemical it is that they stained my skin with, I had a bit of an allergic reaction to."

"That explains the swelling." Wakefield said, wide-eyed as Moe tapped the puffy skin around his left eye. "It looks awful, Moe. You're sure you're not hurt."

"If it convinces you, it should convince everyone at work." Moe said.

Ellie reached out and touched a long scratch on Moe's left temple and forehead.

"Ouch!" He winced and pulled away from her. "That one is real. I added it myself, and the cuts on my hands." He held them up.

"They are so tiny. They look like papercuts." Ellie observed closely.

"They are. Papercuts are harder to achieve than one might think, unless you don't want one," Moe's mouth twisted to the side.

"Well, you've convinced me. Thoroughly." Judah said. The man looked like he should be in bed, if not a hospital, rather than being sent into a warzone as an agent for the enemy. It was odd to think of herself as someone's enemy.

They stood in the main meeting room instead of interrogation as they spoke together for perhaps the last time. "Tech went over with you how to deactivate the tracker in case you are swept for bugs, right?"

"I spent hours going over the call-in details, the code words, the devices yesterday. They even woke me in the early morning before the sun to test me with loud sirens going."

Wakefield felt her eyes go wide.

Moe grinned widely through his heavy beard. It was incongruous with his fake-beaten face. "I got it *all* right. And very fast. God will help me with this assignment." He nodded confidently. "And my family will be safe from Islam."

"Did you mention it to him yet?" Judah asked Ellie.

"What is it?" Moe asked Wakefield.

"We are having some difficulty distinguishing others who are requesting religious asylum from people who may be trying to infiltrate us or just trying to get out of bad national circumstances."

"How can I help?"

"As we speak, all the men and three women claiming Christian persecution are being moved into the four interrogation rooms."

"Oh. Stop!" he interrupted. "If you have fakes among the real and then they are sent back, they will be murdered for sure."

That made more sense than anything the man had said so far. Judah rushed to the rooms' central viewing station downstairs. Three men already occupied room C. Two women were in room B and one man each in A and D.

Judah stepped quickly into the stairwell and even as the guard's hand was on one man's arm and the key was sliding into the lock. "Change of plans." She said with authority. "Please return this man to his cell. And anyone else who is out." she added.

"Yes, ma'am." The army guard didn't even flinch as he secured the key and turned the detainee around to climb two flights of stairs.

"Come back and see me when you are finished." Judah ordered him.

"Yes, ma'am." The linebacker-sized man in his early 20s nodded in affirmation.

Judah reentered the central viewing room and peered into the one-way glass of the different rooms. Room C with the three men in it caught her attention. Two of the men obviously knew each other and were trying not to show it. The third man sat looking bored at the table. Each of the men alone in a room were wandering around. One was examining everything, including the one-way glass, the other was just pacing. The two women were both seated in the two chairs at the table, facing the door, somewhat sideways in those chairs. Judah cocked her head to the side; their positions changed the way the whole room looked to her. Normally one chair was for the interrogator and the other for the detainee. Each translator brought his or her chair in as needed. The women held hands across the table; the younger one was biting her lip while the older one by less than a decade crossed her legs at the knee under the heavy hijab and her dangling foot swung out once every second.

"This is all being recorded, correct?" Wakefield asked Lieutenant (j.g.) Wilson who sat quietly sipping from a water bottle in the control center.

"Of course, ma'am." He screwed the plastic bottle top back in place with a tiny click

"Great. I'm going to want to see footage of when each person was brought into the rooms containing another person."

LCDR Wakefield climbed the dimly lit stairs to the main floor. The air was almost cool and she let her hands slide over the smooth, bare-concrete wall on her way up.

"Continue waiting here just one more minute, if you would," she instructed Dayan and Moe who chatted at the table/door.

At the top of the stairwell to the second floor, Wakefield motioned to the guard she had spoken to moments earlier. "I was just on my way." His mouth twisted and he licked his lips twice.

"No matter." She waved a hand in the air as if to erase any offense. She stepped down four steps and stopped mid-floor. Turning around, Wakefield had to wave him to follow her. "I need you to bring the Christian asylum-seekers down one at a time. They should not be able to see one another unless an interrogator is present. Can you organize that for me?"

He nodded quickly. "We will return each one to their cell individually. But what about those who came in together or—" he grimaced as if he had made a mistake. "What about those already together downstairs?"

"Not your problem. No contact without an interrogator present."

"Yes, ma'am."

Wakefield smoothed back a piece of hair that had worked itself loose and was tickling her cheek as she trotted back down to the main level.

"Thanks, guys." At the landing she poked her head in to tell Dayan and Moe, "Let's go." and continued to the basement.

"Anything change while I was gone?" Wakefield asked Wilson as she reentered the central room.

"Hardly ma'am. It's been about 30 seconds."

"Right."

The wheels on the tech's chair spun and rattled as he shot back from the desktop and leapt to his feet. "What's he doing in here, ma'am? Are you—" The wide-eyed young man was reaching for his sidearm.

"It's fine. He is helping us." Wakefield smoothed over. "I'd introduce you, but the less he knows…" she shrugged.

"Can we start with the women?" Ellie Dayan asked.

Wakefield shrugged and walked to the glass. She looked back at the IT tech. He was still standing somewhat slack-jawed and eyes now squinted. Wakefield saw his pupils darting among the three of them and the glass window to his right before he noticed her watching him and he schooled his features. A caution

93

came over her. Not a tingle in the spine or a word of knowledge, just a funny little, "hmmm?" in her heart. "Do you know either of these women?" she asked Moe, switching to Arabic.

"You know it is not like we have a regular church where we go and all the Christians worship together. I understand it is not even like that in America," he said in Arabic as well. Moe showed no sign of even noticing that he had switched languages, but Wakefield saw Ellie cut her eyes to look at her in the slight glass reflection.

"The young one looks familiar, but I cannot tell you where I have seen her." Moe squinted and leaned in as if it would help him remember, and Wakefield could no longer see Dayan's questioning look. "Besides my family," Moe rambled a bit, "I meet with just 11 others weekly to worship. Our pastor really did die on the second day of the air attacks. That is how my wife and I got the idea for me to pretend to die."

"He has only been gone a week or so." Ellie said softly. "I'm sorry for your loss. I know it is hard."

Wakefield watched him allow himself a single moment to feel the pain. As quickly as the etching in his forehead and cheeks was there, it disappeared. Perhaps stuffed back into the little grief-box that lives in everyone's soul. Wakefield knew, even as a little girl sitting at her daddy's funeral trying to rub the pain out of her heart, that grief always remains, just as memories remain. Through healing and even regaining relationships that were lost, grief lived in corner of the soul in a box with a lid that opened and closed. She tried to live with the lid open all the time, allowing loss to breathe as needed so that even in healing, her soul didn't fester. But there were times in life to close the lid and lock it down with a key so that one could survive to open the box later. Times like this, when Moe was locking it down for his pastor so his family could live. Times like the grief of missing a long-awaited honeymoon to fight for one's country in a warzone.

For Judah, the single second stretched long. And then it was over, buttoned up like a good marine.

In Room A, the single man who examined the room was still wandering around touching everything. "Hey! It's Chucky." Moe's face lit up as he turned to Wakefield.

"Chucky doesn't sound very Arabic." Wakefield squinted and shook her head in mirth.

"Oh, his name is really...Um, actually I don't remember his real name. He got kicked in the head by a mule when he was about 8. It was 12-15 years ago, at least. The mule knocked him around. He is fully blind in one eye and very nearly blind in the other. But he definitely loves Jesus. He actually goes up to the imams and clerics and challenges them on their faith to their faces. There was this one time—"

"But why is he called Chucky?"

"The donkey who kicked him blind."

"What about it?" Wakefield felt so confused by Moe's jumping storyline. It was obvious from his face that he was being truthful. But truth didn't mean she could understand his story.

"The donkey's name was Chuck Norris, Missy Judah. He loved that donkey, but his aby sold him immediately, so to remember the donkey and to help Chucky feel strong without his eye, everybody who knows him started calling him Chucky, after Chuck Norris."

"Oh." Wakefield smiled lightly and squeezed her brow together as she shook her head. She couldn't imagine being nicknamed after a mule, especially one that had nearly blinded her. And why was the mule named Chuck Norris? "Must be a cultural thing." She said as she glanced sideways at Ellie.

"Don't ask me." Ellie shrugged and laughed. "Balaam's donkey spoke. Probably would have probably talked himself out of being sold in my country." She ran a hand through her dark curls.

As Wakefield threw her head back to laugh, she caught a glimpse of the bewildered Wilson staring at the trio. "It's about a donkey named Chuck Norris in Baghdad," she tried to explain, but then just shook her head as Wilson's eyebrows became lost in his hairline.

"So Chucky's okay." Wakefield giggled once more before directing the group to the three men in Room D. All three of them were curiously peering at the glass. They couldn't see in; Wakefield had tried herself when they were first built, even peering under the shadow her hand against the glass, she couldn't penetrate the one-way's glare. But they must have heard the laughter.

Under the curiosity presented in the features of a man called Saul, Wakefield saw flashes of resentment that she filed away for later. She and Ellie had interviewed Saul twice already, and she had not picked up any resentment from him before. The guy sitting at the table looking bored only looked slightly less bored. His eyes flicked back and forth between the glass, which Wakefield knew reflected the room, and his sleeve where he picked at fabric pills.

Moe was quiet as he studied the men. Finally he spoke. "I know the man there with the beard and blue turban. I, uh, owe him some money. I would not have thought of him as a believer in Jesus. We never talked about Jesus. But he is not a bad man. What has he done? As much as I'd like to tell you he is a bad one so I do not have to repay him, if you let him go, even in collecting my debt, he would never hurt me or my family."

"What? Is he like a loan shark enforcer or something?" Wakefield asked.

Moe frowned. "Sort of."

That made Wakefield pause uneasily. An informant who was in debt made him not only a target for others to squeeze, but it made him vulnerable to being forced into becoming a double agent if he was ever found out.

Moe was not slow. "If my family is out and safe, Missy Judah, you have nothing to fear from me."

Judah only nodded. "What about the other two?"

"Nothing." Moe said shaking his head.

The pacer in Room C was still pacing, just a bit slower. Moe shrugged and shook his head.

The women in B had been swapped out for a short man by the time they worked back around to that window. "Him, I know." Moe took a shuffling step backward as he spoke. He pointed at the man. "He is no Jesus follower. Not even secretly. He is in the palace with the Husseins. Does something in the finance department." Moe's eyes rolled to the ceiling as if trying to remember. "He has been on Al Jazeera TV demanding that all Iraqi Christians pay the Dhimmi tax, convert to Islam, or die. I cannot remember now if he actually crucified some Christians in one of the rural provinces or if he just threatened to. It was not even a year ago." Moe was shaking his head, with shallow breathing, and moving on to view Room B before there was even anyone in it.

Wakefield waited next to Moe and watched his pulse pound in his throat. He rubbed his fingers softly, first the right hand, then the left. You can't make up that kind of fear, she decided.

What neither Moe nor Ellie realized was that Wakefield had arranged for some of the unwillingly captured detainees to be mixed in with the Christians seeking asylum as a final test of Moe's integrity as an intelligence source.

So far, he was passing with flying colors, just as she'd hoped.

The next round of men filled up the rooms at a perfect pace for her, Dayan, and Moe to study them and get Moe's assessment of each of them. Wakefield caught an occasional glimpse of the guards as they relocked each door. Doing the math in her head, between the two guards, they had already made eight trips each up and down the two steep flights of stairs. Neither of them even looked winded. Go Army! Training and early morning PT refreshers were working.

It was at least forty-five minutes later and countless trips around the circle of windows. "It seems to me," Ellie said as the guard signaled them that this was the last of the detainees, "that we need a more on-the-ground real way of checking out claims of Christianity beyond asking about conversion moments and Bible character quizzes." She snorted. "Which have certainly had their place of disqualifying some."

"What you need," Moe began, "is to contact the man Pastor Baruk was training as his associate. He has been to most of the house churches, at least once, I should think. He only came to us once though, a few months back. So I do not know this man's name. He was medium height, a bit poochy in the middle. Of course I never saw him in Western clothing, and he has a beard and dark hair and eyes. Really thick hair it looked like under his kufiyah."

"Okay" Wakefield said. "I hate to sound American, but that describes about 30% of the population in Baghdad. And 50% of the remaining are women, and the other 20% are children or old people."

"Your population figures are a bit skewed, but point taken." Moe said. "I will make it a priority to find him when I get back and connect everybody up so you can get background checks on the people you need. I have heard there are at least 14 house churches that were all linked together through Pastor Baruk."

Chapter Eleven

"I hope they will only escort him part-way back," Wakefield balanced the sandwich on top of the apple juice box so she could scratch her nose. She carried back a little early dinner for Moe before he headed into the lions' den of Baghdad.

In the twilight, the whole distant city glowed against the dark cloud cover which was more smoke than cloud. Judah had resigned herself to the constant sound of the bombing, the airplanes taking off or flying over, the smell of dirt and jet fuel, helicopters whirring up. Noise, wind, and sand in equal measures.

Ellie walked beside her from the tent city back the few hundred yards to the Intelligence House, as it was coming to be known. One arm comfortably resting on her Uzi, the other swinging as if she had not a care in the world. "I think they will be driving over near the airport and dropping Moe off near the back of the hospital. We know that both of those are still operational. I hear whispers that command wants to keep the tarmac in good shape for bringing in the larger C-5s and C-130s to deliver troops and tanks as the ground war gets underway."

"Whew," Wakefield sighed. "That would be interesting, to see the airport liberated. You know it's called Saddam International Airport. With all the cultural pride attached to that name, you *know* it's not going down without a fight."

Ellie grinned, her short curls frizzed in the constant wind. "I once helped draw up a battle plan for taking over an un-named airport near us. You'd be surprised at how many options there are. So why didn't you mention you are married? And newly married at that."

Wakefield winced; she knew this was coming eventually after that look earlier. "Honestly. I forgot." Wakefield shook her head. "It sounds strange, even to me. I try to be fully present wherever I am. And to do these evaluations and interrogations at the volume we are running through them, it is taking all my energy and brain RAM. If I mess up, somebody's life is on the line. Maybe lots of somebodies."

They rounded the edge of the bombed-out village street and showed their passes to the guard who challenged them just by stepping in front of them, as Judah kept talking.

"It kind of just feels like the wedding was a dream, and now I've woken up. I've not spoken to David since the reception when I was flown to my duty station. And we've not had any contact, even email, since I left the aircraft carrier."

"So what is your new name?"

"Judah Rivers." She gave her new friend a half-smile. "It is a pretty great name." Her smile grew more rounded as she remembered practicing her new signature in the weeks she made their wedding plans. "But it doesn't feel like me yet."

There was a small entourage of people standing at the two-story building across from Intelligence House. Wakefield heard a double sneeze from someone in the group as a helo departed leaving a lighter blanket of sound over the base.

"Oh, yes, sir. Welcome to Forward Operating Base Beta. This will be your new headquarters."

"But, but where are all the people? The equipment?" Judah heard a familiar voice and smiled as she snapped out of her revelry.

Another big sneeze was followed by, "I don't know what you mean, Commander Grady. This is an FOB, we don't have a many of the comforts of home, but we can probably jury rig you a tarp to sleep under in your personal quarters right next door to the HQ here."

Wakefield hurried her pace so she could see. PO Bailey was gesturing across the street from her building to a little stone shack which did look slightly less porous than the building Bailey was offering the base's new C.O. as his headquarters. But it was tiny, and had what the soldiers referred to as "natural air conditioning."

"You are located right across from Intel House, and look here comes some of those folks right now." Bailey winked at Wakefield, but he stood closer to her than Grady did, so Grady didn't see it.

"Brady Grady. How long has it been?" Judah walked up and saluted as she saw he had indeed picked up the extra half stripe to full commander. "Oh, sorry, sir. Congratulations on the promotion."

He snapped off a salute, and she relaxed her stance. The six men with him sort of milled around, all of them carrying something. All but one of the men looked more administrative than soldier-y.

"Welcome to FOB Beta. It looks like we are neighbors. I see your place has a bit more natural air conditioning than mine." Judah smirked.

In truth, the two-story building was uninhabitable. The front doorway was blocked with at least two feet of rubble where a concrete wall had fallen from the top of a windowsill.

Black-soot-covered clothes or curtains or cushions mounded underneath each window. Now that she was standing close to the building, it also smelled like something larger than a rat had died inside too.

The breeze must have floated the smell to everyone at once, because one of the pencil pushers stretched his neck forward and his shoulders bunched as he leaned over, his face greening in a way that did not look right.

PO Bailey sneezed again. Judah could not stifle a choked cough as she pulled Moe's dinner into her chest to keep it from contamination. The sandwich was only wrapped in a paper napkin.

"You'll probably want to do something about that smell, neighbor." Wakefield gave him a cheeky grin.

Grady looked a bit green himself. "This will not do," he said. "This simply will not do." Judah couldn't tell if he was going to scream or cry, but something was happening on his face.

"I'll take it from here, Petty Officer. Go on back to your post." She ordered.

The young man flashed her a shaky smile that of course she could only see in his eyes because the kerchief covered the lower half of his face. "Thank you," he sneezed. "Ma'am." Bailey disappeared between the buildings faster than a surface-to-air missile.

Wakefield had caught on quickly to the petty officer's plan, but from the look on Grady's face, his anger was mounting. He was muttering, "This will not do. General Franks will hear about this directly." He gestured for one of his men to bring him a satellite phone that he had pulled out of a briefcase. The aide engaged the antennae before passing over the phone.

Wakefield knew that supreme command of the Iraq Invasion had been handed over to General Tommy Franks weeks earlier. He was in the same position that Judah's stepdad had been in at the beginning of the Afghanistan operation and while the Navy was leading. Though both men were still in the area. Franks did *not* need to be bothered with a practical joke gone awry. "Commander Grady, would you come with me before you make that call?"

"What for?" He was gruff and walking away from the putrid smell with the phone in hand.

"Let me drop this off for one of my guys." She gestured to the sandwich and apple juice in her hands. "Right here across the way." Moe was actually standing in the doorway by this time. 'And I'll show you."

Ellie's thin eyebrows peaked high on her forehead and she said, "I'm just going to stay here with Moe, if you don't mind, Judah."

"Course. I'll be right back." Judah handed Moe's sandwich and juice to Ellie.

"What is it, Wakefield?" Brady Grady huffed. "What can't wait until I get the ball rolling on getting some decent—uh everything—in here. This place is a disgrace."

"You can leave your guys here if you want." Judah suggested.

"I'm not going anywhere in this god-forsaken place without my team." CDR Grady growled.

This was not going well. Brady had always been so happy and carefree. "Then bring them along. How have you been, sir?" It felt funny to address him as a senior officer now.

"Where are we going?"

"I hear you when you say this won't do, so before you make that call, I wanted to show you the rest of the place."

"The rest, you say?"

"That sneezy petty officer told me this was it."

"There is a bit more. And a hot dinner is already on."

"Oh, thank God!" one of Grady's aides moan softly.

"There's a chow line?" Grady asked just before they turned the corner where Wakefield knew to expect the guard to ask for ID, but Grady and his men didn't.

"Where do they do any sanitary cooking in this place? It's not MREs is it?" Grady asked as the guard materialized in front of them, just as he always did. Grady started, but caught himself before actually drawing his weapon. Judah thought she might have even heard a whimper from one of the men immediately behind her.

They showed ID all around, even though it had been less than three minutes since Judah had come past the guard in the opposite direction.

"Is this a regular thing around here?" Grady asked the guard directly.

"Oh, yes, sir."

"Well, it's annoying."

"Yes, sir." The young man's face fell.

"But an important layer of security when coming from FOB command and the intel wing where the detainees are held into the rest of the base," Judah stated.

A smile, though smaller, perked up the young man's face again.

"What rest of the base?" Grady asked frustration coloring his words.

The guard allowed them to pass, and up two stairs later the entire group could see the giant tent city with cars, trucks, and about 6,000 people. "This rest of the base, sir."

After a flash of relief in her old buddy's face, Judah saw anger set in.

"I think the petty officer was just having you on, sir. Don't hold it against him. It was my fault." Judah said.

Grady's once fun-loving face turned a mottled red. "How was this, this *lie*, your fault?"

"I'm sure he meant it as a prank, Commander. Not as a lie. The petty officer was standing there when I first heard you were coming in slated as the base commander, and I told him about some of the crazy pranks that were pulled in OCS."

Wakefield could feel her face pinking with embarrassment. For the first time since arriving in-country she wondered if her scar showed. It was new since Grady last saw her. Just before Christmas before last, Wakefield had been attacked by a madman with a knife in Afghanistan when she had been sent in by the CIA to both rescue a handful of men being held hostage as leverage and to search for some nuclear weapons that had gone missing from Russia. It was where she had met David Rivers, and the rest of that was history—sort of—but why was she thinking of that scar now? Did she care what Brady Grady thought of her face? She hoped not.

"This isn't high school, Lieutenant Commander. Let's leave the gossip and the pranks behind, shall we?" His voice had a razor sharpness that Judah had never heard in him before. "This is a war zone. War is serious business, and people die when they aren't focused. I'm sending that kid away from the front. Games are a menace to good order and discipline.

"Surely, sir—" Wakefield tried to gather up the fraying straw of the conversation before it was entirely unraveled.

"Zalusky, take down his name and get the orders drawn up," Grady ordered one of his marionettes.

Wakefield eased her finger between the sweaty chin strap of her cover and jaw to loosen its suction grip. Zalusky's mouth opened, presumably to ask his name, but Judah jumped in quicker. "Commander Grady, let me show you and your aides the chow line." She began walking back the way she had come without waiting for a response.

Grady swung in right next to her.

"If you need anything while you're here, please let me know. I've only been here a week or so, but I've gotten a pretty good lay of the land. The Seabees are great. And the coffee is drinkable. However, it is better at the Intel House, so drop by whenever you'd like. One of the wives is supplying Starbucks, and she promised weekly shipments."

Grady snorted. "You're stationed in the Middle East, the home of some of the finest roasters of Arabica beans in the world, and you're excited about Starbucks? Wakefield, you stick with me, kid, and I'll introduce you to real coffee."

The entourage followed a polite 3-5 steps behind. Obviously they were not a body guard, more of a reputation-enhancement detachment. Grady was describing a coffee den he had visited in Baghdad last time he was there when she tuned back in.

"Superb," he declared. "If we have any choice, we can set up a perimeter around that block, and take it first. It is only a half a klick from the Republican Palace's West Entrance."

"Are we really going after the palace?" Wakefield felt her eyes widen. She knew of the deep security and impact on the people that would have as a sign of American military might. Oh right, *Coalition* military might.

"Eventually we will have no choice. If only as a symbolic gesture of removing this regime from power. But securing the airport is our first mission."

Wakefield nodded. Of course. She'd been hearing the rumblings around the base of the Third Infantry Division being called up for primary action. "It'll come soon enough."

They were just a hundred yards from the mess tent entrance, when Wakefield turned to Grady, "Sir, you're not really going to can Petty Officer Bailey, are you? He has been so helpful here, and it really was my fault for telling him you enjoyed practical jokes."

The easy comradery melted in the sun as quickly as it had appeared, and shadow lines creased Grady's brow and eyes.

"You know what it will do to his career to be sent home in disgrace from the front. He is a life-er."

"Wakefield, he is obviously allergic to something here. He could never serve in a combat unit because he can't stop sneezing. It would be a mercy to send him elsewhere."

Hmm, Brady Grady might have misplaced his sense of humor, but he had not lost his keen insight and sharp people assessment skills.

Chapter Twelve

The senior staff meeting was breaking up. "Commander Grady?" Wakefield called out. It had been his first morning briefing at the Intel House. The room was overcrowded by the pencil pushers he had brought along, but at least they seemed to be filing out into the early sunshine in a quick flowing current.

Grady turned and cocked an eyebrow.

"If I could have a moment, sir."

Brady Grady patted the shoulder of the admin officer who was following him in the line out the door, and Judah read his lips from across the room as he spoke softly to his aide, "I'll be right behind you. Just give me a minute."

Judah walked toward him around Ellie who gave her a lip-only smile that implied, *good luck, you're gonna need it.*

"What is it, Wakefield? I don't want any further arguments about this Moe's family."

"I understand, sir." Judah seethed inside.

Grady gestured for LT Miller to walk around him as he waited for Judah to thread her way over to him. There were entirely too many people in the room for her liking because of the security level of the items they had been discussing. "Well?"

He was in a hurry, Wakefield could feel the tension around him. "I just wanted to apologize. I hope I didn't cross the line back there, sir. We've had a more relaxed chain of command until—" oops, she broke off her sentence. She'd walked right into that one.

"Until I arrived?" Grady's face was expressionless.

"Well, yes, sir. And it's been working pretty well." She'd already stuck a foot in, might as well, jump in with both feet. She did try to keep her voice low so as not to provoke the man into asserting authority to save face.

"Is that how you came to your conclusions on Moe?" he asked.

"No, sir. Ellie and I questioned him extensively." Judah smoothed her hair back to its bun, none was out of place, but she recognized her own self-soothing gesture. Why was she nervous speaking to Brady Grady? "He's only been back in Baghdad 12 hours or so, there is no reason for him to have checked in with intel yet."

"Then why do you think him a valuable asset, enough to risk a convoy of Americans going into the hot zone to pick up his family if they don't arrive in their own in another 24 hours?"

"He gave us plenty on men we've already sent ahead to long-term detainment. Gitmo."

Grady broke his fierce stare to glance over her shoulder. Men still jostled out of the room to their duty stations for the day shift or to their beds for the night shift. "Walk with me."

Wakefield followed Grady toward the doorway that always felt a bit short to Wakefield. She ducked going out instinctively.

A path cleared around them. Everybody wanted to get out of the way of the big boss.

"I understand your attachment to this guy, Judah. I do. I just wish you had checked with me before sending him in last night."

"But, sir." Grady had not even been officially in the chain of communication until this morning. Why did he expect to be notified or have requests sent through him?

"Look." Grady's voice dropped low. "There is going to be an assault on the airport for a first attempt to capture. Tomorrow."

Judah's mind whirled. "Why didn't I know about this? Moe's house is in the airport zone."

"Now you see why we can't just pop in and get his family out."

"But we've got to get them out before the attack, sir. We made a deal. And why didn't you say something just now when we were all together? The interrogators could be trying today to get more high-level target locations from our already identified Tangoes today."

"Wakefield, you know as well as I that information from Tangoes is only about 20-30 percent reliable. And it is rarely the info we really need in a situation like this."

"But what about questioning some of the vetted Christians? Surely the younger guy Moe ID'ed and trusts, Chucky, might know something. Blind or not, he seems connected and observant from my interviews with him. But either way, we needed to know this." Wakefield accused.

"No." Grady growled. "Your office has a leak."

Judah's breath stuck behind her windpipe. "How do you know?" She asked softly, without bothering to clarify that it wasn't her office. Surely they had not been wrong on Moe.

No, she dismissed the thought. There had not been time to assess him, even if he had been a leak. There was something else.

"Emails have been exchanged, Judah. They were short, encrypted, and routed through more than two dozen countries, but, NSA traced them back to originating between this FOB and being picked up in a café in Baghdad." Grady turned to Judah with a pained expression. "You know the rule about emails out here."

"Couldn't it have been—" Judah racked her brain for some reasonable explanation that did not include espionage. She saw a glimmer of hope touch Grady's eyes as he waited. "I've got nothing," she finally said. The rule was no emails outside the network. Nothing personal, nothing but business, and then business *only* on the network which copied everything to the dedicated server which was reviewed in D.C. in real time for red flags. Or semi-real time. It always seemed to be several hours behind.

Grady continued walking, and Judah hurried to catch up. "Who do they think it is?"

"We are working on it."

Judah frowned. What did that mean?

"Who do you think has the means, Judah?"

"You're sure it's Intel House?" Judah clarified as her heart fell. There were a couple of folks she didn't really like, but she didn't see any of them being spies. That they had narrowed the source down to the Intelligence unit of FOB Beta meant something specific had been compromised.

Grady slowed his walk to a stop when he reached the shade line of the building across from Intel House, which at 0730 hours, put them squarely in the middle of the street. It wasn't hot yet, but something in the quality of the atmosphere told Judah it was going to be warm later.

"Why aren't you talking to Captain George about this, Grady?"

"I think you know, Judah." Grady frowned meaningfully. "The leaks started right after he arrived."

Wakefield shook her head. "Of course they did. The whole base of thousands of people has only been here for a few days. He arrived only a day or so after I did." She refused to believe that freckle-faced CAPT George would compromise soldiers' lives. Or risk his own life. Committing treason during wartime. That was literally a death sentence. "Anyone could be the leak. We're *all* new." Judah said even realizing the implications as she said the words aloud. She'd accepted the premise that there was a leak while trying to defend her senior officer.

"Look, Wakefield, I'm loath to ask after the way you mouthed off in the meeting, but you were always better at accurately profiling people than me in school. I need the best on this. I don't want it to be George. But to me it is safer to consider him guilty unless you can prove him innocent to my satisfaction."

"I didn't mean to be mouthy, but we were chasing a rabbit trail that didn't matter, sir. And it was going on and on. I was just trying to bring us back on track, but, you're right. I see now what you were trying to do, in planting some information." Wakefield shook her head. "But there is no way it could be true. And how are you going to narrow down the culprit if you feed misinformation to the whole intel staff?"

"Well, that's why I need your help. And it wasn't the whole staff. It was just senior staff and my guys, who are looking into this as well, you might as well know."

"Commander Wakefield," CAPT George bellowed from the Intel House doorway. "Are you planning to join us for work today?"

Wakefield felt her eyes startle wide.

Grady snorted. "Don't ever play poker, Wakefield. You don't have the face for it." He paused while she frowned. He reached out and traced the three-inch scar on her cheek. "Although this is quite curious. I don't remember it being there in OSC."

Wakefield turned her head to break the uncomfortable connection and saw CAPT George standing only 40 feet away. Ellie was standing just beyond his shoulder in the sun that lit the entry.

Judah felt her face heat. "Let me just grab *Seren* Ellie Dayan to help. And I'll have to tell George something, of course."

"That IDF chic? No way, Judah. I need people I can trust. *Americans* I can trust." He emphasized with a wrinkled brow. She remembered those wrinkles from their school days; they were deeper now. "You can give George whatever excuse you want."

"You want the best and the fastest? She is it, Grady."

"No." If possible, Grady's wrinkles dug deeper. "Just you."

Judah held her breath for a moment as she assessed Grady's motivations. "Okay fine. But she is better than I am, even at her age." Wakefield nodded once in decision and began to walk back toward Intel House before tossing her head around, meeting Grady's eyes and saying, "But I'm not giving up on Moe and his family. Not by a long shot!"

Grady chuckled so softly she saw it rather than heard it. "If I remember correctly, you were a better-than-superior marksman at the long shot," he said.

"Still am, sir."

"What was that about?" Ellie asked suspiciously before Judah even had time to open her mouth.

Judah pulled out her best poker face, met Ellie's eyes briefly, shrugged and addressed CAPT George. "Grady wants me to work from his office on a special project today. It sounds like he'll send me back over here tomorrow."

"Where is his office, Wakefield? And where is the protocol?"

"I believe Brady had his guys set him up two doors up from the joke headquarters." She pointed across the street at the tumbling-down two story and then to the right two doorways. Within hours, the whole base had heard about the welcome Commander Brady Grady had received. "Would you like me to have him call you with those TAD orders, sir?"

"Watch it, Lieutenant Commander. I'm still your supervisor even if you're on a first name basis with the base commander."

"I'm sorry, sir." Judah sighed. "You're right. I shouldn't have said it like that. I'm not mad at you. I was counting on working on some of Moe's leads today with Ellie. And seeing if we could back-channel some help getting his family out." Judah cut her eyes to Dayan over George's shoulder where she still stood taking in the entire performance. "But it looks like you're going to have to do it on your own, Ellie."

The expression on Ellie's face told Judah she was not fooled in the least. Wakefield turned around before the blush she felt coming made its way to her neck. She folded her arms across her chest and pinched her waist to distract her mind and try to avoid the blush. She couldn't remember a time when she had blushed as often as she had been the last few days. Even as a teenager. It annoyed her.

115

Chapter Thirteen

The muezzin began to wail the mid-morning call to prayer. Number two of five had begun for the day. The sound Moe had grown up loving when he was called Muhammad, grated on his nerves and sent fear into his belly now that he was called Moses, or Moe, for short and for safety.

After the early morning drop off, Moe had scurried through the streets, making his way on foot through hometown neighborhoods he scarcely recognized anymore.

The coalition forces were thorough, he would give them that. For perhaps the thousandth time since being deposited west and south of town, Moe prayed, "Oh God of Abraham, Isaac, and Jacob, please help me and let this plan work."

Moe had skirted around the edge of the city and was approaching his district in the west by the airport from the direction of Ibn Al-Bitar Hospital near the river. He hoped the hours of walking added to his disguise, though the exhaustion was not fake by any means.

Fear was like a dark, wet, wool blanket adding weight to every step. Moe scurried from corner to corner and slunk along crumbling walls of the city of his birth to avoid the blanket of fear being tossed over his head to smother him.

He was afraid he would be caught, that his family would be caught, that he would never see them. Actually, he expected that. He was afraid that he would not hold up under torture when the Iraqi Republican Guard captured him. He was afraid that he would get caught in a bombing run by the Americans. Sometimes he could hear them coming; sometimes they were too high to hear them, and only a slight high-pitched whistle was followed by the explosion of some building or street. He wasn't sure which he preferred. He was afraid of the looters. Of not finding water soon. He was afraid he couldn't help bring freedom to his city. Fear exhausted him, weighed him down.

From two blocks away, Moe could see a hole in the city's block of buildings where there shouldn't have been a hole. The views of this route that he had memorized from walking home from work every day for years.

He quickened his step but the heat from the blanket of fear drew even closer to him.

The structure of the city block to his right looked correct. A few more windows broken than he remembered. The al Mahdavi family had boarded over both their front entryway and their downstairs windows with new beams of wood in an X.

Closer to his fifth-floor flat at the corner of the 900 block of Seventh Street, Moe stopped stock still in the center of the street.

He could see at an angle the ceiling of the bedroom he had shared with his wife for 12 of their 17 years of marriage. The outer wall was missing from the roof-top terrace and fifth floor all the way down to the second floor. The innards of everyone's private lives lay exposed to anyone who happened past. The concrete rubble lay where it had fallen mixed with the fabrics that had brought comfort to him, his family, and his neighbors.

By the time Moe realized his feet were moving again, he stood at a pile of rubble he recognized. Fastened in place among chunks of stone and concrete and twisted rebar, lay charred bedding and clothing that had survived. If you could call it surviving.

He felt a tickle in his beard, and when reaching to scratch it away, his fingertips came back wet. *Blood?* But no, his hand was not red with death, it was wet with sadness. *Where are you, my Liliya? Do you have the children? Are you safe?*

"Oh, Isa, I need you." Moe barely whispered. So many memories in their small little home, now uninhabitable. Moe stared up at the gaping hole and raised his sleeve to dry his face.

He felt his heart start to grow angry. Of all the blocks, why his house? Why his family? Why did the Americans come in and destroy his city? As Moe opened his mouth to curse them, he remembered the vision God had revealed to him four months earlier: What a free Iraq could look like. How the Kingdom of God could be revealed and spread like wildfire. He had seen the cleansing fire that had to precede that building of the Kingdom. "I just didn't expect it to start at my house." Moe's strength of stature crumbled into the dusty intersection and he mourned his former life.

FOB Beta
Female Officer Quarters
April 5, 2003
2245 hours

Judah lay on her side willing herself to relax into the cot. It was the first early night she'd seen since arriving in country.

Everyone still on the FOB was aware of the day-break mission. At late chow some of the young soldiers were jacked up

118

on bravado, others displayed the short jerky movements she associated with fear. The old hands had forgone the extra cuppa joe and headed back to give their weapons and boots one more polish. She knew the exercise was more about setting the soul right than the shine.

Wakefield and Intel House would spend the next morning getting caught up on paperwork, clearing the cells, sending confirmed Tangos on to Gitmo, and rearranging those still being pumped for intelligence, to make room for high-value Tangos who would soon be brought in for questioning.

She breathed deeply, trying not to listen to conversations outside the canvas walls that even the generators' noise couldn't mask. She relaxed her toes, then her calves, her knees, but by the time she forced the tension out of her thighs, her feet were tight again.

"Lieutenant Commander Wakefield?" A female voice called softly from the dimly lit tent flap.

"Over here." Judah sighed and threw back the covers. Sleep would be postponed until later after all. She jutted her chin toward the outside, and the girl must have seen her even in the ambient light, for she stepped outside to wait. Judah wrapped her uniform jacket around her and didn't bother lacing her boots as she sank her feet back into them and walked outside. No one in the tent was actually sleeping she knew, but taking business outside was a courtesy the officers had all come to observe in order to preserve a semblance of work life versus home life.

It wasn't fooling any of them though.

Wakefield raked fingers through her hair, which really needed a shampoo. She pulled it away from her face and twisted it once before tossing it over her shoulder.

An enlisted woman, whom Wakefield assumed worked the night shift because she had not seen her before, waited a few feet from the tent flap in the middle of what would have been the road, if this tent city had been a brick-and-mortar village.

"I'm sorry to interrupt your sleep, ma'am, but Commander Grady asked to see you."

Wakefield's face must have reflected her incredulity at the timing, because the petty officer said. "He got a phone call and then ordered me to get you ASAP, ma'am."

Oh boy! This didn't sound good. "Are you to escort me, or am I free to make my way there on my own?" Wakefield grumbled.

"He didn't say, but I'll wait for you, ma'am. More for my own safety than anything else." The young woman smiled.

Judah nodded once. Sounded like a good idea. She turned and lifted the tent flap and began buttoning her uniform as she shuffled to get her cover and weapon. Stopping only to tie her boots, Wakefield was ready in 30 seconds.

She wound her hair into a low bun, securing it with the black elastic band she kept on her wrist at all times, as she walked to Grady's office. The petty officer followed in her wake.

At least I had time to brush my teeth and wash my face before lying down this time, she thought. It was the third time this week she had been called back to an office after her shift.

CDR Grady looked up at her as he finished signing his name to the middle of a sheet of paper. Hair askew, the garish lights the Seabees had rigged to the ceiling in the FOB Beta commander's office magnified wrinkles around Grady's eyes.

She stiffened to attention and waited silently for him to address her.

Brady Grady pushed the paper to the right corner of his desk without breaking eye contact and laid the pen on top. He took a breath, held it two beats and exhaled as he slowly leaned back into his folding metal chair.

Judah felt like she was being sized up, and wasn't sure which way the judgement was falling. Was it about the practical joke again?

"Is that aim of yours still as dead-on as I remember from OCS, Wakefield?"

"Sir?"

"Sit." He threw a hand toward a metal folding chair. "I've got a problem. The advance team of sniper cover for the assault in—" He broke off to look at his watch, "six hours is down by four men. The one with the fever going around said he can still go, but the ones puking their guts up—" Grady just shook his head. We cannot advance without sniper overwatch. Originally we called for ten, but Blount thinks he can make do with eight. I'm down to the dregs, Commander. Can you do it?"

Wakefield squinted and gave him a reserved half-smile. The adrenaline had already begun to shoot through her body. "The dregs, eh? Thanks for the vote of confidence, sir." She shrugged. "Sure, I can do it."

"Good. I'll read you in right now." Grady reached for his metal briefcase before the words were out of his mouth. For seven minutes he read the battle plan and objectives to her.

Wakefield closed her eyes and listened. Committing the details to memory. While she catalogued the plan, and even assessed it a bit for flaws, she transitioned to battle mode. She would be on her own, unaccompanied even by a spotter. This was not a CIA mission that had thousands of man-hours built into it and back up via satellite coms in real time. This was not a desk job or an interview. This was the real thing. War. Raw and ambiguous. One shot-one kill. Perhaps over and over again.

Wakefield felt the odd sensation in her nervous system of an increased heart rate while the steely calm of confidence built on 100,000-plus shots fired that had found their targets settled over her.

He checked his watch again. "You'll have just about thirty minutes to zero your weapon, review the other firing positions, and hop the transport."

"I'll also have to go put my contacts back in." Wakefield stood. "Combat, huh?"

Grady reached out to shake her hand. "Let's not mention that until it's over. Officially, I cannot order you into combat. Thanks, Wakefield. Keep your head down."

"Aye, aye, sir."

As Judah double-timed it back to FOQ, her mind was shifting into prioritizing overdrive. Contacts first, change socks and double up on them. It would get chilly lying still, in wait for sunrise. Get to the armory, sign out an L115A3 long range rifle, a laser range finder, and practice ammo, and then get more .338 Lapua Magnum rounds and a ghilli suit for the watch. Check the atmospheric conditions for herself. Had she updated her "just-in-case" letter? Were the Iraqis expecting them? Would there be anti-sniper measures in place around the airport? How long would the mission take? Take water for sure, but MREs or bars? Oh, grease paint for skin camouflage. At least clean hair with a shampoo scent wouldn't give her away.

So many things to bring order to.

The thirty-four minutes passed like a smear.

And Wakefield, covered in a lumpy suit of grasses to disguise her figure and carrying her rifle and pack, climbed aboard the back of the transport truck with the other seven sharp shooters.

She smiled inside. Not a single man offered to help her with the four-foot leap up with her pack. The ghilli suit was a great equalizer. She knew that until she opened her mouth to speak, they would be none the wiser as to her gender.

The team leader distributed coms ear pieces, and went over the plan one last time, complete with maps, on the ride to the ridge entry point. "Remember no more than three shots from any location," SGT Harvey said. "Shoot and move, then reload. And these coms are for *us* to speak to *you*. Only. Capiche?"

Wakefield was assigned to the west company.

Hopping down, she reached back for her thirty-pound pack, mostly ammunition, and slung it to her back for the three-quarter-mile hike to their positions around the ridge. Her team of four stood still allowing their eyes to adjust to the moon-lit night. Smoke hung like a coat over the city. It plumed upward reflecting the little light in varying shades of deep gray.

Donning night-vision goggles from their packs, Wakefield's world turned to shades of green with three red and orange body-shaped blobs showing the heat signature of her surroundings.

Denning hunkered down first. The west team leader, U.S. Army SGT Harvey pointed to Wakefield next, and she peeled off from the group about 1000 yards west of where Denning did.

Slowly she made her way up the backside of the treed ridge toward the glow of the airport until she could see pinpoints of light dotting her vision. Constantly sweeping side to side looking for trip wires or IEDs, listening for the tiny click of landmines. All of which would give away the team's position, and most likely kill her.

She wasn't seeing anything out of the ordinary in nature.

Dropping to her knees, she slowly crawled with a low profile to avoid attention, to peek up over the edge of the rise. There she was: Saddam International Airport ablaze in lights appeared just over a mile away. One of the runways ended about 10 degrees to her left and approximately 80 yards away. She would measure the distances when she settled.

The scraggly cover of trees looked just right, so Wakefield pulled off her pack. Taking out the laser range finder, and stowing the goggles, she pushed the pack forward of her position to act as a sandbag to steady her aim. She stretched her long body out prone.

Fitting the stock into her shoulder and leaning her face to the cold plastic cheek piece, Wakefield closed her left eye and peered through the scope.

The circle of her world got very small as she viewed the landscape a mile away. In her mind she overlaid the map grid of her responsibility for the coming dawn on the live airport location: the entry road, the terminal doors and canopies, the terminal buildings and landscaping, the helo pads, a small portion of the baggage inner-workings she could see from her position, and the runways that stretched like claws toward her.

A windsock lay against a flag pole like an orange peel ready for the garbage.

The haze of Baghdad's earlier carpet bombing still hung over the concrete city, reflecting yellow street lamps in some areas and leaving deep gray holes over areas that had no longer had power.

The lack of wind will make calculations and compensation easier, Wakefield assessed as she began the precise measurement of distance with the laser. But when the airport liberation, courtesy of the Third Infantry Division began to kick up dust, she knew the lack of wind would leave a deep haze covering her targets.

General calculations and all scope adjustments for wind, elevation, magnification, and focus complete, Wakefield screwed her silencer in place, and pulled down the bi-pod for additional stabilization when firing. She loaded the magazine with a metallic clicking sequence so familiar.

LCDR Judah Wakefield began the watching and waiting.

She focused on her breathing, her heart rate, the slightest stirrings of the natural inhabitants of small wooded area she was using as her hide. An occasional nocturnal bird or rat would move in the more-soft-than-crunchy leaves that had been on the ground for nearly six months. Traffic still buzzed around the city, though there was not too much civilian movement around the airport, an occasional delivery truck or grey military transporter lumbered through the simple circle to the terminal. She thought she heard a train whistle, but it would have been miles away according to the map she'd studied.

By the moonlight she checked her watch slowly and silently. Three more hours to wait.

"Oh, Father," Judah whispered in her soul. "I didn't even take the time to address you in this. I just got caught up with the preparations. Would you help me function at my best? Give me wisdom and guide my hands and heart. Show me what you would have me to do. I'm sorry I will probably kill some of the people you love and have died for in a few hours."

Judah's heart was heavy. "If there is any other way, Father…" she left the prayer hanging.

"Jesus, I know you've been at work bringing your Kingdom in this city. Would you send dreams and visions to those who might accept your offer of salvation? Would you remind them of

125

times you've ministered to them and cared for them? Soften hearts all over Baghdad tonight to receive you before it is too late for some of them at dawn."

Chapter Fourteen

Moe awoke with a start. Something sounded different. Straining his eyes against the black night he searched, "Liliya?" he called softly. "Girls? Amil? Is that you?" No reply.

A thought that he would like to take a walk on the quiet streets before sun up crossed his mind. Nothing urgent, more like an invitation from the Lord. He had felt this idea before and learned to follow the prompting.

Rising, Moe used the bedclothes to swipe his face dry from the dew and oily smoke residue that had settled on him in the night from the al fresco condition of his bedroom. It was hard to breathe in the thick air. His nose wrinkled of its own accord. Those tires were still burning, and somewhere close. The oil refinery had been burning for two days already and the smoke enveloped the whole of the city.

Putting a fresh long outer robe and the traditional kufiyah for warmth and blending-in ability, Moe traversed the broken stairwell carefully and let himself out the shared outer door to his apartment building. Not another soul stirred in his view, though a vehicle cranked up a little slow a few streets over—his

127

spark plugs need cleaning, Moe assessed easily—and the eternal whir of traffic from the highway provided white noise as it did at any hour in a city of seven million people.

Moe had an urge to run, but didn't know where to go. He felt like his face was a beacon screaming "SPY" but knew if he tried to stick to the shadows guilt would be more pronounced, at least to anyone who knew him.

If he couldn't find his wife and children, it wouldn't make a difference anyway. He was stuck here. His beloved hometown was coming down around his ears, and the Americans wanted him to be their inside man. He shook his head at the lunacy his life had become. Just a month earlier he never dreamed he would be living like this.

He kept walking in the middle of the darkened street, partly to avoid the random rubble piles of neighborhood apartment homes and storefronts on the lower levels. They lived too near the bridge, the probable American target. And partly he walked in the middle because the street was empty.

The sound of the highway became deeper, more throaty. Heavy trucks. He recognized the sound. But whose?

Having just passed the Al Wadi Garden pass-through, Moe reversed his path and made his way to the alley-shaped garden with the hand-dug creek bed between two 6-story buildings. It was Liliya's favorite little walk in the city. So unexpected, not gated, and had never been vandalized, at least that Moe had ever seen.

Even in the dark, the single-block-long meandering snake-path was easy to traverse because he had walked it so often, and he enjoyed breathing deeply of the night scents.

Exiting the peaceful garden, Moe's pace quickened. The sound of heavy trucks was actually multiplying. Two more blocks to his right and one block closer to the highway and he'd be able to see whose military was coming through town and which direction they were heading. From the time he left the garden pass-through, Moe decided to stick to the shadows, but forced himself not to scurry like he wanted to. That always attracted more attention and was so much more difficult to explain away when one was delayed for questioning.

Moe began to pray. It was under his breath and he wasn't even sure it was in any language he spoke. He felt his city deteriorating around him. He felt the helplessness and hate in the atmosphere. "Oh Lord, have your way in me. Have your way in this city."

He took a right one street early to zig zag the blocks to the little neighborhood rise where he knew he could see the highway.

One city block later, making a left back toward the highway, Moe pulled up short.

There was no break in the truck convoy noise, but when he started around the corner the sound of deep anger enveloped him. The buildings had funneled the noise away from him until then.

Moe edged half his face around the chipped-plaster corner.

There were at least three separate fires licking at the street. Though the smallest one, unattended, looked on the verge of going out. Maybe two dozen men jostled each other in a cluster around the largest fire, the one closest to him. Fortunately, most of the men faced the fire, not him.

Moe squinted to try to identify two overly-animated young men in front of the fire facing the men and him. They both gestured with raised rifles and jerky movements, one following slightly behind the other in his movements. They even poked at some of the people around them with the butts of those weapons. From the staggering back of one of the men who was not expecting to be singled out, the leader was not gently motioning to them. The two men did seem to take turns speaking emphatically—okay, yelling—at the group. Most of whom would bark some phrase Moe couldn't quite untangle from the night noises. The leader of average height held himself as though he had formal military training, though like the rest of the crowd, he was dressed in civilian clothes more Western than cultural.

An old Toyota mini-truck was parked sideways as a barrier between Moe and the group and he could see the front grill of an Iraqi Army Jeep reflecting firelight, though it was mostly hidden by a building. A few of the thousands of leaflets that had canvassed the city with fair warning of the bombing runs still skittered around the edges of street.

With the firelight destroying the group's night vision and their attention firmly distributed among themselves, Moe decided it was probably safe to just cross the street where he was.

The first step was the hardest. "Straight shoulders. Deep breath," he coached himself. He hummed a lullaby his mother used to sing him to sleep in order to help pace himself on the longest 70-meter walk of his life. The adrenaline surged and sparked in his extremities; fear gripped his belly and urged him to run. He could taste the sour desire to hide. Five more paces. Finally, the corner of the building hide him from the crowd's view. He knew that crowd could become a mob in seconds.

Keeping his head lowered, he looked for any movement on the ground in the street in front of him, and on the first two stories of the buildings that lined the street. Those not brave enough to be at the impromptu street meeting of young men, also seemed wise enough to stay behind closed curtains.

Step by trembling step, the sounds of the incited neighbors began to give way to the highway noise that had sent Moe on his mission in the first place.

Cutting through one more alleyway, deserted, thank the Lord, Moe pulled up on the tree branch that allowed him to swing his legs up slightly to steady himself atop a left-behind concrete highway divider from before the tall sound barriers had been erected for the neighborhood in 1997.

The view was comforting, even more so than he thought it might be. "They are coming!" he breathed as he stretched to see if he could spot the end of the convoy. It continued as far as he could see at very nice pace.

"Now to find a phone." Moe muttered.

Chapter Fifteen

Overwatch rise above
Saddam International Airport
6 April 2003
0500 hours local time

A third set of headlights in a row broke over the edge of the airport entry road that curved toward the terminal.

Wakefield glanced at her watch simultaneously with the first sounds of the convoy reaching her ears. *Right on time.*

After the first U.S. Marines' M1 Abrams tank's top gunner received a volley of automatic fire from a pair of security officers at the main gate, the tank returned fire, sending the trio of security huts and striped traffic arms into an inferno. Wakefield shook her head. She had thought the Iraqis would be more prepared than what appeared to be security guards. A shoulder-mounted rocket launcher at the very least.

The U.S. convoy melted into a three-wide band of strength that took up all lanes of the paved road. Because of the only slightly curved roads, they progressed, Wakefield guessed, around 35 miles an hour.

She tore her eyes away to hone in on the quadrant she was responsible to cover.

All movement was proceeding normally. Only two people were even visible within her whole zone. Based on their early-morning sluggish movement, they probably could not hear anything out of the ordinary with the jet engines idling on the tarmac and the general hangar noise of repairs being conducted for completion by morning to get an international airport ready for a day of moving passengers from the terminal to the sky and onward to their destinations.

It was funny how many rich or desperate people, or both, found that they had business to conduct abroad during tumultuous times in their nation. Even when their airport was being shelled on a schedule. Flights out of Baghdad had been overbooked for weeks, Wakefield had heard it from dozens of her interviewees since arriving in country.

Once the pop-pop-pop of shooting started, the cacophony of war compounded on itself. Based on the sounds echoing back up to her position, the Marines had moved into Denning's zone on her right. Still, she swept her area left to right and back again through her scope. With the naked eye, people who now scurried through her zone were the size of very small ants. Through the scope though, she could choose to hit the head or chest.

There was not a single weapon in sight in any of the square footage of Wakefield's zone, so she raised her head slightly in the raggedy ghilli suit's fringe to take in another overview of the area.

"Oh no." Wakefield felt her body tense and her eyes go wide. A stream of those ants was now moving out from a door on the tarmac-side of a small hangar adjacent to the airport's main building, hidden from the U.S. ground troop's view. It was only a two-story Butler building with a couple of windows and a large hangar door on rollers immediately next to another regular-sized aluminum door which had been propped open and had a second, thinner line of ants pouring out.

Black-clad and heavily armed soldiers were now a steady stream merging together.

U.S. forces, First Brigade, Third Infantry Division amassed in the front of the airport with little resistance, but Judah knew there was no way they could see the enemy forces building behind the airport.

Wakefield peered through her scope again and swept her area of responsibility. Marine vehicles were filling in the space in front of the airport terminal, but no fighting had begun there. Hardly even giving it a second thought, Wakefield looked down to her notes on distance to get the trajectory correct and adjusted her sight to the small propped-open hangar door that faced her directly. A flood of men still poured out the exit. More than a hundred Republican Guardsmen had begun to spread out and were approaching the edge of the large airport building as a disciplined and practiced unit.

They were still outside the view of the marines.

A very large clash was coming.

Wakefield zeroed her gaze through the scope back to the door and then side to side. "What can I use to block that hole? Come on, come on."

Her words were under her breath, maybe even just lip movement.

And then she saw it.

A fuel tanker streaked into her scope from the left.

When she had last seen it, the tanker driver was at the pump refueling the truck, a distance from anything. But he must have received a warning, because he was booking it out of the way of the U.S. Marines. A door on a second small hanger began to roll back to accept the tanker.

However, to get there, he would have to roll right in front of Wakefield's line of sight between her and the building where the Republican Guard was gushing from what could only be an underground bunker. The men kept coming and coming. The group had swelled past her guess of 250 or 275 men. Well-armed men.

One more check of the wind sock. Just the tiniest gusts of wind. "No problem," Wakefield's mouth pulled up on one side and her grease paint felt thick on her skin. "It's a pretty large target."

With the ease of hundreds of hours of moving-target practice, Wakefield tightened the stock in on her shoulder, held her breath. This shot would coincide with her heartbeat rather than fall in between the heartbeats, as she preferred. She could feel the correct timing rather than all the fancy calculations.

Three, two, and on one, she pulled the trigger.

On the imaginary zero-count the tanker truck driving squarely in front of the small hanger door exploded.

Many of the guardsmen had seen the truck coming and had scattered out of its path already. More than a few were caught in the immediate fireball formed by the full tanker truck.

The tower of flames taller than the airport terminal reminded Wakefield of the Children of Israel in the desert being led by a pillar of fire.

No time for remorse or celebration. The deep percussion alerted the Third Infantry Division out front of the activity stirring on the unseen side of the airport. But the Butler-building bunker doorway was jammed with fiery debris, as she had hoped. Paint peeled and dripped as it changed color in the heat.

A quick check of her zone saw troops beginning to clash. An RPG launcher appeared on the shoulder of one of the men in black garb. Men scattered out from behind and in front of him. They had seen this before.

Wakefield clicked her scope focus back to her previous settings as he leaned his head into the long thin launcher to verify his aim.

Don't do it, she begged him silently. Holding her breath again, when he leaned forward and braced his back leg, she fired.

He went down without firing his RPG, but someone else just picked it up. The trigger must have tangled in his dead fingers because the man who picked it up jerked it once with no success and then stepped on the man's arm and yanked it away, leaving the dead man's forearm to flop to the tarmac.

That was two shots from this position. Wakefield felt like she could risk one more, counting on the chaos of the first minutes of shooting and the Iraqis entering the field to cover her.

The U.S. tanks now began to round the corner onto the airfield.

Wakefield risked a quick look at the burning tanker to see if the stream of soldiers had been stymied.

Her heart sank.

The little door was certainly disabled, but now the hangar door was rolling open. Not only were twice as many Iraqi Republican Guards pouring out as before, but armored vehicles were driving out two at a time in columns from the wider opening.

The vehicles and the men simply skirted around the tanker's column of fire.

It appeared the trucks drove up out of the hangar as if from an underground parking garage.

And the soldiers, trucks, and now armored vehicles kept coming.

Wakefield returned her over-watch to her zone to look for some advantage for her side. Scanning left and right, up and down to cover all the space.

The entire backside of the airport was now alive with activity.

Wakefield focused and then saw it. An Iraqi was edging his way toward a U.S. Marines' troop transport truck idling near a wall. The truck had a light guard around it as U.S. troops dropped down from the back of the truck three by three in full gear. The Marines held their weapons upright for their four-foot jump to the ground and immediately moved to patrol-ready level as they scurried to surround their vehicle.

The Iraqi had a grenade and it would be a fairly easy toss, even though it would be suicide for him with so many Marines who would be facing him when he stepped out of cover to make his throw.

Wakefield watched his facial features through her scope and knew from the narrowing of his eyes and pull of his lips that he had pulled the pin. She let her bullet fly. The man dropped to the concrete and no one on either side seemed to take note, until the concussion followed four seconds later. Not only was the man in pieces, but he had managed to put a hole in the lower level of the airport with the grenade. Bricks from the façade tumbled and a pouf of dust rose.

Not a single American was harmed.

Third shot, gotta move, Wakefield prompted herself. Under cover of brush, she scooted slowly to a new position 25 feet from her previous hide. She found a large fresh divot in the woods' floor. Wakefield assumed it was American-made from one of the softening-up bombing runs of the previous two days.

She lay herself back down, prone, facing the activity of the airport.

No flashlight, no sudden moves, no night vision goggles that might reflect and give away her new position.

Rechecking her distance with the laser Wakefield wondered how this battle might have gone without the air raids preceding their ground liberation.

This airport was a stronghold not only in the way it had been dug in and built up militarily, but also, it was a person's only way out of the country without attempting a *Sound-of-Music*-esq tromp over the border.

And that oppressive raised-arm statue of Saddam Hussein out front in the arrivals/departures traffic circle was lording over the territory. Wakefield was glad it wasn't facing her position because it really felt like it could see everything going on and was disapproving deeply with an anger stirring in its molten brass belly. Creepy!

"It's probably just cameras I am sensing." Judah swallowed and focused on her zone again.

An hour and two more position changes later the sky was just beginning to streak grey. Sunrise would be coming at 0647 hours according to the briefing on their way in.

On her next visual pass over the flat roofline of the airport terminal that was in her zone, Wakefield saw a ghost of shadow movement. She backtracked and waited for it again. Tactically, she assessed, it was the perfect place to attack the U.S. troops. High ground, defensible, at lease for a little while, and plenty of protected space with the lip-wall that protruded above the flat roof.

The only problem was there was no emergency exit.

She scanned the space of the roofline within her jurisdiction. Still nothing else. Maybe it was just her imagination.

A quick glance to check for emergency needs on ground level. They seemed to be holding their own.

Back to the rooftop. "Where are you? I know you're up there." She murmured. "Come on show your head."

She waited.

Then there was movement. A lot of movement. The roofline came alive in a coordinated fashion. Six crooked chimneys peeked up through the smoke crowning the main terminal. Three of them were in her zone. Each of the men held RPG launchers at the ready on their shoulders. She zeroed in on the one closest to her scope crosshairs when they appeared. But her shot did not come in time.

Six dragon tails of fire leapt into the air and spit sparks as they zoomed toward the Bradley Fighting Vehicles that were inflicting their own damage into the airport's main floor.

Wakefield felt like Elisha not able to watch the progress of the RPG like Elijah's chariot-of-fire distraction from the main event. She made a minor adjustment of her aim and took a third shot from this location. The shot she had just fired must have found its mark, because she could only see five marks on the rooftop now, but it was too late to avoid the discharging of his weapon.

Without waiting for the body to drop, Wakefield adjusted her weapon a quarter inch to her right and a millimeter down to take out the target nearest to the close-side corner of the rooftop.

Crosshairs aligned on his chest about the time she realized she was not taking a profile shot this time, but a full body shot.

Even as she gave the trigger a firm pull she focused on the man's lips. He was yelling something, and his eyes moved down as if he was giving instruction to someone below him.

He already had another weapon on his shoulder, and it appeared as if a third one was being shoved toward him from an unseen assistant hunkered down below the four-foot-high lip of the roof.

Her bullet found its mark.

The shooter flew backward out of the circle of her scope.

But he had discharged his weapon toward her already.

The large RPG was slower than the force behind her .50 caliber ammunition. But still only gave her about two seconds to gather her rifle under her arm and throw herself two giant leaps and about 12 feet at an angle to higher ground, trying to avoid jostling her weapon's calibration while keeping herself alive.

She fell hard on her left side and curled her knees to her chest, tucked her head inside her left armpit and toward the dirt as she held her breath and remembered SGT Harvey's warning "no more than three shots from any location. They *will* find you."

The rocket propelled grenade detonated about 35 feet down the slight incline from her new position. Dirt clods and splinters rained around her. The ghilli suit did offer a little padding protection. A single mid-sized tree was felled by the blast and shook the earth around her again as it cracked and boomed to the ground.

Somehow even being chunked out on the airport-side of the tree, it fell downhill and away from her and did not even cause a disruption to her line of sight after it settled in place. Wakefield looked at the quivering leaves for a moment, puzzled because she felt like it should have fallen toward her, especially with the direction of the blast force.

"Thanks for sending angels to push it away from me, Lord."

Wakefield repositioned herself to face the airport again. The angle was awkward and pinched her spine, so she belly crawled to a lesser incline.

Wakefield scoped the roof again. It was getting lighter out by the moment. She hoped there was something left of her gear-pack to salvage. And it would be really nice to have the laser distance finder available too. After the sun was up, she'd see what she could see. She sighed. Her canteen, if it had survived, was over there too.

Chapter Sixteen

The pounding American war machine had not allowed him even a moment of sleep. Saddam Hussein swung his feet to the floor, shuffling until he found his slippers. Aides had come every hour, on the hour, to update him on how well the airport was holding. Other aides had updated him just before midnight that the final truck routing for movement of the chemical weapons they had been working hard to complete were in place. They had never been able to duplicate the exact formula that that retched Filasek had sold him, but in the trying, his scientists had produced one that spread just as easily, was nearly as deadly and took only a few steps to lay in a supply.

Saddam twisted on the lamp switch next to his bed. For today, this place seemed the most secure location from which to command his troops and look over the route to memorize the pattern or some common stopping point so he could access a batch or two as needed. If he had to go underground to chop off the Great Satan's filthy hand which had dared reach into his sovereign nation, so be it. But next week or next month, "Even if it takes a year," he shuffled to the door, "I will reign from my own

142

palace once more. The Americans will run home with their tails between their legs." It was inevitable, he knew, just as he had known his taking up power as king of Iraq was inevitable. Just as he knew in his heart that he was King Nebuchadnezzar reincarnate and would soon rule from Ancient Babylon. It was never something he reduced to words; he just knew. His people would never bow to the Americans, never cooperate with them, except maybe on the surface and then, only for a little while, in order to set them up for defeat. Every last one of them would stand and fight until they had no breath left in their bodies.

But better to have them make a stand at the airport, than in the city where rebuilding was already going to be time- and resource-consuming. Not bothering to dress, he grabbed a heavy robe and threw it over his shoulders as he walked to the Generals' alcove, the East Wing addition. He would send in more troops. There was no sense defending the borders around an entire city when the Americans had already showed where their greatest interest lay: travel capabilities.

The call to prayer began to wail insistently. Saddam huffed. He picked up his pace and tied his flapping robe in the middle. The only reason he allowed the annoying cacophony was the great way it kept the masses in check.

FOB-Camp Liberty North
6 April 2003
0705 hours

"Today's the day." Rivers announced to the entire Echo Company and Delta Company assigned to train at and insert from Camp Liberty. The SEALs stirred with whispers and good-natured shoulder punches.

"Hope you enjoyed your breakfast. I want everybody carb-loading at lunch and eating a moderate dinner. We go after Saddam tonight. In about twenty-four hours we will be back in this spot to debrief. This is *the* mission of our lifetime, men. The one we will remember for the rest of our lives. Hopefully our success will be declassified in twenty years so we can tell our grandchildren all about how we took down a madman monster."

"Or gave him his face-to-face introduction-to-Jesus meeting!" came a call-out from the second row of the metal folding chairs.

"Or that." Rivers nodded. "But we do prefer to bring him for tribunal in an international court. Remember that. The airport raid began last night and is going well so far. We should have another update on that before we pull out at sunset."

**Saddam International Airport
6 April 2003
0930 hours**

A lull came in the intense fighting. The airfield was by no means quiet, just a little less movement, a little less smoke and sound. Wakefield watched a pair of medics race into her zone toward one of the boys she had been keeping an eye on. "Go guys go! I've got you covered from here." The lower half of the soldier's leg was gushing blood. Even with her limited medical training in battlefield assessment, she knew he could lose part of his leg.

Ten minutes earlier, the soldier had crawled, using only his upper body strength, and an occasional left leg thrust, dragging his right leg behind; his weapon on its bandolier hung underneath him. A streak of red led directly to his hiding place behind a stack of orange loading-zone cones. He was hidden—

sort of—from the action, but visible to her. The marine had maintained his weapon and laid it across his lap as he leaned against the stack of cones. He had pulled off his own belt, wrapped it around his thigh, just above the knee, and fastened it tightly. He had struggled. As Judah watched him through her scope the marine had used something that looked like a pen or a stick to twist the tourniquet so that it turned off his blood flow to his leg from the knee, down. And he waited. Wakefield could see him struggle to retain consciousness and hold onto the twisted belt.

Judah broke radio silence to pass on the man's position when she saw he had the constitution to make it. Someone had relayed it to the medical unit on scene. And here they were. "Come on, hurry," Wakefield urged them on.

Not a single shot was fired at the medics. Unusual. Wakefield paused in her constant scoping over her zone. When the lull reached two minutes, Judah wondered if this was her chance to go back for her equipment pack and water.

She had already started to move when she felt a tug on her ankle hold her back. It was a physical tug. Wakefield dropped back to her prone position, still and silent for half a minute. She slowly wiggled her ankle to free herself from underbrush or vines. Nothing was touching her.

Did I imagine it? she wondered.

Slowly, slowly she zoned in on her environment. The lighter gunfire at the battle scene made it easier to hear. But that could pick back up any second. The Republican Guard was regrouping.

The chirping birds from pre-dawn had long since abandoned the noisy area. The few sounds she could hear felt eerie. Truck noises in the distance grew and faded and grew and faded. Something was not quite right about it. Were the sounds coming from behind the little hill in the woods where she and the other snipers were hiding?

Reinforcements or an attack?

The commander would have warned them over coms if help was being brought in, to avoid friendly fire. Was this about to become fire…and not so friendly?

She tapped her ear piece four times and went perfectly still. Short shallow breaths that offered no movement.

She was still facing the airport runway and terminal building, but now she could hear them coming behind her.

Boots tromping loamy earth and old soft leaves. Still a little way away. *How many? How many?* The demand to know ran through her head on a loop.

More than a dozen for sure.

Moving only her eyes, Wakefield assessed her position. The fight-or-flight mechanism pumping chemicals into her blood stream was shrieking, "Run!"

She still couldn't see the men coming, but they sounded as if at least some of them had crested the hill about fifty yards behind her.

Wakefield's rifle was covered in tied-on brush. She knew the cumbersome ghilli suit would appear to be a heap of dried grasses and leaves that lay partially under a short but dense evergreen tree. She hoped her boots were covered. It was too late to check now or to pull her legs in.

All of her concentration converged in listening and breathing without moving.

Chapter Seventeen

Making his way through many streets on foot toward the palace garage to check for work, and to see if he could siphon any Republican Guard plans for a counter-move after the American invasion on the west and south of Baghdad, Moe walked in contemplation. Some streets felt deserted even by air, others he avoided when he was able to, because they were crammed with rioting crowds being shot on sight more often than being hauled in for questioning by the king's merry men.

Moe kept his eyes peeled for a way to establish contact on the phone number he had memorized along with all the proper protocols to connect him to Missy Judah's base.

Whether he ever found his family again or not, he had determined at some point just after dawn that helping to free his nation from Saddam's tyranny was why he had been placed here on this earth. He would put his sadness and panic away and help funnel information to the right people.

Then he walked straight by her. A heavy-set grandma perched outside just away from the curb on a corner of two blasted-out sidewalks, balancing well in a plastic chair while watching the little activity of her street. With her thin silver hair mostly covered in a triangle-folded scarf that tied under her chin, she looked to him more like she should be sitting in Russia than Iraq. Presiding over a few boys playing ball using a red kickball and two pair of 50-gallon drums as goals, the woman held a distant gaze, that seemed more like she was looking into the past than focused on the cross traffic about four blocks up from them.

Moe doubled back. "Hello, mother." He greeted her gently. Acknowledgement flicked in her eye but she made no effort at a verbal response.

Moe squatted down instead of towering over her. Still her gaze was far from where she was. "Mother? Mother," Moe cooed again. "Can I help you get somewhere safer?" He picked up one of her limp hands that laid in her lap and rubbed the back of her liver-spotted and veined knuckles.

Whether it was the comfort or something else, Moe couldn't tell, but the woman finally looked at him.

"My grandson has deserted me to go fight with the resistance. I know what happens when you fight." She shook her head once, as if twice would take too much from her. Her deep-set eyes contained a lifetime of sorrow. "I have no one left to call."

Her other hand flopped over to reveal a small flip phone that had been hidden underneath.

Moe's heart bounced. What a provider his God was!

Now, how to buy it without further damaging the wrecked soul in front of him?

"My family is missing too." Moe shared without guile. "But I still hope and pray that they will be found living."

"If Allah wills it," she mumbled.

Ah, now I know why I was sent. Moe smiled.

"No, mother," Moe said while he still had her attention and her hand. "Allah has no power over me or my family. Isa has all power over us. You know Isa?" Moe asked. "The Son of the God of Abraham, Isaac, and Jacob."

"The Jewish God?" The woman looked like she wanted to spit out a curse, but it would take too much effort.

Moe nodded, "And the Christian God." He felt her muscles jerk under her papery thin skin. "Isa came to earth to erase our sin. All of it. Forever. If we ask him to forgive us and live with us."

The old lady moved her hand that had covered the cell phone to stroke her coat-covered mid-section roll, but left her other hand in Moe's much larger paws. Her head shook in the tiniest of trembling motions left to right.

"But He did. He came because the God of the Bible *loves* you."

Moe reached into his robe's pocket and pulled out the last banana his wife had purchased and put away in their kitchen. He handed it to the woman.

She didn't seem to have the strength to take it from him, so he laid it on her leg and placed her hand on top of it to hold it in place and gave her a double pat as he straightened up and shook his legs behind him to get the blood flowing into them again.

He chuckled a bit at himself. "Not getting any younger, are we?"

No emotional or verbal response from her, but she did follow him with her eyes. He supposed that was something. Moe waved good-bye and started to walk away.

"You take phone. Maybe you call your family to find them."

Moe caught his breath. "That would be such a blessing," he smiled. "Thank you very much, mother."

She jutted her chin out at him, effectively dismissing him.

Moe smiled and took the hint. He grasped her hand. She was holding out to him her last connection to her family. He received the phone in both of his hands and gently rocked her hands and released her.

Moe walked around the children's match and stood on the sidewalk across the street to make his call in private. He would not call his wife's number in case she was in hiding. Their plan was always to wait until any emergency was settled down before contacting one another if they were ever separated. When they had sat across from one another cross-legged on their bed making those particular plans, he had never dreamed it would feel like this.

Wakefield's hide above
Saddam International Airport
0947 hours local time

Wakefield could sense the Iraqi soldiers getting closer and closer. She willed her thrashing heart to settle to a quieter beat, but it would not comply. The adrenaline screamed at her to jump up and run away. But that would mean certain death.

They were taking their sweet time coming down the hill. Little whispers under their breath were being passed back and forth in Arabic, she recognized the tones and nuances, but couldn't distinguish any words.

Her short breaths were too hard to maintain while laying prone, pressing weight on her lungs over such an extended time. Wakefield was starting to feel light headed. So, ever so slowly, she grabbed more oxygen with her next breath.

Centimeter by centimeter her movement shifted more weight onto her elbows allowing her back to rise, giving space for her lungs to expand beneath her without the tell-tale movement of breathing.

Finally in position, she allowed a slow, full, open-mouthed breath large enough for her chest to touch the ground. Still slow, avoiding any sound, she felt her head clear.

The steady plod plod of dozens of boots advanced closer and closer.

She cut her eyes to the side, now that her body had oxygen again. Fifty yards to her right the first of the men crouched into her peripheral vision one step and at time. Based on sound, the others were not far behind him.

Keeping her vision cut to the east, there was plenty of movement between her position and Denning's position. At least eight different Guardsmen she counted. *Keep still, Denning!* she pleaded with him in her mind.

Since the Iraqis had entered the wood not a single shot had been fired by the West-hill sniper crew. Even if none of the four American snipers were discovered, which was highly unlikely odds, they had been effectively shut down by the troops walking down the hill among them.

While they were there, Wakefield and the others could not even keep an eye on the action on the airfield for fear of being discovered at their slightest adjustments of the body and rifle that were made on automatic when zeroing in on a target.

Jittery did not describe her insides fully enough when a pair of heavy black boots stopped close enough to her slightly projected elbow to feel the dirt move. She could just see the scuffed toe of the boot.

"Where are you? I know you're here" the man muttered under his breath along with a few colorful phrases about her ancestry.

"Hide me in the shadow of your wings, Father." Wakefield prayed more in a picture in her mind than in actual words. It was a wonder that the man couldn't smell her stress sweat that left her chilled. Goosebumps pressed against her uniform and she had to suppress a shiver that crawled up her spine.

The boots shifted to balance the man's weight on the foot closest to her while the right boot kicked a pile of dirt, twigs and leaves away from them toward the airport.

He cursed again. The boots stomped and the weight shifted between his feet as he turned in a slight circle as if looking back up the rise. Then he stomped away. Many of the other Guardsmen were farther on ahead of him in the rugged line-search they were conducting, she saw as she dared take her eyes off the man's back.

She blew out the stress through pursed lips and her eyes fluttered closed of their own volition. She saw a close-up of the scuffed toe of the black leather boot, smelled the old shoe polish again, and thanked God that she had never seen his face. She was sure it would have been etched into her memory for a lifetime. A scruffy boot was enough.

Not a single shot was fired as the troops made their way down the hillside to the level ground of the runway.

Wakefield assumed there had been some sort of signal when the man had been standing next to her, because all the troops had picked up a much faster pace at that moment. Or maybe time had just slowed down before that because she couldn't see what was going on.

She shrugged more in her mind than in her shoulders, she was just glad to see the back of them. There were no orders over their coms as to whether her team would remain hidden or take out the troops with about 6-7 clean shots each. At this close range, that would be no problem for the sharpshooters hidden on this hill.

But no orders meant stay put on primary mission: Overwatch.

The black-clad men were now 10 yards onto the flat. There was a single word grunted out and they turned as one, facing back toward the hill hiding the four snipers, and began emptying their clips of ammunition into the woods.

The roar of 25-30 large-caliber automatic weapons spitting fire toward her brought on a flinch she could not hold back. She pressed one ear into the dirt and covered the other by pressing into the little flap of her ear with her trigger finger.

As the sound dissipated to the background attt-tatt-tatt of gunfire at the airport that she'd been hearing all morning, Wakefield looked up slowly, releasing her right ear, in time to see a well-organized movement of the troops. Half faced forward walking, weapons held across their bodies as they loaded new magazines. Though she couldn't hear it aloud, Wakefield knew the sound of metal sliding across metal and the satisfying pop as each magazine clicked into its groove.

The other half of the men seemed to have already reloaded, except one man, second to the end on Denning's side, who fumbled with his equipment. This string of men were walking backward about 15 yards behind their brothers-in-arms, weapons at the ready, while they fixed their gaze on the hill where the snipers lay buried in cover leaves. Wakefield was sure she could see the whites of their eyes moving in a disciplined grid, searching for any stray movement. Never mind that they were now hundreds of feet away and their black scarves covered most of their facial features.

As much as she needed a stretch from all the tension of the past few hours and the intensity of the past however-many-minutes it had taken for the Iraqis to filter down the hill, she willed her body to be still, relaxing, forcibly, each large muscle group one at a time, starting with a shoulder, without moving an inch.

By the time the Iraqi's figures had become indistinguishable from each other, Wakefield exhaled fully, then lowered her head to the scope again. The troops were closer to the noise of the fighting at the airport than they were to the over-watch hill, so resuming cover fire for her grid was an acceptable risk, especially with the suppressor she was using. They would not be able to hear her fire.

After her second shot from that position found its mark, Wakefield lifted her head to search for her pack that she would need to recover, before she began to scope out her next hide.

Only 20 feet to her right and slightly downhill from her current spot she saw her gear. Exposed as you please, right in the path that Scruffy-Shoe the Iraqi had taken down the hill. The small branch of leaves she had tied to the gear stuck up from the pack unnaturally. *How could he not have noticed?* She wondered.

She exhaled again as she saw in her mind a heavy ghosty hand shape covering the whole pack and at least a foot around it in all directions. Because she knew it was there and what she was looking for, Wakefield could still distinguish a rather crude outline of her pack, but it was almost like the whole area was pixilated and shadowed for a couple of moments. She blinked and it was clear again.

"You hid me in your shadow, didn't you, Lord?"

She heard no audible answer, but felt peace. Then she began to inch toward her bag to retrieve it just as the sound of fighting ticked upward again.

Chapter Eighteen

Moe punched the end button on the cell phone he had bought from the grandma for a word of comfort and a banana. Life was certainly unexpected. He began the protocol of erasing all traces of the number he had dialed, entered a false number and shut it down.

Moe watched the grandma from across the street where he had retreated. He took one step away toward the palace garage to see about work. That plan had just been confirmed by the Americans as a good move. She still just sat there. The banana he had traded her for the phone laid on her thigh covered by a single gnarled hand.

Moe walked back to her around the boys and their kickball-futbol match, and laid the phone back on her lap. "Thank you."

Moe kissed her hairline and felt the silk of her old scarf from the motherland under his lips. "Don't forget, Isa loves you, mother." He whispered. "He wants you in His family forever. Just ask Him to take you into His family."

The old grandma never said another word that Moe was aware of, but he had felt the love of God that was present on the street while the boys played with a kickball, and he was pretty sure he saw a glimmer of a tear in her rheumy eyes.

Moe walked on toward the palace. As the morning progressed, the side streets he traversed were more likely to have people wandering like him. They looked aimless, though Moe was not. But on blocks nearest to the main arteries of the city, where American troops were streaming in their troop carriers with tanks riding aloft flatbeds, not a soul stirred at ground level.

Though there were steady trickles of cloaked individuals making their way into the stairwells of buildings tall enough to offer views of the highways over the sound-barrier walls. Once he happened to be looking up at the right time to see a curtain wiggle to unveil two emotionless faces, one over the other, observing the American parade into town. Then the curtain was snapped back in place.

Moe continued walking right down the middle of the side streets. No traffic breathed to move, save the Americans, this morning.

Wakefield's Over-watch Assignment
6 April 2003
1117 hours

Wakefield wiped her brow this time as she repositioned in her thirteenth new hide, or was it fourteenth? Slowly adjusting her ghilli suit's pile of camouflaging fabric, strings, grasses, and leaves, to avoid observation even under binocular surveillance, hunger hit her with an unexpected vengeance. Unusual during the stress of battle, she assessed. Fighting to focus her concentration on covering her over-watch grid, Wakefield could not recall another sniper assignment whether for Naval

Intelligence or when she had moonlighted for Richmond Dietz at the CIA over the years in which her stomach had growled with that sunken-in, feed-me feeling.

A low rumble reached her ears, snapping her back to the scratchy hill at present. Raising her head slightly from the scope, she spotted the source of the noise right away.

Vehicles clogged the airport road, driving four across in a semblance of formation. They were not military vehicles.

As one, the vehicles turned off-road at the first curve in the entry road, and Wakefield felt her mouth tighten. The pack of trucks sped across the manicured lawn, cutting brown ditches into the green and tossing dirt clods into the air. They were firing at the American troops from guns mounted in the back of trucks.

"You've got company at your six, First Battalion!" Wakefield heard the announcement go over the secured channel in her ear.

She leaned back into the scope and focused her eyes back on her responsibility grid. No emergencies. Oops, just as she was about to glance back at the impending forces, Wakefield saw at the edge of her field of vision through the scope, an Iraqi in profile, leaning out from behind the same barrels where the injured soldier had been picked up by medics.

Were they gaining ground?

The Iraqi was taking careful aim. She watched as he trailed whatever his subject was. Without needing to check what the man was targeting, Wakefield pulled against the trigger.

One shot, one kill.

Then she took a moment to verify what he had been aiming at. A troop carrier was moving into parallel position from where the man had previously crouched to unload its precious human cargo. He had been tracing its movement, waiting for the correct angle for the fuel tank.

Wakefield breathed deeply.

She cut her eyes back to check on the progress of the pack of trucks coming for the American troops at the main terminal. The smoke of the advancing guns dirtied the air, and Wakefield squinted to try to distinguish how many there were and the threat at this distance.

Several Bradley tanks had been diverted from the American advance toward the airport's main terminal to cover their flank.

Wakefield recognized a chemical reconnaissance vehicle rolling to a new position out of the advance of the Iraqi line. This team, now standard with any troop roll out, would sound the alarm for gas masks or retreat if they identified any chemical weapons in the vicinity with their super-sniffer equipment. The highly equipped van with its plate armor nose-dived like a kneeling elephant. It could only be a tire blowout.

An Iraqi gunman had found a target.

Just then a flame irrupted from the underside of one of the Bradleys that had turned around to hold the American flank. The driver began to turn the tracks of his vehicle into the pack of trucks. Head on, the vehicle would present both a smaller target for more incoming fire, but would also make itself into a shield for the commander, gunner, and driver to exit the burning vehicle.

Wakefield watched through her scope to get a better view. The shot was out of her zone and unmeasured for accuracy, but she watched anyway. The gunner reached down and gave another soldier an arm up. The man sprawled toward the back of the tank while the gunner kept the bullets spitting out the front side. The first escapee slid down the backside and landed feet-first between the tracks of the advancing Bradley. The second man bounced to the ground three seconds later landing on his back side. Both ran for cover as the other troops fired continuously into the truck-pack to keep the Iraqis busy avoiding shells and misaligning any firing coordinates so as to keep the men on the ground safe.

The gunner on the Bradley still rode the top of vehicle driving toward the Iraqi line. The driver must have jury rigged the gas pedal to the floor before evacuating his post. The gunner still stood, firing the gun, shifting this way and that, his gun shooting trucks through the fire on the front end of the vehicle.

He disabled at least three trucks in the front of the line. They in turn, held up the traffic behind them.

One truck and its attached gun exploded.

The sound and visual distraction of the huge explosion allowed the gunner to follow his division-mates off the back end of the vehicle. This man hit the ground running.

Hunched and scurrying like an opossum crossing a highway during the morning commute, the soldier ran an unpredictable zigzag all the way past the American line.

Wakefield lost him in the crowd of soldiers after someone pressed a sidearm into the man's hands.

She was just letting her breath out when a massive explosion stopped her.

The Bradley still running on auto pilot, and its gun firing at a constant angle was now firing over the top of the converging Iraqi truck pack. Three of those trucks' drivers had headed straight for the Bradley in a crazy game of chicken. They must not have seen the men slide down the rear in the haze.

The three trucks were run just about underneath the Bradley about the same time the fuel tank finally surrendered to the blazing fire. The right-most driver tried to swerve at the last second, losing the game of chicken to an empty American tank, and also losing to the flames that licked out and consumed the whole truck, driver, gunner and replacement gunner who had been hanging on for dear life. A second and third concussion followed as shrapnel from the trucks and the Bradley penetrated the Iraqi truck pack.

Only the outer third of the trucks remained unmarred and undeterred. They flowed around the mess in the middle of their group as a stream flows around a boulder. Eventually some of the trucks in the back of the pack picked their way forward, but that quick-thinking Bradley driver and brave gunner stopped more enemy combatants in their abandoned vehicle than they could have if they had maintained possession.

And the vehicle was now in millions of pieces so there was no chance of compromising the proprietary technology.

Well-done! Wakefield smiled to be on the same side with those men.

Baghdad Streets, Amil District
6 April 2003
11:47 AM local time

Moe shifted on his perch overlooking the orderly advance of the Americans' lorries still rolling into Baghdad. His stomach rumbled in protest of the early departure and giving away his breakfast.

"I can't sit here just watching forever," he chided himself. The man on the phone had pushed for information. Moe's forehead wrinkled as he recalled the odd conversation. Missy Judah was not on the other end of the line as he had expected.

161

And the man who answered the call kept asking for names and his location. The officer who had reviewed protocols with him for hours had said they would not ask for his location over an unsecured line. Ever. And yet they had broken their promise on the first call. The phone operator wouldn't even let Moe finish asking any of three attempts to query about his wife and daughters and beloved son.

A plan materialized in his mind. There was no end to it, but he had a solid first few steps. So, Moe rose to his feet and carefully picked his way down the tree-shaded embankment. The heat mirage on the blacktop shifted like steam. He blew out his breath before stepping into the street. The trip back to his neighborhood would be longer and hotter than the trip out, that's for sure.

Five buildings before his, Moe knocked on an acquaintance's first floor door. "Here we go," he breathed. He didn't have to fake his concern. Moe pushed back his kufiyah a little and swiped with an open palm some of the dampness that had soaked him on the walk.

The dark curtain jostled in his peripheral vision. And then a scraping noise and the metal bolts began clunking. He couldn't determine which direction for sure, but his breath caught in his throat, because it wasn't likely that the door had been *un*locked before his approach. Not in this environment.

The door inched open. He could only see darkness in the doorjamb. Then a little voice called up from about three and a half feet high. "Hi Mister," a young boy said. "You're my friend Aroosh's Aby. What happened to you?"

Moe smiled in spite of himself. "Yes, I am. I got a little hurt" He bent down. "You must be in Aroosh's class as school."

The little boy's loose brown curls wobbled back and forth before he squinted his eyes with a grin. "No," he laughed. "She babysits me sometimes."

"Have you seen Aroosh or Rohi or their Omy since all the noise started?"

Wide eyed, the boy shook his head slowly. "It sure has been loud out there." His little face fell with the memory.

"Is your Aby or Omy here with you?" Moe asked.

"Omy is getting bread and Aby is sleeping."

"Mahmoud, who are you talking to?" a voice bellowed from deep inside the apartment.

"It is okay. It is Aroosh's Aby." The little boy threw back the door. A man Moe had only spoken to once or twice walked toward the door yawning widely and scratching his chest under an open bathrobe.

"I'm sorry to wake you." Moe called out and bowed his head in deference. "I'm looking for my wife Liliya and our two daughters and little son. They went out for food almost two days ago and, and never came home." The stutter wasn't even planned.

The barefoot man whose name Moe could not recall sloughed forward. Then his eyes popped wide open. "What happened to you, man? Are you all right?" His neighbor was wide awake now and ushering Moe inside.

"Sit, sit." He urged. "Let me make you some tea."

"Thank you, but no. I must find my wife. Have you seen her?"

"Not since all this began. I am sorry. My wife should be home soon. We can ask her. Please sit."

"I thank you but I cannot. I must search for Liliya and the children." Moe backed toward the still open door. "If your wife

163

knows where they are. Please send word to my home." Moe rattled off the address.

"I know it." The man nodded and pointed in the correct direction. "If you have a photograph, I can help you look. I will be out in the early evening."

"You are very kind. Our apartment was struck and I am sure she is in the neighborhood staying with friends somewhere." Moe's heart squeezed from the man's generosity.

"We must stick together in these uncertain times." He nodded briefly. "*Saalam Alikum.*"

"*Alikum a Salaam.*" Moe heard the door latch behind him.

Moe's knuckles burned as he scraped them across one more door. He propped an elbow against the frame. He had lost count of the doors long before he lost heart. But his hope had pretty well dissolved before lunch time. *What is happening to my country? My countrymen?* He wondered silently.

A sundown curfew had been decreed. Moe tried to hurry toward home, not wanting to test the Husseins' resolve for enforcing it. It took so much effort to move.

So many people not at home. His head wavered back and forth hardly able to control it in his emotional exhaustion. "Did that many people make it out?" he asked himself as he turned onto his own block. Golden light still danced across the crowns of the tallest buildings, but shadows on the ground deepened by the minute. "Were that many people in hiding or displaced to the countryside already? Or were they just not answering their doors to an unfamiliar and bruised face?" he mused and picked up his pace as another pickup truck rounded a corner. This one was driving away from him two blocks ahead.

After at least five offers to help search for Liliya and the children, and one offer to drive him to the hospital, Moe collapsed back in his apartment. Moe sat cross-legged on his and Liliya's double bed and bored holes with his eyes in the nightscape. The air was cooling quickly after dark, but still felt muggy.

His head had begun pounding. He rubbed his forehead to try to relax the tight muscles around his eyes. "Where are you, my love?" he whispered. He climbed off the bed and began pacing their al fresco apartment. Not a soul on their street had seen his wife or children in at least six days.

The story of his demise had never even circulated. He sat heavily in his favorite arm chair—now his only arm chair—determined to break through the fog encroaching on his mind, so he could think. Moe rubbed a circle into his warm forehead just above his eyes with his thumb. Over and over he pressed that little circle to try to press away the pain. "Where are you, my Lilly?"

Moe lifted his eyes toward the heavens, which were less impeded now without things like walls. "God, what do I do now?" The question felt like it clawed its way out from the bottom of his belly. It made him want to wail and kick and scream in emotions he didn't have the energy to identify.

Then he remembered when the disciples of Jesus had asked each other a similar question borne of anguish and grief. They went back to their work fishing.

Moe's head pounded harder as he felt an urgency in his heart. He shook his head and tried to massage the tight muscles on his forehead. "My wife and children are missing, and you are seriously asking me to go back to work?" he couldn't contain himself. "For a madman, a killer, a psychopath?" But it was words like *unjust*, *unfair*, and *no way* that were actually floating through his mind.

165

"Have I ever not cared for you?" Moe heard in his heart.

"If you care so much, where are Liliya, Aroosh and Rohi, and Amil?"

"I've got them safe under my protective wing."

A strange peace settled over him and the words penetrated his body, even his headache. He wasn't sure even what they meant. Was his family safe, as in being hidden some place even he could not find them? Or were they "safe with Jesus" as in *dead?*

But strangely, that peace cut through all the questions. Moe pushed himself out of his favorite and only chair on gnarled hands.

"All right," Moe said, feeling the power of those words of response in his chest. "I will go back to work, like your disciples."

Chapter Nineteen

Wakefield completed her third shot from her current position. A slight kick from her rifle pushed into her sore shoulder once more. One shot. One kill.

Throughout the afternoon she had scooted approximately 300 yards to her left a few feet at a time and now the sky was starting to change hues. The fierce fighting on the ground kept the Republican Guard from noticing that men were dying from more sources than the Americans on the tarmac, so there had been no repeat of visitors looking to take out the American sniper team.

Wakefield felt around inside of her pack for more loaded clips as she settled into her next hide. Jerky movements searching the innards of her pack brought nothing except a melty protein bar. Out of ammo. She was reaching for her ear coms to tap "out" when she heard a voice in her ear ask jovially, "Anybody around here ready for a coffee break?"

"Oh, yes, please." Came someone's reply on the question's heels.

"Reinforcements are here. Begin retreat protocol," came the order. She recognized her temporary duty C.O.'s voice from the instruction period nearly twenty hours earlier.

Relief poured through her veins.

She began an awkward backward crawl toward the crest of the hill. Eyes on the field except to check her path. Once she got behind the rise, she would be able to stand and walk back to the road. But switching out was always a bit tricky for snipers. The ones coming into place were jittery because they had not yet settled into the rhythm of the particular battle and the battlefield sounds, and the ones coming off duty were low on supplies and hyped on adrenaline.

Wakefield was more than ready for the chow line and the ladies' room, but she schooled her thoughts to remain alert where she was, so she would make it to the facilities. She didn't see a soul until she hit the road. It gave her confidence in the next team.

At the back of the vehicle, by the pink light of the setting sun 25 minutes later, Wakefield released her last magazine into her hand before climbing aboard. Only two bullets remained nestled tightly in their beds.

"We timed that about right," she said to no one in particular.

"Ma'am?" came a hesitant voice from the left bench of the dark interior of the vehicle.

"Yes?" she asked. "What is it?" she asked again when no answer came.

Wakefield shoved her nearly empty pack and rifle in ahead of her.

"Have you been out here all day, ma'am?"

"And much of last night." she grunted as she hauled herself aboard in the heavy body armor and stringy ghilli suit.

Wakefield could only hear the sound of two people breathing inside the canvas-topped truck.

168

Finally a deep throated, "Huh," sounded.

Wakefield half smiled in the dark interior as she began to unscrew her silencer and break down the scope on her rifle and place them back into the pack between her feet. She had a pretty good idea of what they might be thinking, but didn't even care. It was too much effort to challenge anything at the moment. After today she actually had a much better argument against women in combat than any feminist women who were fighting *for* it.

It wasn't physiological or psychological fitness. It wasn't physical strength, upper body or otherwise. It wasn't women's lower aerobic capacity and higher body fat percentage that made combat a more difficult place for females to serve. In Wakefield's now experienced opinion, it was simple anatomy. Her bladder reinforced this point with every bump all the way back to FOB Beta.

Moe's Baghdad Apartment
6 April 2003
6:45 PM local time

There were a few roadblocks, but after showing his palace mechanic ID papers, and a few guards giving double takes at his battered face, the roadblocks seemed to melt away. He didn't see any patrols roaming the streets to enforce the curfew. The distant sound of gunfire and occasional larger explosions told him the Americans were still at work on the airport.

On Moe's long walk his mind was clear and he began to assess all the information, spoken and unspoken, that he had gathered by talking to his neighbors. One thing was certain. People were afraid. But it wasn't the Americans they were afraid of. Sure, people had mentioned the stray bomb possibility. But a few discreet questions showed Moe it was the Hussein family's grip on the government of their country and their wholesale slaughter of people who disagreed with anything they said or did that had people cowering behind their curtains and bolted doors.

"Where have you been?" thundered a gruff greeting as he entered the half-rolled-up garage door just before seven o'clock. It was the bossman, Dabir al Hamdani.

And here was where his story had to be flawless. Moe rubbed his twitching nose. "Had an accident. But I'm okay." He held up his "injured" arm at the elbow and said, "It'll be good as new in a couple of days. But I can work one-handed until then. You know that."

Seven duplicate Hummers stood in a row with hoods raised on all but two of them.

"Looks like you need some help getting these ready." Moe frowned. Why couldn't he remember how he normally behaved around these men he had worked with for years?

Moe gingerly shrugged out of his outer robe and exchanged it on his hook for his apron. The small shelf above his hook was empty. He had not brought a lunch with him today. But it was way past lunchtime. The echoes were getting quieter and quieter, but he chose not to notice the men staring.

"Tonight's the night!" From the half-rolled door Moe had just entered, another voice broke the quiet of a place normally filled with clinking tools and Riyad's strange taste in music. It was Akeem, Moe's closest workmate.

Akeem froze as he straightened up from slipping under the door. "What's going on?" He asked more quietly.

"Moe here was just explaining where he's been for the last week." There was an undercurrent to his boss's voice that made Moe feel squirmy.

Akeem's face lit up as his eyes traced around the garage for Moe. "You're not dead, my brother!" He said as soon as he laid eyes on him. But then his jaw slackened. "But you look about half dead. What happened to you?" Akeem walked over to lay a gentle hand on his shoulder.

Moe winced even though it didn't really hurt. "If I had a dinar for every time I've answered that question since my wife found me..." Moe tried to smile, but it felt stiff.

The garage was nearly silent, except for the fan already blowing air with a steady hum.

"I got caught in the blast of the Americans on the first night. I laid in a ditch, mostly unconscious, for two days and nights. I must have been pinned under something, because I can hardly remember anything except being very cold and very hot and very thirsty. And that I couldn't move. My wife said she and our neighbor friend found me and brought me to our apartment on a wagon. She was scared to go back out to take me to a hospital because of the bombings. They got our apartment at some point; I'm not sure when that happened. But it's a wreck!"

Moe told himself to slow down and take a breath. It could not sound as rehearsed as it actually was.

"I remember just bits and pieces. The girls arguing in the next room and Liliya shushing them. Sleeping a lot. A few evenings ago, she came and said she was taking the kids to find some bread to buy." Moe paused. "But, um, she never came back."

The silence and wide eyes told Moe they were buying it, just like Judah said they would. Perhaps it helped that part of it—Liliya and his children actually being missing—was true.

"Yesterday I was finally able to get down the stairs and asked my neighbors. Everybody is so scared." Moe didn't mention of whom or what. "No one has seen her for five or six days. I didn't think it had been *that* long. I didn't know what else to do." Moe leaned against one of the pillars for support. "She could be trapped anywhere. So, I thought I'd come to work. I will need money for food when they are found and come home." He trailed off. "I didn't know what else to do."

Akeem grabbed his good arm and pumped his hand up and down. "I'll do whatever I can to help you find her, buddy. To help you find *them*."

Al Hamdani's was the only skeptical face in the room. "Everybody back to work. We have a short turn around tonight."

The crew responded immediately. Apparently they already had instructions. Moe looked this way and that. The Hummers—all of them—were the only vehicles in the shop today. He decided he would normally ask, so he did, "What's going on? How can I help, boss?"

The 37-year-old, full-bearded al Hamdani, who had been working for the Hussein family for about half his life, was running the mechanic shop because of his loyalty and administrative skill, not any great knowledge of gas or diesel engines. Al Hamdani motioned Moe over to the side with a quick flip of his neck.

Moe moved as quickly as he thought he should, and looked up at al Hamdani expectantly.

"Who was your neighbor that helped your wife dig you out? Why don't you ask him where she is?"

Moe's heartrate jumped, and he was sure his boss could see his pulse pounding in his throat. He shrugged both shoulders slowly. "I don't know. I don't recall my wife ever mentioning who it was. Musta been someone we know pretty well, to carry this old body up five steep flights of stairs." Moe gestured to himself. "I talked to everybody who would answer their doors yesterday. Lots of people not at home though."

Moe watched the man waver between two decisions. He seemed to know more than he was letting on, but Moe wasn't sure what gave him that impression.

Finally he said, "Go see if you can help Akeem with the electronics in number 6. He's never any good at that."

Moe gave a quick nod and immediately regretted it. With all his pretending to be hurting and sore, he had tensed his neck and shoulders into a *real* stiff neck. He used his healthy arm to massage his neck on the short walk to the sixth of seven identical cars. They even had matching license plates. Each Hummer was labeled while in the shop though with a round magnetic number near the fuel door according to the final digit in its VIN number to maintain proper upkeep records.

Moe recognized them as the king's personal fleet of armored Hummers. And with all of them being prepped, something big was going down. This fleet was used for misdirection surrounding the king.

This was the kind of thing the Americans wanted to know. Moe glanced back at his boss. He was following his progress across the shop with narrowed eyes.

Chapter Twenty

Rivers tossed his waterproof rucksack into the back of the first of the painted-on-dust trucks in the convoy, laid his sniper rifle next to it, and walked back to the last truck to oversee loading.

En route from the mess hall which had offered the entire SEAL team an early-seating evening meal, Rivers had walked by the airfield to see the Black Hawks being fueled under guard and behind temporary fencing. Delta Company, who would be driving various factions of Echo Company into their insertion points, had left their training and accommodation FOB mid-afternoon, arriving right on schedule, according to Alpha company which was already on-assignment in TOC (Tactical Operations Center) monitoring communications.

Rivers had arranged with CDR Jackson to pipe in all coms to the earpiece he was already wearing so he could monitor all progress live.

There was little chatter right now. But one of the trucks idled a little bumpy and loud from Camp Liberty East and one lorry truck with Charlie Company had breaks that had begun squealing.

"Don't worry about it," Jackson intoned himself rather than farming out the early coms to his team. "It will just give you more authentic cover."

"Aye, sir. Delta 455 out."

Rivers smiled. Trust Jackson's experience to settle the frayed nerves of the younger set.

Rivers' survey brought him back to his ride in the first truck. His 18-truck convoy was well ordered and bravado comments were traded back and forth all the way up and down the line. From experience he knew that when the wheels started turning, it would get quiet, not because of the sound or wind, but that is when it would suddenly get very real that the vow each sailor had made to protect and defend might cost the greatest sacrifice. It might be the guy sitting next to him. It might be the one sitting toe to toe with him. They would avoid each other's eyes while those thoughts spun in their heads.

It might be me. That would be the thought that would turn a man one of two directions: either toward remembering his family, or rehearsing the waypoints assigned to that mission. Rivers also liked to rehearse stripping down and reconstructing his service pistol in his mind, then his sniper rifle. It was a soothing ritual that actually slowed his heart rate.

But all that could come in a moment.

Rivers pounded a fist on the cab of the lead truck. The signal to advance. Three and a half weeks of plotting, rehearsing, and replotting were now behind them. The mission was now!

The wheels rolled forward, and the anticipated silence commenced.

He flipped his mic switch to ON and said, "Echo 31 to Alpha 1. Do you read me?"

"Five by five, Echo 31."

"Can you pipe me into everyone's ear?"

"Sure thing, Echo 31." There was a slight pause. "You're a go, Echo 31. Good luck, Commander. Ooh-rah! Alpha 1 out." Jackson said.

"Welcome to the most important mission of your life," Rivers began. He could see that the coms check from the late morning had held. Every SEAL in the truck bed with him sat up a little straighter.

When Rivers turned off his mic four minutes later and slid to a seat facing the billowing dust and convoy following them, he counted it as his best pre-mission speech ever.

Staring at the scuffs on his neoprene dive booties, David slipped away in his mind to unhitch the disassembly latch on his service pistol. Press the release button with the first finger, turn the pistol over to unhitch the disassembly latch down to 90 degrees, the slide coughed forward on its own. Remove the slide from the frame. The sound of oiled metal against metal was comforting somehow, even in his mind. Set the frame aside. It would plunk against the table. Press forward on the coil with just enough pressure to remove the spring recoil and guide rod, then pressing the lug to release the barrel, pull it out of the hole and set all four pieces separately on the cotton cloth that covered the table in his mind.

Rebuild it in reverse.

When he focused again on the men in the back of the truck, Delta and Echo both, he saw strange hand twitches among the men of Delta Company, not a comforting sight for the demolitions team.

Rivers nudged the boot of a Delta man next to him. "Schaefer, right?" The man nodded. "What's going on?" Rivers asked and jutted his bristly chin at Schaefer's hands.

The dark-haired man with a wide jaw rubbed his mouth. "Lieutenant Jonsey had Delta drill setting all our bridge demolition charges blindfolded. Said we could avoid using flashlights at all that way."

Rivers cocked his head to the side. "Did it work?"

"Most of the time." Schaefer grimaced at some memory. "Can I let you know tomorrow?"

FOB B Entry Gate
6 April 2003
1825 hours

The team of nine, eight snipers and one commander, were let out at the gate to FOB Beta with a double horn hoot and a hard tap of the brakes.

Wakefield slammed her feet into the floor to keep from ending up in her neighbor's lap. Before walking inside the gate that had been erected since her departure 21 hours earlier, she flashed her dogtags. The gate was only as wide as a transport truck and four men stood guard. One man not dressed head to toe in body armor sat inside a little shack. Perhaps an interpreter, she thought.

She stopped at Intel House first. Mostly because it was the closest bathroom she knew of and partly because she wanted to check for information from Moe.

Wakefield recognized Ellie's silhouette just coming out the door against the backlight from inside. She held a file folder.

"Hey! Are you heading out for food?" Wakefield called out across the makeshift street.

"You're back!" Ellie said. "Yes. Heard there is spaghetti and bug juice on the menu tonight. Not sure that sounds terribly appetizing though."

"Wait up and I'll come with you. I just have to make a pit stop."

Ellie looked up and down the street. "Don't you need to debrief with your team?" Everyone was scattering.

Wakefield also looked around. The team had virtually disappeared. There was only one man still visible, and he was headed around the corner where the security officer seemed to take joy starling people. "I guess not." She shrugged. No one had mentioned anything about it during the ride home.

"Let me just run in here." Wakefield squeezed past Ellie already beginning to untie her ghilli suit. She shrugged out of her pack and slung it down onto the door-table used in their Intel staff meeting, laid the empty rifle next to it, then untwisted herself from the suit and let it fall into a heap on the dusty concrete floor.

Wakefield raced for the restroom.

When Judah walked back in, Ellie was leaning casually against the open door frame with her eyes closed. "I really wasn't sure I was going to make it." Judah confided. "I haven't taken a sip for the last several hours."

Ellie smiled with her eyes still closed. She emanated peace. With a deep breath, her eyes flew open. "So what is this bug juice they were talking about?" she asked. "I couldn't tell if they were joking with me or not."

Judah chuckled. "Don't worry. There are no actual bugs. No actual juice either, as it happens. It's Kool-Aid." Ellie's features didn't gain any clarity of understanding, so Judah continued, "A kid's drink, like flavored sugar water. Usually we get a red fruit punch flavor, sometimes orange."

"Fruit *punch*?"

Wakefield immediately saw the language gap reflected in Ellie's dark brows wrinkling. "*Punch* like the party drink not *punch* like in a fight," she added.

"Are you sure Americans speak English?" Ellie laughed.

"We do seem to have our own dialect." Wakefield agreed. She picked up the rucksack, rifle, and ghilli suit and followed her friend out the door. "I've got to drop this stuff back at the armory. But it can wait until after we eat. There is probably a line right now to check things in."

"You might want to hit the showers immediately after that." Ellie nodded wrinkling her pert nose.

"Pretty ripe, huh?" Wakefield's lips twisted. "Sorry. It was a hot day in April. In the sun in body armor and the suit." She lifted her elbow where the mass of stringy material lay. "Have we heard anything from Moe yet?"

"No." Ellie adjusted her Uzi across her front. "And your friend Grady is pretty jumpy about it. He was over 'just checking in with intel' at least four separate times that I saw today."

The mess hall tent was louder than usual, and Wakefield found herself annoyed by it. She avoided the officers' tables choosing instead to sit near the canvas wall with her double serving of spaghetti with meat sauce. Ellie sat across from her, pronouncing the bug juice, "barely drinkable" by the end of the meal.

"Then why did you finish it?" Judah prodded.

"It kind of grows on you, and I didn't want to get up to get something else." Ellie shrugged.

Judah huffed. "I'm sorry but I've got to get out of here."

"The noise." Ellie nodded knowingly. "You need that shower. I'll see what I can do about getting it cleared of people for you to have a few moments alone."

"How'd you know?" Wakefield balled her fists at her side and clawed at her collar. "I just feel so...I don't know. Ready to eat someone alive or burst into tears. And I'm not sure which I prefer." Judah chuffed, uncomfortable with admitting it aloud.

"It's the combat stress catching up with you."

"But I wasn't exactly in combat." Judah tried to excuse it. "And I have been in today's situation before, more or less."

"For that length of time?" Ellie asked. "With the same stress load as you've been carrying for weeks?"

"I suppose not. David, my husband—it still feels odd to call him that—he says that he reacts differently depending on the number of stressors he is carrying too. He compared it to his SCUBA diving. If he is well rested, has had no alcohol and eaten properly, has felt physically well, and is comfortable with the environment, equipment and company, he gets much better bottom times on the air tank he is using. But adding one or two stressors diminishes how he is able to perform and how much effort is required."

"He's right." Ellie agreed. "You can cut yourself a little slack and still be a good officer."

Judah sighed. "I suppose some sleep would help too."

After signing in her equipment, she dug deep to find a smile for the sergeant at arms. Then Judah went to gather her shower things. Ellie, as promised, cleared the female shower cubical. Of everyone.

Standing in the spray, not exactly hot, but warmer than chilly, she was grateful. Men had come before her to set up showers. They had done their job with excellence. She leaned both hands against the wall and let the water rush over her scalp creating a pocket of air as her long hair streamed like a fountain around her head.

It was cleansing, inside and out. "God, the pressure is building up inside and I just want to cry. I'm so tired. And I'm concerned about Moe. And his family. And all those men. All those men I killed today." And that's when the dam burst inside.

"Today, was a really hard day, Lord." It was the truth in simplest form. The few tears that streamed down her cheeks joined the solar heated water and escaped without shame. "I need your help. Come and fill me up with your presence, your peace again."

"Sorry, ladies, the showers are closed for a while tonight." Judah heard Ellie's lyrical voice intone over the falling spray, but she purposefully blocked out what was sure to be complaints from the women.

Dear Ellie. She was as good as her word. Wakefield managed a weak smile. "She is a real gift from you, Father. Thank you." The tears came again.

Wakefield strode across the lots toward her bed still wringing out her hair. The eight-minute shower was long by military standards, but well worth the restoration Wakefield found in the stolen moments with the Lord in a camp crammed with soldiers.

Judah never did see Ellie, but thought she heard her come in just before she drifted off.

Chapter Twenty One

In his element, Rivers felt the swell of euphoria as if he was listening to a symphony orchestra as all the threads of the attack played out in his ear. The coordination among the myriad of teams within the overall plan using the three-minute waypoints was working better than he had dreamed. Even Howard had tempered his attitude problem for the most part, once Rivers had given him some leadership autonomy and control.

In the shadow of a bridge and brush, Rivers tapped his microphone ON switch, "Echo 31 going dark." He hated to miss the next 12 waypoint check-ins, which would include the first bridge being demolished behind them. But these coms were not designed for underwater use.

"Catch you on the other side. Alpha 1 out."

Rivers removed his earwig and sealed it in a quart-sized Ziploc freezer bag with all the air pressed out. Rivers pulled the neoprene hood that dangled down his neck up and over the top of his head. Then he put the Ziploc bag in the front breast pocket of his Kevlar vest, crammed it into his rucksack and sealed all the waterproofing zippers, and hoisted it to his shoulders.

While working, Rivers observed the progress of his team and Howard's men. In the dark he couldn't really tell who was who among the twelve. Two were already slouching in the weeds at the shore. Another pair were already feet-wet. All he could see were two head-shaped lumps crossing the edge of the reeds into open water, when they disappeared, he knew they were two of Howard's men. His team would descend for their longer swim together. The other seven men hustled in various states of ready or inching toward the waterline.

Rivers crouched low in his all black wetsuit and left Delta Company to their bridge work. In the brush that surrounded a trio of mid-sized trees, Rivers steadied himself by holding onto a branch the size of a Kindergarten crayon as he stepped into the water.

The Tigris was not quite at flood stage from the snow run-off in the Taurus Mountains 1,200 miles away in eastern Turkey, but it was certainly colder and faster flowing than the practice pools of still water that heated up all day. Rivers was glad that he had opted for the 5/4 mil wetsuit to insulate against the cold instead of the more maneuverable 2/3 suits. The neoprene tear at his ankle that he had repaired with duct tape and a black Sharpie marker let in more cold water than the rest of the suit. While the shock of the temperature actually soothed for a second, Rivers could feel the battered joint begin to stiffen quickly.

Mass was immediately beside Rivers as their feet, covered in dive booties, sank into the cold clay bottom of the ancient river of fables, and perhaps even an ancient boundary of the Garden of Eden. Rivers shook his head to loosen the awe of where he was diving to focus on the monumental tasks ahead.

183

He took two full breaths on his rebreathing equipment while his eyes were still above water and his mask around his neck. Mass signaled his equipment test success by a fist resting over his head, and Rivers assed the team in a single glance as he moved his arm into the same OK position.

Everyone was a go.

Each of the three pairs was responsible for their own navigation, side-by-side, and Rivers waited for the last person besides his own partner to disappear under the surface before he descended.

The sensory deprivation of a night dive was always the same. No sight. No sound. Well, there was the murky-green glow of his dive watch which contained a digital compass, and the steady rhythm of his own breathing. But *almost* no sight and no sound.

Except the temperature difference he could be back in the tropics on his honeymoon dive. The indelible imprint on his neurological pathways of "Find the light, find the light" from the dive down the Devil's Throat made unexpected appearances in his mind. He still couldn't grasp why the Lord had asked him to go. Rivers shrugged against the water as Mass signaled that he was ready to swim. If the Lord thought it was important, whether he could see the outcome immediately—or ever—or not, it was the right thing to do.

The shock of the cold water wore off quickly as Rivers kicked beside Mass. The edges of Rivers' face and his hands were his only exposed flesh. He had opted for no gloves since it was to be a short swim. Everything under the neoprene, except his ankle, warmed nicely as his body temperature heated the thin layer of water trapped against his skin.

Mass navigated with Rivers on his left shoulder. Directly on schedule they ascended with the river bottom on the Al Faw side of the Tigris. No physical security fencing had been built underwater. No alarms had been triggered that he was aware of. No repeat of the getting lost in a dark, overhead environment.

P.O. Allen had invited Mac, LT (j.g.) Johnny McDaniel, to accompany him on the initial insertion across 400 yards of manicured-grass no-man's-land to the Al Faw Palace alcove. They crouched, fully out of the water, leaving their rebreathers on the bank.

Rivers disengaged himself from his rebreather and rucksack too. He slid his Kevlar vest over his head and stuck his left arm through the arm hole and fastened the Velcro sides firmly against the wet neoprene on his right side in one attempt. This was a practiced move so that opening and re-closing the tight weave-Velcro would not give away a position. Faster even than the rehearsal that had played in his mind earlier, Rivers unwrapped his sniper rifle, screwed in the night vision and digital site. He inched up from the water to the small ridge to offer Allen and Mac cover if needed.

Mass, Hayes, and Birdie waited in the water for one more three-minute waypoint while Allen and Mac marched confidently across the yard in their wetsuits and Kevlar vests stuffed with explosives and ammo clips, with rifles against their shoulders, pretending to be Republican Guardsmen even if the tight-fitting neoprene presented a silhouette quite different than the loose fitting uniform of the Iraqi military.

Rivers eyes were on constant swivel. The place was lit like the Crown Jewels but they had been aware of that from the nighttime satellite photos that Intel had collected for them.

185

Allen and Mac strolled from left to right in only about 20 degrees of Rivers' vision. The rest of the track was in line toward the palace alcove garden.

Rivers sucked in his breath. They had been right. A pair of sentries patrolled the grounds. In fact, they were moving in the same left-right direction, counter-clockwise, as Allen and Mac. The Iraqis were 255 yards ahead of the Americans, according to his distance finder's measurements. Not far enough away by half in Rivers' estimation.

Then the sentries stopped. Rivers held his breath and tightened up on his weapon. When the two turned around, he placed the cross-shaped reticle in the middle of the forehead of the soldier closer to the water.

Allen and Mac hesitated slightly at the very edge of the Rivers' scope's round and very limited field of sight. Then the two kept walking toward the Iraqis. It looked to Rivers as if the Iraqis were waiting for them at first, but then they began to advance toward Allen and Mac.

The Iraqis took two steps back the way they had come, slowly, then three. Rivers trailed the one closer to him, adjusting his aim with each step the man took toward his men.

Allen and Mac kept walking too. Rivers' blood pounded behind his ears. He took a deep cleansing breath and felt his heart rate slow back down from 76 BPM back into the optimum range of 50-70 BPM. A heartrate over 70 beats per minutes threw off a sniper's targeting accuracy. The higher it ran the more the hands moved with each pump.

Then Mac raised one arm with the simplest of wrist-flipping gestures, and it looked like he was shooing the Iraqis off.

The soldier Rivers trailed with his crosshairs shrugged and punched the shoulder of the other one and they turned around and returned to patrol their previous counterclockwise route.

Rivers allowed himself a long blink and another controlled, quiet exhale. That had been close. He continued trailing the guardsmen with the back of the same man's head centered in his crosshairs.

That was when he saw it. It would not have been visible with the naked eye. It would have appeared that the Iraqi was scratching his chin or gesturing to emphasize some point he was making to his fellow guardsman. But in the scope, Rivers viewed the set of his head and the placement of his wrist. The man turned slightly, probably unconsciously, back to gesture behind him, and in the move, Rivers saw a furrowed brow and tight lips moving fast. The Iraqi soldier was definitely alerting someone on the other end of his wrist mic.

Chapter Twenty Two

M oe wiped his chilly fingers on a grease rag. "This one is good to go too." He announced to Dabir. Moe closed the Hummer's hood and tapped it with his fist. The seven Republican Guard drivers had been anxiously waiting while throwing around threats and foul language for at least two hours.

Dabir al Hamdani spoke to the team of drivers, "You may now take the fleet to the East Entrance." The drivers were already moving toward their vehicles before Dabir opened his mouth. "Take good care of our sovereign and his family!" Dabir charged them too loudly

Moe wasn't fooled. His boss was trying to show off that he had enough authority and trust in his position to be made privy to the plan. The younger man was foolish like that. Moe had watched the resentment build the whole two hours while the uniformed soldiers waited so impatiently.

The Powertrain V-8 diesel engines growled to a start one after another. Moe recognized the senior driver of the group by his uniform insignia as he walked toward Dabir. He thought the man was going to shake Dabir's hand.

As the soldier got closer though, Moe couldn't tear his eyes from the exchange. The man leaned the slightest bit to his right. Moe melted back into the shadows near the huge air compressor. Quick as an adder, the solder reached down to the top of his boot and straightened up.

It appeared to Moe that the soldier punched Dabir once and stepped back. Moe couldn't hear any blow, though he wouldn't over the massive horsepower being generated in the enclosed space as the shop door rattled and clanked upward.

Dabir crumbled to the floor as the uniformed man turned 180 degrees. "Anybody else have anything smart to say?" He asked. A dagger shimmered in his upraised fist under the lights near where Dabir always did the paper work.

Moe caught his breath.

"Everybody go home. We will recall you to work when the enemy has been destroyed."

Moe nodded quickly and saw that the handful of mechanics who had not yet been sent home were doing the same, but nobody moved.

Apparently that was just fine with the senior driver who mounted the Hummer and slammed the vehicle into reverse. As soon as the vehicle disappeared from view, but before the sound of it had died away, the mechanical crew sprang to grab personal items from their hooks and shoot for the door. Two of them even stepped over their former bossman with blood in an ever expanding pool around his body.

Akeem slowed at the door and turned back to Moe. "Come, friend. You can't stay here. My son will share with his brother, and you can have his bed tonight."

"I, I" Moe was just able to put one foot in front of the other to move out of the shadows. "I need a minute to rest." It was all

189

he could think of to say. And it was true. Akeem must not have seen what he did, not if he was inviting him into his home.

"It is not safe here, Mohammad! You must come."

"I can't go. Not yet." Moe pleaded for understanding. "You go ahead and I will follow you as soon as," an idea hit him as he looked at the mess on Dabir's upfront desk, "I will take care of all the records. If the Americans do come, we will not want our names found on the records as royal staff members." Moe motioned with his broken-wing arm toward the file cabinets against the wall to Dabir al Hamdani's private office, and just past their boss's body. "You go ahead. Don't risk not getting back to your family."

"Thank you, friend! We will wait for you at our home. Come quickly."

Akeem fled into the darkness, leaving the door open behind him.

Moe walked around Dabir's lifeless body and moved not toward the filing cabinet, but back to the telephone.

Al Faw Palace
7 April 2003
0055 hours

"Birdie, get them back here." Rivers whispered. He didn't take his eyes off his target. The sound of moving water behind him told Rivers that Birdie had heard his instruction and was moving up his flank so his call would carry over the riverbank.

The two men on patrol were still walking away, but the man in Rivers' crosshairs was also still speaking to his wrist. The patrol could not be allowed to disclose their position to the rest of the guard who was sure to come running at the alert. Rivers gave 5.5 pounds of pressure to the trigger, absorbed the recoil and pumm of the suppressed shot, then redirected his crosshairs to the second man. He aimed a fraction lower on this man, putting the cross in the middle of the back of his neck. Rivers pulled the trigger again, one heartbeat later. He kept his eye on the movement in his little circle of vision scope.

As anticipated from experience in multiple shots of two or more targets, the second man's body jerked at the sound of the suppressed rifle shot traveling over the grass, amplified by the proximity of the water. The first man keeled forward cleanly. The second one had just enough warning to start ducking down in the open air with no cover to hide himself. Just like all the others before him in Rivers' sites, the man actually ducked into a headshot.

Rivers followed the second man's fall through the scope. He fell at the same angle away from the water as the first man. There was not even a twitch between them for the three seconds David watched. But their angle would have shouted to Rivers which direction the shots came from and allow any guardsman to trace a line to their riverbank hideaway.

"Exfil, exfil." Rivers scrambled backward, not caring that he was leaving smashed grass as evidence of his location. At this point he just hoped to be gone before anyone else arrived. He wasn't worried about them knowing where he *had* been. But it would alert the entire palace guard and be more difficult all around. *Howard may not welcome us attaching to his unit, but he will appreciate the heads up and extra bodies now that it is not a quiet entry,* Rivers knew.

Allen and Mac tore across the manicured lawn and slid down the embankment, arms flailing and breath heaving like kids on a playground too long.

Birdie came back to the edge of the water and held open Rivers' waterproof rucksack so he could more easily breakdown the hot rifle barrel and suppressor and pack the equipment away in a hurry. Rivers sure wished he had those gloves now. He slid the scope away from the body of the rifle and used quick touches with his fingertips to unscrew the silencer.

Velcro crackled as Allen and Mac undressed. They shoved their vests full of ammo and explosives into rucksacks, shrugging into them as they scurried to the water's edge.

The water was anything but calm. Hayes and Mass had quickly gotten out and grabbed everyone's rebreathers. Water dripped everywhere, making mud of the bank. Mass positioned one for Birdie who took it and waded back into the Tigris.

That was when the alarm screeched out a pulsating warning. Strobe lights and circling spotlights joined the grounds of the well-lit palace compound. If the palace grounds had looked like a Crown-Jewels display upon the SEALs' entry, it looked and sounded like a Barnum and Bailey's Circus upon their exit.

Good for Birdie, Rivers thought, *he never looked back*. Mass got back out of the water to haul Rivers' rebreather to the shoreline. Rivers motioned his partner to head out into deeper water with it.

Mac and Allen each took a rebreather that Hayes had held for them in waist deep river water.

Rivers counted five heads while on the move as he whipped his zipped rucksack onto his back while passing his rifle back and forth between hands and not dropping the waterproof bag for it.

"Go, go," he called, not having the luxury of hand signals right then. Not that it mattered over the incessant siren "Back to plan A."

Four hands signaled ok with a quick fist to the top of their neoprene hoods and slipped beneath the surface. Mass waited, neck deep, holding Rivers' rebreather with the mouthpiece in position to nearly swim into it. Rivers slipped on the mud with his sore ankle leading. He felt himself skid, but caught himself before falling.

Leaning over knee-deep in the Tigris and just three feet from the bank, Rivers squatted and leaned into the water for leverage. As abruptly as the clamor rang out over the palace campus, it stopped. For a moment there was dead silence and Rivers was tempted to peek over the embankment to see what was happening. Then human shouts filled the air, still some distance away. Lots of them. So, he returned to his objective and flung a few quick sheets of water toward the muddy bank to destroy as many footprints as possible. No sense advertising that there were six of them, and now they were gone.

Rivers began sucking air from his rebreather before descending under the cloudy Tigris waters. He closed the file in his mind that housed plan B and pulled plan A into the forefront. As he kicked against the current back to the entry point of the underground labyrinth, he rehearsed the order of the steps his team would now take from the tunnels into the connection points to the main structure. They would enter and search the palace for Saddam and his sons and their wives and other key Ba'ath Party leaders who had been living at their offices for weeks now.

Chapter Twenty Three

Rivers struggled hard against the Tigris current. On the one hand it used more energy, but on the other, it kept his muscles warm and joints loose in the chilly water. He was pretty sure he was swimming with a bubble of air trapped in his rucksack. He had not taken the time to roll the air out before zipping it watertight with all that was going on. The extra buoyancy would cause problems when he could no longer swim at a constant down angle. He would just have to figure out how to compensate when the time came.

Mass signaled a slow down with a quick tap to Rivers' shoulder.

They had arrived at the underwater tube, and there was a line to get inside.

The four-foot diameter concrete pipe the top of which measured out at a depth of eight feet underwater was sealed just as their intelligence source had described: a hatch grid made of one-inch-wide steel bands about a half-centimeter thick. What the source had not described was the messy welding job at each joint, the three inches between each weld, the outflow of greywater coming from the palace, and several items that probably used to be clothing caught in the grid and

194

current. Weird. How did clothes get introduced into the water system?

There was a man-sized hole sliced through the bands and bent outward on the top right section of the grid. Rivers could see the torch burn marks where Howard's team had gained entry even in the dim light from Birdie's flashlight.

Rivers fought against current and buoyancy as he tried to figure out what was taking his men so long. Finally, he swam down to 12 feet and grasped onto the bottom of the pipe by one of the grid welds. Looking above his position he saw Birdie shining his light on the hole, and Hayes wiggling out of his backpack and passing it off to Allen while trying not to lose the rebreather in his mouth. The hole Howard's team had cut was too small for his team to make it through expediently.

Hayes pushed through. He received his bag from Allen as each man wiggled out of his backpack hurriedly. The water churned more than Rivers liked, and he felt the three-minute waypoints slipping away from them. Mac was next and he gripped the top of the concrete tube and sailed through feet first. Allen passed Mac his pack and handed him his own pack at the same time. He followed through in the same feet-first manner. Birdie noticed the time he had made up and followed suit, then Mass, and finally Rivers.

Once inside the confines, Rivers didn't bother to expend the energy he knew it would take to get his air-filled pack situated on his back again. He settled it under his midsection and kicked hard to catch his team.

Birdie was leading this leg with the dim flashlight. Even in the distance it appeared to Rivers that he was mostly shining on the ceiling of the pipe. He was watching for the break that according the sewer builder's schematic should have been 120 feet from the end of the greywater pipe. *Find the light, find the light.* The mantra was back again.

The six kept swimming and swimming.

Inside the four-foot pipe was gloomier than the river. Built-up silt raised the floor several inches. Then the light disappeared altogether. Rivers moved his left hand in front to let the tiny glow from his watch keep him from barging into Mass's feet which were churning fast enough to concuss him if he wasn't careful. Then Mass's feet scissor kicked and disappeared too.

It must be the joint in the pipes. "That was 120 meters, not feet." He grimaced around his mouthpiece wondering how many more cultural mistakes there were like that in their planning. Rivers released his pack and the air bubble inside ran for the surface. It blocked the intermittent light above him. Then the glow returned, so Rivers followed his bag through the small man-hole-sized joint straight up. Two scissor kicks later, his head broke the surface. He was facing a hewn stone wall and only had time to look to his right as arms threaded under his arm pits and hauled him out of the water and backward. Allen and Hayes deposited him on his rear in a splash of water next to the hole.

It was a small cavern more like a wide tunnel. Slick floors with water dripping from walls and collecting in small imperfections in the floor. Rivers fixed his eyes on the source of light that allowed them to explore their surroundings. It was a live flame fixed to the wall and shaped like a torch.

Hayes began to stack their rebreather equipment in a shadowy corner with Howard's team's equipment as each man disengaged from his unit, hoses, and mask. Even in their soft-bottom dive booties, every movement echoed in the chamber. They would have to slow down once they entered an actual tunnel so they didn't give away their position.

The six entered the tunnel shown on the memorized map to lead to the closest entry point to the palace.

They slunk along the damp passageway. It felt ancient inside, yet Rivers knew it couldn't be any older than the late 1980s. The Al Faw Palace had been completed in 1990.

Rivers replaced his earwig before the next waypoint sounded. Everything was on schedule for check in #93 of 180, except Rivers' unit. They were just beyond the halfway mark and had yet to accomplish anything meaningful.

Hayes' light disappeared. He must have gone around the final bend before he would run into the stairs to the inside. Rivers loosed a little bird whistle, and the men returned to the little chamber where he stood.

"We've not yet met any resistance nor seen Howard's—ugh, what is that smell?"

"That's decomp." Birdie wrinkled his nose.

"It's coming from back here." Allen entered a tunnel at the back of the little chamber. "Oh." He stated. "I guess we can mark the Nine of Hearts off our list. He's not going anywhere."

Allen referred to the deck of cards all military personnel going in country received. The cards faces and numbers had been replaced with the top 52 wanted terrorists in the Middle East. The image of Ali Zuzchen, the Grand Imam of Iraq, occupied the Nine of Hearts card.

Rivers saw the black line of blood across the large man's throat through the locked cell where he had been left to decompose on the floor, with fingers of one hand still wrapped around the bars of his captivity.

"Let's catch up with Howard's team so we can be of some help. We will send someone back to bring him up for burial and update the database when we return. I'll lead to breach the door."

The doorway didn't require breaching. Howard's team, presumably, had left it gaping open.

Then a volley of fire erupted. *That should make it easier to find them*, Rivers thought as he took off toward the sound, knowing his men would follow.

Doubling-timing, they weaved their way through corridors, clearing rooms big and small one after another. They continued to follow the sound of the dozens of rounds being fired. It was definitely on this floor.

When Rivers picked up the unique smell of a flash bang still lingering and saw smoke seeping out from the bottom of a wall, he felt the wall for heat and then a seam. It had to be a door.

Howard's team was right on the other side, under fire.

Rivers pushed and pressed the wall, and when his men saw what he was doing, they copied him. Finally hands pressed the right combination of places and the door sprang inward. The SEALs jumped out of the open doorway putting their backs against the stone wall, but not before Rivers saw through the smoke black-dressed Special Republican Guardsmen backing toward them while firing at Howard's men who advanced from two other entrances to the large room that appeared to be a library of sorts.

The dozen or so soldiers seemed to be making a last stand. Where were the rest of them? There should have been men by the hundreds guarding the palace.

Rivers motioned Birdie to move near the break in the wall and call out for surrender. He was their best Arabic speaker. "Hey there!" Birdie spoke in English first so the Howard's guys would not assume they were more of the enemy and fire on them through the smoke before he could get the words out. "You're surrounded. Give up!" He called loudly. Several of the Special Guardsmen turned toward the sound of his voice and Rivers' team began taking fire.

"Advance as you're able, and stay out of Howard's line of fire." Rivers called out. He and Mass went one high/one low using the edge of the wall for cover. Allen and Birdie did the same on the other side. There were a few substantial looking couches around the room, but most of them were quickly used for cover by the guardsmen now. They hid behind the furniture and kept firing their automatic weapons in steady spitting streams at the three entry points. Surely they would have to stop and reload any second.

Rivers counted his fifteenth shot fired, only two bullets had found a mark, both in appendages. He said, "Reloading," and rolled out of the way to let Hayes take his position.

Rivers' clip clicked into place and he shoved his empty into the Velcro pocket on his Kevlar vest. Before he could move into position on the far side to relieve Allen or Birdie, the automatic fire had slowed considerably. Maybe two rifles were still in play. Slow steady pop, pop, pops of suppressed pistol fire continued until the last Iraqi Guardsman had released his trigger finger.

Rivers waited three full seconds of silence, did a quick gofer head-out-of-the-hole move and ducked back down to see if he would draw any fire. Silence.

"All clear." Rivers recognized Howard's tenor call out from the far side of the room.

Mass said, "Confirm. All clear," at regular volume.

Rivers straightened up and strode into the smoky room thick with cordite. Howard and Garcia led the rest of their team into the room from the other doors.

"They tried to lead us into a trap in the hall back there, but we turned the tables on them."

Rivers recognized Burns' voice. He was the youngest member of Echo Company-Al Faw. While Rivers appreciated his enthusiasm, he wanted to hear from Howard or one of the other senior members.

Rivers surveyed the room, not one guardsman had surrendered his post. That was disappointing. It would have been nice to have a weak link to question.

"I think we're done here." Howard said as he moved toward Rivers. They met in the middle at a bookshelf along the wall. Feathers from couch stuffing still floated down to rest like patchy snow over the massacre in the center of the room.

"Is anybody hit?" Rivers asked.

The group looked around to assess each other. "I have a little scratch." Lettuce said pulling the substantial bulk of his right arm forward to show a four inch long pink burn where a bullet had just missed him. "I don't think it even touched me, just gave me a bit of wind burn."

A couple of guys laughed. Rivers heard a radio squelch in his ear. "Shh." He waved them quiet and cupped his ear so he could hear. Howard also pushed his earwig further into his ear canal to listen.

"All ears, attention, all ears, attention!" It was CDR Jackson himself back at TOC. Echo Company at the Republican Palace is requesting any and all assistance. They are meeting much resistance. If you can assist, begin making your way there ASAP and report in your strength and ETA en route. Alpha 1, over."

Rivers looked at Howard in question.

"This palace was nearly evacuated before we arrived. Only a small contingent remained. This is all that we saw. Even after the siren was tripped earlier. There was no rush, no movement of troops. I haven't even seen any maids or anything."

"I cleared the kitchen with Bags, Commander." Garcia said as he was checking all of his pocket closures. "It was empty."

"And the soup on the stove was stone cold." PO Bagsby said. "That says to me this palace is shut down at least for tonight."

"Only you would stop to eat in the middle of liberating a palace and searching for a fugitive king." Lettuce teased.

"I just touched the pot!" Bags threw Lettuce a dirty look.

"Let's go lend a hand over at the Republican Palace then." Rivers about-faced to return where he had come from.

"The bridge is faster this way," Howard started back the way he had come in.

"I wasn't going to go over ground." Rivers countered. "It will be faster and a straight shot if we use the tunnels."

"We might meet resistance." Someone said.

"Or get lost."

Rivers eyes swept around the room at all the eyes glued to his. Some were wide, but most were confident. "We will probably meet resistance either way. I don't want to argue over this and lose time, Howard." Rivers hitched up his rifle slung across his chest. "Mass and I are going back to the tunnels. You men are free to choose whichever direction you want to go."

To Howard's credit, he didn't give the others a chance to start after Rivers before calling toward Rivers' backside, "I'm with you, commander. I just didn't think of going back down."

Rivers smiled.

If Rivers thought the 120-meter swim was long, the four-kilometer run over uneven, damp excavation was interminable.

There were so many side chambers and splits in the tunnel. They had to slow down for each one to check the compass heading. The tunnel from the map Rivers had studied showed that Al Faw Palace sat at a southwest angle from the Republican Palace. So they kept their compass heading as close to dead on northeast as any split allowed.

Twenty-four minutes after the first call went out, 12 more Echo Company men arrived to help. Rivers had listened to their own Bravo Company helo extraction team and all the factions of Delta Company from around the city be re-routed over his earpiece.

Waypoints were completely obliterated now.

Chapter Twenty Four

"This should be it." Rivers slowed to check his compass one last time when they came upon a crude set of stairs, much more worn than the stairs at Al Faw. "Wait here. Mass with me." Rivers said and began to climb the stairs while the team milled behind. Mass followed and the sounds of outside became clearer with every step away from the corridor filled with heaving SEALs.

At the top of four flights of stairs, Rivers and Mass finally reach a landing. Fifty feet away was a light spot in the otherwise dark space. The light was interrupted by vertical bars spaced about three inches apart and a few horizontal bars. Rivers and Mass stole up to the gate from the cover of the shadowed wall even though the whole area felt as deserted as the Al Faw Palace had.

The waist high horizontal bar had a massive ancient lock that looked rusted in place. Rivers shook the gate. Not even a rattle so firmly was it stuck.

On the other side it appeared that there was another small landing and half a dozen steep wooden stairs leading up to a grassy area. There was more light and a lot more noise up there. He couldn't see anything other than shadows that didn't make sense, but from the roar of sound, Rivers picked out occasional gun fire and voices and motorized vehicles, heavy ones.

He looked at Mass who shrugged. "It looks like as good a place as any."

Rivers nodded once. "Go get Howard and Allen. I'll be right behind you as soon as I check in with Alpha 1."

Rivers was still talking to Jackson when Howard and Allen arrived and began molding their C-4 plastic to the hinges of the old iron gate. He kept an eye on the volume Howard was using. He did not relish dying at the bottom of a cave in because of an over-zealous officer. Howard was unwrapping a radio from plastic to use as a signal receiver to ignite the C-4 when Rivers signed off his radio. Since Howard appeared finished forming the explosives, and it didn't look over packed, Rivers said, "See you at the bottom boys." And his feet flitted down the four flights.

Twenty seconds later, Howard and Allen were huddled in the bottom with the rest of them. "Fire in the hole." Howard said, and pressed the button.

Underground it sounded like a pretty terrific boom followed by a cascade of gravel shaken loose by the explosion. Rivers wasn't sure how it would play against all the noise on the surface.

The 12 SEALs surfaced. They stepped over the fallen gate and stealthily moved up the small stairs. Rivers needn't have been concerned about being observed.

He stared at the chaos on the grounds. Uniformed and armed-to-the-teeth Special Republican Guards ran everywhere.

Four American Black Hawks sat in a sea of spotlights on the rooftop, and though men from the ground had loosed AK-47 fire at the choppers, the aircraft were protected by the angle.

It looked like every light in the palace was on. Loose papers and chunky file folders flew out of a couple of windows by the arm load while he watched. Multiple fire barrels surrounded the main building and were manned by a few people who would pick up the papers and stuff them into the fires. Destroying evidence, Rivers presumed. There was lots of yelling, even a bit of screaming. There were men being scurried out of several exits under protection of the guards and the dark. A line of vehicles with exhaust pouring from their mufflers inched forward on the left side of the palace. That must be some sort of bigger exit that he couldn't observe from his vantage point.

Rivers wondered why the guards did not extinguish the floodlights all over the place. He shrugged, it would make it simple for him to lie in the grass and fire at targets all night long, or until he ran out of rounds.

Saddam Hussein's Republican Palace
7 April 2003
2:30 AM local time

"We should have left hours ago, like our sisters. Or even days ago, like I told you." Uday screeched at his father.

"You were welcome to go at any time. No one forced you to return here. In fact, with your behavior—"

"It's too late for arguments now." Qusay stepped between the two vats of boiling stubborn blood. "We need to get out at once. The Americans have dared to enter the west wing, but they still have to make it down the corridor, past all the guards."

Hussein's youngest son pleaded with him. "Didn't you always say after that visit to Camp David in America where they tricked you into being in the same house with a Zionist that you'd never occupy the same house as an American again?"

Saddam felt the ire of that afternoon thrash through his veins again as fresh as the insult had been that day.

Uday saw his disgust and exploited it. "Well, dear old Ab, they are here. In your house. They'll probably drink all your tea and milk. And have their way with Waf."

Saddam dropped his briefcase and valise bag with twin thunks. The boy needed his jaw knocked out of place.

"Let's get out of here." Qusay urged. His youngest child sat on his hip, still in footed pajamas peeking at the exchange between uncle and grandfather with his head buried in his father's shoulder full of military medals.

"I should have never come back to this place," Uday snarled and stepped toward his father while pulling back his right arm. All six bodyguards drew their side arms.

"You are each as bad as the other." Qusay huffed and walked out the door where his family waited for him.

"Come on." Saddam heard the younger son gather his young family and lead them toward the east wing where the party leaders and their staffs were being evacuated from the city.

"Get lost!" Glowered Saddam to his eldest.

With the guards holding him in place at gunpoint, Uday would not be able to follow. Saddam followed Qusay and his family's scramble through the corridors of the east wing. He hoped the whole house didn't come crashing down around him before he got there. He was glad the Americans had not set fire to the building; that's what we would have done: sent all the little rats scurrying out into an ambush ring of soldiers.

Ahead of them, two to three hundred people pushed forward toward the East Exit that appeared to pop out one or two at a time into the dark night. The corridor was packed with clamoring monkeys. Qusay skidded into the back of the pack before he could stop himself in the dress shoes he wore. His wife wore more practical tennis shoes under her long skirts. But several people sprawled forward with the impact, causing more people to fall against others.

The horde mutinied, shoving and screaming against those they thought were trying to push ahead. The fire of angry fear spread like stage-IV cancer toward the door in the jostling crowd.

Saddam wasn't sure they would have stopped even if they had paused to look at the faces of their prince and his young family as being the accidental first hit. So he drew his weapon and fired three times into the ceiling. For a brief moment the noise increased, but then as everyone tried to cower into corners of a hallway or break into rooms on the side, the sound died down.

"Make way!" A voice bellowed behind him.

A nice pathway parted in front of Qusay, who by this time had drawn his weapon with his right hand and carried his son on his left arm.

A young man broke away from the whimpering lowly multitude and sprinted up the pathway cleared for the royal family.

"I've got it." Saddam said. Qusay twisted to the side and nudged back with his pistol one of his walking-age children. Saddam centered the fleeing target in his metal sites and pulled the trigger. An explosion of red rained on the huddled throng, and the traitor slid to a stop leaving a slippery red trail on the marble pathway.

Qusay shuffled his family forward. Saddam holstered his pistol and picked up his leather valise and followed them. Men of all shapes and sizes at this end of the crowd were still stuffing themselves into vehicles that stopped barely long enough to jump inside.

Qusay elbowed forward, barking orders like he did at his military men. A small man Saddam recognized as an under-secretary to one of his counselors got Qusay's elbow right in the mouth. He skittered sideways into the crowd like a bowling pin, taking a few people to the floor with him.

Saddam made his way close enough to see out the East Exit. Chaos reigned. Even the vehicles looked funny, like they were leaning toward the palace.

A man pushed in front of him, even while daring to say, "Excuse me, sir."

Saddam was loosening his grip on the valise in his right hand again to shoot the man when he recognized his own face looking back at him.

Saddam saw Qusay shove his wife and two children into an SUV and pound the back panel to send it off. Then he stepped toward the next vehicle with the other two children when Saddam lost track of them. His six look-alikes had surrounded him.

"Sir, you should go right in the middle of us. The Hummer parade is pulling around from the garage this second. It is just outside this line of vehicles, so we will thread through the SUVs. Each of us can take one bodyguard with us, so there is no way the enemy can tell who is who." One of the mirror men shoved the information at him all in one breath. He was obviously the one in charge. "Each driver is fully armed and has the evac route assigned to him. We will split as we leave the gates."

Since Saddam couldn't think of anything better than their regular protocol, he nodded.

The group of seven men and seven soldiers surged forward in a V, pressing people into the wall who stood in their path toward the clearing outside.

The look-alikes and their bodyguards moved forward stepping between some black SUVs toward the military-painted Hummers. The SUV drivers stopped in recognition of the identical faces being shuffled forward.

At the same moment the second look-alike's driver skidded away from the curb, an explosion rocked the night. One of the black SUVs five or six back in the line waiting to move into the loading zone, exploded in flames and jumped tail-first into the air flipping the back end forward so severely that it landed upside down, crushing the roof of the vehicle in front of it.

Saddam sank backward into the palace again. So close to escape. "Follow me!" He called to the look-alikes who remained.

Chapter Twenty Five

As the action swirled in front of him, Rivers' fingers tightened around his weapon. There were so many courses of action where they could make a big difference in how the future of the war would play out.

Echo Company requested help, but now that they were here, Rivers needed more information. Specific information. The grounds were like a college campus with dozens and dozens of buildings of various size. But even as Rivers assessed and categorized the action by a hundred different priorities, he restrained his own leadership. He reached up to engage his mic.

But he couldn't tear his eyes off the line of vehicles at the left of the building. All those leaders were melting away. And who knows who else. Any one of them might have the charisma to reform the same sick government that they were here to relieve of their power. But the Teams were not authorized to use lethal force on unknown entities. Rivers' unit was not under any threat where they were. Saddam was the number one objective.

Maybe if they just slowed down the leadership leak over there, and then they could investigate.

Rivers turned to see, that to a man, his team stood in a posture of restrained readiness, waiting for instruction. "Take out as many tires as you can," Rivers pointed to the left of the building, "while I get further orders and priorities from TOC. Tires, not people." He clarified.

The SEALs went right to work, some threw themselves down prone, others took a knee to broaden their firing stability base while Rivers tried to raise Jackson's team on the radio.

"Echo 31 to Alpha. Twelve souls have arrived at site. Over."

"Alpha 14 to Echo 31." Rivers was delighted to hear an immediate answer. "Where are you located? Over."

Rivers glanced around behind him for an accurate description. "Echo 31 is at an outbuilding about twenty yards from a back-yard enclosure. Do you have an update for us? Over."

"We just sent three Delta units from the treeline and the street into the palace from the west. Lemme find your building on the satellite photos of the property."

"It should look like a glorified shed, maybe 10x10 with a hole for a stairway. Most of the space is underground." Rivers said. "I see two Delta Company units on my right. They're making good time toward the palace. Hardly any resistance yet." He knew that would change as the team stepped from the shadows into the floodlights of the yard.

"I found you, Echo 31."

Birdie interrupted just then. "Ok, Boss, what now?"

Rivers glanced toward the line of vehicles, they all sat at an angle leaning toward them, but they were still rolling forward, perhaps even faster now.

Rivers saw Howard fire again, but in the opposite direction. His aim was right toward where Delta was streaming toward the building. "Got him!" Howard said.

Rivers eyes went wide. When Howard turned around, he must have seen the accusation growing in Rivers' features.

"He had a shoulder-fired grenade launcher. Aimed at the roof. From his angle, he probably would have made it."

Rivers sucked in air. "Great. Keep an eye on those birds, men. I don't relish another run through the city just to catch a ride home."

The rat-tat-tat of multiple weapons firing simultaneously told Rivers that Delta had breached the palace.

Saddam Hussein led the way through another corridor with his weapon drawn. He had tossed his valise to one of his men. The briefcase though would not leave his left hand.

They snaked through main corridors and hidden hallways until they arrived at the concealed panel that led to a little-used stairway. It was steep and a cool draft sent an involuntary shiver up his spine. The legend his men loved to retell about this underground portion of the extensive tunnel-works put a curse of death on anyone who dared enter. Both previous rulers before Saddam, Qasim in 1963 and Saadi in 1968 had reinforced the validity of those stories when each of them tried to flee opposition forces from this exact tunnel. Now standing in their same circumstances, he knew why they had chosen this cursed tunnel.

Saddam had allowed the rumors to persist over the years to keep the route and its exit point as secret as possible. But he had explored it himself in the mid-1980s as he discussed architecture plans for the Al Faw Palace. He knew its exit, a little shed on the edge of the grounds near a gate nearly encased in vines, would be the perfect way out for him. It was located right on a road. And if that exit did not appear safe, this corridor led all the way the Al Faw Palace. Not that he would need to go that far. Multitudes of staircases along the way led to homes he had emptied of their inhabitants. Mysteriously those buildings never went up for sale again. Their doors were locked and window security maintained. Anytime squatters tried to gain access, it was the last time they tried anything. He could escape up and out at any one of them. And the entourage could come too.

Four remaining look-alikes in military-green garb and the five bodyguards in black scampered quickly down the stairs into the semi-lit earth. He hated being forced to hide underground like a rat to evacuate his palace, his city, his *capital* city of his country. Rage ebbed and flowed in this chest like tides in a time-lapse movie, so far he had kept it under control.

Saddam waited at the top of the stairs for the sounds of the men reaching the bottom. He reached for the switch to the gas line and plunged the tunnel into utter darkness. He could do the 56 steps to the bottom by feel now.

He started to pull the door shaped like a wall panel closed behind him when he heard running steps. "Wait, wait!" it was the voice of his latest wife, Waf.

They had no children together so he had never updated the evacuation plan to include her.

Saddam peeked around the wall panel and saw that she was close. Close enough to have seen them filing in. It was too late.

Waf held an overnight bag to her chest like a child. It shifted side to side as she ran full stride, her abaya loose on one side and flying with her dark hair behind her.

"Hurry!" he called out. "Where have you been?"

She didn't say a word but slipped in front of him and he could hear her tiny sandals making good time down the wooden stairs. But not before Saddam saw where she had been. Her neck and fingers were covered with gold and platinum jewelry, and her bag rattled with each step.

Well, jewelry could come in handy, Saddam thought. He tugged at the heavy panel to close the break in the wall. Then the entire party was encased in thick, moist darkness, but he kept moving. Someone flipped on a flashlight ahead.

Chapter Twenty Six

Rivers watched a line of matching Hummers move into place behind the SUVs with all passenger-side tires flat. He elbowed Mass to take a look and quickly outlined a plan to Alpha 14 as it formed in his mind.

"Let's go!" Rivers sprinted off over the spongy lawn even before he had the go-ahead from TOC. "Too many people leaking through our fingers unchecked over there. The flat tires didn't slow them." He heard his team behind him.

Rivers pulled up short just before they broke into the floodlight area. "Keep going." Rivers motioned with his right hand. His lifted his rifle and sited the digital crosshairs on one of the SUVs, not a tire this time, but the fuel tank.

He pulled the trigger and two seconds later he heard the shot find its mark. One second after that, a fireball lifted the rear end of the vehicle high into the air flipping it forward to land on top of an identical one in front of it in the line.

Rivers started running again. The SUV behind the fireball slammed on its breaks, which even at the 5-7 miles per hour they were rolling caused a significant jostling of the driver.

Then the SUV behind that one smashed into its bumper and the SUV bounced forward like a bumper car perhaps eight feet.

The fireball SUV crushed the roof of the SUV it had fallen on, but didn't settle immediately. It rocked forward, slid down the windshield, crushing it and dropping onto the hood. The momentum shifted as the driver's side of the engine compartment gave way before the passenger's side and the fireball rolled away from the palace into the line of Hummers.

Another vehicle crashed into the back of the one in front of it. In the line, the third Hummer's rear skidded sideways; Rivers was pretty sure those would be reinforced and nothing would penetrate their hull. All the vehicles in front of the fireball speeded up their progress, but for those behind it, effectively both lanes of traffic were now blocked. The skidding Hummer's heavy tires found traction in the grass and turned back into the concrete lane.

Rivers smiled. He stopped his unit with a fist in the air hidden by the corner of the main Republican Palace structure. If he had been on Saddam's security detail, he would have never allowed bushes and trees to be planted in such a place. But they worked nicely for his purposes.

"Nice fireworks." Someone said. The SEALs didn't have to worry about being heard. Among the roaring fire, all the engines revving, and the screaming people, it was loud. Half-a-dozen drivers had jumped out of their SUVs, and they were yelling too. Madness.

In all the commotion Rivers spotted a familiar figure. The Ace of Spades, Saddam Hussein. Mass must have seen him at the same time, because his massive paw on Rivers' shoulder dug into his joint.

"There's our target." Rivers said. "Howard, you've got Echo team. Mass, Mac, and Allen, with me. Birdie and Hayes, you're with Howard." Then Rivers stepped out from the shadows provided by the bushes. The four jogged behind the fire that gorged itself on two vehicles now. Several armed guards were pressing a blanket and rolling a screaming man on the concrete to smother flames. He must have been the driver of the SUV with the caved-in roof, Rivers assessed.

The SEALs jogged past unscathed. Perhaps unnoticed.

Rivers motioned Mac with him, Mass and Allen would take the passenger side. As they moved to go behind the Hummer, the first Hummer in line screeched away, but Rivers saw the unmistakable face from the Ace of Spades only feet away from him. Saddam climbed in the back. A bodyguard shoved him quickly from behind, and met Rivers' eyes as he scrambled in after his president, screaming, "Go! Go! Go!" His voice cut off with the slamming reinforced steel door and screeching tires.

The driver of the last Hummer in front of the roadblock must have read the fear in the bedlam because he was moving forward even before the Hummer with Saddam in it was rolling. Rivers grabbed his side arm from his left thigh holster as he ran in the Hummer driver's blind spot until Mac was also in position.

"Go!" Mass shouted the signal from the exposed side of the Hummer.

All four SEALs opened the doors of the rolling vehicle simultaneously. Mac jumped in the back seat and held his pistol to the driver's right temple. Rivers yanked the driver's door open and inserted himself inside the little alcove there, jogging along at pace. As the driver was turning toward him and stomping the accelerator in surprise, Rivers jerked the man's elbow with his right arm while holding his Glock with his left.

Rivers jumped back out of the way as the man's body tumbled unwillingly out of the driver's seat. His legs flailed and he bumped Mac's door closed with his head on the lower panel. His head bounce was actually fortunate; it kept him from being thrown under the tires. But in his fighting the fall, he twisted a leg underneath himself. Rivers was pretty sure he heard a bone snap when the man hit the concrete driveway lane.

Rivers caught up to the open driver's door in two giant leaps and pulled himself into the driver's seat, his sidearm still in his left hand. Mass's meaty fist gripped the steering wheel from the passenger's seat until Rivers was able to down shift and take advantage of the powerful engine. He took the wheel. Mass adjusted to grab the dashboard and seatback in order to give a powerful right-footed kick to some poor guard's chest. The man disappeared from view.

Rivers grinned. They had commandeered a military vehicle in the Iraqi Royal Motorcade in front of the Presidential Palace without firing a shot! *Well, not firing a shot once the plan materialized,* he acquiesced. His last shot, had been a beauty!

The mess behind them turned to pandemonium that shrank in his rearview mirror when as many as three dozen weapons, both automatic and single shot, released their anger in a barrage of bullets in their direction.

The body of the reinforced steel held, but it would certainly be a mess of dents and scratches. Once Rivers began the drive, the bulletproof glass windows were at inaccessible angles to the guardsmen in line, so they also held.

Saddam's Hummer followed the curved concrete road. One black SUV made it out of the disarray, and followed the Hummer. Rivers' only obstacle to getting to Saddam. And the SUV driver was driving like it was Sunday afternoon.

Saddam's Humvee neared the palace compound's gate. "Keep your eye on the first Hummer, Mass." Rivers instructed, "Everybody brace." Rivers tugged the wheel left and accelerated up over the curb. The deep-carpet grass was nothing for the thick tread of the tires. They flew past the SUV as if it were parked.

"My Hummer just passed the through gate." Mass informed them. "Looks like he is going straight. But my view is blocked now."

Rivers bumped back onto the concrete road going about 55 mph, though the speedometer registered in KMs so the indicator had already inched past 85. He shifted into fourth gear and the engine strain lessened.

"She's purring like a kitten, sir," Allen said from the backseat. "A very large tiger kind of kitty."

"I wish our Humvees were this new." Rivers said. "It drives like a dream." He managed to keep himself from caressing the leather wheel with molded finger grips.

He could see the second Hummer, the one carrying Saddam, now only half a football field ahead. The guard whose duty post had been to keep the arm of the gate that night had long since abandoned his raising and lowering of the arm between vehicles. Rivers saw him touch his ear and turn around quickly to his little gate shack.

"Looks like the guard just got word of our escapade." Rivers commented. He pushed the pedal to the floor and the Hummer roared forward in response.

Saddam's Hummer fishtailed to the left one block past the gate.

The striped guard-arm with a universal red octagon fixed to the middle of it loomed closer.

A chain link fence began rolling right to left across their path, courtesy of the guard who was now picking up an H&K XM-29. Rivers immediately recognized the weapon's futuristic body's appearance from the thorough testing two back-to-back squads of SEAL trainees had performed for the manufacturer. It had failed muster, but now Rivers knew which weapons had been sent as part of the late-90s arms deals. "Thanks for arming our enemies," he muttered.

Republican Palace Garage
7 April 2003
2:57 AM

The shop was eerie now. No voices, no motors, no music. Moe could hear his beloved city not at rest tonight. His shaky fingers missed a digit on the shop phone as he punched in the number from memory. He hung up and picked up the receiver again and began the series of numbers from the beginning.

He stumbled through his identity confirmation, then gave the officer who answered his urgent information on the motorcade and explained how the look-alikes worked.

"Look, I need to know if you ever got my family out. I can't find them."

"I don't see a record of it here." The voice was slow as if reading a screen.

"It was part of my deal. I inform, and my family gets a place in the City of Kansas."

"I don't know what to tell you. The last entry here under your name is a call in from you yesterday, and before that it lists that you were released from FOB Beta."

"I need to speak to Missy Judah." Moe was as firm as he could muster against the fear assaulting his thin courage. He didn't even realize he had been holding out hope that the Americans had already picked them up until he had asked the question.

"Judah Wakefield? Is that your handler? I see the lieutenant commander's signature on your paperwork, but you don't get to talk to him." Moe could hear impatience in the young voice.

"Missy Judah is a her not a him." Moe corrected in case his identity was being tested.

"Well, you don't get to speak to *her*, then. She is in the field half a world away. You've called Washington D.C."

Moe calmed himself. "I am in the field, also half a world away, a few kilometers from her base. Can you get a message to her, to call me back on this number?"

Moe licked his thumb and smudged oily residue from the number under the plastic cover near the dial pad. He read off the number.

"I will do my best. Are you secure at your location?"

"Thanks for asking." Moe shook his head at the irony. "Not particularly secure, no. There is a war going on outside my door."

Moe heard a sharp intake of breath on the line as a giant explosion seemed perfectly timed to emphasize his statement. The young man's words came more quickly now. "If you can move to a more secure location and contact us again, go ahead. Otherwise, hunker down, and I will try to get your number to your handler, uh, Lieutenant Commander Wakefield."

At least he sounds a little bit more alive now, Moe thought. "Thank you. I am going to need you to get me out of here!"

221

Chapter Twenty Seven

As he shifted into fifth gear and pressed the accelerator back to the floor, Rivers' dive watch buzzed his arm in triplicate to indicate their final waypoint time had been completed. They had missed their Black Hawk ride, but had picked up an alternate route home, if they made it that far. The windshield spider-webbed in three places, but it held, throwing off more than a dozen rounds from the guard's AR-15.

"We're running this stop sign boys!" Rivers squinted against the splintered glass. The grill of the Hummer bashed through the guard arm like it was a toothpick. The red wooden block sign held together and smacked the windshield right at Mass's face.

Mass winced involuntarily though the sign slid off and hit the street without even scratching the glass.

The fence was closing in front of them.

Rivers hit the horn to warn any pedestrians off who were stupid enough to be wandering the streets during a full-scale evacuation.

The Hummer's front grill caught the stabilizing pole of the closing gate and the Powertrain engine charged through it as simply as a bull sliding through a red cape.

The 12-foot-wide gate flung backward and snapped out of its chain-guided channel. It bounced and skittered to a landing right in the middle of the road. The twisted metal see-sawed in the SEALs' wake.

Rivers spun the wheel to the left and pressed his right foot hard to catch up to their target.

Seatbelt flashed in his mind. But all his front-strapped gear. Un-belting time. *We're going to have to chase on foot*, he justified. Rivers leaned into the steering wheel, and threw another wide left as he pushed the limits of the new machine against the surprisingly clean Baghdad streets around the Republican Palace. Adrenaline rushed. The monster vehicle ate up yards between them in seconds.

Baghdad Streets
0327 hours
SEAL Team Waypoint +9

Rivers tore his com mic over his head and shoved it toward Mass. "Update TOC." He re-gripped the wheel with both hands never letting his eyes stray from the narrowing roads.

They were pushing 95 kms in city streets better suited for donkey-speed. Saddam's driver weaved the pair of Hummers expertly through neighborhoods with tiny alleys and bomb rubble lying in the streets. "As soon as we come to some space, fire. Try the tires first, though I suspect they have the self-healing tires. Make your shots count."

The Hummer became a wind tunnel as Mac and Allen opened the windows to prepare. Rivers weaved back and forth trying to get an edge on Saddam's Hummer. He blasted the horn again and again, flashed the lights, and gave them an occasional bump as he waited for his chance. The driver certainly knew how to avoid the bridges that Rivers had been counting on to stop them in their tracks.

Mass was chattering away to Alpha Company, but all Rivers could afford to hear was Mass's vocal tones. He drew within a few inches of Saddam's rear bumper again. *God, please don't let a child stick his curious head out of any alleyways to see what all the noise is.*

A slight rise in the narrow street showed a heap of rubble and a missing building in the tight lane ahead on the left. Rivers gunned the engine. The Powertrain responded and they surged forward. Rivers steered right and bumped the front Hummer forward and slightly left.

He wanted to shake up the driver. Disorienting the passengers would be a side benefit. Rivers came at the Hummer again. This time he was able to maneuver the vehicles side by side 16 inches into the first vehicle's rear panel. That was all the leverage he needed. Rivers braced himself and slammed his vehicle hard to the left into Saddam's Hummer for the kill shot.

The Hummer proved its all-terrain advertising as it scraped its left side against the concrete block building and kept moving. Sparks flew behind Saddam's vehicle like a rooster tail. Rivers did not let up. He kept the wheel hard left. Pushing, pushing.

The drag against the buildings slowed the front vehicle significantly and Rivers matched his speed. They were hurdling straight for the 10- to 15-foot hill of rubble blocking the street. Then Rivers saw exactly what he had been waiting for ahead. A tiny break between buildings. Not even an alley. More like a footpath.

He waited one everlasting second, then came off the Hummer a couple inches to the right, accelerated, and smashed his hummer left again into Saddam's vehicle with all his strength on the wheel.

The first driver plowed into the footpath about eight inches deep. But it was enough. The corner of the building held, and Saddam's vehicle endured an immediate stop. Rivers flew by, still traveling at least 40 kms. He slammed on his breaks and pitched all of them forward. They stopped three feet into the edge of the pile of debris. He nearly ate the steering wheel like corn-on-the-cob.

Rivers threw the shifter into reverse and the wheels whirred. Backing about fifteen feet, "Exit to your right," he announced as he stopped the vehicle. He had effectively double parked with about one inch between the left side of his Hummer and the right side of Saddam's Hummer.

As if it been part of their original rehearsals, Allen and Mass jumped out and covered the vehicles. Mass took the front windshield, and Allen aimed from in front of Rivers' Hummer, ready to escort the first person to exit to his cuffs. Mac shifted from behind Rivers' seat and followed the others, setting up to the rear. He surveyed the darkened windows of the street for any movement.

When the three were in place, with two weapons drawing little red dancing laser sites on Saddam's vehicle, Rivers waved his first finger at the occupants and shook his head, encouraging them not to resist. He revved his engine, and slowly backed up two more feet, to clear the front door.

No one occupied the front passenger seat. Mass motioned to the driver to climb over and open the door. He had a significant amount of blood streaming down his face, but he was conscious.

225

The driver dug down, leaning forward. Mass called in English, "Show me your hands!" The driver moved slowly, but complied, bringing up a pistol, held by the muzzle in his fist, to show no threat. He kept it as steady as Rivers could expect given the crash they had just experienced.

The driver reached down to open the door with his other hand, keeping the pistol visible. The door didn't open on the first try, so the driver bumped it with his shoulder. From just three feet behind him Rivers could see the driver's shoulders tense in pain at the impact. The door did screech open though.

"Toss it on the ground." Mass instructed. The driver complied and the metal clattered against the road. "We are liberating this very fine vehicle for use by the American military. Come on down." Mass told him and the man fairly melted out of the passenger's seat to the ground. Rivers lost sight of him in front of his vehicle, but kept his eyes moving among all three of his men and the two remaining occupants of the backseat who were arguing.

The argument kept Rivers' attention an extra beat. Then he returned to monitoring the situation.

Finally Mass straightened up from PlastiCuffing the driver and motioned Rivers to move the Hummer a little further back to release the two in the backseat. Mac was alert and vigilant on the neighborhood. Rivers eased off the brake and rolled the diesel back.

Underground Labyrinth

Saddam quickened his pace and pushed forward past the look-alikes and the men assigned to guard them, leaving Waf to lug the heavy bag at the rear of the line. The men at the front should be getting close to the turn off he wanted to use. Quietness was paramount, so, though he wanted to yell out, he refrained, resorting to shoving men out of his way in the narrow tunnel. The grunts and smacks they made as they bounced off the hewn walls lent a satisfaction to his need for control.

The ugly thirst rose in him.

He would be able to put it aside for a while, but not for too long. He knew from experience

Only one man was still ahead of him just as the turn off to the little shed exit appeared on their right. "We stop here," he announced to Yazeen, the man in front. Saddam smiled at the man's luck. If it had been anyone else, he would have just let him keep walking away.

The little alcove at the bottom of the staircase was smaller than he remembered. Sounds of automatic and semi-automatic gunfire slithered down the stairway. "You." He pointed to one of the uniformed men, "Go see what it looks like up there."

The man took the stairs two at a time, quickly disappearing from view.

The number of people surrounding him began to close in on him. He growled lightly as he stretched out his arms to either side. "Give me some space." A couple of people tumbled into one another with the unexpected movement until everyone moved back.

Saddam sank to the floor, hating that he was sinking so low beneath his God-given station. A king. Sitting on a floor. Under the ground. He growled again.

Waf squeezed around the bodyguards toward him. He pushed his palm into the air to stop her. Apparently she didn't see his signal to leave him alone. She kept coming and crouched down facing him on her toes, preparing to swing around and seat herself next to him.

Mid-swing when she was perfectly off balance, he shoved her. Away she scattered, her bag falling neatly next to him and her body, lovely as it was, slamming into the rock floor with a happy smack.

As she should have done earlier, the woman crawled into the darkness on her hands and knees.

Chapter Twenty Eight

Through the window Mass flitted his rifle's red laser on the backseat bodyguard's chest like he was playing with a cat until he finally looked down at it. Mass brought it slowly up to center on the man's forehead. Deep wrinkles formed there while Rivers watched.

The bodyguard raised his hands above his head. Rivers could have sworn he saw a lip tremble just a little bit.

Rivers reversed the Hummer until his door was free to open fully. Four on three sounded more secure than three on three, even if one was already secured on the ground. He secured his rifle across his chest and hopped down. "Hold up." He called to Mass.

Mass immediately held up a hand to the bodyguard and told him to stop. The laser never wavered from the man's forehead.

The man froze.

Rivers said, "Have him open his shirt, I don't relish any suicide bombers climbing aboard our train." The argument he had witnessed still played at the edge of his mind. It didn't fit. A bodyguard did not argue with a king, or president, or whatever Saddam was calling himself these days.

The bodyguard must have heard Rivers through the open front door, for he quickly began unbuttoning his black uniform.

229

His white t-shirt still glowed in the moonlight but Rivers could see heavy sweat stains around the neck. Good, that meant he was scared, hopefully scared enough to be compliant even in front of Saddam.

Rivers pantomimed lifting up the t-shirt. He was taking no chances. The man bared his chest. All clear. He removed his beret and tossed it in the front seat without being asked and replaced his hands stiffly in the air.

"Saddam is getting shifty in the backseat," Allen warned.

Out of the corner of his eye, Rivers saw Mac's body shift toward them. "Stay sharp, Petty Officer." Rivers warned him. "Get them out of there, now." Rivers instructed Mass.

"You heard him. Come out with your hands up. Don't try anything funny, because I have a bullet with your name on it." Mass deadpanned.

All three of his men were performing perfectly, calmly. Even trigger fingers that he could see on Mass and Allen in the Hummer's headlamps appeared loose but alert.

The back door opened without incident and the bodyguard tossed his two side arms and a blade as long as a butcher knife to the street.

"Ankle holster." Mass said knowingly. A smaller gun clunked as its solid barrel hit the pavement. "Now hold onto the top of the door and kick them aside." The man complied, his untucked uniform waving open in the chilly air.

There seemed to be no communication issues in English. Rivers was glad of that. It had caused many a problem and hot-headed misunderstandings in the past.

As Mass took another pair of PlastiCuffs from his pack for the bodyguard, Rivers used Mass's laser-pointer-to-the-chest technique on Saddam.

The man scooted across the back seat pretty nimbly for a heavy man who would be 66 in a few days, Rivers observed.

"I am arresting you for crimes against humanity." Rivers said. "You will be treated in compliance with the Geneva Convention of 1949 until such a time as an international tribunal court can be convened for trial." Rivers paused and looked at the old man from bushy eyebrows to chestful of service medals. "After that, I don't hold much hope for your future."

The man's lips pursed beneath his beard. It looked like he was taking a right to remain silent seriously.

Rivers motioned Saddam out of the Hummer then. Something still wasn't sitting right with him. Rivers frisked the man, relieved him of his service pistol at his right thigh, a nasty blade from his boot, some hand written notes and five 25,000 Iraqi dinar notes from a front pocket, and a little pill in a tiny plastic bag in his left sleeve. "Cyanide?" Rivers asked?

Saddam shrugged.

"What are we gonna do with them?" Allen asked softly.

Rivers had been thinking on that since leaving the palace courtyard to strike out on their own. There were seven bodies and a vehicle designed to transport four. Maybe five if they really liked each other. And he wasn't really sure where in the city they were.

"Secure all those weapons and we will see." Rivers told him. "Mass, get on the horn to TOC and let them know we have the Ace of Spades plus two and have our own ride home."

"With pleasure, sir!" Mass reached up to engage the mic at his throat.

"And Mass," Rivers lowered his brow a bit as he searched stories of dark windows that lined the street, "don't smile so big.

231

Those teeth of yours are like a beacon if any tangoes are watching us."

Underground Labyrinth

Saddam drifted in his mind to massage a dream he had since boyhood. The great golden statue of himself set up on an empty plain. Droves of people flowed from cities and villages alike and as one bowed to the statue. With a glance of his eye he could command his soldiers to eliminate anyone who did not bow quickly enough.

In moments of quiet like these, he felt the ancientness in himself. He knew he was once a king of a great empire. He would be again and would rule as he once had from the seat of the empire: Babylon.

The deep knowing, no one understood. But it was the reason behind the great expense of resurrecting the former Babylon from the desert sands south of Baghdad. He had accomplished it under the guise of tourism. But someday it would once again be his home, and he would retake his real name: Nebuchadnezzar the Great.

He found the deep breathing and complete relaxation of meditating on these precious visions relaxing. These American Infidel invaders were just a blip on the timeline of his life. He was so close to his destiny.

"Where did that soldier go? What is taking him so long to bring back a report?" Saddam snapped out of his revelry when he realized his feet had gone numb.

"It has been about an hour and a half," he recognized Yazeen's voice out of the dark recesses of the passageway. "I don't think he is coming back."

"Fine. You go up." He ordered. "But if you leave me, I will come and strangle you to death the first time you try to sleep."

"Don't worry." Yazeen appeared on the edge of the dim circle of light. He held up a hand. "I'll be right back." The young soldier ran his hand through his longish dark hair and began to climb.

True to his word, he was back in less than four minutes.

"We are not going anywhere tonight." All his features frowned wryly as he reported. "And I believe Al Bashani is gone for good. I didn't see hide nor hair of him. We are still defending the palace, sir."

Chapter Twenty Nine

Mass walked toward the relative shelter of the building that had withheld the Hummer's force trying to raise TOC on the coms unit.

Rivers scanned the shadows up and down the street. "Guys, get them up. I don't like being this exposed."

Mac reached for Saddam's arm, secured behind his back as he lay flat on the street scattered with gravel and concrete chips. Saddam's head was positioned to watch the action and his cheek pressed to the ground in compliance. Mac pulled him up, giving the old man time to rock back to his knees before staggering to his feet.

Allen was less gentle with the much younger bodyguard. The man spewed a string of English expletives that he could have only learned from the masters in Hollywood.

"Switch." Rivers told Allen. Allen's face registered his surprise and slight offense, but he immediately released the bodyguard's arm and took up the weapon slung around his neck and shoulder and diligently began to scan the street in a random pattern.

Rivers stepped into the foul-mouthed bodyguard's personal space, even by Middle Eastern standards, but did not touch him. He stood silently nose to nose with the younger man who started his string of curses over from the beginning.

When he took a breath, Rivers asked, "Are you finished?" and without allowing him time to answer he went on, "because it is obvious that you don't even know what those words mean, because they don't make sense the way that you are using them. What would your fellow officers think of you if they knew you'd been enjoying movies made by the Great Satan? If you can speak civilly, I will not use the duct tape on your mouth. With that mustache and beard stubble taking it off is going to feel a lot like waxing your face."

The man didn't break eye contact and started over on his memorized cursing syllables.

"So you are ill-mannered as well as unintelligent. Thank you, you are telling me much about your weaknesses." Rivers' lips turned down. He hated vulgar language. He reached into his vest for the special-sized roll of black, non-reflective duct tape. Because the facial hair would allow slight movement of the tape, Rivers secured the end to the bodyguard's right cheek and ripped tape away from the roll a few inches at a time. He wrapped it all the way around the back of his head in the short neck hairs and back around the front to end at his left ear.

Rivers saw Saddam watching the exchange unemotionally. Mass called out, "Commander."

At the same time Allen began walking backward from his position. Mass's voice was flat and his eyes fixated at ground level, 400 yards, "Fall back to cover. I've got movement."

"Mass get the driver. Mac protect the asset." Rivers assessed the street with a new objective, not just cover, but also avoiding civilian casualties, and escape route options.

235

"We've got movement from the south as well." Mass said calmly.

Everyone was backing toward the building the Hummer had crashed into with guns at the ready. The 30-inch gap in the façade of the block that had stopped the first vehicle was blocked up by that vehicle. They could try moving the prisoners under the carriage or over an accordion-shaped hood. It would be slow and everyone would be exposed too long. Rivers rejected the option.

The other cover was a door that remained unboarded by plywood like most of the other doorways of this block. There were two more unboarded doors on the far side of the street too. Or they could climb the rubble pile and enter the cover of the building that remained. Too risky for ankles on the rubble and too unsecured in the structure. Too exposed to cross the street, and then too far away from their vehicle if they got there.

Closest door it is, Rivers decided. The first burst of bullets arrived at that moment. They slammed harmlessly into the concrete building above their heads from their exposed north side. The steel-plated Hummers provided slight shelter from the threat on the south, until the threat came closer.

Rivers reached the door first and tried the door knob. Locked. He back up a step, shifted his angle and fired. The brass knob flew off toward the rubble pile and he heard the inside knob ping off the tile floor inside. He pushed the door in and stood back against the frame.

No gunshots. The most dangerous moment was when he was silhouetted against the open door. Even the smoke- and fog-covered moonlight would offer his impression against the full dark of the interior.

Rivers pushed his weapon away from his body and into the void of the doorway. A shrill scream rang out. He could hear labored puffs of pint-sized breaths like a hand was over a mouth of a baby who had a stuffy nose. A little whimper, but in a different tone than the scream. At least three souls in the house. The sound of gravel being traveled over quickly also registered on his brain. The men from the north were gaining ground. His men were returning fire in regular bursts.

"It's ok. It's ok. We are not here to hurt you." Rivers formed a few of the Arabic phrases he had practiced.

"Here!" he whisper-called to his men. Saddam was the first one to join him in the house followed quickly by Mac. The scream sounded again, only it sounded like strangled words. The woman's voice fell in volume but continued mumbling the same syllables over and over. Rivers heard dry feet pushing against tile and knew the woman was on the floor scooting away from them.

"What's she saying?" Rivers asked Mac.

Allen pushed the driver into the house in front of him. "Stay down and stay quiet." He commanded the Iraqi.

The driver's silhouette ducked down before even clearing the doorway and crumbled to the side. "Take that window." Rivers told Allen. "Do you have any grenades left?"

"Of course, sir. I always over pack."

"I think she's saying 'the devil, don't let the devil get my baby.'" Mac answered.

A deep growl and yell came from the floor near Allen at the curtained window. "Sorry." He said.

"Me fingas!" The driver squalled in British tones.

"I said sorry." Allen repeated. "Now get out of the way."

Mass entered, dragging the bodyguard under his arm. "Where do you want this one, Commander?"

"Is he dead?" Rivers asked. Allen returned fire from the window and the driver shuffled on hands and knees on the tile.

"No, sir, just uncooperative, so my fist gave him a little kiss on the jaw."

"Make sure he is breathing, Mass, and set him out of the way against the back wall."

The main door of the domicile opened into a parlor-like room for receiving guests. Rivers could pick out the furniture now that his eyes had adjusted fully. There were now 10 souls in the room. "Mac, get the civilians out of here to cover."

"I'll move them upstairs as far back in the house as we can."

"And tell them to keep quiet." Rivers moved for the door.

"I think she's talking about Saddam when she's saying 'the devil,' sir. I'll need to move him before she'll go up the stairs."

"Move him. Carry her. Just clear this room of civilians." Rivers followed through his scope a hunched-over man scurrying from the rubble pile to another unboarded door close to his position. Rivers fired and the man sprawled forward in the street. "How many tangoes do you count?" he asked Allen.

"At least four left to the north and a couple to the south. I can't see around our Hummer. But I saw two muzzle flashes at once a second ago. "

Mass loosened a double-shot from his prone position. "Make that three to the north. Nope, two more just came over the top of the rubble. So five."

Rivers glanced back at Saddam sitting on the floor, wedged into the corner. The driver was resituating himself immediately next to his leader with no reaction from Saddam. The duct-taped bodyguard was draped across a velvet setee, unconscious. It was a quality piece of furniture. Furnishing his new house over the last few months had given him a new appreciation for quality. The wallpaper and a painting above the setee looked quality too.

One stray bullet, while good that it would miss a body in the house, would ruin the artwork. It might be all they have left after this firestorm. In three large strides Rivers was at the far side of the room. He leaned across the unconscious driver and lifted the painting off its mounting.

"You thief!" hissed Saddam.

"I'm protecting it." Rivers said, yet a wave of guilt washed over him.

"Right! Like you are 'liberating' the car?"

"Take it up at the tribunal." Rivers said and stepped sideways to get through the narrow doorway leading to the back of the house. He stepped into a room that felt like a kitchen though he could see nothing. "Coming through," he called, just in case. It felt strange to announce himself. SEAL missions were generally carried out in silence. Civilians and working out of their homes changed things up tremendously. He didn't like it at all. He set the frame flat on the floor and shoved it away from him. Its heavy weight only sent it a few feet. That was good enough. Mac was clomping down the stairs to his left when Rivers turned around. "Commander?" he asked. "What are you doing?" Gunfire erupted in the front room.

"You help Allen at the window." Rivers hustled at half-stature into the room that reminded him briefly of a disco with its flashing muzzle lights and racket of firing on auto and slugs finding their marks to chip away at the concrete.

"Reloading." Mass said right as Rivers crouched over him. "Left side!" he warned. "At least seven within forty yards."

"I'm waiting until they get a little closer." Allen said from the window.

"Toss it over here."

"Toss you a grenade, sir?" Allen asked.

"For Pete's sake! Somebody do something. I need help keeping them at bay." Mac fired two double shots in a row.

"Here." Rivers had covered the tile between them and took the hand grenade from Allen when he saw the pin still in place.

"Oh this is too easy." Rivers chuckled softly. In the soft light of the waning moon low on the horizon now, a group of tangos was scuttling across the street. Two on the front side carried metal trashcan lids as shields. Double muzzles flashing from a second story window pinpointed the man left behind to lay down cover fire. The flashes were too close in proximity to have room for two bodies behind the triggers. It was one man holding a full-auto rifle in each hand. The bullets were scattering everywhere because he didn't have the strength and coordination to fire two weapons simultaneously.

Rivers pulled the pin, waited two beats and wound up to pitch it at 80 mph into the center of the group. With the intense darkness inside the house, he did not even have to worry about them seeing him in the doorway or having any idea it was coming.

"Fire in the hole!" Rivers called as soon as he released the ball. He pressed his fingers into his ears and squeezed his eyes shut. The four SEALs had time to take cover behind the wall. The concussion rocked the whole street.

"What did you pack those things with?" Rivers asked shaking his head to clear his vision.

"My special recipe." Rivers could hear the smile of pride in Allen's voice. "That was some throw."

"Starting pitcher at Annapolis all three years as a midshipman."

Allen whistled. "Go Navy!"

"Speaking of 'go Navy'—" Mass interrupted. "We need to get out of here."

"I'll get the Hummer. Cover me."

They were in place in seconds. Rivers raced to the Hummer and threw himself inside. The windows on the passenger side lay in chunks in the seat. "Great."

The engine turned over on the first twist of the key. Smoothly Rivers executed a tight U-turn from standing still and then once facing back the way they had come into the street, he swerved backward toward the door as if he was parallel parking.

"Curb service." He called through the window hole. "If there was a curb." He added unnecessarily.

"Where are we putting everyone?" Mac asked.

"Driver on the back floor, passenger side. I need Mass up front with the bodyguard's old red beret on. Window is broken.

"You think his hat's gonna fit this head?" Mass chuckled.

"You're gonna try."

"I think we should pull the ammunition from the turret gun on top and put Saddam and the driver standing through the top." Mac said. "They can smile and wave like it is a V-E Day parade. They can be properly motivated." He patted his weapon across his chest. "Duct tape them if we have to. We have a long way to go and not too many friendlies."

"Bad, bad idea, friends." It was the driver who spoke up then. They were all shuffling out the door and into the Humvee.

"Bodyguard in the back back. Pull out anything in there." Rivers said. "Why is that a bad idea? Because this is not really Saddam?"

"Well. Yes." Sputtered the driver. He reached up with both hands to remove his cap too. "That and parading Saddam through the streets is more likely to get us shot than not. He is hated here." The driver's voice had dropped to a whisper, like he was trying to keep from hurting the look-alike's feelings. "You have not understood Iraq at all. Most of us are very glad to have you Americans here. Even if we're not dressed like it."

Rivers took in the driver's words and decided on a plan as he stared at him. *Is he playing me?* Rivers wanted to trust his unprompted support. For now the man was staying, he'd let intel sort out the motives in camp. All he said was, "Well, you don't hear those words in a British accent every day."

"The shadows toward the south are moving again," Allen announced. "Better load up pronto."

"Sit on each other's laps and use the floorboards." Rivers instructed.

Mac took the bodyguard's elbow and took him to the back of the Hummer. The gear space was slanted like a sharpened pencil. It was going to be a tight fit.

The man began shaking his head, his eyes became wild. His body stiffened. "A little claustrophobic, are we?" asked Mac. "It'll be ok, just close your eyes."

While the words themselves were decent enough, Mac sounded like he was addressing a two-year-old. "Mac." Rivers called him out.

"Sorry." Mac said immediately, though Rivers wasn't sure to whom the man was apologizing. "He'll have more space back here than we will up there, crammed in like sardines." Then Mac addressed the prisoner, "Get in or I can make you get in. Your choice."

It was probably as good as Rivers was going to get from him. "Where'd those bank notes you had on you go?" he addressed their fake Saddam.

The old man didn't even look up at him from the floorboard at the driver's feet where Mass had stuffed him.

"Hey." Rivers tapped his knuckles against the man's shoulder. "Where'd the money go?"

The man just sealed his lips tighter.

"I don't think he speaks English," the helpful driver said. "You want me to ask?"

Rivers shrugged.

A few words in Arabic and the old man reached two fingers into the front pocket opposite from his chest full of colorful war medals. The disdain in his rheumy eyes made Rivers feel defensive. The old man made a disapproving sound deep in his throat, and he tossed the bills out of the vehicle like flinging a spent cigarette.

"I'm not a thief." Rivers couldn't help himself. He leaned down and swiped it off the gravel as Mac slammed the trunk lid. "Five 25,000s" he ruffled through them. "It's only about a hundred bucks. But it is more than nothing." Maybe the woman could sell the painting too. Mac tucked himself into the tiny remaining space, and slammed the scraped Hummer door behind him.

"I'd be happy drive." Rivers heard him say because there was no window.

Rivers chuckled, glad for the legroom up front. "Thanks. I've got this," he said as he reentered the home. Bending down, Rivers picked up a bread-loaf sized chunk of concrete that had fallen in the fire-exchange and stuffed the cash under it on the cracked tile floor to keep it from blowing away. "We are leaving now, ma'am. Sorry about the mess." He called out, knowing she probably couldn't hear him from whatever second floor back closet Mac had stuffed the cowering little family.

Chapter Thirty

Republican Palace Garage
7 April 2003
5:20 AM

Moe's eyes flashed open. He froze, sitting there on the garage floor, propped in the small corner between the outside wall and the air compressor. Only his eyes moved, roving back and forth in the little bit of light. When had he fallen asleep and what had awakened him?

The sounds of battle had fairly well quieted down. Just an occasional burst of flak. And while it didn't quite feel peaceful, the bit of sky he could view through the row of high rectangular windows in the closed garage door was tinged with pink. A new day. What would it hold for him? For his city? For dear Liliya and the children?

Moe shivered and shifted on the concrete. He wrapped himself tighter in the quilted pad they used to soften the concrete floor when taking a quick peek under the skirt of one of the fleet vehicles and didn't want to fire up the hydraulic lift. His whole body ached. "I'm getting too old for this," he mumbled under his breath and tried to massage the swelling out of his gnarled knuckles in the slight warmth that had accumulated under the blanket.

A tinkling of metal slipping off metal sounded again. Moe froze again. He recognized the sound that had awakened him.

The slipping metal clinked again. It sounded to him like a 29 mm wrench slipping off a bolt. *What has a ¾ inch bolt in a garage?* He searched his brain.

Sit still or investigate? He asked the Lord silently as he looked around his little hideaway. It was a pretty good spot. Moe tilted his head. Unless someone was searching for something, they wouldn't see him in a once-over of a deserted mechanical shop.

Go look and see what I've brought you.

Moe felt the words expand in his heart as he sensed the Father's delight. "What are you up to?" Moe's energy surged in wonder as he smiled. He pushed himself up from the floor and wrapped the blue, oil-stained, industrial quilt around his shoulders like a thick cape. Because of its dense padding and small zig zag sewing pattern, it flared at his shoulders and swung in a flapping motion with each step. It was kind of fun.

That's one of my favorite things about you, Moe, Moe heard the words form in his heart not aloud, but they were just as clear to him as if they had been aloud. *I love the way you find joy in simple pleasures.*

Moe didn't even try to stifle the grin that stretched toward his ears as he moved toward the sound. "You have favorite things about me? You've thought about me enough to have favorite things? That makes me happy too."

Moe felt his shoulders straighten taller under his flapping cape. The sound of metal started to chink, like metal hitting metal, but it was kind of muffled. He had crossed over the entire pit area of the garage. He could tell he was getting closer, but he couldn't see anything moving in the electronics area, or the open office area. Nothing near the chairs or the coat pegs and lunchbox area.

Maybe al Hamdani's private office? The door was ajar at least a foot. Moe would have to step over Dabir to get there though. The chinking persisted, but with no discernable rhythm.

Blood had congealed in a brown oval around Dabir al Hamdani's upper body. The bossman's suspicious young face held no color, and his dark brown eyes stared toward the ceiling.

Moe reached down to close the cold eyelids so al Hamdani couldn't see him. It didn't make sense, but the eyes creeped him out. Moe saw the man's fine leather jacket hanging just outside his rarely used private office's door on a coatrack that only he was allowed to use. Moe strode over quickly and grabbed the coat by the collar. The wooden hanger slipped off the rack and clattered to the concrete.

The chinking metal stopped abruptly. It was definitely coming from inside the office.

Moe squatted to spread the coat over the man's upper half. He pulled the collar up over Dabir's head, leaving the bottom half of his bloody midsection exposed. Moe shrugged. Better than his face.

The wrench sounds remained silent. Moe pushed open the office door silently.

North of Baghdad
7 April 2003
0547 hours

Mass reached up to click the microphone he now wore on. "Echo 34 to Alpha 1. Copy. Is Alpha 14 available on the maps again to re-direct us?"

"What now?" Rivers asked. Mass's posture had changed.

"Thank you, Alpha 1. Echo 34 out." Mass said and clicked off the microphone. "Jackson is grabbing Lucky off Howard's call in a minute. We are going to have to loop around the airport and drop these guys off at FOB Beta. The inn is full at home. Howard will beat us home and is bringing in, um, quite a few long-term guests from our secondary target."

The sun streaked the grey sky pink near the eastern horizon.

"What's the new ETA?" Mac groaned.

Rivers drummed his fingers on the steering wheel. It had been a nerve-wracking drive, with three re-routes from Luckhardt to get out of Baghdad on the north side where they were based at Camp Liberty. "From what I gather it will probably be another 25 to 35 minutes. Did Jackson say how the airport is progressing?"

"We have taken it!" Mass grinned.

A whoop went up from the back seat.

"Outstanding." Rivers pumped his fist in a single jerk.

Al Hamdani's Private Office
6:10 AM

The office was empty. A fancy table set up as a desk with a straight-legged fancy chair behind it. No noise, no curtains or windows, except the ones that opened into the shop. Nowhere to hide.

The office had a dampened silence about it.

Moe slipped back into the shop and picked up a wrench from the pile of them scattered on the desk where he had made his phone call. In the middle of his pivot toward the office, Moe turned back to the desk. He spread out the cold wrench set. The 29 mm was missing. "Hmm." Moe nodded.

Walking back into the office, Moe no longer tried to keep quiet. He had not heard any gunfire in almost ten minutes. Starting with the wall directly behind the door, Moe tapped the plasterboard wall. He shuffled a few inches forward and tapped again. At the corner, the whole wall had sounded the same. He didn't even hear the sound of wooden studs at 16-inch intervals.

But about a meter into the long wall of the bossman's office the pitch of the clunky metal wrench resounding changed. For 75 centimeters the higher sound remained and then the original thudding pitch returned.

The striped wallpapered wall had a hollow behind it.

"Hello?" Moe called out and returned to tapping the hollow space. Something, no some*one* was back there. He ran bitten-down fingernails horizontally at shoulder height and waist height trying to feel for a seam in the paper.

"Is anybody there?" he pounded on the plaster board with the side of his closed fist. That was when the wall sprang toward him.

Moe jumped back out of its way. He must have released some weighted spring or trigger. The seam, camouflaged by the stripes in the paper, was obvious now.

Moe gasped at the scene revealed.

Round rusty bars ran vertically from the top of the new hole in the wall to the floor. Above his head a heavy lock was inset into a reinforcing horizontal stabilizer bar. It looked like it would take pirate-type skeleton key to open it. Damp, foul air washed over him.

"Ugh," he groaned. "That is rank!"

A stirring sounded in the darkness of the space that could only be called a cave jail. "Is someone there?" he called. "Show yourself." How he knew to call gently, Moe never considered.

A rag of a person slunk toward the light. A thin arm was thrown over the face. "Please don't hurt me." A shallow voice begged.

"What are you doing back there?" Moe couldn't believe his eyes. He had heard about the underground labyrinth prison of Saddam Hussein, but always considered it a legend.

The little voice offered no reply, but the waif did come closer. "It's a little bright out there mister. Where did the other man go?"

"Um. I don't know." Moe was at a loss for words. It was a child. Dressed in rags with short, hacked hair. "Are you alright? Are you hungry?"

Boney shoulders shrugged in a careless move he had seen both his daughters make often since they became teenagers, when they really did care very much.

"I don't want nothing from you, mister. Just leave me alone."

Moe stepped back at the fierce vehemence emanating from her slender body. He saw the morning light glint off the 29 mm wrench in her right hand then. "I'm not going to hurt you, girl." He said softly.

"I ain't a girl, you idiot." The small creature tried to laugh but ended up coughing. She pulled her left hand through her chunky close haircut as if to prove her gender.

"You're going to be ok. I'm not going to hurt you." He said again. "I've got two daughters of my own. Well, I *think* I have two daughters. I haven't seen them for a week today."

His tone must have broken through the girl's shell. She moved closer to stand at the bars. "I hope they're ok, mister. Have you got any food?"

Her clothes were filthy, though they looked like they had been of decent quality in some distant past, and her feet were bare.

"I don't have any food on me, but what do you say we work on those hinges together and see if we can find something in the shop after we get you out of there?"

"You're gonna get me free?" The girl's light brown eyes found a sparkle of life.

Moe removed his cape blanket and stuffed it through the bars toward her, "Why don't you wrap up in this and see if you can warm up a little?"

"Thanks, mister. Is there a bathroom out there? I don't think I've ever been so dirty in my life."

"Yep. We will get you some water. Hot water. All you want. And drinking water too." Moe was already measuring the waist-level hinge with his thumb to go get the proper tool to pound it out.

He brought back a sledge hammer and a paper cup full of water which he passed through the bars.

"What's your name?" Moe asked. He took a practice swing as if he was on the golf course. The hinge would have to be pounded out from underneath.

"I'm Takita."

Two strikes on the middle and bottom hinges each, and they only hung on by a few centimeters.

I'm Moe," he said as he dragged the office chair from behind the desk. It would give him a better angle at the highest hinge. "What's your family name, Takita?"

The girl sank into blue-blanketed heap on the floor of the stinky cave-jail on the far side of where he was swinging the sledge hammer. "I don't have a family anymore, mister."

Moe paused, but barely. A lot of people would make that statement in the coming months. "What happened to them?" he asked. The chair scrapped against the floor as he lined it up with where he thought it would work best for his swing.

"Qusay got 'em," she said dully.

The top hinge pin came all the way out and crashed onto the floor with one blow. Takita recoiled.

"I'll just grab some pliers and we'll have you right out of there." Moe said. He plucked the bottom pin out first. "Can you hold the bars while I get this last hinge, so the door doesn't fall on either of us?"

"Sure." The girl gripped the bars just wider than he shoulders and braced her feet. Moe wiggled the pin from the top of the hinge and tugged it right out. "Better hurry, mister. It's heavy!" Takita warned.

Moe took the door that leaned in towering above her head and pulled it back toward himself. A single clanging yank had it fully inside the room. He set it against the solid wall and turned back to see that Takita had already scampered out of the cave.

"You don't mind if we close this thing off again do you?"

Takita shook her head in little movements. "I never wanna see that place again."

"I'll do my best to make sure you never do." Moe promised the urchin girl with hunks of hair chopped off. "Bathroom's just through there." Moe pointed. "You take your time, Takita. And there's a lock on the door."

When she returned, Moe had found three lunches that had never been eaten in the craziness of the day before and all of the food was laid out on the desk near the phone.

Takita froze at the entry to the shop from the back hallway. The body lay between them. Moe had not foreseen that.

"He can't hurt you." Moe said. "But I don't want to move him. In case somebody comes to inspect the place." The girl was shivering even under the oil-stained blanket. "Come take a look." he invited.

Takita took the smallest steps possible and still be considered moving.

"Is this him?" Moe uncovered Dabir al Hamdani's face. And looked expectantly at the youngster.

"Yes." She trembled nodding in a quick motion and looking away.

"Well, he had a pretty bad day yesterday, Takita. So I don't think he'll be causing you any more trouble. How about you pick what you want to eat first." Moe gestured with an open hand to the food items on the desk as if he were showcasing a new car for the girl with his bent fingers.

She sighed big and fingered each thing before picking up the orange and inhaling its sweet scent. She set it back down and then tore one of the pitas in half and offered part to him as she sank even teeth into its softness.

Chapter Thirty One

FOB Beta Front Gate
7 April 2003
0625 hours

"What is with all the people?" Mac asked.

Rivers shifted into fourth gear on the secondary road that lead to FOB Beta. He had found a nice rhythm on the loop road, despite the traffic, and he had begun to relax just a little as the mission wound down. It would still be hours before he got some sleep, he knew, but he was ready to get looped in on the full picture of what had been accomplished—and not accomplished—by each team in the field.

"Those would be refugees." Mass answered him from the passenger's seat.

"What? Where are they going?" Mac asked.

People had been walking alongside the highway during most of their route. Singles, couples, and family groups. Some wheeled a single suitcase, but nearly everyone had a backpack, down to the youngest walking-age child, Rivers recalled. The crowd began to thicken about the time Mac had asked his question. Every civilian car was packed to the roof with bags and people. Most had random items strapped to the roof. Rivers couldn't keep from a two-second stare as he passed a bicycle held to the roof of a small two-door car with belts fastened together end-to-end and looped through open car windows. "That's pretty cleaver." He remarked and nodded to the driver when he got caught staring. He passed orderly traffic of motorcycles and bicycles that looked as overloaded as he had seen them in regularly India and Africa.

"Away," the driver spoke up. "They will go visit friends. Stay with an aunt or cousin away from the city. Try to get to an airport, perhaps. Baghdad has been leaking people for months. They will return when they feel it is safe." In the rearview mirror Rivers saw the driver shrug sadly in the confined back seat of the Hummer with the fake Saddam sitting on his lap. "Or not." He went on in his cultured British accent as if lecturing a classroom full of students. "According to my studies of world history when faced with danger or uncomfortable living conditions, since the dawn of time people have fled to more stable environments. Once they get there, migrants usually stay, especially if they can get work. Whole populations shift. Look at the entire Middle East post World War One. When the Ottoman Empire collapsed, and everything shifted."

"Are you a driver or a professor?" Rivers asked making eye contact in the mirror.

"I was a professor of ancient history at Merton College in Oxford for six years after I completed my graduate studies," the man sounded wistful. "Until my father needed me to return home. Since he had paid my tuition, I was obligated. This driving was the only job I could find."

The Hummer's deep engine and an occasional thump from the bodyguard in the trunk were all Rivers could hear as they pulled up to the end of a line of eight vehicles at FOB Beta's gate.

"Looks new." Rivers said of the gate's shiny links.

"Everything is new." The driver shrugged again.

An old truck at the front of the line made a U-turn and passed them. Its dirt looked real, not painted on.

The lorry passed through the gate next, then the second lorry turned in. Rivers rolled the Hummer forward with a slight flexing of his ankle. A woman cradling a newborn in her arms trudged past them. Rivers remembered passing her earlier on the main road.

As Rivers finally rolled up to the gate twenty minutes later, he could see the woman with the baby still being interviewed. With his window down as the day was beginning to heat, he heard her black abaya ripple in the wind.

The two Army guards speaking to her split up. One spoke into his walkie, the other led her to a bench on the shadier north side of the little guard shack, motioned her to sit down, and offered her a bottle of water which she accepted and then set on the bench beside her to jostle the baby gently.

A private second class according to his insignia worked the gate in mirrored aviator sunglasses against the early piercing sun. He hooked a finger over the temple bar and pulled them low them on his nose as he looked the Hummer up and down. He whistled one long note and glanced at Rivers over the top of the lenses. "What did she ever do to you?" he asked in a mid-western twang.

Rivers stuck his head out the window to view the Humvee's paint gouges and body dents in the daylight. "You should see the other guy." He leaned back in. Another guard in heavier body armor over his BDUs swung a mirror on a long stick to inspect the underside of the Hummer on the passenger side. He moved around to the back.

"All right. Whatcha got for us, Lieutenant Commander?" The first guard held out his hand for a manifest or identification.

Rivers loosened his dog tags at his neck. "You should have received a reservation for three new detainees from Commander Jackson at Camp Liberty North."

"We're not expecting anyone." The private first class pushed the aviators back onto his face with his middle finger. "No one past the gate without authorization." he said. "Sir." He shrugged.

The guard with the mirror called out "all clea—" and was interrupted. The bodyguard in the trunk chose that moment to give a thump hard enough to bounce the back end of the vehicle, punctuated by a muffled grunt.

Everyone at the gate went on alert.

"U-turn, Commander. Park it over there," the PFC circled one finger in the air and pointed and then placed both hands on his M-4 carbine, one finger conveniently near the safety switch. "And everybody out!"

Tension whitened the young man's fingertips on the Colt slung across his chest.

"PFC Astor." The guard with the walkie leaned the upper part of his body out of the little shack to yell to the guard. The woman on the bench next to the door with the baby jumped.

A female soldier approached the gate from inside. Rivers noted the non-U.S. uniform as he turned the Hummer around to park it and the woman was blocked from his view for a moment. Was that an Israeli?

"You heard the man." Rivers disengaged the engine and depressed the emergency brake pedal. "Everybody out."

The U.S. Navy men and Iraqis fairly spilled out the back passenger doors. Mass hauled a very rumpled bodyguard from the trunk.

"Commander Rivers," the guard with the walkie hailed him from the doorway twenty yards away. "I'll be right with you."

Rivers saw the man lift his hand in a slow-down motion toward the pair of PFCs running the line of traffic at the gate. Rivers stretched his lower back as the walkie man then turned to the female soldier flashing her credentials from inside the gate. He pointed to the lady with the baby. The woman on the inside spoke to the woman on the outside in Arabic and motioned her over. The soldier was definitely Israeli. Rivers would recognize that accent anywhere.

The lady with the baby started at least as violently as she had when the guard had called out next to her a moment before. Her head snapped around to see where the voice had come from. She must have recognized the accent too.

Rivers couldn't hear any further conversation over the two cars and a mini-truck idling at the gate, but he could see the Israeli speaking gently and inviting the woman to come in. But the woman stiffened her posture and turned her face toward Baghdad.

After another minute and a half, Rivers took two steps toward the gate. "Please return to your vehicle, Commander." The guard with the walkie held up a hand to stop him. "I will be right with you."

Rivers turned back and leaned against the driver's door to wait. Another car joined the line at the gate. His guys wandered around. Mac and Allen were talking, but alertly watching the driver, the bodyguard whose mouth was still taped shut, and the fake Saddam, who had sunk to the ground almost as soon as they got out of the vehicle to await his fate.

It was a full eight minutes later before a Marine and a Navy man carrying something joined the Israeli. The Israeli spoke and demonstrated largely with her hands.

Both of the new guys moved their overloaded fists out to their sides to allow the guard with the walkie to examine their ID cards dangling around their necks. The man in charge of the gate nodded toward Rivers and escorted the pair toward him.

At thirty feet Rivers finally identified the objects the men were carrying. A young Navy ensign with a broad grin and a scruffy chin held up a cup in his right hand. "A Commander Jackson from your TOC suggested four coffees, strong and black, might go a long way this morning."

Bless Jackson, Rivers thought. *He knew it was a disappointing night for us.* He reached for a cup with steam pouring out the sipping hole in the lid.

ENS Anderson pressed a cup into Mass's big paws while the Marine with him handed his cups to Allen and Mac.

Mac actually sighed with his first sip. "Where did you get Starbucks?" he asked.

Anderson unfolded a piece of paper from his back pocket while Rivers took a big gulp. "You don't have a Starbucks on your base?" Anderson laughed. "Actually one of the guy's wives from Intel House is our generous supplier."

"What's going on over there?" Rivers asked the walkie man still watching the Israeli standing inside the fence and the woman seated on the bench jouncing her baby. The water bottle sweated beside her, unopened.

"The mother refuses to walk with an Israeli. Since these guys were coming anyway," the man shrugged, "I decided to send them all together to be interviewed."

Rivers tore his eyes from the two women and signed the paperwork. "Thanks for this." He hoisted the paper cup of coffee. "I'd suggest leaving the bodyguard's mouthpiece in place for the trip back to the cells, but the other two have been pretty cooperative."

Anderson must have really looked at the prisoner sitting on the ground for the first time. "Holy cow, Commander!" Anderson stepped back and then asked in a softer voice, "Is that who I think it is?"

Rivers cleared his throat. "Cows are not holy. Pretty certain he is not." Rivers helped the old man up from the ground. Anderson and a Marine from Intel escorted the three prisoners toward the gate.

The walkie guy ran his fingers over a deep dent in the back panel of the Hummer. "You sure about that, commander? This vehicle is part of the royal motorcade according to its license plate. We were all briefed on what to watch for two nights ago."

"I'm sure." Rivers said. The man was out of earshot now. "He wasn't nearly arrogant enough to be Saddam. Mount up, folks. Let's go home."

Chapter Thirty Two

Ellie untangled her fingers from the fence links and turned to trail after Anderson and the others. "A complete waste of time." She muttered and scratched her head under the required pith helmet-looking ensemble she had borrowed from one of the American guys on her way out the door to meet the woman from Baghdad who showed up at dawn with an infant. The gate had requested a female escort, and she was available.

Ellie tried not to take offense at the woman's abject rejection of her race. She lined up her steps to kick a little rock off their path from the gate to the broken-down street that housed the base HQ and Intel House. Some other group had moved into another ramshackle hut on the row, but without putting her head in to ask, she didn't know what they did.

Something didn't sit right about the woman. She squinted against the rising sun and the memory of two suicide bombers who had walked up to the check point crossing between the Palestinian Territory and Israel one Tuesday afternoon when she had been on duty. They had each disguised their explosive weapon as a baby bump. They used the excuse of a clinic appointment in Jerusalem to get through the first layers of security approaching the actual check point.

Ellie had noticed immediately that neither of them had swollen facial features or fingers. They both waddled a little, but it had not looked quite right. They had been sent to her kiosk after the metal detector. She had thrown up the red light as they approached.

They obeyed the traffic signal, but inside her reinforced steel and Plexiglas kiosk Ellie had monitored their reaction on the video screen next to her for just this reason. They had looked at each other and then around behind them and to the guards on the other side of the check point. They did not have the board, tired-of-standing-in-line look about them that others crossing over displayed.

Ellie felt the same uneasy jumpiness in her belly with this lady with an infant as she had with those two pregnant women.

Just as Ellie had been reaching for the red button to alarm the entire check point into Jerusalem and send it into lockdown, those two ladies on the monitor held hands and dropped their handbags. Then she saw plastic detonator buttons dangling from their sleeves.

She ducked down in her chair as she fist-pounded the panic button. The siren wailed, and then the blast of whiteness and sound were the last she remembered.

Ellie had woken some time later maybe seconds, maybe minutes. All but one duty officer inside kiosks had survived. Everyone outside, Israeli guards and Palestinian people, along with a few tourists, had died.

Ellie shook herself from the memories. It had taken a while to recover both physically and mentally from that one. She over-studied every pregnant woman, fat people, even stocky people,

people carrying parcels, luggage, babies, children that came across her path. "Anderson." She called him back while the group continued down the road, only 100 meters or so to processing at the Intel House.

"Do you smell anything?"

Anderson screwed up his face at her. "Uhh, dust, diesel, and outside smells." He shrugged. "What are you getting at?"

"We are slightly downwind from a baby who hasn't been changed in hours because the mother doesn't have a diaper bag with her, and I don't smell anything."

Anderson still stared as they kept walking. "It is suspicious." Ellie widened her eyes.

"Maybe they are both dehydrated." Anderson loosened his helmet strap. "I heard it crying earlier."

"I did too," Ellie remembered. "But that could have been a mechanism. Wouldn't it be better to double check? We don't even have X-rays set up to screen people at the gate yet."

"Okay, Dayan. What do you suggest?" He sounded put out, but he did refasten his helmet strap as she explained. He walked to the front of the group and said, "I'll take it from here."

They walked right past Intel House and the C.O.'s HQ and continued right around the edge of the last building on their little village street. The main area of the base was still hidden to the left, and they headed toward the open airfield.

Ellie quickened her pace now and came up behind the woman's left elbow, she reached across the woman's shoulders and pinched her right bicep and then quick as a wink reached in with both hands from the left and snatched the baby as the woman's head whipped to the right. Ellie was careful to cradle the infant's neck in her left hand if indeed it was a newborn.

As soon as she touched the blanket though, she knew.

"Somebody call the bomb squad!" Ellie announced turning away. She began to run from the group, trying not to jostle her arms. The woman chased her and pounded on her back. She scratched and clawed at her sleeves to retrieve the baby blanket.

Someone pulled the woman off abruptly. Ellie stopped and unwrapped the blanket.

It was a realistic looking doll head attached to a body-shaped, old-fashioned dynamite bomb. Ellie didn't see a timer. She flipped it over and let the blanket drop to the dirt. Just then the sound of a chopper on approach was added to the dangerous mix.

"Get that guy out of here." Ellie ordered. She didn't care that she didn't have the authority. She had the experience.

Anderson waved his hands over his head running toward the landing pad and yelling to the pilot and the soldier guiding him in with landing clearance on the radio.

On the back of the bundle was a little finger depression on a flesh-colored box. It had to be the crying mechanism. The woman could activate the crying to discourage onlookers.

Ellie's eyes followed the wires to the clip-like detonator. It looked simple enough to disarm, but she would wait for the pros.

She checked on Anderson again. The helicopter was dipping into a 180 turn away and Anderson's arms dropped to his side. A successful wave-off. When Ellie saw him begin to talk to the radio guy, she placed the baby on the ground and backed away.

The woman was struggling against the marine who held her tightly. The prisoner with his mouth taped shut had eyes that were bugging out of his face. The old man who looked like Saddam stood still, slightly bent at the waist, watching the action with tired eyes, and the third prisoner was trying to convince everyone to back up from the danger in British-accented English.

Fifteen minutes later, back at Intel House, processing the four new prisoners, a boom erupted and the ground and air shook from the force.

"Turns out the bomb squad likes to blow things up." Ellie smiled at the woman who refused to give her name. "I'm sure you'll enjoy Guantanamo Bay. We don't require a name to give you a reservation."

FOB Beta
Female Officers' Quarters
7 April 2003

Judah stretched long against the end of her bed and her heels bumped into a metal bar about the same time her wrists, stretching over her head ran into the tent canvas. "Hmm," she sighed, remembering where she was before opening her eyes. Her body's stiffness told her she had been asleep a long while.

She rolled to her left to thank Ellie for arranging the alone time the night before. But Ellie's bed was empty again. She had just decided her friend had gone for a run when she realized that she could see clear across the officer's quarters tent and there was not another person in the tent.

Throwing back the blanket, Judah stood up and looked at her watch in a single fluid motion. "Zero-eight-ten!" Judah inhaled quickly. "I'm so late."

Slow down, she heard in her spirit.

"I suppose a few more minutes are not going to make any difference now." Wakefield assessed. "The staff meeting is over by now anyway. And no one came looking for me." Judah shrugged.

Then she smiled. It wasn't as if she could luxuriate with the time, but a few moments in the Word would care for her soul more than breakfast—if it was even still being served—would care for her body. She opened to the Psalms and crawled back onto her squeaky cot to sit cross-legged with the scripture across her lap.

Leaning forward she closed her eyes and inhaled slowly. "Feed me with your sweet words today, Lord." She flipped open to Psalm 51:10 and read barely aloud, "'Create in me a clean heart, Oh God, and renew a steadfast spirit within me. Do not cast me away from your presence and do not take your Holy Spirit from me. Restore to me the joy of your salvation and uphold me by your generous spirit.'"

Then Psalm 55:16, which was underlined, caught her eye. "'As for me, I will call upon God, and the Lord shall save me. Evening and morning and at noon I will pray and cry aloud, and He shall hear my voice. He has redeemed my soul in peace from the battle that was against me. For there were many who were against me...'"

Then Psalm 57:1-2 penetrated her spirit, and she read aloud, "'Be merciful to me, O God, be merciful to me. For my soul trusts in you. And in the shadow of your wings I will make my refuge.'" A picture of her pack covered by an angelic hand formed in her mind and she continued reading aloud. "'Until these calamities have passed by. I will cry out to God Most High, to God who performs all things for me. He reproaches the one who would swallow me up. God shall send forth his mercy and his truth.'"

Judah felt the time getting away from her, but chose one more minute. "My soul is among the lions..." she started to read and then skipped down, "Oh, there it is," she said. "'My heart is

265

steadfast, O God, my heart is steadfast. I will sing and give praise. Awake my glory...I will sing praise to you among the peoples, I will sing to you among the nations.'" Judah felt her heart singing praise as she identified herself among the nations while there outside of Baghdad among the Coalition Forces from around the world. "'For your mercy reaches unto the heavens, and your truth unto the clouds. Be exalted O God above the heavens. Let your glory be above all the earth.'

"That's just beautiful. I feel so much more alive after some food last night, a good sleep—" she remembered waking a couple of times, "well, a *decent* sleep anyway, and strength from aligning my heart with the truth of your word. Father, you are good and you kept me alive yesterday." A picture of the scuffed boot inches from her slammed into the edges of her mind. "Thank you, thank you."

Uniform, teeth, hair, and boots later, Wakefield walked into the bright 0840 sunshine from her tent.

She nearly collided with an out-of-breath Ellie Dayan.

"Good morning. Sleep well?"

"I feel much more like myself this morning. Thank you for last night." Judah touched Ellie's shoulder. "Only a true friend would stand guard on the showers for you."

"Oh, you heard that, did you?" Ellie shook her dark curls back from her face and laughed. "A true friend also comes to wake you up when you're about to be late for a meeting too." She smiled.

"Staff was postponed after 0700?" Wakefield wondered. It had always occurred on some quarter hour between 0600 and 0700.

"Nope. Your debrief from yesterday. Grady dropped by during staff to inform you to be in his office with the others by 0900."

Wakefield glanced at her watch again. Six minutes to go. "I hope he is providing the coffee." Wakefield said. "Thanks for everything, Ellie. I'd better dash." Judah threw an arm around the Israeli's shoulders and took off double speed.

"Wait!" Ellie called. "There's something you should know."

Wakefield came back a few steps, so Ellie didn't have to raise her voice. "Come on. I'll walk with you," she said, setting a clipped pace to CDR Brady Grady's offices. "We lost some guys yesterday." Ellie began.

"I assumed as much." I saw a lot of it through my scope.

"After you were headed back here, at approximately 1755 hours, a U.S. Air Force F-15 misidentified the enemy at the airport and attacked Battery C, First Battalion." Ellie's voice was emotionless like a reporter. "Two Humvees were totally destroyed. Three Americans were killed. Five are in hospital, recovering. That was the big news at breakfast this morning. That and you."

"Me? What did I do this time?" Wakefield sighed, remembering the awkward office buzz during her Article 31 hearing a year ago, after her and David's first encounter with Filasek in Afghanistan.

"Apparently you broke the glass ceiling. First woman in combat and all that." Wakefield saw Ellie grin as she rolled her eyes. "Don't worry, you're still the same nobody to me." Ellie shrugged as they stopped short and presented their badges to get past the security zone guard. "We've had women on the front lines since the 1940s in Israel. I think it is about time you all caught up."

267

"Well, I just hope it doesn't get blown out of proportion. I was just filling in where needed. Not trying to make some sort of social equality statement. If women were smart, they'd rather *not* be in combat."

Wakefield and Ellie stood in the dirt street between Intel House and the base C.O.'s HQ. "One last thing," Ellie said. "Your SEALs attempted a major raid to get Saddam Hussein last night."

Judah immediately thought of David. He was sure to have been part of anything *major* with his teams. He was in the area! "You said 'attempted'?"

"Yes. They brought in a couple of lower-level guys. We received a few of them for interviews in our lock-up. Including one of the Saddam look-alikes they used. Several photos and DNA samples are in the lab to confirm identities of others. But none of the Husseins were captured or killed."

Wakefield's shoulders sank. She managed a weak smile as they parted to go their separate ways. "Thanks for telling me." *Lord, help David and give him wisdom, peace, and whatever else he needs to deal with this disappointment and failure.* It was all she had time to pray between the dusty street and the doorknob of her debrief.

Chapter Thirty Three

"Everybody take your seats and settle down. We've got some work to do here this morning."

Wakefield heard the call-to-order as she entered the room. CDR Grady was already seated and watching closely from the rear of the room while U.S. Army Captain Harvey lead the debrief from the front. She slid into a metal folding chair in the second to last row. In the office there was only space for four rows of three chairs each. She hooked her booted feet into the support bar of the chair in front of her and leaned back, glad she wasn't as tall as the guy to her right. He was disturbing the precise military rows to make room for his knees by slowly walking the chair backward and sideways out of alignment, one little scoot at a time.

"It seems we have a celebrity here among us today." Harvey began. "Welcome to the boy's club on the other side of the glass ceiling Navy Lieutenant Commander Wakefield."

Oh boy! Everyone was turning around to stare. She smiled wanly and gave a tiny single wave.

"How's it feel to be the first female sniper to have been sent into combat?" the captain kept pushing.

Wakefield could see he wasn't going to just pass it by. So she said, "Rather blown out of proportion. I go where my country needs me. Many times it is analyzing data. Yesterday it happened to be on a hillside atop an airport. It could have just as likely been cleaning the head. The call of duty is whatever my C.O. says it is." She shrugged, hoping that would be enough to get her out of the spotlight and back to work as quickly as possible.

A few of the men clapped. "Well said!" Someone pipped up from the front row.

"Well, I think you went beyond the call of duty, Commander. And I appreciate your willingness to step in with real skill."

Judah felt her face soften at his kind words. She hadn't been sure that was where this meeting was going to go, in the five minutes she had had to think about it. But it felt strange to be welcomed "up" by a man whose rank was under hers.

"Many of us have not worked together before, but one of the things I value," Harvey paused to include everyone in his glance around the room, "is celebrating wins, even partial ones. When someone does well, we will celebrate him," he paused again, "or her, as an example. And when things get screwed up, we'll talk about that just as freely, so everyone can learn from a single person's mistake. In this room we are all learners, and leave our ranks at the door. Sound fair enough?"

As a chorus of "yes, sirs" filled the room, Judah remembered breaking the radio silence order to call in the corpsmen for the soldier with the injured leg.

Gonna get used as an example on that one, she thought. But she didn't mind. Having led and having followed, sometimes you had to make a call. Having already experienced that there was no negative outcome to their mission from her decision, Wakefield came to the same decision. A man's life had been spared. A man was still breathing and a family was not grieving the loss of a son and a husband, perhaps a father even, at only the cost of disobeying an order that would probably have been rescinded if Capt. Harvey had known the outcome from the beginning.

She could defend her decision with experience being a corpsman, an officer, or in the CIA if necessary, but maybe it wouldn't be.

The debrief had gone on without her, she noticed when she zoned back in. "We should have had more ammunition stores available. A way to replenish our supplies." The tall man was speaking.

Harvey asked, "How did the length of time you were out there work for you?"

Another very young-looking sergeant raised his hand. "I had some trouble remaining alert. My coverage zone was probably the one with the least amount of action once the front gate was breached."

A voice she recognized as Denning started to speak next, "It seems to me—"

Denning was cut off by CDR Grady's SatFone trilling.

He walked out of the meeting to take it, but Wakefield was lost in thought again. When Grady opened the door, he set the SatFone on the metal chair he had occupied and continued to the front of the room.

Capt. Harvey yielded the floor, and took two steps to the side.

"We have more to cover then we previously thought. That was word from Maj. Buford's yeoman that last night we lost one of the reporters who had embedded with the first division. Michael Kelly died yesterday along with Sergeant 1st Class Wilbert Davis while trying to secure the airport for Coalition Forces' use.

"I told Kelly in my office before he went in that it was a real war with real bullets that could actually kill him." Grady frowned. He shook his head. "What a waste." A moment later he continued, "Before sunrise this morning we came under fierce counter-attack by Iraqi troops. The First Brigade's Tactical Operations Center began taking small arms fire and mortar fire. While it was still dark, several T-72 tanks managed to get within several hundred meters of their position. A chemical reconnaissance vehicle was fired on and disabled, but no one was killed. That is besides the Bradley that Capt. Harvey reported lost while this team was out. That's the bad news.

"The good news is that reports are that we have taken the airport and the Seabees are currently jury-rigging a way to topple that god-awful statue of Saddam."

The room burst into cheers before the words were out of his mouth!

"Thank God!" Wakefield said. "That thing creeped me out!"

Grady let the jubilant high fives make their way around the room before calling them back to order. "Can anyone shed more light on the embedded reporter's death? Since he is one of their own, you can be sure the media will have a field day with this one."

"What did he look like, sir?"

"Last seen in my office wearing khaki from head to toe, including one of those floppy hats that archeologists favor. He was issued black body armor with PRESS written on a large

Velcro patch across his chest." Grady shrugged. "Don't know yet if he was wearing it."

"I am pretty sure I saw him out there." A young man in the second row raised his hand to speak as if he was still in school. "But he was still alive when I saw him. Looked like he was hunkered down with his minder, both behind a pile of something, extra airplane parts maybe? He was tossing his camera up above the pile every few seconds to snap off a shot or two for his paper. Didn't look too shy and cautious, nor too foolhardy either. He was keeping his head down pretty good when I saw him. But you know, sir, how these things go. If there is a bullet with your name on it, you ain't leaving the field of battle without it."

Wakefield swallowed hard. The speaker looked so young, maybe 24 years old she guessed, to be so experienced with battlefield death and sound so matter of fact about it.

By 1300 hours, a number of stomachs had begun to make noise. When a gurgle reached Wakefield's ears from the front of the room, Harvey cleared his throat and patted his flat abs. "Well, that one was me, and I think we've covered everything to my satisfaction. Commander Grady?" Harvey acquiesced to the base commander as final authority. Wakefield could hear Grady's chair squeaking as he stood, effectively dismissing the debrief. The room came alive with chairs scraping the bare concrete floor in front of her.

Harvey nodded his head. "Dismissed."

"If anything comes of the reporter we can do follow up as needed individually. Let's get some chow." Grady said over the sounds of packing up to leave.

Judah Wakefield slid into a chair front of her computer, still munching a sandwich and potato chips she had snagged to take back to her desk. She had not checked her email in more than 30 hours.

Ellie popped her head into the main room on the second floor of Intel House. "I thought I might find you here." She smiled. "How'd it go?"

Judah frowned and tilted her head. "Not too bad. Harvey was fair." She thought of the broken radio silence defense she had given. Wakefield had served under men of higher rank who were less comfortable with authority than Harvey seemed to be.

Together they had come to the conclusion that perhaps, in future, Morse code could be used in a similar situation. Wakefield smiled then. Actually code tapping was Capt. Harvey's idea, and she had seen the wisdom of it, when not in the actual stress of battle.

"Yes," Wakefield nodded connecting to their dedicated system. "Harvey is a very fair-minded officer. For the Army," Judah winked, before remembering that Ellie was an IDF officer.

Ellie ran fingers through her short curls, puffing them out to nearly stand on end as she laughed. "We have a little competition among rival IDF branches too."

Wakefield tilted her head. "Wait. I know you have an army, but?" She reached for the largest ripple chip on the plate and took a bite. It broke in three pieces and one dropped to her desert BDU jacket.

"We also have a navy and an air force." Ellie shook her head. "You may have heard the story of Entebbe?" Wakefield shook her head. "How about the Six Day War when we made a preemptive strike against the Egyptian Air Force and destroyed 222 of their planes before they could act against us the next day as planned?"

Wakefield popped the remainder of the giant chip into her mouth and reached for the second half of her tuna sandwich. She held out the white plastic plate of chips toward Ellie who shook her head. "That one, I've heard of." Wakefield nodded. She began typing in her password.

"Oh good," Ellie walked over and sat next to her just as her email was popping up. "I had heard that your Naval Academy and war colleges refuse to study Israeli wars for strategy because the outcomes always include the miraculous." She smirked. "That's why I like them so much."

"Oh boy!" Wakefield's eyes widened. "I can see we need to sit down for a story or two." She loved military history. "Combining war stories and miracles? That sounds just about perfect."

Ellie's lyrical laugh echoed around the room. "With the airport captured, maybe tonight will be a little lighter," she offered.

"What's been going on around here? Have we heard from Moe?"

"Well, it's about time you came back to work, Lieutenant Commander." CAPT George filled the inner doorway with a grin plastered on his lips. "I heard you did us proud out there."

"Scuttlebutt on a FOB is faster than on a navy patrol boat." Wakefield said. "It *was* a nice little fieldtrip, but I'm ready to get back to my nice, cushy, air-conditioned office job." She snorted

275

in the back of her throat. Nothing was air conditioned as yet. When she left they had been promised an a/c unit for four days in a row. *Tomorrow's transport,* was promised each time they asked. "I see we will still be receiving that unit tomorrow." She rolled her eyes.

"They've given up tomorrow." Anderson said from behind George. "Yesterday they started saying 'next week.' Seems the base C.O. gets precedence."

"Well, having just come from Grady's office where ten of us crammed in for four hours, I can agree with that assessment. At least he hasn't commandeered our fan or our basement." Wakefield shrugged.

"Speaking of basement." George trailed off. "We had a development this morning."

"Oh? Besides the baby bomb?" Ellie pipped in.

"The what?" Judah whipped her head around to stare at Ellie.

"There was a little incident with one of our new guests this morning out on the airfield." Ellie grimaced. "Let's just say I don't think she'll be in house here for long."

George turned his back to the main room and spoke something to Anderson that Judah couldn't hear. The lieutenant took off in the direction of the basement stairs.

George turned back around. He glanced around the room. LT John Miller and his translator Sahir Abu Jamal were trying to ignore the distraction of the senior officers going line by line through a transcript in the corner nearest the window. "With me." George turned around and followed Anderson toward the stairs.

Chapter Thirty Four

Wakefield shut the door behind CAPT George and smiled at Ellie. "'My best team' is what he said, huh? So how are we going to play this?"

"Let's play to the man's ego." Ellie suggested. "We are the B team of women sent to clean up tiny details after the men are done."

"Works for me. You'll have to help me with language nuance in real time. Knee tapping for pursue a line of questioning, hand to throat or face on specific words that are standing out to you." Wakefield instructed.

"Shall I be an equal or hired translator?" Ellie asked.

"Let's go with hired so that you can clarify words with him even before 'translating' for me and use it to help relax him into thinking he has the wool completely over our eyes and will be granted asylum."

"I think we should even help him assume we heard that his asylum will be inside the U.S. That is the golden egg for terrorists; free access to anywhere inside your borders."

277

Wakefield nodded. "Make sure your necklace stays tucked in this time. We'll only use that as a last resort."

Ellie touched her uniform collar at her throat, and buttoned up just as the marine escort pounded on the door to deliver a fairly average-looking Middle Eastern man dressed in Western clothing.

His clothes were unexpected. He was Wakefield's first refugee seeker in non-Muslim-compliant dress.

"Welcome, Khayyat ibn Al-Awad." Wakefield began and moved toward the chair facing the wall, leaving Al-Awad the seat facing the camera behind the one-way glass. "We just have a few more routine questions to wrap up for my commanding officer." Wakefield gestured upstairs, even though she knew very well that CAPT George was watching from behind the glass. But it would give Al-Awad the impression that Blackstone, who had previously questioned him, was of higher rank than she was since all identifying insignia were purposefully removed from uniforms before interrogation. "You may translate." Wakefield told Ellie.

Ellie bobbed her head quickly. "Yes, ma'am." Then she repeated the words in Arabic slowly and deliberately. Even Judah had trouble believing she was not a nervous rookie.

Back and forth they went for three quarters of an hour, re-asking the questions Wakefield had skimmed in the transcript from the day before. So far the man was as patient as Job, repeating nearly word for word what he had told Blackstone and Bousaid.

Judah noted minor corrections in his speech. Clarifications that really were not important, but to an inexperienced profiler would lend veracity to his persona and story.

But neither Judah Wakefield nor Elishava Dayan were inexperienced.

The details were too rehearsed. It took him too long to think between events when asked to tell his story backward with the most recent events first.

"Tell me, Al-Awad, if you are given asylum in the U.S.—and we are not promising what we've heard is true—where would you want to go?" Wakefield asked him while picking up her ink pen as if to record his answer on her form.

As rehearsed and signaled, Ellie questioned her revealing the military's plan for this man before it was official. Wakefield gave her a simple nod and said, "We're not promising. Just getting a head start on housing. You may translate my original statement."

Wakefield stared at the edge of tabletop during this English interaction, but sharply focused on the tiny muscles around Al-Awad's eyes. The tiniest of involuntary micro expression there showed surprise and happiness before he was able to school his features.

It was assumed that he spoke at least some English. Ninety-five percent of those seeking asylum would.

Ellie repeated the question exactly.

This time when Al-Awad heard the news he let his face light up and started chattering away like a magpie. "Oh, it would be my dream to go to America one day, to live by the Statue of Liberty and see freedom every day."

Wakefield put up an open palm when he hadn't given Ellie a chance to translate for twenty seconds or more. He did quiet down and Ellie translated his sentiment if not word for word, but Wakefield wasn't listening. And Ellie was scratching her neck telling Wakefield to focus on the words. That was exactly what she was doing. The vast majority of refugees, especially political ones such as this man claimed to be, but religious ones fleeing for safety too, they almost always had one thing in common.

279

They didn't want to move too far away. They held onto hope that their countrymen would be freed, that things in their homeland would change for the better, that their families could be re-united.

This man had not mentioned a single family member that he wanted to take with him.

Since Judah knew he would understand, she said to Ellie. "If only we had a way to corroborate his identity beyond the papers he has given us. An address or a family member or even a friend who could verify his story, prove that he is in danger from Saddam's regime. That is the only box left to tick." Wakefield shrugged and held up the prop clipboard with the notes many teams had used during interrogations in the last week in country.

The impression Wakefield was gathering from this man's words, body language, and micro-facial expressions was confidence. He had been well trained. But who did the training? Why? What was Al-Awad's purpose? He was obviously in inner conflict with the words he spoke, perhaps as strong as hatred for Western values. His lips had curled back and his nose wrinkled like a bad smell had entered the room in a very fast universal expression of disgust when speaking of the Statue of Liberty and freedom.

Wakefield's mind spun with more questions than answers as Ellie continued translating. Why had someone, presumably with plenty of money, taken on the expense to groom Al-Awad so thoroughly to pass *this* gateway of asylum seekers? Because he was really good. There were plenty of other ways to gain entry into the U.S. It could be as simple as overstaying a visa. There was no strategy in place within U.S. borders to follow up with someone after they left their port of entry.

Wakefield stilled her movement. Unless. Someone was ineligible for a visa. Or they needed to be able to move about as a legitimate citizen without fear of being asked for papers. If there was some plan in place that required a particular skill set that they could not recruit within the U.S. What kind of a skill set could a man possess that would prompt him to be sent through this kind of screening process?

Wakefield knew she would be able to run the tape back and show CAPT George all that.

Let's check his attitude when I send him back to holding without confirming his next step, she thought. "I need some time to consider." Wakefield said. Then she remembered who she was supposed to be playing. "I will have to talk to my commanding officer and get his opinion," she corrected. "Marine?" she called out to the guard on the other side of the door.

Wakefield watched the reflection for Al-Awad's reaction. He didn't disappoint. His clean-shaven cheeks, Western-style, couldn't hide a flicker of movement, then his neck twisted as he seemed to search for another option. His back stiffened in frustration as the door knob twisted and the marine guard stepped inside.

But he went.

At the last second, he turned back and spoke to Ellie, "Tell her thank you from me, for all she can do to save my life."

Again unexpected, but the kind of thing that could be drilled into a training program: always remain grateful and respectful. The interchange was off camera, so she couldn't rewind and examine his face for signs of deception.

Wakefield waited to nod to him until after Ellie completed the English translation.

In the background she saw another marine escorting another man slowly down the stairs. His feet appeared first, taking each stair right foot, left foot before moving down to the next plateau. When his face came into view she caught her breath.

The marine escorts placed themselves between the two prisoners as they passed each other. But it wasn't enough to keep Al-Awad from snarling at the man.

"It's remarkable, isn't it, ma'am?" The guard asked while escorting Saddam Hussein toward the interrogation room.

"I thought we didn't get him." Judah felt her eyes bugging out. Perhaps the word had been put out as misinformation.

"Says he was employed as a look-alike."

"Oh." Wakefield blinked and looked at Ellie. "Is this the one you were talking about?"

Ellie nodded.

"Well somebody get the poor man a shave and a new haircut or he won't survive another twenty-four hours." Wakefield was aghast. Most of the world wanted this man dead. Well, the man whose face he was walking around wearing. "I'm sorry." Wakefield apologized to the old man.

The marines guarding the doors while their prisoners were interrogated stood looking at one another in silent confusion. Finally, the one who had brought the man downstairs said, "I brought an electric razor with me. Would that help?"

"Yes, Marine. Go get it. I'll stand your watch." Wakefield said. To the old man she asked in English, "Would you like to sit down?" and motioned for Ellie to translate when it was obvious he didn't understand.

Chapter Thirty Five

Wakefield leaned back against the warm metal chair in the main room and smoothed her hair back into its regulation bun. The fan worked it loose again immediately. "That's the fourth time all the way through the interview tape. I don't think it has anything left to reveal that we have not already discussed."

"We all feel uneasy." Blackstone retorted. "Uneasiness is all the information we have. We had that last night. That's why you guys were called in." Blackstone seemed kind of edgy toward her, but maybe she was just low on compassion today.

"It is obvious that there is some sort of deception with this guy." CAPT George rubbed the top of his head in frustration. "But I don't want to just kick him back to Baghdad, like we've done with some of the others we have rejected."

"He is obviously well groomed for something. But we haven't been able to even get a hint of what it might be." Ellie said. "Judah laid down the honey, now let's see if he bites the trap."

"What trap?" Blackstone asked.

"Are you serious?" Ellie looked at the man like he was ignorant. "We just watched it four times. We told him that in order to get a *yes* to go to the U.S. we had to be able to verify his story with someone on the ground here."

"Like it or not, the ball is now in his court. If we're finished here, I'm going to try to get to my email again."

Wakefield walked to the far side of the room to her laptop when a double tap came at the doorframe to the stairwell corridor. "Sir?" Wakefield recognized the voice of one of the marine guards and turned toward him as he addressed CAPT George. "Al-Awad is asking to speak to Blackstone. Says he just remembered something. He wouldn't be persuaded to wait until morning." The hefty guard shook his shaved head, "I can't bear to hear 'em whine like babies, sir." His left cheek and lips puffed out to the side in disgust.

CAPT George cleared his throat as he stood, "Who can't you bear to hear whine like babies?" His tone suggested warning, and Wakefield glanced over at him.

"Men, sir. *Men* should not whine. No matter their circumstances."

"That I agree with, marine." The captain's voice softened. "You did right by coming down to let us know."

Wakefield felt her cheeks bunch up in pleasure. She wished she could let the marine guard know just how right his action had been, whatever his motivation. But he wasn't cleared for details, so she just caught his eye before he left and mouthed, "Thank you."

Al-Awad had taken the bait!

When the marine had left to order one of his men to escort the man back to the interrogation room, Wakefield said, "Are we taking bets on whether he has remembered a long-lost cousin or auntie or brother?"

Ellie smiled "I think it will be an uncle, who is not his uncle."

**Republican Palace Labyrinth
7 April 2003
8:30 PM**

"It's just me. Don't shoot!" The voice echoed through the stone and earthen tunnels.

Saddam found it slightly easier to breathe. Yazeen made it back a second time. His threat must have been very effective.

Several oil lanterns cast flickering shadows and every sound someone made in the too-small space felt too loud. Boredom had outweighed fear three hours after sunrise. Well, for everyone except Waf. She trembled still and had whimpered at random moments throughout their short night. Saddam squirmed. Even his clothes felt too tight.

"Did you get any food?" he fingered the chunks of fallen ceiling on the floor next to him as the young Republican Guard officer came into view wearing the mismatch of civilian clothes they had managed to hobble together from the eight underground refugees. Saddam didn't even give Yazeen a moment to answer. "What took so long?" He demanded.

"The Americans are everywhere!" Yazeen spread a bundle which turned out to be a ladies' silk scarf on the hewn floor near the lantern at Saddams's feet. "I had to go all the way around to the Ibn Sima Hospital steam plant tunnel exit/entrance, and then make my way this direction." Yazeen sorted the fruits, vegetables, and breads as he spoke. "I got turned around once too," he admitted. The young man handed a bottle of water to him and then to each other person.

Saddam pushed his back away from the chilly wall to take first pick of the food. His hands roved over the bread, apples, and dates, popping one into his mouth. He picked up an onion with crispy golden skin. "Really?" he asked. "How are we supposed to eat this? Where's the meat?"

"Nothing is open out there, your majesty." Yazeen shook his head. "I snuck into a tiny neighborhood market and had to dust this stuff off."

Saddam grimaced down at the pita he had just bitten, and his jaw slowed its chewing. He swept his fingers over the remaining bread, but it was difficult to distinguish what was dust and what was flour.

"Here's the good news." Yazeen glanced over toward his fellow guardsmen and the look-alikes to include them. "Having to go around to the hospital gave me a chance to spread our story. I planted it four different times. Once with some other folks out scrounging for food and three times in the hospital itself before I made it to the steam plant."

"Did they buy it?" Saddam wondered aloud.

"Seemed to. It made sense, to the doctor at least, that you had set up a place to rule from before the Americans arrived. I told everyone the same thing. That I had heard you made it safely to a new secret location in the mountains with your full entourage. You'll be issuing orders and ruling from there until the army can purge our land from the Great Satan.

Saddam nodded as he snapped off a mouthful of apple. "We will evacuate tonight."

"I had an idea about that too." Yazeen caught his eye. No other bodyguards ever dared do that. Saddam kind of like this new boldness, but other times he wanted to wipe the insubordination off the young one's face.

"Go on." He was feeling generous today.

Yazeen slowly pulled out a pair of sheers from the pocket of his baggy pants. "We've got to change your look. Do you want to escape as an old lady or a bald old man?"

The little cavern went silent. Even the sounds of chewing stopped. It was a relief to Saddam's ears and nerves.

"We can't do anything about a famous face, but we can change what people see with clothing, hair, and makeup. Waf, I assume you have some makeup in that bag of yours."

She nodded three quick times from where she had inched forward toward the food. She held her water bottle in both hands in front of her drawn up knees.

Yazeen went on painting the picture for the group. "The only people who are out right now and not being bothered by the Americans are old people and children. People whom they don't perceive as a threat. If we can disguise you, we may be able to whisk you out, right under their noses."

It was perfection. However, even *pretending* to be a woman was out of the question. "Waf, do you think you can make me appear like a little old man with some makeup?"

She shrugged and nodded.

"I'll also add a limp to my gait."

"You might practice, and you'll want to tie something on your leg to help you remember." Yazeen nodded, "just in case we run into the pressure of soldiers watching."

"Very well." Saddam tossed his apple core toward the corner of their little crowded hideaway. "Let's get this hair off."

Chapter Thirty Six

Ellie had been right. Wakefield now sat in the back of the third Humvee in a convoy of six driving off campus again, dressed in full battle gear, with a side arm and a rifle equipped with a scope. Al-Awad had given them an address of an 'uncle' in Baghdad whom he was sure would verify his story and identity. "But you must call out to him very loud at his door. He's a little hard of hearing," were Al-Awad's instructions.

Wakefield shook her head at the memory. "Yeah, right, hard of hearing. More like give him warning to hide stuff he doesn't want seen."

Ellie sat next to her in the Humvee behind two other U.S. Army soldiers, besides the gunner standing half in and half out of the round turret affixed to the roof. "You would think he would want to keep his uncle from the prejudice of inviting the Americans into his home. His neighbors are going to think he is cavorting with the enemy."

Wakefield had no trouble discerning Ellie's underlying meaning: this was not an uncle they were about to interview.

"Who knows what the mood is like in any given neighborhood. It is different from house to house, ma'am," First Lieutenant Walls said from the front passenger seat. "I've been out on patrols nearly every night since I arrived, and every night is different."

"What should we expect?" Wakefield asked. This was her first such patrol.

"The unexpected, ma'am." The man was leading his fourth day of patrols in Baghdad, but he seemed to have a pretty good grasp of what it took to get everybody back to base at night.

"Well, I am not expecting a wizened old uncle with Al-Awad's picture on his refrigerator, I'll tell you that. Though it would be a nice surprise."

The tactics had already been drilled with everyone in the convoy and twice with the drivers.

"How doable is that five to ten minutes we need to talk to this man, once we verify who *he* is? Is that going to put your men at too much risk?" Wakefield was rethinking their strategy.

"These guys will give you their best, ma'am. But if I need to call it, I will." Walls' confidence reassured her. "Don't worry about that. We can always toss this 'uncle' in the back seat and question him back on base."

"I hope it doesn't come to that. Just in case he really is an innocent little old man." Wakefield frowned. There was always the off chance.

The rhythm of the convoy changed once they left the main road for the tight Baghdad city streets. The Humvees ran closer together at a steady 40 miles per hour, which to Wakefield, felt incredibly fast for the narrow streets.

She wanted to call out "Watch for kids in the street!" but as she looked around, the one thing that wasn't in the street was kids. Rocks and rubble, yes. Abandoned vehicles, yes. Even some 50-gallon drums and piles of clothes that she couldn't imagine where they had come from.

She couldn't tear her eyes from the road. Minus the mud it reminded her of photos she had seen of hurricane aftermath. White dust covered everything. Buildings were missing sides where they had collapsed after an explosion of ordinance. Men stood in open doorways, some congregated, some alone. She couldn't determine where one neighborhood ended and another began.

They passed through what must have been a nicer area at one time. Shopping and residential seemed to be mixed. Young planted trees lined the street, but they were choking on dust and debris.

Wakefield heard the pop-pop-pop of small arms fire. Perhaps as close as one street west of them. She glanced at Walls. He seemed alert, but unbothered by the gunfire.

"Beta Three, copy. Following your lead." It came from the driver who to this point had been silent. Wakefield guessed he was speaking into his coms unit to the front driver.

The gun fire increased in volume and in number of weapons. The at-tt-tt of automatic gunfire volleyed in front of them. It became accompanied by squealing tires and flashes of light. The legs of the soldier on gunner duty stiffened where he stood on alert between her and Ellie. Fires of varying intensity and size burned at irregular intervals on the sidewalk, in the street.

The driver accelerated slightly.

The increased jounciness at which they were now dodging debris and abandon or burned out vehicles in the road did help Wakefield release her tunnel vision of the roadside which was lit by the headlight behind them in the convoy. Sitting in the backseat was not her favorite place in life or in an actual vehicle. Nausea came in little waves with every jerk of the wheel.

Wakefield glanced over at Ellie. Her eyes were closed and her head rested against the seat back. Was she praying? Trying to keep from throwing up?

Wakefield forced her shoulders to relax and closed her eyes to try it. Hmm, she frowned, it did help the nausea. But it turned her focus to the sounds of war too much.

"Copy that." Floated back from the front seat. "It's the next block, sir." The driver relayed.

"Thank you, Smith." Walls said. The familiar clicking of an ammunition clip sliding into place from the front seat dissolved all nausea. This she was familiar with.

Wakefield touched the sidearm, pre-loaded with a 15-bullet magazine, safety on, strapped to her thigh. She made eye contact with Ellie as they both released the magazine catch in their rifles, pointed toward the Humvee's ceiling, at the same moment. The double click as they both shoved them back in place was satisfying.

The Humvee driver came to a quick stop. Wakefield opened her door at the same time the First Lieutenant did.

"Just a moment, ma'am, while we establish a perimeter." He pushed her door back closed.

Since she had been about the step out, she yanked her legs back and sprawled back in her seat to not get crushed by the heavy door. "He did not." Anger rose in her belly. "Either I am part of this convoy or I am not," she seethed.

"Relax, Judah." Ellie's voice carried a note of laughter and Judah whipped her head around to see. "I think it has less to do with you being a woman needing extra protection than you being a senior officer he doesn't want to come up dead on his watch."

As Judah processed the Israeli's assessment, Ellie raised a slim eyebrow. "Okay, that makes sense." Wakefield acquiesced. "It gets so drilled into us as women in the military, the double standard, and that we have to work twice as hard, I forget sometimes, that maybe there are other motivations for people's actions."

And then he opened her door.

Judah laughed as she slipped out of the backseat, her weapon at the ready. She clicked off the safety and said to Walls, "I hope your timing is generally better than that."

Ellie walked around the Humvee and joined Wakefield for the short march to the front door of the apartment building.

"How could the driver tell that this was the address?" Wakefield wondered aloud. She felt completely turned around.

"GPS verified by a physical map before we left FOB Beta." The answer came from just behind her.

"Thanks." Everything looked so much like everyplace else in the city. Covered in dust. She touched the wall as she was checking the obviously dysfunctional buzzer system for the flat number for Al-Awad's uncle. She rubbed her fingers. The dust was mixed with ash from the bombing campaign over the last weeks. She pointed back to the probable smudgy name next to a 3 and an Arabic letter. "I can't tell if this is a ta or a tha." She spit on her finger and pushed it against the dirty plastic cover. "It is only one dot difference. Based on location, I'm gonna go with a tha."

No electric light burned on the whole block. Wakefield flipped on her helmet light as the others did the same.

Up to the third floor, which was actually the fourth floor for their legs, they trooped. Not worried about noise.

Wakefield knocked and called out. Loudly, just in case, "Muhamad ibn Allah al Kitir? Are you home, sir? We need to have a word." Then she nodded to Ellie who repeated the phrases in Arabic and Kurdish.

That kicked off scrapes and whispers and what Wakefield could only imagine was a mad scramble to make some people disappear. She turned to Ellie. "What a great uncle Al-Awad has."

The escort soldier tensed at the sounds inside. He had experience in these situations, Wakefield could feel it, but held up her hand to stand the men down. "Just a second." She whispered.

"But ma'am—"

"Give them time to situate themselves the way they *want* us to see them. Call out again." She pointed at Ellie.

While Ellie repeated her hail, Wakefield whispered to the escort leader. "The guys on the ground will arrest the people who it sounds like are scrambling through the windows. I want information, and this man at ease as we can make him so I can extract that information from him."

The young man's eyes went wide as he nodded in agreement.

A voice called in Arabic from inside, "One moment please. Have mercy."

"Here we go." Wakefield mouthed. She motioned two men to accompany her inside and the remaining two to park outside the door. And the last one to look out at the ready at the stair landing where he was.

The door cracked open and a thin nose appeared out of the darkness first. "Yes?" He asked.

The scent of burning paper and many candles wafted out the door.

He was younger than Judah anticipated. Perhaps ten years older than Al-Awad's years. "Hello, sir. How are you tonight?" Her cultural training took over and she nodded deeply toward him. Arabic peoples are very hospitable, and she aimed to encourage that.

Ellie translated.

The man's head came further out the door, and he looked left and right at the soldiers, and didn't seemed bothered by them in the least. "I am good tonight. Thank you, ma'am. How are you?"

Maybe we should have brought more reinforcements, Wakefield thought, *I wouldn't be happy and relaxed if seven armed uniformed men showed up on my doorstep after dark.* "I am doing well, too, thank you for asking. I do apologize for the hour. We have come because we need some information about your nephew," Wakefield said. She was sure she heard a snort of disapproval from one of the men in the hallway. She cleared her throat in his direction and hoped hear meaning of "Button it up, soldier," came through to him clearly.

As Ellie began to translate Wakefield's statement, al Katir held up both hands in what looked like folding them for prayer. The door was opening wider and wider next to him and the room was dark, save a single candle burning next to a chair. A ceiling-to-floor curtain shifted slightly. "Is okay," al Katir took a step back and shrugged. "I speak English." He said with only a slight accent. "Would you come in for tea?"

"We wouldn't want to put you to any trouble." Wakefield said shaking her head as the cultural dance continued even in English. Where Western cultures expected you to accept an offering even if you didn't want it, Eastern ones expected that you turn down the first two offers and accept the third offer with gratitude.

So, at al Katir's offer which included, "please, I insist, the water is already on," to his offer of tea, Wakefield said, "Yes, thank you very much. That would be nice." They followed him inside. Indeed a kettle was already warming over a little flame on a mobile cooking stove that she had not been able to see from the doorway.

"Please, can we shut the door?" al Katir asked. "The neighbors, you see."

Wakefield nodded once. The soldier closest to the door pulled it to, but Wakefield did not hear the latch engage. Good.

"Sit, sit." He gestured toward the small common area. Al Katir putzed around the tiny kitchenette, taking out tea and bringing down teacups for all of them. He favored his left leg slightly, Wakefield noted. But his eyes were quite sharp.

"We didn't interrupt anything did we?" Wakefield prodded gently.

When al Katir turned at her question, she gestured toward the kettle. "Your water was already heating."

"Oh no. It is an evening ritual I enjoy alone each night," he shrugged slowly. And it seemed to Wakefield that al Katir began emphasizing his limp more profoundly after that.

Finally the water was poured over crushed tea leaves, one mesh metal strainer sufficed for all five cups.

As Wakefield glanced around she noticed the tips of a pair of sandaled feet peeking out from under the curtain. Poor thing was probably suffocating from the dust back there. One of the men also pointed it out to her while al Katir's back was toward the cupboard pouring.

Wakefield gave an almost unperceivable shake of her head. Ellie's grin suggested that she seemed to be enjoying her glimpse into the inner-workings of an American military operation. Judah guessed this was a pretty low-key interview for her experience.

Al Katir brought the tea on a tray and served each of them. "Ladies first." He said approaching Wakefield and then Ellie.

Wakefield did not allow her features to show surprise as she said thank you when she accepted the closest cup of steaming light brown tea. That was definitely outside the normal Arabic and Muslim cultural norm. He had to have been taught that, perhaps while he was studying English.

"Where did you study English?" she asked as he continued serving tea around the room. She and Ellie had been seated, the two men, one behind Wakefield's chair and the other still at the door remained standing, but loosened their grip on their weapons to accept the tiny teacups into their large hands.

"I took a night class across the river here in Baghdad at first, ma'am." Al Katir took the last cup for himself, set the tray on the cabinet, and limped over to the chair by the candle which was still burning. "Then I continued my studies at Oxford. Do you know it?"

Wakefield smiled. "Yes. I am familiar with Oxford. Nice place." She wondered at how he had afforded the massive expense and now lived like a pauper.

More gun fire and sounds of a crowd gathering outside distracted Judah momentarily, as they all looked toward the window which of course was covered with the curtain they were avoiding looking at.

"You said you have a question about my nephew," al Katir prompted. "Which one? Please. I help."

"You have more than one that would stir up enough trouble to illicit an American investigation?" Wakefield asked lightly.

"I have many nephews." Al Katir shrugged.

"Tell me about them," Wakefield asked over the edge of the teacup and she sipped, letting the silence settle in the room.

"I have many older sisters who produce many sons." Al Katir shrugged again. "I am the only boy of all my father's children, the youngest, and I, broken since birth. No sons for me. My father could not be more disappointed."

"Tell me about your nephews," Wakefield prompted again. She was going to force Al-Awad to name him or not.

Al Katir reached for paper. "I will write them down for you." He smiled a gray smile. Probably from bad anti-biotics in the 1970s, Judah assessed clinically

"That's okay," Wakefield shook her head. "I have a pretty good memory." She shrugged back at him. No need to write them down. I am sure you know them all very well."

She was not allowing him to have a cheat sheet to reference once he had named them all when Wakefield went back to question him—but he didn't know that part was coming, yet. However, his eyes started when she refused, so maybe he had guessed.

"Start with your oldest sister," she invited him. "You can tell me about your nieces too."

As he rattled off each name, Judah pictured the name written in a family tree of sorts in her mind. He only offered a little tidbit about a few of the nephews, but Judah recorded it all.

There did not seem to be a pattern emerging that would help him remember the order, so either he really did have eight

297

prolific sisters, or he was providing information on many people he was connected to.

Wakefield went back to the second sister and questioned the common names between sister 2 and sister 7. "Do the nephews not mind being named the same? My sisters always consult each other before naming their children," she stated, before asking him to begin repeating the information but out of order.

The names were all accurate, though somewhat out of order within the family groups. Al-Awad was not mentioned.

After twenty minutes of questioning, and no hurry-up from Walls, their tea was cold. Judah had started making connections and asking little telling inquiries about ages. She was building quite a picture of this family group.

Wakefield carefully placed her teacup on the small table at her elbow and leaned forward. That the names al Katir gave her were actual people he was very familiar with was not a question in her mind. This man was very well connected.

"Are there any nephews you've left out?" She asked.

"Not purposefully." Al Katir shook his head also placing his teacup on the small table, though there was still half left.

Wakefield rose to her feet. "Are you familiar with the name Al-Awad?"

"Al-Awad?" He asked. "Yes of course. He is my step-nephew," al Katir smiled.

"Oh?" Wakefield stood. "From which sister? I thought Islam frowned on divorce."

"Not divorce, you understand. Sister number 5, her husband died and she became second wife of Al-Awad. He already had two sons you see. My sister is the step mother.

"And both sons are still living?" Wakefield asked.

Al Katir nodded. "Yes, as far as I know."

"And the father is well? Your sister is still married?"

"Yes, I think. They live in a village outside Baghdad now. I have not seen them since all this started." He gestured toward the window.

"Oh, what's their address?"

"I don't know exactly. I only know how to get there from the bus stop. But we have no more busses running." Al Katir shrugged. "I am sorry," his voice said but his eyes did not match. He seemed to be getting exhausted by their memory games.

Judah was just getting started with this gold mine of information, but she had enough for tonight. She ticked her head toward the door.

At the signal, the others put their teacups on the tray at the tiny sink. Wakefield noted that neither of the guards with her had even taken a sip. Good men!

"Thank you for the tea, Mr. al Katir. I'll see that your step-nephew is given every consideration he is due."

Wakefield made sure she was the last person out the door. With a hand on the door handle, she turned back and said, "By the way, it's ok to tell your previous guest he can come out now." Then she closed the door behind herself with a click.

She didn't dare look at Ellie lest she burst out laughing.

Chapter Thirty Seven

Takita stirred. Her whole body ached with stiffness as she stretched and then quickly rolled back into a ball. Her mind ached too. She winced and rubbed the sleep from her eyes then strained against the darkness. It smelled greasy. Not food grease, but metal parts kind of grease. Like the one time she had helped her Abi work on the car when she was about six years old.

Her life rushed at her like a tsunami. It sucked the breath out of her to remember her parents' murders, then overwhelmed her as flashes of the horrors of the last few weeks invaded her mind. The shame of Qusay's rooms. The transformation in moments from ultimate young femininity to a shorn and filthy boy. Then the dungeons: the hunger, the cold, the smell of death that threatened to strangle her. Being discovered. The death march past mounds of bodies. Her stomach ached as fear shook her. Being given like spare change to a man she had never seen late at night and then shoved into a wall-prison in absolute darkness. Then no one came and no one came.

Takita's eyes adjusted to the darkness. But she was now longer in her prison within the wall. The man with the kind eyes had rescued her. Her belly ached, but not because it was empty this time. It ached from stretching from a shrunken state to accommodate the food she'd tried to eat so delicately. It had not worked.

"Takita?" It was the man's voice. Takita realized he must have been calling her for a while. It was his voice that had cut through her dreams.

She just wanted to shrink back inside her body, make herself as small as possible, close her eyes and sleep forever, never to dream. "I'm awake," she mumbled, forcing her voice through her throat with great effort.

"Oh good. I was getting worried." He had such a fatherly tone, it made her want to cry with the ache of missing her Abi. "Here is the apple. We need to get out of here. I've packed the rest of the food to take with us."

Her mind wanted to know when she would be able to curl up in a ball again, but it felt too much effort to ask. So she just stood. She dragged one heavy, bare foot behind the other toward the moonlit window of the door.

The man came up behind her and she trembled at the sound.

"It's okay. Take the blanket with you." He tossed it around her shoulders without touching her. "It's chilly outside tonight."

Then he opened the door and she followed him into the night, staring at the backs of his heels for guidance.

Republican Palace Labyrinth
7 April 2003
10:45 PM

"I want one more look at my home before the American filth destroy it." Saddam growled. "We will be using this garden-shed exit in the yard." He was not arguing with them anymore.

The eight of them stood at the bottom of the landing, four stories beneath the earth. No gunfire resonation. No tanks or even close small-arms fire that he could hear. It certainly sounded clear.

Saddam's hand went to his bald head again. He felt so exposed with no kufiyah and no hair. Even the lightly circulating air in the protected tunnels felt strange against his bare scalp. Eyebrows were gone too. "I probably look like a cancer patient." he grumbled.

"Oh, no," came quick but unconvincing reassurance from several of the men.

"But you are going to have to stop touching your head, sir. It looks weird." Yazeen coached him.

Saddam shoved his hand into pockets hidden in the long brown robe. He preferred white, but brown was more generic, they said. Plus it was all the two guards had brought back from their twilight scavenger hunt.

It had been fully dark for hours now. It was time to go. Saddam began to climb the staircase. The tight scarf around his ankle did indeed help him limp. It hurt.

Seven pairs of feet followed him up the stairs, squeak for squeak. He had waited until now, to announce the final addition to his plan.

He pushed open the bars at the top landing and walked into the night air, still below ground. Inhaling the sweet scent of freedom he closed his eyes and pictured his home in his mind. He took a few more of the earthen stairs and peeked up over the grass.

The entire yard was dark and quiet. The Americans had turned out the lights.

Saddam turned around to face his seven followers. "Change of plans." He announced. "Yazeen and al Fadil, we will walk closely together to the garage, pick up a car, and head south to the desert safe house of Al Muthana. The two of you," Saddam pointed to the look-alikes who had not changed their appearances from the military uniform, except to add dark blankets to their shoulders, so that they appeared to be trying to disguise themselves. "You will go first, one right and one left. You guards stick close to them. If you make it to your original safe space without interference, you are released from your duty with my thanks. When I have reclaimed my power in fullness, we will renegotiate your salary."

No one was saying a word or even wiggling. They had all crowded onto the landing just below the surface, and Saddam alone towered over them three steps higher.

"In the event you are captured, you have one job. Keep your mouth sealed. You know this and have trained for it. Your families will be compensated out of the royal treasury for your time of incarceration, and a double pay-out protocol is in force should you choose to give up your life for our cause. Your names will be recorded with the grand martyrs of Islam. The same goes for you," he pointed to the two bodyguards for the look-alikes whose names he was not even sure of.

Waf pushed to the front of the group then. She had aged herself with brown eye shadow and eye liner to create liver spots and wrinkles on her eyes and mouth. A plain scarf covered her luscious dark hair. She had practiced a stooped walk with Yazeen in the tunnels.

"Waf, hand me your case." Saddam had watched her organize and hide in the secret bottom of her satchel all the gold and jewels that had hung around her neck the night before. She mounted the first earthen stair and handed it up to him handle first. When she relinquished her grip he added, "You will need to stay here. I will send for you when it is safe."

The savage rage in her eye made him glad he had decided to leave her behind. She had always tried to conceal a self-regarding greedy streak in her character that probably would have sold him out one day. Now it would never be a problem.

Saddam directed the first look-alike and his bodyguard up and out. Not a sound beyond everyone's breathing.

"Next set." He motioned to them. They disappeared into the darkness.

Four remained. Saddam placed his right hand on his thigh where his pistol was normally strapped and shoed Waf back down the stairs where the lanterns were still lit below.

She went. But he didn't trust her for long. He should have pushed her backward down the long flight of stairs. But she was gone, and a king did not chase anyone.

"Now another change in plans." Saddam whispered to the two men just in case Waf was still listening. "We will be heading to the mountains of the north as our first destination. But we are making a few stops along the way. First stop is the National Museum. The girl did have a good idea every once in a while." He held up the case with possibly a million U.S. dollars-worth of jewelry in the bottom of it. "There are a few items on display at the museum which will transport well. Yazeen, you will precede me, and al Fadhil, you will follow. You will maintain a discrete seventy to one hundred meters between each of us, and my limp will set the pace."

Saddam walked back toward the actual garden shed part of their hiding place and shoved aside an ancient push mower and some empty jerry cans. He placed his fine leather briefcase with all his important papers, culled from the myriad of important papers he had burned or destroyed, on a dark little shelf and pulled the junk back in front of it. Nothing but his fingerprints and DNA could identify him as the king or president of Iraq any longer.

"Yazeen, let's go."

The lawn was squishy under his sandaled feet. It felt good to be moving; no longer cowering in a grave. They walked in a line under the trees and then slipped out the side gate past the vines and into an empty street one by one.

There was definitely more going on in the neighborhood than met the eye. Saddam could feel it, and sounds of people echoed off the stone structures.

Step one in rising back to his Babylonian throne and power: complete.

Chapter Thirty Eight

"Something big is going down, ma'am." An excited voice greeted her as she exited the four flights of stairs. Of the six Humvees in the convoy, three remained.

"I sent the six men fleeing the apartment window coming to ground level on the fire escape back to base holding for questioning," Walls, who had remained outside during the entire tea escapade, explained. "That's where the rest of the convoy went."

"We just picked 'em up one at a time, Plasti-Cuffed them, and tossed them in the back." It was the same young voice that spoke a second before. Wakefield glanced over at him.

"Private Martin," she addressed him formally, as she assessed the 19-year-old sandy blond who already was showing signs of a receding hairline. "What really big is going down?" She echoed his words back to him.

"Well," Martin drawled and pulled in his excitement to a degree, "I'm not really sure, but the foot traffic has been heavy through here. Everybody going the same direction. You hear that big noisy crowd? That's where they're going. There's gotta be thousands of 'em."

Wakefield had noticed that people were out, if not in droves, at least in a steady trickle. They did cross to the other side of the street, but did not seem concerned enough about the American convoy to alter their courses to another block. Many used a pace that resembled excitement in their steps. There were even a few children among the groups she could see from where she was standing.

"What's going on? What are you hearing?" she addressed Walls.

Martin broke in before he could answer, "That's what some of us were hoping we could go and check out, ma'am."

His chubby cheeks looked so hopeful, Wakefield couldn't help a little chuckle at his expense.

"We have a few more FOBs providing security in the square. It is about a half a klick straight up this street and one block north." Walls pointed, which helped Wakefield; she still felt a little directionally disoriented in this city. It was pretty loud for being that distance.

"Do you have any objection, Walls?"

He frowned, "Nah. I'd kinda like to see it myself."

"Then let's go see what's going on." Wakefield smiled and opened her own door.

She and Ellie watched the crowds swell the closer they got. In the front seat Walls was on the driver's com system letting the other operators on scene know that a few more friendly faces were coming in from the south.

The people were holding hands and swinging them back and forth, some appeared to be singing. Wakefield saw some children skipping. All three Humvee gunners in their convoy stood in their turrets at the ready though. The convoy crawled through the crowds while the vehicle in the front honked its horn, but Judah could barely hear it over the cheering people.

"What are they so excited about?" Ellie asked.

Walls said, "I don't want to spoil it, because you're gonna want to see this!" His grin as he turned around looked like he was cheering on his favorite college football team, not clearing crowds in Iraq.

When they had not inched forward in over two minutes because of the pressing people, Walls got on his coms with the Humvee in front of and behind them. "Drivers and gunners," he ordered, "I need you to secure the vehicles, but you can put them in park. We're not going to be able to drive any closer. And this is about them tonight."

Wakefield still couldn't tell what the man was talking about. "The rest of us, let's walk in pairs. Meet back here at midnight, and for heaven's sake make sure your safety is on. We don't want any accidents tonight."

Wakefield and Ellie quickly lost sight of the rest of their team as they shuffled forward in the crowd, but they occasionally saw other armed U.S. service members in their desert camo BDUs, keeping watch over the crowd of revelers.

The noise of the crowd pressed against her body and her mind. Scanning for trouble spots was fairly easy at Judah's height. That was when she spotted some people pointing. She followed their gaze and caught her breath.

She tapped Ellie on the shoulder and pointed too. "Look! They are putting ropes on the Saddam statue in the traffic circle there. They are gonna hang him or topple him!"

The crowd frenzied with pointing and pressing forward into the open area from the streets that swept into the traffic circle.

Wakefield was pretty sure with the slim ropes and only people to do the pulling, it would take a while to accomplish their goal. "I'd feel more comfortable with my back planted against a wall, so I only have to keep an eye in one direction," she yelled to Ellie and pointed about seventy yards away. Ellie nodded once and the pair threaded the crowd with Wakefield's shoulder leading the way.

**Firdos Square
7 April 2003
11:45 PM local time**

He kept his body as still as a city boy can imagine that a hunter might when stalking his prey. "That was definitely a person." Moe identified. "And there is another."

When he focused on a single spot—and determined not to become distracted by perceived motion in the corner of his eye which was always gone by the time he focused his 55-year-old eyes in the darkness—it was obvious that people were out. All the movement he could see was heading in the same direction too. They were converging on Firdos Square from all directions. The square that he and Takita needed to cross to get home.

Dozens of people grew to a hundred before his eyes. They seemed oblivious to the gunfire echoing in the city. Some were armed, most were not.

His countrymen were streaming into Firdos Square, and the more that appeared the more a sound was generated. Moe felt the emotional brain fog dissipating. Was that excitement and fire in their eyes? Hope?

Something was afoote. He could feel it in the atmosphere as tangible as, well, as tangible as the little rocks of concrete rubble he now noticed were digging into his knees.

And he knew he needed to be part of it. Whatever *it* was.

He looked around for somewhere to hide the girl where she wouldn't be seen, where she would be safe. The concrete stairway was not enough. He spotted a pair of trash bins on little wheels in the teensy alleyway across the street from their current hiding spot. Scores of people streamed up the street, but he decided they could make it across.

They moved across the foot traffic like fording a wide and shallow stream.

He rolled the two trash bins slightly apart to create a hole for the girl. "Takita, hide here in this little alcove, he pointed to the little hole where she could rest with her back against the wall, covered by her blue blanket. "I'm sorry about the smell." He frowned. His heart wavered between getting the girl to his safe home and being part of whatever was going on in the square. But she did need to rest. Her feet. He shook his head and winced. She had not given one sound of pain through their entire trek.

"You hold onto the food, take a little nap if you can, and I will be back soon."

The girl sank into the space between the garbage cans and fairly well disappeared under the oil-stained blanket. Her eyes closed even before she covered her head with the blanket.

Moe's heart sank as he realized that she now looked like a lump of garbage between the two bins.

He shook his head but had to leave. "Lord, if she'll let us, we will restore this little one to wholeness. She is so important to you." Following the sounds of chatter and laughter, Moe merged into the traffic flowing toward the square.

Chapter Thirty Nine

The statue of Saddam Hussein rocked back into place. The men on the ground heaved again on the ropes that had been cast over the statue. As they pulled, Saddam— or his likeness anyway—leaned further and further forward, bowing, as it were, to the will of the people.

Judah grinned widely. "Here it comes!" She poked Ellie, as if she wasn't watching with every other eye in the square. "It is so exciting." She yelled to make herself heard over the great cheering and jeering. "It reminds me of King Nebuchadnezzar's evil statue the three Hebrew children refused to bow to.

"Children?" Ellie yelled back. "Those guys were government officials who had risen to great power, especially for a bunch of foreign slaves!"

"I can't hear you!" Judah yelled. "There it goes!" The statue did not rise back on its own this time but came apart at the rebar-reinforced center.

The head and torso popped off, and the grandest cheer yet swelled to deafening decibels.

Judah covered her ears and laughed with joy at the people's excitement at being free from the oppressive man and his government machine. At least in this section of Baghdad.

311

Firdos Square
8 April 2003
12:05 AM local time

Excitement bubbled in Moe's soul as he came closer and closer to the pulsing crowd of his countrymen. He couldn't remember the last time he had seen such happiness in Iraq. "Oh my Father in Heaven!" he praised aloud without fear. His skin felt stretched at his cheeks and lips from smiling. "Thank you for not letting me miss this joy of joys!"

Passing a hand over his face to touch his cheeks that had not smiled so wide since his son was born. He found tears streaming down to his simple round collar. This joy could not be contained and Moe roared as he thrust his fists into the air.

He was overcome by the magnitude of the miracle of freedom he was experiencing and opened his fists to palms of praise to the Almighty One Who Sees. As his ancestor Hagar had acknowledged, "*Adonai El Roi!*" Moe called out. "You are good!"

He surged forward until he squeezed close enough to grab one of the ropes used to pull the former king's graven image down. A group had begun to drag the golden statue around the traffic circle. It was heavy, but several dozen men made it light work once a jogging momentum had been attained.

Moe ran and pulled and cried with excitement, loping like the kid of a goat in spring sunshine.

He opened his eyes wide to take in all the shining faces and fix them in his memory. And also to search for Liliya. She should be here. If she wasn't, he wanted to recall every detail to paint the picture for her soon.

Then he spotted a familiar white face in the sea of dark complected people. "Missy Judah!" He grinned, then remembered that while people might not be able to distinguish his words in all the noise they would not mistake his joining a uniformed American female soldier. He couldn't tell what his countrymen would think of that. Even a crowd of happy topplers was sure to contain spies for the Hussein family. They were not ones to go down quietly.

But he needed to get her the information too. And maybe she had seen to his family and knew where they were now. But how? He acknowledged her with a wink as he and the runners passed right by her pulling the statue behind them. "Stay," he mouthed. Hoping she understood.

A plan began to form in his mind. He got about hundred feet away before he let his portion of the rope drop, and gradually slowed his run, then quickly stepped out of line to avoid being trampled. Truth be told, he was quite winded.

He placed one hand to his heaving stomach and with the other pressed a few fingers into his neck. His pulse was wild.

Moe shuffled his fingers through his many pockets looking for just the right thing. He crawled as quickly as possible back through the crowd that had definite momentum going the opposite direction as they paraded behind the dragging golden torso.

"Do you have a pen? A pencil?" He asked over and over between heaving breathes.

Someone finally pressed a pen with smudged advertising into his fingers. "*Shokran!*" he called to his unseen benefactor. No one was even looking at him that he could tell.

Moe slipped out of the swarm and scribbled a few words of explanation on a piece of paper he had been carrying around. That would be enough. Now to get back to her. Going against the traffic surge was like threading the eye of one of Liliya's needles with gloves on.

The crowd seemed to be dispersing now and everyone was coming his direction.

He could see the top of her mottled tan helmet and pressed the people until he finally popped out right in front of the helmet, but the helmet was perched on the Israeli translation lady's head. She was very brave to be out in this crowd. Missy Judah was nowhere to be seen, so Moe quickly slipped the note to the Israeli as he passed by her and melted into the crowd on a side street. He would circle the block and pick up Takita. Together they would go back to his flat to await further instruction.

Baghdad City Square
8 April 2003
0018 hours

Seren Elishava Dayan felt alive in this surging crowd of celebrants. She watched history forming and freedom being found in front of her eyes. It reminded her of what her grandparents and famous uncle, Moshe Dayan, must have felt on that first evening of independence on May 14, 1948 when the streets of Jerusalem and Tel Aviv were filled with dancing, laughter, and praise such as this.

She knew she was staring as she secured the little details in her mind. But she didn't mind. No one seemed to mind anything tonight. Judah was more carefree than she had been all day.

"I think they are trying to run through the crowd dragging that statue like a dogsled," Wakefield yelled while laughing at the same time.

They both saw Moe at the same moment among the runners. Wakefield grabbed her shoulder. They saw him recognize them, wink, and say something they couldn't hear.

Wakefield clipped her on the shoulder. You stay here in case he comes back. I am going to try to follow him.

There wasn't time to disagree before Judah had slipped into the effervescing throng at half speed.

But Ellie could see with the people jumping in front of her, she was never going to be able to keep up with the runners who had people out front clearing the way for them. Judah would be back soon.

She looked at her watch out of habit to establish a sequence. 12:27 AM. "Oh! we are so late!" And there was still the trek back through the crowd to the Humvees.

Ellie pressed against the building and stretched as tall as she could to look for Judah coming back. Just the crowd.

She could now see, with the slight thinning of people in the wake of the runners, a line of Coalition soldiers in two different locations around the perimeter of the area. The light color of their head gear reflected nicely in the subtle moonlight that was mostly blocked due to the ever-present dust and smoke.

There was also a Hummer like the one they had ridden in with a soldier alert but casual in the turret. The vehicle was fully on the far side of the square from where they had ended up.

12:31.

12:33.

Standing on tip-toe Ellie surveyed the crowd again. There had probably been nearly two hundred thousand people crammed into this space at peak. Thousands had drifted back toward their homes and the volume had begun to dissipate, Ellie assessed.

As she dropped back to normal height to keep her calves from cramping, Moe materialized in front of her for two seconds. Just long enough to press a crumpled piece of paper into her hands. Then he was gone.

Ellie rose up again to look for Judah who should have been close behind him.

She couldn't see any faces coming toward her from that direction. It was all backs of heads and head scarves as the square and traffic circle emptied for the night.

She didn't know whatever happened to the top of the statue, maybe they were still chasing after it and that's where the crowd was emptying like a drain for a city square.

12:40.

Still no sign of Judah.

12:50.

Ellie looked this way and that. Giving slight little jumps to try to see over heads and find the desert camo helmet. More than half the crowd had thinned out. Judah should be back by now.

She wasn't sure what the American protocol was for this situation. But she was pretty sure something had gone wrong.

She bit her lower lip.

Gunfire irrupted about three to four blocks over. The Republican Guard must have gotten wind of the celebration and were going to try to break it up and impose order.

With that Ellie, pushed against the foot she had been resting on the wall and made a beeline for the last place she knew the Humvees to have been parked. They were nearly an hour overdue, and *they* was now just her.

Dodging slower walkers Ellie double timed it back. First Lieutenant Walls was scowling at his watch when she jogged up.

He looked up and glared as he identified her. His jaw moved forward, and he looked ready to explode at the mouth.

She cut him off. "I think we have a problem," she said. In the distance gunfire erupted. Heavy artillery. "Make that two problems."

"Get in!" Walls yelled to the soldiers who had been milling about, apparently waiting for her and Wakefield to return.

Chapter Forty

"Stop here." Ellie ordered the driver from the back seat of the Hummer. The driver looked at his C.O. for confirmation as he took his foot off the gas, but didn't break. "Right here!" Ellie repeated. "Let me out." She leaned forward in her seat and reached for the door handle.

"We're in the middle of the street." But LT Walls nodded short at the driver, who began to brake.

"We are between Intel House and the Commander's HQ." Ellie retorted. Throwing open the door, she put her boots on the ground while they were still rolling. "Thanks for the ride," she called, slamming the door behind her.

Surging through the door, Ellie took in the layout of the darkened room. Only one lamp cast light. The bluish glow of a computer screen reflected off one of Grady's pencil pushers at a desk immediately to her right. An orange on-light of a coffee pot gleamed in the far corner of the make-shift reception area.

"I need the Captain. Immediately!"

"Who are you?" Ellie felt the man's hackles rise.

She powered down and took a deep breath, only because it would save time in the long run. "I'm *Seren* Dayan, IDF, assigned to Intel House."

"A translator? What makes you think you can burst in here demanding to see Grady?" The young ensign was on his feet now.

"I'm an interrogator, actually. And why don't you let me worry about that?" Ellie challenged him. She recognized that his rank was at least four grades below hers.

"Because I'm the one that has to wake him up, and he said not to disturb him unless the house was on fire."

"Well, consider the house on fire."

"Interrogator, you said?" The distain in the young man's lips lessened. "With the IDF?"

Ellie could see he was putting together who she was, remembering the bombing incident from earlier in the day, and moving toward judging her wild interruption as more legitimate with every second. Ellie nodded. "Yes, *that* Ellie Dayan. Now get moving. And I suggest a fresh pot of coffee too. I'm going to get CAPT George while you get Grady."

The kid started moving then. Rolling two senior officers out of bed was probably akin to a three-alarm house fire.

Eighteen minutes later, CDR Brady Grady held open the door for CAPT George. Ellie stopped her pacing. "This had better be good!" Bellowed Grady.

"This way, sirs." She led them into the debrief room, snapping the door closed against prying ears. Without preamble she said, "Wakefield didn't make it back."

The shock loosened both men's mid-night stubbled jaws. She could see the questions about to spew, so she held up her palm and unloaded her story for them.

"So, she's still alive?" Grady asked.

"Last time I saw her. But that has been nearly two hours now." Ellie emphasized. "And she disappeared in the direction of all the noise of the firefight."

"So the op was a complete waste of time, *and* I lost my best interrogator and profiler?" George rubbed his short haircut.

"Not a complete waste, sir. We got a veritable family tree on the guy we couldn't figure out. But it is in Wakefield's head, and her head is in danger. We've got to go back in for her!"

Grady strode over to the door and poked his head out. "I need coffee and a sit-rep on Baghdad's Firdos Square. ASAP." His voice was too loud. He pushed the door closed, and Ellie saw him take a beat to compose himself before turning around to them.

"We will find her." Ellie assured him, pushing her own clamoring what-ifs back in her mind.

"There was a note from Moe?" CAPT George had seated himself, leaning forward and rubbing his palms together as if the room was 30 degrees instead of 60. "What did it say?"

Ellie patted her pockets. She had completely forgotten it. She had not even read it. Her right olive-green pant pocket crinkled when she touched it. She withdrew the crumpled paper.

Smoothing it out, she read the Arabic aloud. Her shoulders dropped in disappointment. Ellie looked up as she translated to English for Grady and George. "There are seven identical unmarked military Humvees from the Royal Caravan. Six look-alike men plus the king will be deployed and sent out of the city in all different directions. Moe is returning to his flat."

"Old news. It's useless!" pronounced a frustrated George at the same time as Grady said, "Just simple misdirection."

A quick knock sounded, and Grady's night yeoman, an ensign, entered the room carefully balancing a tray with three white porcelain mugs and a silver carafe. He slid it onto the table and straightened up. "Commander Grady, I have the latest fighting reports printing right now and another pot brewing." Then he looked at Ellie, "If you want cream and sugar, they are out here."

Ellie narrowed her eyes at the young man. "I take it black," she announced and half-smiled at his attempted slight backfiring.

"Oh, Captain, I have a couple of notes that came in for you a couple of hours ago. I was going to deliver them in the morning."

"I'll take them now, son. Not going back to sleep tonight."

When the ensign returned a moment later, he handed two phone memos to George.

"That'll be all." George dismissed Grady's yeoman as he read the first note silently. His head snapped up and his lips pursed until the door closed. "Seems Moe tried to get the intel to us earlier." George folded the memo in half and held it up between his first two fingers. "He is requesting a call from Judah. This came through the call center nearly 20 hours ago. It would have been helpful *then*." George sighed. "This system needs an overhaul. It takes too long to get the right info into the right hands."

"What are we doing about Judah?" Ellie redirected the conversation that could rabbit trail easily.

For twenty minutes, the two officers read through after-action reports and the latest intelligence briefings while Ellie typed in her report describing Judah's disappearance. She added as many details as she could on location and direction the crowd was moving.

"There's some pretty intense exchanges going on in the neighborhood you mentioned, Dayan." Grady wiggled a couple of pages in the air. "We've gotta get her out of there!" His eyes darted back and forth between them.

"That's what I was saying, sir." Ellie calmly enunciated. The man needed to settle down.

"There are several SEAL Teams in the area. Closest one is stationed over at Camp Liberty North." Grady's tense shoulders made the officer's uniform shoulder boards tilt down toward his collar bone like angry eyebrows. "The base commander owes me a favor." Grady stood up suddenly, bellowing, "Ensign, get me Commander O'Reilly on the horn." He walked over and threw open the door. "He's the C.O. at Camp Liberty North."

"Aye, sir!" Ellie could see the ensign reaching for the phone even as he spoke.

"I'm *not* losing another officer that I sent into harm's way!" Grady vowed shaking his head hard and then turning to walk into the reception area. "I'll take it in my office." He growled.

The night yeoman gave him a thumbs-up acknowledgement as he spoke to his counterpart a few miles away on the north side of the besieged city.

When he had gone Ellie whispered, "Well, that explains a lot."

"Hmm?" George looked lost in thought.

"Judah told me when she knew Brady before he was a huge practical jokester. Now he's so stern." She grimaced. "He lost someone or someones, and he thinks it is his fault."

CAPT George slurped his coffee. "I think in this case, it will work to our advantage."

"True, sir." Ellie hit send on her report. It was as complete as it would ever be, and now it was available for the SEAL team

322

Brady was going to send after Judah. She turned to look at the man at least a decade and a half her senior. "But we both know, unresolved guilt can turn into reckless behavior or timid leadership if not dealt with."

George looked long at her with eyes that knew she was correct. "You are an old soul, Ellie Dayan." He stood. "And you've had quite a day. See if you can catch a few winks and report at 0645 for staff. I'll have breakfast and coffee delivered, and you can tell the team your story."

She nodded. George left the door open behind him.

Ellie turned the events over in her mind looking for something she could have done differently. Namely she could have gone with Judah. But that would probably mean two of them lost, and no one to report any details.

Ellie sighed. "I can think lying flat and out of these boots, and at least pretend to get some rest." She refocused her far-off stare and trudged out of HQ and into the street. The light at Intel House was burning as always, but she turned away and walked toward her cot. Her new friend wouldn't have a cot tonight. Would she have any sleep at all? Was she captured and thrown in a nasty cell? Ellie's eyes watered; she'd been briefed years before on the condition of the underground prisons in Iraq. Iran, Iraq, and Saudi Arabia, those were the ones to avoid, they had drilled into her during basic training eight years ago. Maybe Judah hadn't survived the firefight. Was she lying dead in the street somewhere? Had she found protection in someone's home?

Questions chased each other in Ellie's mind all the way back to her tent.

Chapter Forty One

Judah Wakefield tapped Ellie on the shoulder to get her attention over the noisy throng. "I'm going to follow him. Stay here in case he comes back. I'll be right back." Then she slipped into the stream of people moving quickly in the direction of the top half of the Saddam statue being dragged.

The top of Moe's brown kufiyah-covered head bounced into and out of view several dozen yards in front of her. With its rust colored bands, it was distinctive in this sea of humanity.

People dodged and jostled all vying for the same piece of pavement that kept moving forward as the statue bumped and scraped against the blacktop. Wakefield tried to shoulder forward, but even the wideness lent by the uniform, stiff Kevlar vest, and weapon was not enough to displace the excitement of these crowds. *I ought to just turn around and go back*, the thought crossed through her mind.

She lost sight of him momentarily.

"There you are!" She saw him over to the right side of the sea of people, even further ahead. "Slow down, man!" she grumbled.

324

Picking up her pace as much as she could, Judah pushed forward by swinging her arms and pushing people behind her, as long as they didn't have children in tow. She didn't want to cause panic among families. Even though everyone was going the same direction, navigating the volume of the mass at this speed was like trying to swim upstream.

Then a bulky man in flowing robes passed her at a near jog. He was calling out in a sort of sing-songy way in words that didn't make any sense to Judah in any of the ten languages she understood. The crowds parted for him.

Wakefield snorted, "Oh, yeah!" She didn't care what he was singing about. She stepped into his draft and followed a quarter step behind, just far enough to not trample on the hem of his robe and trip them both.

Every third or fourth step she bounce a little higher to see over his shoulder and most of the time she caught a glimpse of Moe's brown and rust colored head covering. Sometimes she was gaining on him, other times, holding an even twenty yards to the rear.

The men who were running while dragging the statue's ropes didn't seem to be losing any steam.

Based on her normal jogging speed, Wakefield guessed the crowd had been moving at this pace for more than half a kilometer since they left the city square on the wide paved boulevard. She shook her head, *only I would be running the numbers while jogging after a suspect in a crowd.*

Wait! When did Moe become a suspect? She asked herself as she glimpsed his bobbing head gaining on her again. *Probably about the time he winked at me and started running for his life.* "Ugh! Come on." This chase was getting annoying.

The crowds were thinning though. Hundreds of people poured down several side streets at a growing number of intersections. The main thrust of people was still intact and still at speed. The group began a turn down a side street. And then another.

Actually there were three street intersections in a row—a right, left, right—where the bulk of thousands of jubilant runners made quick turns in succession.

"Maybe I ought to start reading the street signs." Judah looked around for signage and landmarks to navigate her return as the lane began to narrow. Hardly any directional signs were available. Plenty of food advertising and Imam faces on posters though.

Then finally up ahead she spotted a sign she recognized as green civil-government color and branding. In another forty-five seconds she was close enough to recognize the icons on the right side of the large sign. The universal P for parking was the easy one. The second sign took another few steps to work out. It was the Republican Palace icon.

This frenzied crowd was delivering the deposed statue as a message to the palace!

In the few seconds after Judah realized where they were running, and that it was probably not a good idea for her—especially in uniform—to appear with this crowd at that location, two things happened at once. Moe, who had been slowing down little by little, was now only two steps ahead of her. She called out, "Moe. Wait!" as she reached around the man who had been leading her and clearing her path. And the sound of coordinated gunfire on three sides assaulted her ears.

"Down!" She called out in English and then Arabic. "Everybody get down."

The crowd was having none of that. They knew better than to become that last person standing—or ducking down—in circumstances such as these! Too much experience where friends or family didn't survive the experience. The crowd bolted like a school of fish breaking apart.

Revving truck engines and squealing tires increased the ruckus of automatic gunfire. Moe was within her grasp. Wakefield lunged forward and grabbed his arm.

Her arm jerked as he shook her off. "Moe! It's me!" She yelled. But when Moe turned around, it wasn't Moe.

The man shook her off and ran away.

Three-quarters of the crowd had melted into side streets, shops, apartments, and alleyways. She wasn't sure where they had all gone, just that the target-rich environment for the black-uniformed Republican Guard was quickly leaving her as a prime bullseye.

Wakefield felt her eyes go wide and her lips pull back as she spun around looking for the best direction to run.

This block had been on the Coalition Forces to-do list sometime in the past week, and many shops on the first level and residences on the second and even third levels were empty shells. Some were gaping holes blacker than the night.

Bright headlights from two and three deep and three directions threw their beams across one another creating confusing shadows.

Wakefield shook herself from her stupor. Anyplace was better than the empty street. She dodged left and slightly back in the direction she had come from. That direction avoided the string of headlights racing toward her from a side street.

She flung her rifle on its sling to her back as she ran. Then planted both hands on a four-foot high concrete road barrier

327

presumably used to protect the sidewalks and shops from runaway traffic. She swung both feet up and over to her right and sailed over the barricade, letting go at the right moment as had been drilled into her in basic training so many years ago. Her body still remembered what to do. She landed in a crouch on both feet and scurried fifteen steps to a gaping doorway. A single step up. Wakefield hurled herself inside and behind a wall that was still standing.

Crawling further inside, she plopped heavily on the floor. It appeared to have been inlaid tiles earlier this week. Today it was sharp ceramic rubble. She jumped back up and cleared away the sharp pieces in a few quick sweeps with her open palm, then returned to sit, her back against the wall.

The sounds outside crawled through the openings and slurried around the room, amplifying until she put her hands over her ears. Wakefield pulled her boots as close to her body as she could and rested her forehead against her knees.

"Oh, Lord! I should have turned around when You sent me that tiny little thought to turn around. Oh, help me get out of this one."

Burning lungs and throat were Judah's first reminder that she should breathe. She sucked in great lungsful of air then, and threw her head back against the wall, her helmet clinking.

Camp Liberty North
8 April 2003
0250 hours

"Wakey, wakey, eggs and bakey."

Rivers groaned in his cot as squeaks like a pack of rats grew in the room from the 24 other SEALs' cots in their shared barracks. They slept in a tent that was set up for 120 men. Those men would be deplaning in Baghdad in a few days at the former Saddam International Airport. But for now, the Team had a little space to spread out as they dealt with the disappointment of missing Saddam and both of his sons. The high-profile leaders that Howard had detained were a boon, but Rivers was having a hard time shaking his disappointment over leaving the action at the palace to follow a dead-end look-alike puppet.

"Got ourselves an O-5 sailor who got herself lost behind the greenline." It was the same voice that had announced breakfast, but with no pungent smell of bacon or coffee to punctuate his statement.

Rivers opened his eyes to a single lightbulb lighting the room shining near the door flap opening. An O-5 was a lieutenant commander in the Navy, same rank as him. Not good. Definitely not good. He sat up, his own cot squeaking in protest. He swung his feet to the floor as his head cleared. "Hmm, we have a greenline established." He mumbled. "That's a good start."

Rivers stood, scratched his chest, and looked at the messenger across Mass's and Birdie's cots where they were both awake but had made no move to get up yet. "Where are our orders and briefing material?"

"I'm sorry, did you say 'her'?" It was Howard, Rivers identified as he received the envelope of sealed papers.

"Yes. I did." The messenger, a U.S. Marine, a lance corporal, gave a little chuckle.

"Since it was *your* female officer that got lost," the enlisted Marine Corps man emphasized that it was the Navy who had gotten lost with his tone of voice. "The C.O. thought you SEALs might want to go and fish her out."

329

"What was a woman doing behind the line? That's a combat zone." Rivers tore the envelope's seal. "That'll be all. Thanks, lance corporal." Rivers dismissed the young marine.

He took a moment to read just the first summary paragraph and then looked up. "Everybody up and dressed. We have another long day of ahead of us."

The area stirred immediately. The squeaky cots faded as Rivers sat on his cot and read the fullness of the briefing.

His breath caught in his throat as his eye took in the familiar shape of a name on the line below the one he was reading. He could not keep from skipping to that name: Wakefield. His eyes lingered there, knowing she was involved, but not how.

Rivers forced himself to return to the line above and read through the information.

"Oh Judah, what have you gotten yourself into?" Rivers' eyes raced through the packet of pages, one sliding behind the other as he finished.

He finally looked up at the quietness. Half of the SEALs were already headed out to grab some coffee and something to eat from the 24-hour cantina. But the dozen men from Echo Company that had trained together for the two palace assaults stood staring at him.

Rivers schooled his features, but couldn't slow his heart rate as he usually could.

"What is it that has you so spooked, Boss?"

Rivers studied their concerned faces but couldn't even discern who had spoken. He swallowed hard against the lump in his throat that was keeping the bile from spewing itself across the floor.

"It's my wife. Judah is the missing officer."

Chapter Forty Two

At the tree whose branches overhung the main entrance from the sidewalk to the national museum's expansive front lawn, Saddam watched Yazeen lean casually as if he was resting. Yazeen lightly motioned with his head.

Saddam hobbled forward in the dark humid night. A bit of fog must have rolled in off the Tigris because everything felt damp, especially his naked scalp.

"How are we going to get inside?" Yazeen asked? "That front door looks pretty solid. I don't think I can get us in that way."

"Have you never been here before?" Saddam asked confused.

"Never had the time. Until now, I assumed the front doors would be glass and we could smash right through."

"That would not be very secure for safeguarding my treasures." Saddam shook his head at the young soldier's lack of round thinking. "But we *will* go through the front door."

The young al Fadhil had caught up by then but was hanging back a few yards as if he could distance himself from the other two by proximity even though the three of them were

331

the only living beings on the street at that dark hour. "Your treasures? But I thought—" The young man behind him choked off, but not before Saddam caught the hard look Yazeen had shot at him.

He moved through the gate in the iron fence and mounted each step firmly, leaving his limp behind at the street. His guardsmen followed.

At the top step, Saddam raised his arm high to knock on the heavy wooden door.

"Who are ya and whadda want?" a voice came from his right followed quickly by the cocking of three weapons.

Saddam turned slowly toward the voice keeping his hands away from his body. He knew two of the weapons belonged to Yazeen and al Fadhil. Leaving a third that was probably in the hands under the voice.

In the hazy moonlight and black shadows of the lawn trees it was hard to distinguish the man's shape from the tree trunk, but the rifle barrel was unmistakable.

"Come out from there." Saddam commanded him.

"No way. You state your business or be on your way." The barrel jerked to show them the way to the street.

Saddam breathed deeply to calm his rage. "I think if you will come out, you will recognize what I'm here for."

The silhouette of a man separated itself away from the tree trunk with sloth slowness. He grew larger as he stepped closer.

The rifle lowered all at once. The man clutched his heart and his whole body lowered actually. He melted in place all the way to the grass.

Two hand guns uncocked with a metal click. "Get him up." Saddam ordered when the man had not moved even to breathe in more than ten seconds.

Pistols were holstered and the two passed by him to pick up the old man using his armpits as leverage.

"I apologize, your majesty, for not recognizing you right away." The man's head was bowed low. "You are correct, as you should be, I *do* know what you are here for."

When the man didn't move, Saddam sighed shortly. "Would you lead the way?"

"Oh yes, sir. I would be delighted to show you what you already know." When the man reached for his robe's pocket, the young guards stiffened. Saddam lifted a hand to stand them down. He could see the old man's ridiculous grin; they could not. "The key." The guard smiled as he pulled out a key as long as his whole hand from the gnarled tip of his middle finger to his wrist. His right canine tooth was missing.

The double click in the lock as the key was twisted released a burning sensation in Saddam's chest, and as the old guard pulled the heavy door toward them, Saddam brushed past making his way to the largest artifact displayed partially right there in the lobby. A giant stone gate of the original city of Babylon. When it had been unearthed in the excavations, Saddam had had it moved here for safe keeping and so he could visit it at his convenience. When the city was complete and the reproduction gates based on this one lined the city walls, this original piece would be replaced, moved stone by stone, back to its resting place. Saddam smiled as he rubbed his palms across the smooth surface, gaining a recharge with every second.

It might be weeks or months even before he could breathe this deeply of its ancient powers again.

The smaller items he had in mind would have to suffice him until then. He released the stone wall and hurried back toward the Babylonian displays. The entourage followed him.

Standing before one of the glass cases, Saddam glanced at the security guard, ridiculous grin with the missing tooth still plastered to his face, and motioned for him to unlock it.

"Oh, I don't have keys to the cases, your majesty. I do apologize if I gave you that impression. The board thought—"

The old man stopped as Saddam put his elbow through the glass with a mighty crash.

Minutes later, Saddam's bulging pockets kept bumping into display cases and the weight on his shoulders compressed his sore lower back as he hurried back to the front. He wished he could take the Babylon gate with him like the rest of the valuable pieces of ancient Babylon in his pockets. But the brown robe was worth its ugliness for the depth of its reinforced pockets. He smoothed war-torn hands over the swell of necklaces, medallions, signet rings and giant jeweled rings, coins, and bracelets of antiquity mixed in with beautiful—and valuable—modern pieces the security guard had convinced him to take for "safekeeping."

Saddam's nose crinkled in contempt. Safekeeping indeed. Nothing modern would be allowed to enter the gates of Babylon once it was rebuilt. But these ugly rings and diamond bracelets would help finance his next weeks in forced exile because of those horrid Infidels who dared challenge his plans.

The masterful prize Saddam clutched in his right hand: an eight-inch-long clay cylinder covered in Cuneiform writing. It described Nebuchadnezzar's conquering of the Hebrew lands including Jerusalem. An event Saddam hoped to one day repeat in his modern body. He could almost feel the heat radiate off the piece in connection to his previous life as that man.

Saddam stopped at the ancient gate to suck the nectar of its power once more. He opened his one eye when he heard the rustle of plastic next to him.

The old security guard had brought out large plastic bags with the Iraq Museum logo emblazoned on them and was handing them out to the two guards and then to him.

To his surprise, he took the bag, and followed the old man back into the museum proper when he beckoned them to come after him.

"And take these." The man indicated at another display with many small items. Saddam and the guardsmen mostly filled up on objects of metal or jewels that would not crush in the days of travel they had ahead of them. The guard lifted a trio of paintings from a wall and gave one to each of them.

"That is all." Saddam turned on his heel and walked back to the front. He smiled again at the man's over-helpfulness in packing their pockets. He insisted on sending some weird mask that he insisted was from ancient Babylon and should be protected from the Americans. So the mask ended up in a little padding in his plastic bag, even though he did not feel a tangible connection with it and did not think it could possibly be from his former kingdom.

**First-floor Tile Shop
8 April 2003
0325 hours**

Judah Wakefield leaned back against the hard surface at her back to catch her breath. The incessant atkk-tak-tak of weapon's fire just outside set to auto-fire mode drilled into her mind. As she drew her knees up to her chest to make herself smaller, her fingers played across the floor. Looking for further protection in the room where she sat Wakefield assessed her surroundings with a critical eye.

"A bombed-out tile shop. Are you kidding me?" She rolled her eyes. Any further blast inside the shop would shatter the tiled walls and samples, sending tiny ceramic shards through every surface, including her.

In considering moving to an upper floor, Wakefield glanced up. Chandeliers. A hundred glass chandeliers on display. *Get out! Get out!* Her mind screamed at her. She already had enough scars on her face.

She scrambled on hands and knees through junk on the tile floor to the next room back, away from the breach in the front window where she had first entered. She dove behind some sort of barrier and looked around. Another showroom. One spray of a machine gun…not safe, she shook her head and kept moving further back into the building. It got darker and darker.

Finally, from the light of the moon filtering in an unshuttered window in the back office, Wakefield saw a back door. She flung it open. No response. So she stuck her head out. The slim alleyway was empty, and, she smiled widely, there was a rickety looking fire escape connected to the upper floors.

She took the stairs two at a time to the top floor. Unfortunately, there was no roof access; that would have been ideal for what she needed.

She tapped on the window with her knuckle, and stood to the side with her back flat on the wall, just in case. No response. Hopefully, no one was home.

Wakefield pressed her fingers against the glass and tried to force it open. It wouldn't budge. Then she saw that the lock was engaged on the wooden window casing with layers and layers of paint covering the locking system and each panel of the windowsill.

"Sorry, about this," she breathed. Protecting her face by turning her head, she punched the butt of her rifle through the glass. The tinkling sound let her know she was not going to be stepping into a long drop.

Wakefield hurried to squat with her back against the concrete-block wall waiting for any sound from inside. Nothing. She peered around the sill. Now that the reflecting glass was out of the way, she saw a wingback chair right in front of the window. She stood and quickly tapped the rest of the sharp edges out of her path with her rifle. There was some movement in the alley below, but the pair of people seemed focused on their own business.

Ducking inside, Wakefield stepped into the seat of the wingback and easily down to the floor of what must have been a study. A Persian rug dulled her footsteps, if anyone was listening over the firefight in the front street.

Wakefield weaved her way to the front, clearing every room before putting it behind her. The occupants had left the flat some time earlier. The refrigerator had been emptied and unplugged. It was a nice place though. Wakefield was thankful to borrow it for a little while.

She passed the main entry door on her way to the front room, where a triple window, also painted shut, offered a front row seat to the fireworks below. This room felt stuffy with its heavy curtains and formal antique furniture.

Wakefield leaned her left shoulder into the wall and used the muzzle of her rifle to slide the curtain open a crack. Another volley broke out and Wakefield dropped the curtain back into place until it quieted down.

She tried again, slitting the curtain just enough to let one eye peer out. This time when the muzzles flashed and the tracer bullets revealed their paths, she held her ground and observed.

All the action looked to be on ground level, so she widened her viewing space by pulling back the curtain further. She counted 18 different locations in the northwest firing toward the south and southwest. Three of the Republican Guard trucks that initially sent her running for cover were sprawled in the intersection in front of where the barrage of bullets was coming from. The trucks formed a microscopic cover for a few soldiers.

Wakefield dropped the curtain, crouched down and inched to the far side under the protection of the wall below the windows to peer in the opposite direction.

The return fire did not contain tracer bullets for her to follow, and the disorderly return volleys didn't sound highly trained. Wakefield shook her head as more muzzles flashed. It was not American forces that were engaging the Republican Guard. "It must be resistance forces." Wakefield assessed under her breath. "Maybe some of the men from the Saddam statue pull-apart thing got caught trying to get home. Or maybe it was on purpose."

Just by watching the timing and placement of the rounds from the road and first floors to the southwest, Wakefield knew the resistance was advancing. Or trying to.

It sounded like the Republican Guard ordinance was weakening. Not in power but in number. Wakefield switched sides again. Not even half of the 18 places were still firing. Were the resistance fighters that good a shot? It was impossible, and she had not heard anyone crying out in pain on either side.

338

Then the sound of boots on stairs and whispers in Arabic cut through the sound of bullets flying.

The Republican Guard was dividing their forces and going up, to draw the rebels into a trap. Wakefield had seen the strategy before. Draw the enemy into thinking they are winning while you reposition your troops at elevation. Take them out from above and behind once they move forward in their confidence.

Right now Wakefield's concern was that elevation meant an upper story window, and that was where she was standing. Her heart pounded. Heavy treads were louder.

Move it! She commanded herself. *But where?*

Chapter Forty Three

Rivers looked up to see Camp Liberty North's C.O. duck inside the tent they were using to plan their extraction. When the silver-haired man with a Marine buzz cut just stood in the entrance, Rivers excused himself with a tap his palm on the table and went to meet him.

"New intel, sir?" Rivers was hopeful.

"Yeah. Two things." O'Reilly frowned. "David, I just heard," the man's dark eyes seemed to look through his skin as they crinkled with concern. "I know it's your wife out there, and I'm so sorry. I can't imagine what you're going through."

The shorter senior officer laid a comforting hand on his shoulder.

"I don't even know what I am going through yet, sir. Right now, I've got a job to do, and I'll sort it out later."

"Well, I've reviewed your service history. Which is rather thick." The C.O. quirked a single thick eyebrow at him. "And based on that history and reputation I know you will follow the book on this extraction."

He paused until Rivers knew he was waiting for some sort of confirmation from him, so he nodded slowly.

"To that end, we have some new intel. No coordinates, sorry." He was quick to add. "But the vacuum in leadership had become very apparent in the vicinity around the Republican Palace. Major uptick in fighting, but it appears uncoordinated and random. Reports are coming in of hundreds of civilian casualties. We are moving up our invasion time table to bring it under control and will be working in the corridor of the Republican Palace over to the Al Faw Palace and all the government houses in between to establish what we're hoping to call a Green Zone. That will be where we can establish a ground H.Q. and work from a safe space expanding it either by miles or blocks at a time until the city is fully at rest."

Rivers felt his eyebrows rise higher and higher of their own accord. "When, sir?"

"First official convoy is leaving here at zero six hundred. Think that'll help your Teams out?"

Rivers broke eye contact to glance at his watch. An hour and a half. So many more men available to clear the blocks. "Oh yes, sir. That'll change our strategy. I'd say half of us can accompany the convoy, if you have space to give us a ride, and we can give you some roof-top coverage."

"That'd be helpful. Pretty sure the boys will make room for you, Commander."

Rivers grinned. "Thank you, sir. Really!"

Fourth-floor Flat
8 April 2003
0435 hours

Judah left the bedroom door hanging open, so the room didn't appear to be concealing anything and scampered to the far side

341

of the king-size bed. Trying to be silent and trying to hurry, her heart fluttered like a swarm of butterflies taking over her chest cavity and attacking her throat. She had seen when clearing the space at her arrival, that it was not a platform bed, but raised on a frame, and the flat owners had stored several boxes underneath. There was also a gap where she supposed they had stored suitcases before needing them to vacate the premises.

She shoved her rifle underneath, stripped off her Kevlar vest because she would never fit underneath with it on. The ripping Velcro side sounded like the Great Wall of China breaking open to her. She kicked the vest as far under as she could. Then she lay flat on her tummy, turned her head sideways, and inched under the bed skirt, hoping she would not run into any furry friends or six-legged creepy crawlies. She prayed she was not leaving a tell-tale mark on the bedside area rug by rubbing the pile in the wrong direction.

The front door of the flat crashed open. Too late now.

She pulled her right boot under the bed skirt and lay her cheek flat against the dusty floor. Her eyes shot open and she sucked in her breath; the tile floor was freezing against her face, warm from fear.

The boots methodically cleared the house just as she had done. One of them called a buddy to come check out the broken window at the fire escape in the study. At least one other was still clearing rooms. He was at the bathroom next to the bedroom where she hid. That door slammed against the wall. The small door of the pantry with shelves in the bathroom flew open too. The basket containing laundry creaked as the man dumped it.

Glad I didn't choose to go under the clothes, not that I would have fit exactly.

Then the soldier was at her door. He hummed under his breath. His boots moved through the room. He threw open the wardrobe closet. Metal hangers shuffled on the bar. The vinyl of his old boots creaked as he walked to the far side of the bed.

Hide me Lord, Judah prayed inwardly. *Blind his eyes from seeing me.*

He strode to the other side of the bed. When he bent over things jingled on his uniform. He lifted the bed skirt and saw the same storage boxes she had. Judah pinched her eyes closed so no white reflection would catch his attention.

He muttered something in Arabic that even with superb language skills, Wakefield could not interpret.

The guardsman straightened up with a little huff and left the room. A moment later he called to the other two from the formal living room where she had been standing not fifty-five seconds earlier.

Wakefield forced herself to take deep cleansing breaths. But not so deep that she sucked in dust and would sneeze. This predicament was far from over.

From the sound of their conversation the three men settled in the living room to perch at the windows overlooking the main street the same way she had.

"Here they come." One voice rasped.

"Steady men. Wait until they get out ahead so all of those rebel scum are within our range."

Wakefield bit the inside of her cheek. Should she risk scrambling out from under the bed to retreat downstairs under the cover of the noise when they began the ambush of the poor Iraqis resisting an evil regime to get their nation back? Should she sneak attack behind the three men and take them out as they started to shoot? *Ugh! What do I do?*

"Say, Lieutenant, what are those people doing sneaking out the entrance to the National Museum?" It was the same young yet raspy voice that had spoken first.

"What?"

"Here look through my scope. It is about three blocks up in the same direction the rebels are coming from, but behind the ones we've been tracking." Wakefield heard the clunky sound of a gun exchanging hands.

The lieutenant spewed a vile string of curses in combinations of words Wakefield had never heard before even in interrogation of prisoners.

"You see them?" Raspy voice asked. Wakefield rolled her eyes.

"I wanna see." The third man pushed.

"What are they doing?"

"Keep your mind on the mission. They are taking some of our national treasures to safety." He gave a little chuckle.

Wakefield's mind massaged the new information. It had to be people looting the massive museum. Was it the rebels? Soldiers? Americans? Everyday people from the protest earlier? Some had been headed in that direction when she had had to take cover. She shook her head in the slightest movements allowed by the tight space, they would not have had time to get in, grab stuff, and be back outside by now.

The gun with an apparent scope was put back in Raspy Voice's hands. "Those are our guys." The lieutenant said. "As soon as we clean up this mess, we'll join them." Wakefield could almost hear his salivation from the bedroom. "Tighten up."

The third man chuckled. "They are totally exposed."

"Here we go." The lieutenant counted down. "Three, two, one. Fire at will."

Their guns were set to auto fire and Wakefield's ears pounded with the sound, but she couldn't get her hands into place to protect them. She pressed the right ear into the tile floor and that helped that side a little.

"Enough." Roared the lieutenant.

It was silent as quickly as it had roared to a start.

"That one is still moving." Raspy Voice said. One more pop-pop-pop and the silence expanded in her ears again. "Got him."

"Good work. That is a couple of dozen little ferrets that will not bother us again."

Wakefield groaned inside picturing the bloodbath in the street below. Now she would never know if she could have prevented it and saved some lives.

"Now let's get out of here."

"I'm gonna grab a couple of bags for our little shopping trip." It was the third man. His voice put him walking into the bedroom where she hid. Wakefield shrank inside. He pawed through the wardrobe, tossing things to the floor. Dresser drawers pulled open and the clothing pattered like soft rain as he dropped them by handful on the floor.

"There's a lot of bags in here," called the lieutenant, it sounded like from the kitchen. "Nothing to eat except these old beans though." Dried beans tinkled as they hit the tile.

The man joined the others and seconds later Wakefield was in the room alone again.

Boots descended the stairwell and faded away. She didn't want to move. "Come on." She coached herself. The words sounded loud, though she knew she had not put effort behind them. "Just make the first move, everything else will follow."

Judah stirred up her will and forced her fist out from under the bed skirt. Then her right leg. She pushed her rifle with her right hand ahead of her and inched her body out the same way she had scooted in, only bumping her head once. She dragged her Kevlar behind her.

"Phone. That's my first order of business. I've gotta get out of here." She shook her head. "I'm in way over my head."

Iraqi National Museum
5:50 AM

"Yazeen, you will go first. Al Fadhil, you will follow us, just as we walked on the way here." Saddam commanded. They stood under the ancient arch in the grand entryway of the national museum. Every pocket on the three men bulged with artifacts. Weapons stowed, each hand carried a plastic bag overloaded with more items.

Saddam leaned his back against the stones to pull in one more moment of strength.

The fluttering old security guard with the one missing tooth scurried ahead of them, accommodating as he had been since the first moment of recognition. "Let me get the door. Your hands are so full. One more painting, just here under the arm." He doddered as he lifted al Fadhil's left arm and tucked a 16x20 painting in a gold frame underneath. "You will take such good care of our treasures. I just know."

"Stop it!" Saddam commanded the old man who did exactly as he was told. Sliding an inch or two on the highly polished marble floor.

As Yazeen pushed open the heavy front door, Saddam leaned forward to set his packages on the marble floor, leaning them upright against the door jam.

Irritation that started as an itch in his sandaled toes now made his back crawl with exasperation. His thirst for blood was back with a vengeance. It must be relieved. So he reached for Yazeen's holster and withdrew the man's service pistol.

Saddam turned and fired once.

The old man dropped to the floor.

"You almost hit me!" al Fadhil cradled his ear in his palm.

Saddam shifted the gun a few inches to the right. He pulled the trigger again. Al Fadhil staggered backward and clutched his throat. Red oozed out between his fingers and his next step sent him sprawling back across the heap of the old museum guard. His arms attempted to windmill, but al Fadhil ran out of steam before he hit the marble.

"What was that for?" Yazeen asked wide-eyed. The door was wide open as he held it with his body weight and waited for him to come through.

The young man's eyes widened further and drifted down to where the weapon was pointed at his heart.

"Because I can." Saddam said. He spun the pistol on his finger which was a little fatter than last time he had attempted the finger spin. He handed the gun back to Yazeen butt first. "Let's get out of here."

Five strides down the front steps a volley of gunfire erupted not far away.

Yazeen finished stuffing his holster, but halted on the stairs. Spinning his finger in a circle in the air as he turned his body around, he said, "Back inside. We need another plan. Now."

347

Chapter Forty Four

The early sun cast a depressing grey light, but at least the pitch-blackness of the night was completed. All the chandeliers were destroyed. The tile floor looked like an unfinished mosaic. Judah checked every surface and in every desk drawer in the whole office area.

No computer, no cell phone. Finally, in the back of a storage closet filled with boxed paper records labeled by year, there sat an old yellowed phone with a rotary dial in the handle and a long curly cord wrapped around it.

"Oh boy!" Wakefield sighed then grabbed it and began unwrapping the cord and the grey connection cord. She checked the few inches of wall that were bare; no dice. Heaving the desk along the wall, she looked behind it for the specially shaped telephone plug. Nothing there either. She pushed a hip against a solid wood table full of samples against another wall. It was not going anywhere.

Into the next room. And then the front room. Finally in the corner against the back wall of the main front showroom, Judah spied a circular disk the size of a hockey puck. Keeping her head low and under the line of sight of the concrete barriers guarding outside the glassless showroom windows, Judah scampered over, dragging the curly-corded phone behind her.

She kneeled to reach the outlet and pushed the plug into the disk's opening with a click. As she took a deep breath and melted into a more comfortable position on the floor, Judah noted the sound of early morning birds chirping. It felt incongruous with the sky and the knot in her stomach, as she wondered how this little moment in her life was going to conclude. She pushed aside fear and picked up the phone handset and held it to her ear.

She could still hear the birds outside. The phone line was dead. "Of course it is," she chided herself. "The phone was in a closet. There is no service connection."

Her fingers tightened around the phone and she felt a scream of frustration rise from her belly. She really wanted to throw it into the shredded tile on the floor. Maybe several times. Very forcefully. Instead she tugged the cord from the wall and called upon all of her military bearing to replace the receiver in the cradle.

She straightened her posture to decide what was next, never mind that she was sitting Indian style surrounded by rubble. *Was it military bearing?* The thought crossed her mind.

What else? She shrugged along with her own inner dialogue. Could it be control? A way to maintain one iota of control when everything around is out of control.

Judah smoothed back her tangled hair from the temple and looked at the floor, not enjoying the stab of the truth. She recognized it right away, but felt defensive. "So what's wrong with that?"

"It's not my best for you. Can you give me the final shred of your own control over your life?"

Judah rolled her eyes heavenward, but then felt ashamed. "I don't even know what that looks like." She steeled her features again, locking down her incredulity at God's timing for this conversation.

"If you want to throw the phone, throw the phone."

She shook her head, "Are you kidding me right now!" she hissed.

All was quiet.

Judah threw her hand back over the old phone. She tossed it a foot or so away from her. A picture of King Jehoash of Israel flashed through her mind from a lesson she had taught her first-grade Sunday School class back in Virginia just after Christmas. The prophet Elisha told him to shoot some arrows. Not understanding the significance, the king had shot the arrows a half-hearted three times. Elisha had said, "It's too bad you didn't shoot six arrows, now you'll only defeat your enemies three times."

Judah scooched forward and reached for the phone again. In her current circumstances, following a seemingly foolish bit of instruction from the Lord was a no-brainer, she could not afford to only beat her enemy once or three times. Judah took the phone in both hand and hit it against the tile and concrete and glass rubble on the floor. Timidly on her first blow. The ringer sent out a TING as it vibrated with the movement. The second smash sent a cracked piece of plastic phone casing flying across the room. At throw five, seven seemed like a nice godly number to stop on.

"How was that?" Judah was fully standing now, hands on hips, with the phone in half-a-dozen pieces at her feet, the curly cord adorned the top of the heap.

"One other thing. Your enemy is not the flesh and blood outside these walls you currently struggle against." Before she even had a chance to ask, he continued, "Your need for control is the enemy of your soul."

Strength swelled and indignance rose up in Judah Wakefield like she'd never known before, and she bent at the waist to pick up the phone pieces in both hands again. The motion swung her rifle forward. She caught it with her shoulder and used an elbow to shift it back behind her on its sling. "This thing must die!" Then Judah reared up and slammed the phone to the ground, picked it up and did it again, and then a third time. By the fourth time she felt her grin stretching her filthy facial skin. "Control, you must die!" She growled and the fifth time she threw the whole phone in all of its pieces and cords away from her against the seam where the front wall and the floor met. The plastic shattered and the bouncy cord matted.

Out of breath now with the exertion, Judah looked at the ever-lightening street. The birds had been scared off, but she grinned. She almost wished there had been a witness to her mad-woman, freedom-bringing moment. She felt light, and she knew it had nothing to do with throwing a phone. It was putting to death her need for control, and its hold over her being broken.

"Oh, Lord, help me not give space in my heart over to that enemy ever again."

In front of Wakefield's position more than a dozen lumps scattered on the street in front of the shop came into focus. It was the men of the resistance forces. Would one of them have a cell phone she could use? Seeing as they had the basic same agenda of ousting Saddam Hussein, she didn't think they or their families would mind.

351

One step toward the open door and Wakefield stopped. She remembered a long black tablecloth she had seen up on the fourth floor. She raced up and then back down with the ample cloth in her hand.

She removed her helmet and draped one end over her head, wrapped the cloth around her face just over her nose, then continued around over her shoulders. It wasn't going to work as a disguise when she bent down to check pockets if she was wearing her rifle. She removed the cloth and then the stood her weapon in the corner of the room, feeling very naked without its weight on her shoulder and the protection it offered.

To the soundtrack of an occasional pop-pop-pop of distant gunfire, she rewrapped the cloth. It went faster without the weapon. Holding the tail end of the quality tablecloth in her right hand. She slipped silently out the door of the first-floor tile shop and into the street. She moved slowly, expecting a stray shot to send her either diving back to the shop for cover or to the ground in pain. The second man in her path was face down on the pavement which actually made it easier on her nerves to approach. He wore a black-striped dress shirt, long sleeved, and snug old blue jeans with tell-tale fading on the back pockets. One side stored his wallet, the other a small mobile phone.

Wakefield bit the end of her make-shift abaya/veil combo to keep it from unwinding while she used one hand to pull back on his pocket fabric and the other to reach into his pocket as delicately as she could. He was dead, but it still felt like she was invading his privacy. "I could never be a medical examiner." She huffed out her breath, thankful for the added warmth of the tablecloth before the sun burned off the chill and dew. Digging with her fingers, she was finally able to dislodge the small phone with her middle finger and force it to pop out of his pocket. It slid down on the far side of his hip, and she scrambled after it.

Flipping the phone open while still hunched over the body, she made sure it was operational before she removed herself from the premises. Remarkably, in a section of Baghdad that had not seen electricity for at least 24 hours, the screen showed two bars of cell service.

She hustled back to the tile store and arranged her rifle under the abaya for a walk up the semi-quiet street. She had to get to a place she could offer an address or landmark.

Iraq Museum
6:45 AM

Saddam acquiesced to his bodyguard's assessment, but only because he was right. He stepped over the double decker pile of bodies at the museum entrance, and set the bags that would finance his next phase of life against one of the support pillars. Yazeen whipped out his phone and paced while Saddam spied the snack bar.

"How did we miss this?" he muttered and glanced at Yazeen who had begun yammering into his little black box. Saddam entered the long counter-service area and began throwing open cupboard doors so he could make his best choice for breakfast.

Only minutes later, Yazeen called out, "Sir? Where are you?"

"Over here." He was deliberately calm. He was sitting in a chair he had dragged over from the canteen area to his glorious Babylon Gate. He sipped a cup of piping hot coffee from a pot that was still brewing in the kitchen. He smiled and held up two fistfuls of pastry while a fruit plate balanced on his crossed knee. "Grab some grub, Yazeen, and quiet your screeching."

The young man looked like he swallowed a sharp retort. "My cousin has a vehicle, and he is coming to get us. Don't worry, I didn't say who. But, please, if you could not shoot him, it would be a really big favor to me."

Saddam took an over-sized bite and made no promises.

Chapter Forty Five

Four blocks ahead of Wakefield's trek along the four-lane Baghdad avenue, next to a bright grassy lawn and a spectacular building set back from the road taking up most of the block, she saw people-sized movement coming around a corner. It looked very organized and dark. Angry.

She stopped in decision only a moment, then backtracked toward the intersection she had just passed. The first exit she came to led to the inviting grassy lawn with a few scattered trees in spring-green bloom. A sign identified the building as the Iraq Museum in decorative Arabic writing incorporated into an arch over a substantial iron gate. The paved entrance gate had a chain wrapped around its bars with a lock dangling off the end of it. Its being slightly ajar tempted her, but she also felt uneasy. A museum didn't seem like the best place to call in some help. She smiled, but the green lawn would provide a good landmark for a Search and Rescue pilot to look for in a very grey city.

After thirty more seconds at pace, Wakefield took a quick left around the side of the museum's property, her black tablecloth flapping against her ankles and billowing out behind her. The street looked like so many other streets, but this one had a crater or perhaps two that she could identify. Parts of

355

buildings were missing and chunky debris cluttered the sidewalk and driving space.

Wakefield found a building in the first block that looked stable but quietly abandoned. The ground floor was another shop, but it had a metal rolling door covered in graffiti that shielded the entire store front and was padlocked to a hoop set in the concrete. But near, there was an entryway door that beckoned her up its stairway. The rooftop would give her the best cell reception and view of whatever was going on in the main street. So she climbed, hoping for roof access this time. The building seemed structurally sound. Each floor opened into a carpeted common area for four apartment doors, each labeled with an Arabic letter and number. Judah wondered about the families or offices housed behind those doors. What had become of them?

Five floors up the stairwell, instead of opening up to another carpeted lobby area, Wakefield came to a very solid metal door, labeled "Owners Only" in Arabic, with some legal action threatened in small print underneath for violators. An electronic keypad was at the left of the door immediately next to an industrial silver flange locking system at the door handle.

Wakefield frowned, "What in the world have they got up here that needs so much protection and limited access?" she mumbled, testing the door. Of course it was locked, even with no power running to the box.

The door's hinges fastened to open toward her, so a swift kick would do nothing. She decided to save her joints the impact pressure and skip that option. Shooting the locking mechanism was the only option she could think of, but too noisy and traceable to the place she wanted to hide from the mob of soldiers advancing up the street toward her position. Then she remembered. *Was it one or two floors down?* She wondered even as she took the stairs two at a time.

Just one floor. Wakefield strode across the lobby and picked up two thick decorative pillows from the love seat on the far side. Back up the stairs she awkwardly folded one pillow over her rifle and fired at the doorknob. In the confined concrete-block space it was definitely loud, but the pillow had muffled it enough for her to feel confident the shot would not be traced.

The doorknob clattered to the concrete floor and the door swung slightly toward her as the mechanism released.

Wakefield reached two fingers into the new hole she had created and pulled the door fully open, keeping her body covered behind it. She peeked around it to check for threats and gasped.

It was a whole other world up here.

She steeled herself to clear the space of any danger first, but she was itching to stare at everything. Crouching to make herself a smaller target, Wakefield moved strategically from one place of cover to the next to inspect the entire rooftop.

It had not been touched in days, she assessed from the fine layer of grey concrete dust that covered the entire paradise. Trees and flowers surrounded five pergolas with white gauzy curtains. Twinkle lights reflecting the morning sun made it look like millions of diamonds had encrusted every surface, save the still water features. The pumps to run the cascade that emptied into two shallow pools, one on either end of the roof space needed electricity to create what must have been a magical sound that completed this oasis. Lounge chairs with thick cushions were grouped together under the pergolas and upright seating in pairs and quads were scattered around the deck. Palms and fichus trees grew up to nine feet tall and spread their branches for shade, it was a wonder she had not been able to see them from the ground. Wisteria vines climbed from huge clay pots up each post of the pergolas and covered the roof beams. It a few weeks, this place would be a riot of lavender and purple when the wisteria bloomed like clusters of grapes all over the rooftop Eden.

"This is exquisite." Judah felt she should whisper and could hardly tear her eyes away from the serenity of the place.

She needed to check the progress of the soldiers. "But first." She sighed as she unwound the cumbersome tablecloth from her head and let it fall to the ground in a heap.

Pushing her way through pots full of grasses and flowers growing on trellises interspersed with tall palms to get into the corner at the right end of the roof, Wakefield shook her left boot loose from one of the curling vines that had escaped the trellis in its pot. The four-foot-high stone barrier that surrounded the rooftop had already begun to warm in the sun and felt comforting against her forearms as she transferred her weight to lean cautiously over the ledge.

In the far distance to her one o'clock, Wakefield perceived an exchange of volleys. At her two o'clock just one block forward of her, the soldiers once four blocks away, she could now see through the vertical iron fence that surrounded the Iraqi Museum. In her close vision from about 1:45 to 4:30 sat the huge museum and its grounds. She couldn't see the distance in that direction because of the mature trees on the lawn. Continuing on around, the street filled her vision from the 4:30 mark to 8:00 where she lost visual against the side of her building. The street actually had a few people out at ground level. An old woman beating a rug with a thrasher, a pair of men hurrying away from the main street four or five blocks away, and a little boy playing with a kitten. Resilient Iraqi people.

Returning her vision to the original point of reference at main street, her view was very much obstructed from twelve o'clock back to about ten-thirty, from her height advantage on the roof, she could see over the buildings between her position and the main street down to about the second floor, but not the street itself. Then from 10:30 all the way back to 7:30 all she could see were the trees, pergolas, and water features of the rooftop.

She spun back to check the soldiers again.

"Whoa." Her eye caught movement at one of the windows. The curtain moved. She stared until she saw it again. A thin stick emerged from that curtain and stood out against the light-colored building. A rifle barrel.

She stopped to study each window for a few seconds as she fumbled in her thigh cargo pocket for the flip phone. At least half of the twenty to thirty windows she could see on three different levels had gunmen stationed behind curtains, pointed in the direction on the soldiers outside the Iraqi Museum.

This was going to get ugly really fast. She flicked the phone open. Still two bars.

At the sound of an old car on ancient creaky shocks, Wakefield looked up from entering in the number for Brady Grady's satellite phone she had seen printed on his desk. "Thank you, God, for this photographic memory you gave me. I know I've told you it is annoying sometimes, but today," she nodded deeply as she followed with her eyes a little car with exhaust pluming behind its painstaking maneuvering around the rubble and potholes of the side road toward her and the Iraqi Museum. "Today, I am finding it very useful."

359

She hit the send button at the same moment as the woosh of a shoulder-mounted rocket launcher filled the air moving from her right to her left. The soldiers had fired first.

Ducking immediately in place, Wakefield pressed the phone to her ear. An explosion sounded and then another one half a second later. They must have hit a vehicle which then detonated its fuel tank. The crackle of the resulting fire was unmistakable as the phone got off its first ring.

Chapter Forty Six

"Hunker down in place." Commander Brady Grady ordered. "I'll forward the description of your location to the SEAL Team your husband is leading. They are en route."

Wakefield groaned. "I'm never gonna hear the end of this one, am I, sir?"

Grady gave a little chuckle. "Probably not, Wakefield. But I suggest you do whatever it takes to get it to a place where Rivers is able to tease you about it, because I can more than imagine what is going through his head right now." He paused. "My wife was in a bank hold up a couple years back."

Wakefield strained to hear him against the volley of bullets being exchanged. "I'm really sorry you guys had to go through that, Brady. And I'll do my best to make it up to him. I can hardly hear you. I'll check in when I get back to base." Even if he had said something to sign off she wouldn't have been able to hear him, so Wakefield pressed the end key and snapped the phone closed, and returned it to her thigh pocket.

Rising back up, she checked all the angles. The soldiers had not advanced, but were hunkered down behind several obstruct-

361

ions in the street and in buildings and behind vehicles abandoned in people's rush to leave Baghdad over the previous weeks. So far, no muzzles flashed from any rooftops though. That was reassuring.

Looking down on the street below, one of the cars idled. She couldn't distinguish the sound of the motor, just see the exhaust belching from the tailpipe of a formerly light blue and now more-rust-than-anything model of car she couldn't identify.

The woman with the rug had retreated back indoors, Wakefield assumed, seeing the empty stoop where she had stood. The pair of men had disappeared down the road or some alley. The little boy with the kitten. Wakefield scanned the street and the museum yard. Then movement out of her left eye caught her attention.

The small dark head was about fifty yards from the intersection. The butter-colored kitten playfully cantering head-rump, head-rump just out of the little boy's clutches. They would be in the line of fire in less than a minute! Wakefield's heart pounded.

She turned and leaped over the planters. Grabbing the tablecloth and the spare throw pillow, she bolted to the roof exit door as a plan formed in her mind. It was crazy. Surely some less-reckless plan would materialize before—

Just behind the ground-level stairwell door, her rifle at her side again and helmet in place, Wakefield wrapped the black tablecloth around her head, but when she got to her body, she tucked the extra pillow onto her shoulders and under her nylon rifle sling. The pillow pushed her head and neck forward. She continued the wrapping process as she pushed open the door.

Stepping into the street, she held her head forward, and curled her arms into her body like the old woman she had played earlier. But this time her acting would have to be perfection. The boy and the kitten were forty feet ahead of her and perhaps ten feet from the street, absolutely oblivious to the danger ahead.

Wakefield used a shaky voice to call out in Arabic, "Come back, love. Stop." But she only tried it once since she could hardly hear herself.

She hurried as much as she thought she could get away with as a hunch-backed little old lady.

When she was still twenty feet back from the intersection, the boy followed his kitten into the crossfire. What was wrong with that cat? Didn't they normally shy away from noise? Her cat Bartholomew had always hid under the couch when she had the vacuum cleaner out.

As Wakefield stood at the edge of the corner building ready to step a few feet to the curb and into the street, she mumbled, "Come on culture! Come on culture!"

Exaggerating her hump-back and allowing the quaking on her insides to release through her shaking arms as she fixed her eyes on the boy and reached up with both hands. The position of her arms begged for mercy not to shoot, at the same time as asking both sides to stop all together. She took small shaky steps forward. One foot in front of the other.

Her heart pounded in her ears like a freight train on fast approach. She wanted to dash forward, grab the pair, and retreat. But if there was any hope of successful outcome, this had to be played with equal parts trembling and patience. In a culture that honored elders and hospitality, it actually stood a chance. "Come on culture," Wakefield breathed again.

The gunfire roar did actually lessen, though by no means did it stop all together. Wakefield continued forward, both arms at half-mast with palms flat and fingers curled slightly, as if with age, toward each side of the fighters.

She counted 12 steps into the street before she caught up with the boy, and one more to reach the kitten. She stooped to scoop up the kitten and boy both by their bellies and tottered back to the curb with them both squirming and screeching at having their play interrupted.

Wakefield thought she might have heard a guffaw of laughter from somewhere before the shots erupted again in earnest.

Fifteen to twenty steps out of the line of fire and back in the refuge of the side street, Wakefield straightened up and brought her breath back to its normal rhythm, though her whole body still pounded with her heartbeat.

Judah returned the writhing little paperweight to his feet and turned him around to face her. Squatting to his eye level, she tucked the kitten into her lap, and prepared to scold him soundly. But her heart melted at his precious little face. He couldn't have been a day over four years old with wild large brown curls and liquid fudge eyes. "Where's your mommy?" She asked him in Arabic and then in English while he struggled to un-pry her fingers against the hold she had on his upper arm.

Out of the corner of her eye she saw a flash of movement ahead of her at the fence of the Iraqi Museum. In that moment of distraction, the little imp broke free and sprinted away. He was too fast for her to catch without breaking character, and he was running in the right direction anyway, away from the firefight.

The driver of the rusty car was getting out. He appeared to be shouting at someone on the lawn. Wakefield stood and cuddled the kitten toward her. It had fallen asleep as easily as that. The driver must have seen her and the running boy at the same time for he stopped short and stared at them. Judah moved slow and hunched toward the opposite sidewalk and patted the kitten in long soothing strokes, hoping to ease the man's apprehension. Even though she was looking away from the man, she concentrated all of her powers of observation on the action.

The driver turned back to the lawn, and so did Wakefield's attention. Two men loaded down with bags staggered toward the fence. Wakefield was able to distinguish a small break in the fence after the driver pulled on it. The men would be able to pass through the fence in front of where the rusty car was parked at the curb.

Wakefield kept hobbling forward in her old woman disguise. The little boy got closer and closer to the men and showed no sign of slowing, with his tiny arms and legs pumping for all he was worth. Wakefield looked above his head as the two men forced themselves and their burdens through the small, frameless pass-through in the fence. She caught sight of the old bald man. He wasn't moving quite as slow as his appearance dictated. She gasped too loud.

Wakefield tucked her head, praying they had not heard her over the firefight.

The boy veered in a hard right and disappeared around the corner, hopefully on his way home to safety. Wakefield shuffled down the sidewalk. It was only a few more steps to protection. "Oh, how I wish I had stayed on that rooftop now. I would have perfect cover to take out Saddam from there." She mumbled in her heart not daring even a whisper that might make her recognition known to him.

She turned her back on the three men who were now beginning to argue on the far sidewalk between the car and the now normal-looking fence with no opening evident. She pulled open the bottom stairwell door to the rooftop paradise where she was supposed to be waiting for her pick up." It was Saddam, wasn't it? It had to be him. He looked like a twin of the man from the brig when they had taken the sheers to his Saddam-look-alike haircut.

Instead, Wakefield entered the stairwell and left the door cracked so she could watch what was happening. The younger of the two men took a painting out from under his arm and handed it to the driver while Saddam tossed a pair of huge plastic gift-shop bags that bulged with odd shapes and stretched handles into the back seat.

The driver leaned in and deposited the painting in the front seat, and the trunk sprang open. Saddam shook his head and protested to the man who was with him. The man shook his head right back and spoke emphatically to the king. Maybe it wasn't really Saddam. Wakefield couldn't imagine that the narcissistic king she had once profiled would let anyone speak to him like that and live through the conversation.

And yet. The bald man set his shoulders and walked back to the trunk and climbed in. Judah saw him fold his thick body in half and rest his head on praying hands before they brought the trunk lid down.

The second man started to get in the backseat, but the driver motioned him to sit up front. So he did.

The angle to read the license plate was bad, but it should be clear after they had pulled forward a few dozen feet. Wakefield waited for it, wishing she had glanced at the number on her slow walk back from the intersection.

In a puff of exhaust, the car ground forward. Wakefield blinked quickly to clear and focus her eyes, ready to capture the license number and send it to all the roadblocks the U.S. Army was setting up on routes into and out of Baghdad.

It should have been becoming clear by now. She blinked once more. The space for the license plate was empty.

Wakefield blew out her breath and rolled her eyes. She stripped off the black tablecloth and dislodged the pillow off her hunchback and threw both of them as far and hard as she could. Neither flew very well.

Judah groaned. The man they had been sent in to capture into custody was speeding away right now, and she had done nothing to stop him.

The phone vibrated against Wakefield's leg and she steeled herself in case it was Grady calling back. Wakefield held up the unopened phone to catch enough light to view the front message system that would display the number calling. She groaned again as she read the scrolling message:

REMAINING BATTERY AT 1%. PHONE WILL NOW POWER DOWN.

Chapter Forty Seven

Rivers' SEAL Team observed the men they had attached themselves to, the column of the Third Infantry Division of the Army's XVIII Airborne Corps. Capable men out of Fort Stewart, Hunter Army Air Field, and Fort Benning, Georgia. Rivers smiled as he took in their readiness. It was not a difficulty for the Army's highly mobile, rapid-response unit, to deliver the small SEAL Team to their entry point as the 19,000 soldiers from several FOBs surrounding Baghdad sought to expand U.S. control from the airport into the city center.

The atmosphere was heating up for the day. The entire column ground to a halt. Sweat already rolled down Rivers' back under the full sun where he lay prone on another rooftop providing overwatch for soldiers who had to go house to house in order to clear streets ahead of the column.

He blew out his lips in annoyance at the time it was taking to get to Wakefield. If he had realized they expected his Team to work ahead of them all day with clearing the route, he would have arranged his own ride in. He lost track of the number of men who had fled buildings just ahead of the troops, appearing very ill-at-ease through his scope. But taking men out was not his assignment. His Team was tasked with keeping watch for snipers or any traps being laid ahead of the troops along the roadway. The six SEALs and several Army snipers who were running the show kept leap-frogging each other, moving from rooftop to rooftop to keep ahead of the column. Other Teams were assigned to other city blocks. The Army was determined to clear a four-block-wide swath of safe zone from the airport to the city center where the palaces and other government buildings sat.

Two blocks ahead of Rivers' position tires squealed as a car whipped a right coming out of an underground parking garage. He found them in his scope just as a teddy bear was dropped to the street and bounced once before coming to rest in the middle of the road. Rivers followed the car through his scope but could only pick out two heads through the back window as it sped away.

When the black vehicle turned into a side road, Rivers lost them, so he lowered his vision back to the bear. He frowned. It could be an IED. More likely it was a comfort toy that a child had dropped or a parent had left on the roof of the car in the haste of fleeing.

Either way, Rivers would have to shoot it. So he focused the crosshairs on the butt of the bear which faced him, and it disintegrated before his eyes. White fluff flew into the air and a light breeze scattered it like tumbleweed down the street. Just a teddy bear. And someone else got to shoot it.

"This is taking way too long," Rivers grumbled.

Rivers squawked the radio in his ear as he kept his eyes roving the streets and windows for threats.

"Echo 31 to Alpha 1." Rivers paused. "Jackson, come in." Rivers waited for a reply. They had decided to use the same call signs and TOC team they'd had in place the day before to make it easier on the team working the radio.

"Sorry about that Echo 31. A genius spilled his coffee."

"Must be nice."

"Watcha need, boss?" Jackson asked.

"I am looking for a spare Black Hawk. This advance up airport road is taking too long to get to our package, and this regiment doesn't need six more snipers in over-watch. It has been really quiet for over four hours. Zero incidents."

"Lemme see what kind of bird I can find for you. How many?"

"I'll take three with me to go after the package. Masterson, Hayes, and MacDaniel. Allen will be IC ahead of the regiment, and Birdie will stay here as well." Rivers decided. Allen and Birdie worked well together and would be more than enough to help cover the Army column. "Everybody got that?" Rivers asked.

A series of "Aye, sir"s filled the airwaves.

"I've got it recorded officially here too, commander." Jackson chimed in in his gravelly voice. "Go get your girl, and I'll vector a bird to you a-sap.

"Mass, Hayes, and Mac," Rivers continued, "hydrate up and meet me at street level. We're going to walk in."

Rivers took his own advice, sipping from his canteen, as he packed up his equipment.

All six men met in the street, and Rivers cuffed Allen on the shoulder. It was time for over-watch to move forward a couple of blocks ahead of the Army. "Howard will back you up, just the next block over, if you need anything." Rivers gave Allen the radio frequency Howard and his Echo Company team were using.

For two blocks the half dozen SEALs walked together, then Allen and Birdie broke off, one to each side of the roadway.

The four stood on what used to be a sidewalk under an over-hanging balcony. Two kept an eye out for threats from windows while Rivers took out his city map with green highlighter designating the airport and the block surrounding the Republican Palace as green zones.

"Its six klicks to the Republican Palace from here. Straight up this airport highway until we get to here," Rivers pointed on the map for Mass. Then a right here, and a left here, then the road curves right back around to the green zone. Two turns. The package is in the block that surrounds the Iraqi Museum. Right here." It was easier to refer to Judah as "the package" because it kept his mind from spinning out with the remembrance of every package he had lost over his career. Mass and Mac switched places so Rivers could show Mac the route, and then Hayes.

"I only see two possible LZs if Jackson can reroute one of those birds our direction. Let's get to it."

The quad walked on the edge of the street. Two going forward and two walking mostly backward to cover their rear. They switched positions at random times so as not to form a pattern if anyone was following their progress and was looking for a point to make the biggest destructive impact on the team. Their highest vulnerability was when changing positions.

When Rivers was walking forward two kilometers later, he took his right hand off the trigger to click into the coms system again. "Any word on that helo?"

"Still on the ground out here on base, Boss. Replacing a fuel line that was strafed on her last flight. Seemed kind of important." Rivers could almost see Jackson's nonchalant shrug.

"We are passing our fist rendezvous option now. Continuing to next option. Sure would be handy to have a lift by the time we are coming home with the package. Is there any fresh intel on that front?"

"Nope. Tech pinged the phone and either the battery was removed, or it is dead." Jackson relayed. Rivers told himself that it didn't mean anything bad at least three times before he started to believe it. "They will continue to ping the phone's SIM. But last time it registered was about ten hundred hours this morning from the same location she described, across from the museum."

"Thanks Alpha 1. Echo 31 out.

"Wait," Jackson called.

"What is it?"

"Sir, the fighting is picking up in that area. Intel puts a pretty fierce fire fight between the Republican Guard and the local guys raging all morning in that location."

"Thank you, Jackson. Out. You heard that gentlemen? Let's pick up the pace."

Chapter Forty Eight

Wakefield ducked as a third stray bullet shattered a clay pot on the far side of the rooftop paradise where she had been sitting and waiting for some signal that the cavalry had arrived.

She grabbed the startled kitten, now named Butter, and the seat cushion where she had been sitting and dashed to the stairwell landing for cover. The Republican Guard had spread out all over the neighborhood as she watched from the safety of the roof. She assumed the soldiers were trying to flank the rebels. The sounds of fighting had been sustained so long she had almost become immune to the barrage of concussions and her bubble-hearing.

She leaned the cushion in an L against the wall and floor of the landing under the shelter and cocked her ear for any danger in the concrete echo chamber five flights up.

Even silence sounded muted in her eardrum, and she pressed her finger to the flap of her ear to try to clear the sound. Her hearing was maybe a little clearer, but with the sounds of bullets popping in double shots and AKs spiting their fire at each other just outside the walls, it was hard to tell.

So she sat down and drew Butter into her lap. Threading her fingers through his soft fur, Judah stroked and the kitten purred in contentment until he was again asleep.

Judah leaned her head back against the wall. The stairwell was still nice and cool from the low overnight temperatures. She closed her eyes, scratchy from so many hours awake and in contacts.

Judah awoke with a shudder. Wild-eyed she tried to assess what had shaken her awake. The kitten stretched in her lap with papery claws spread as wide as his tiny pink mouth. The clatter of a door slamming shut under its own weight echoed up from the ground floor through the stairwell.

She must have heard the door opening in her sleep. It sounded like a dozen pairs of boots on the ground floor, several men had already moved into the stairwell to the first floor. Somewhere below a door was kicked in and several shots were fired.

Moving silently and quickly, Wakefield held her rifle close to keep it from clattering as she rose, groaning as she rose as she remembered her black tablecloth was in the middle of the ground floor lobby with the throw pillow from the fourth floor from her temper tantrum earlier. It would certainly raise questions, though this group that had entered the building didn't exactly seem like a talkative bunch. She had not heard a single voice as yet.

Cracking the door, she prayed that a breeze would not curl its way down the stairwell when she opened the door giving her position away. Feet pounded on the concrete stairs.

Wakefield picked up the kitten and the cushion from the floor and silently slipped through the crack. She pulled the door behind her, but left it ajar. It had seemed to work well in the apartment earlier to set the soldiers at ease. There was no way to hide her entry to the roof. She just hoped they would guess the intruder had left a while ago because of the door being open instead of closed as if someone was hiding.

Hurrying across the paradise that now seemed a prison, Wakefield laid the cushion back on the chair so nothing looked disturbed. Now where to hide?

The taller of the stacked stone fountains stood six feet at its highest point and was flanked by palm trees. From the door, one of the pergolas interrupted the line of sight to that fountain. But that would be the obvious place to hide.

Perhaps among the tall grasses? She could lay flat and the grasses' thick overhang could completely cover her. She could even fire from there, taking them out one at a time as they exited onto the roof.

Wakefield walked behind the stairwell that rose from the floor like a little six by six shed which was about the size of the landing she had just occupied. A giant urn and two large clay-potted palm trees with cracks in them and a few other broken odds and ends filled the space.

This is where she would hunker down. She slid down the wall and then moved a quarter turn to face the only avenue of approach. If someone came around the edge of the building, he wouldn't survive, because she would see him first. After that, the most firepower would survive as the victor.

She leaned back against the solid planter, set her rifle butt against the hollow of her shoulder and rested the barrel on her drawn up knee. She waited. Butter had not followed her behind the shelter.

She listened for the change in volume she anticipated when the rooftop door was opened to the chaos below. The guardsmen were making their way apartment to apartment, probably just angry that this building had not suffered damage from the air attacks of the last few weeks.

Then it came. The door opened, and she heard the soldier gasp. She presumed he was as surprised at the landscape as she had been. She heard him yell back into the stairwell, "Akim, come look at this!"

Wakefield felt her pulse quicken. Her breath went short. She focused on breathing deeply and oxygenating her blood to force her heartbeat back into an optimal firing range. Not that she was likely to miss at point blank range.

Akim whistled low. Now there were two. "Anybody up here?" he asked.

"I didn't see anyone." The first soldier stated hesitantly.

"Look what we have here, Ibrahim." Akim remarked. Butter mewed loudly. Akim must have picked him up.

"Awe! how cute. Somebody must be missing this one." Ibrahim gushed. "Or are you here on your own now, king of your own little kingdom?"

"He has to belong to somebody. He is tiny and not starving to death." Akim said. Wakefield could tell he had bent over to put the kitten down.

Please, don't come find me now, little butterball, Wakefield pled in her mind.

Wakefield stiffled her jump as one of the guardsmen attacked the garden with his weapon on full auto. She winced and plugged one ear, then turned the other away from the direction of the noise as far as she could and still watch the corner someone would come around, if they were going to come.

"Hey, grab the cat. And watch this." It was Akim. Four seconds later Wakefield detected a splash over the other sounds she was processing. She tucked her head and grabbed both ears on autopilot. That was going to be a grenade.

Boom! The floor shook unsteadily, and the atmosphere crashed all around her, sucking the air from her lungs.

She shook her head to recalibrate her brain to upright again.

"That was awesome!" The younger man, Ibrahim, shouted too loud. His hearing had been affected by the blast. "Do it again to the other fountain!"

"No need. There's nobody up here. Let the kitty be and let's go."

"Who's gonna stay at this building?" Wakefield heard Ibrahim's voice diminish as they descended the stairs, but did not catch an answer. But it did lay out a new obstacle for when she would need to leave the building to rendezvous with the extraction team. Were they ever coming?

Her stomach rumbled in discontent. Judah pressed her palm into her midsection under her body armor and said a silent prayer of thanks that it had not made any noise while she was hiding.

Wakefield counted off another ten minutes for the building to clear out before budging an inch. When she cautiously peered around the corner of her hiding place with the thrown-out potted plants, her heart sank at the devastation of the beautiful oasis.

Butter seemed untouched by the changes. He batted a displaced fish between his paws in a puddle.

The fountain of stacked stone and the grasses where she had considered hiding would either one have been her last decision. The rooftop was a mess she couldn't bear to look at, so she returned to the broken plants and sat down among them again.

A steady wup-wup-wup got louder. She jumped to her feet, scanning the sky. Finally, she identified it, coming in from her left. Still a klick and a half away but coming in quickly. A helicopter. She had heard so few today, this one gave her hope. Hope that it was coming for her.

Then a swoosh sounded in the main street half a block from her and she recognized the sound, then she saw the tell-tale vapor trail. A surface-to-air missile.

It traced a line to the chopper that didn't have time for evasive maneuvers in the tight airspace. A direct hit. Wakefield felt the impact in her whole being. The brightness of the explosion scorched the back of her eyeballs, but not before she watched the rotor cartwheel away from the body of the helicopter. The molten ball of fire landed with a screech of metal and thick black smoke plumed that expanded as it ascended.

Wakefield's stomach turned when she heard jeers and the celebratory atk-k-k of assault rifles in the street below her.

So many families destroyed by the deaths of the boys on board. They at home would have no idea for days that their lives had already been upended.

Judah sank to a heap and asked God to send those families grace as they grieved. Butter returned to her lap, sans the fish, and butted his head under her hand until she resumed stroking his fur.

Judah frowned. The emotion of this day was intense. "Thanks, Lord, for sending Butter to keep me company."

Chapter Forty Nine

Rivers felt the concussion of the explosion in his bones and groaned. Less than thirty seconds later the telling acrid smoke rose above the buildings on the street where the Team kept moving. They were only about six or eight blocks away.

"We may need to divert as the closest assets," Rivers told his men as he reached for his mic switch to check in with Jackson.

Rivers described what they had witnessed. "Lemme put you on hold there, Boss," Jackson replied in a subdued voice. "I'll see what I can pick up from the chatter on other freqs. Then I'll patch you in. By the way, your bird is still here on the ground. Refueling at last check in."

"We are going to go ahead and move in that direction." Rivers made the decision. Though it hurt fiercely to move away from getting Judah out of harm's way, he had seen her take care of herself in some difficult situations, and knew his team of four might be the difference between life and death for any survivors from the helo. "The package knows what to do, and I'm sure she saw or at least heard the explosion too."

Rivers led the team to the next cross street to their right. Remaining in their diamond formation and on high alert, Rivers set a faster pace to approach the downed helicopter. He could feel eyes on them, but three blocks in there had still been no incidents.

His experienced sixth sense about these things told Rivers the enemy was surrounding them. "I don't like this," he whispered. "We are breaking away. Next left alley, I don't care how small."

A series of small grunts acknowledged their third change of route.

Rivers spotted the next alley when they were only a dozen yards away at the same moment as Mac, the rear guard, shouted, "Incoming!"

Rivers heard his team scramble. The first shots were doled out. Mac returned fire immediately before even making it to cover.

"I'll cover you," Rivers called over the din of slugs being fired and finding new homes in concrete buildings. He stood immediately and from the cover of the corner of the building at the alley pumped two shots into the man standing fully exposed in the street where they had just been walking.

He went down like overdone spaghetti. Mac crawled into the alley as did Mass. "Keep moving," Rivers instructed, "in a switchback pattern. I'm right behind you." He fired another pair of bullets as a man who stood a block to their rear dashed across the road with a grenade launcher on his shoulder looking for a better angle on where the Team was disappearing into the crack of an alley.

"Got it, Boss," Mass took off ahead; Mac and Hayes followed.

Rivers watched the enemy get comfortable enough to begin to slip out of hiding. He waited in the alley an eternal twenty seconds while his men cleared the alley ahead of their path. He heard a couple of shots and thuds as bodies fell behind him.

Then it was time to shoot and scoot.

Eight men were fully exposed in the street converging on his space when he took his next series of shots. One bullet per body would bring the maximum slow down, so Rivers' next eight shots came in less than four seconds, putting each target down in the street. Statistics said at least two of them would survive, but they would not be chasing after him today, and the probable dozens of men hiding in the wings of doorways and windows and behind parked vehicle in the street would hesitate long enough for the four SEALs to avoid the ambush that had been laid ahead of them as Rivers had suspected. Five of the eight men now lying in the street had come from ahead of their route.

A crackle in Rivers' ear told him that Jackson had connected him to a live frequency where the helo pilot had once been connected.

"…a complete loss of equipment. No radio contact. Before SAM impact, the pilot relayed taking small arms fire. Anyone?" There was a tiny pause. "Looking for a response from anyone in the vicinity of the downed Black Hawk with six souls on board. It is a complete loss of equipment. No radio…"

Rivers could tell the man was repeating the same transmission over and over. At the next break Rivers squawked in. "Lieutenant Commander David Rivers, U.S.N., I have a team of four SEALs about four blocks out. Taking light small arms fire but headed toward the crash site to look for survivors. ETA under five minutes."

"Oh, thank God, commander."

"Will relay a sit rep upon arrival."

"Standing by, Navy."

Rivers caught up to Mac, Mass, and Hayes then, but left his mike on open channel to be recorded as they approached. "Men, we are Search and Rescue for the six souls on the Black Hawk. We will also clear the area for a MEDEVAC to fly in. Mass, you maintain contact with TOC and Jackson. I've moved to a new coms channel."

"Aye." Mass said as his hefty bulk led the Team to their left on another switchback down a slightly wider alley, getting them ever closer to the smoke billowing upward.

Rivers could taste the ash in the air and heard the roaring fire before he could see the remains of the helo. It was going to be hot.

Moe's Amil District Neighborhood
8 April 2003
5:30 pm

Moe opened the last cupboard in his kitchen to find only a dusty can of mixed vegetables with a torn label. He sighed and glanced at Takita curled up in the one armchair remaining in the living room. She was covered in the quilt from Aroosh's bed. Takita's eyes were closed, but the tense set of her jaw told Moe the girl was not at rest.

"I'm going to see if I can find some food. Would you like to go or stay, Takita?" Moe asked gently. He remembered just then about Liliya's kitchen money stash under the silverware sorter in the top drawer. It would be helpful to have those small bills for any food he could find. He opened the drawer, and then halted in surprise as Takita answered.

"I still have an orange and a pita." Her tone of voice also suggested a silent "please don't go" tacked onto the end of her statement.

He didn't want to discourage her talking. She had hardly spoken a dozen words to him since they entered the house over 18 hours earlier. She didn't even comment on the natural air-conditioning where the side of the building was missing, or the stairs that were missing on the way in. "You can go ahead and eat them, I will find us some food with God's help and we won't go hungry."

"What God do you believe in?" Takita's breathy voice was barely detectable as she stared beyond a corner in the room.

How much do I say? Moe prayed silently and pulled out Liliya's fabric sachet of money from under the silverware sorter. "I believe in the only True God. God of Abraham, Isaac, and Jacob. The God who made heaven and earth and you and me." He pushed the drawer closed. "The God who sent his Son to die for the forgiveness of sin."

It seemed to Moe that the words sat heavy in the air. The atmosphere had shifted somehow with his declaration. Takita's eyelids blinked like a baby fighting sleep. Moe waited a full minute or more before Takita's voice was able to swim to the surface again.

"The Christian God. My Omy..." she paused in using the little-girl form of referring to her mother. "My Omy told me about Isa. It feels like it was such a long time ago." The girl's voice trailed off again. Moe could tell she was reliving some experience in her mind.

"What was a long time ago?" Moe asked.

"Well. Something strange happened." Takita struggled for words and glanced at him with focused eyes for the first time

383

that he remembered. "I don't think you'll believe me. I don't know if I believe me."

"I'll give it a shot." Moe said and shrugged. He remained standing in the small kitchen area with his hand resting on the counter top over Liliya's money sack while Takita sat in a ball with her feet in the seat under his daughter's blanket. She seemed to be opening up with a little space around her, and he didn't want to shut her down with any movement.

"I think your Jesus got me out of...of." She looked deeper into the corner where she had returned to her 1500-yard stare. "I was in someplace I cannot say. And instead of praying to Allah of my Aby, I prayed to Jesus of my Omy." Takita's hand appeared out of the folds of the blanket and reached up to stroke her short hanks of hair. For a moment Moe thought she might cry, then her face blanked of emotion again.

"What happened?" Moe asked.

"I'm trying to figure out." Her face wrinkled with the effort. "My friend Jocina came in and took me to the dungeon prison, you know, underground."

Moe nodded, though he had only heard horror stories of legend quality about the labyrinth under the palaces and parts of Baghdad. Why would this little one's friend take her there?

"She took me to the east side, where it is not so bad. Well, Jocina said it was not so bad as the west side." Takita's head shook from side to side. "She was a maid. I don't think she was right." Her brow furrowed like an old corn field. "Can it be worse than only bread and water once a day? Being locked away all alone? It was weeks! The sounds and the stench..." The girl shuddered under the quilt.

Moe leaned forward and softly said, "Oh yes, dear one, it could have been much worse. In the west, prisoners do not receive food at all, only water from the river. There are dozens of men crammed in small, damp cells together, and drinking the river water gives them dysentery. Many do not survive the first week, much less several weeks. The um, well, I don't know what the group is called, but Saddam's doctors and scientists team experiment on the western dungeon's population with chemical combinations."

A tiny oh escaped Takita's lips. "I didn't know."

"I wish you had not known either side." Moe bit the inside of his cheek to steel his emotions.

"Why did your Jesus send me there? Why didn't he get me out?" Takita broke the weighty stare again to find his eyes.

"I don't know, Takita. I don't know why you had to suffer all the things you've had to suffer in your short life. Can we find your family?"

"They are all dead." So was her voice.

"Oh." Moe moved toward her then. Unsure how to best comfort one so young who had experienced too much, he placed his hand on the top of her head. "I am so sorry for all you have lost." He couldn't stop himself from turning to the only One who could provide any comfort. "Oh, Holy Spirit of the Living God, bring your comforting presence of peace to restore Takita to life."

Then Moe just stood there. His palm covered her chunky hair. Her chin rested on her drawn up knees. Tears began to slip down her cheeks.

A few minutes later the girl snuffled and raised her head. "I remember this feeling," she said. "From when I was alone in my cell. Sometimes it felt like this. Like I wasn't alone. That's the part I didn't think you'd believe. But you feel it too, don't you, sir?"

"I do. That is the holy presence of the God of Abraham, Isaac, and Jacob. The God who loves you." Moe paused a moment. "And you don't have to call me *sir*. My name is fine."

"Sorry," Takita look up at him. "I forgot your name." She wrinkled her nose, looking present for the first time. "And it seemed awkward to ask after all this time."

Moe couldn't help releasing a deep chuckle. "I imagine that's true." He laughed again and this time Takita actually giggled a little herself. "I'm Moe. You can call me Moe," he said.

"Moe." She tried it out. "I don't think you ever told me your name.

"Sorry about that. I suppose my mother did not teach me the proper rules of introduction to girls who fall out of walls." He shook his head. "You can help me do better next time, eh?" They both laughed at his dad humor. "You ready to go find some food with *Moe*?" He smiled.

"I think I'll stay here. But you will come back?"

"As soon as I can."

Chapter Fifty

Rivers kept a close watch in the deepening shadows as the Team approached the crash site. The fire still roared furiously, throwing a column of dense smoke upward. He wasn't hearing any gunfire, at least none close to them. Occasional pops broke through the sound of the fire from other districts in the city. Especially from the direction of the airport.

Rivers' first look at the wreck reminded him of a dead elephant, down by the trunk, with its rear in the air. The helo skids had either been crushed by the impact or blown off in the explosion, because the helo inferno burned at street level.

The dark shape of a body leaned forward over the stick in the pilot seat. The copilot's door was crushed in an open position, but the seat was empty. The sliding back door lay on the street in two chunks of metal among many other unidentifiable bits and parts and lumps of molten metal that would mean more to a forensic team than it did to him at the moment. Rivers strained to peer through the bright flames and check for more men. Impossible to tell, he decided.

Mac who had led the team around the last corner of protection had already begun a side step into the area with his back against the building, his weapon at the ready. Rivers followed. And the four of them began to work the crash site on critical high alert, watching for threats, high and low, looking for survivors, and looking for bodies.

Mac suddenly crouched down along the perimeter of the scene. Rivers stopped in place but didn't take his eyes off the shadows. It was a perfect time to pick off first responders with a sniper rifle. Even an old AK-47 spraying bullets haphazardly would do the trick if the shooter waited for the right moment.

"Got a live one!" Mac called up, not too loud for the enemy in the shadows to hear, but enough to let the Team know.

The three cocooned around Mac and the man on the ground while Mac assessed him. "I've got movement at my ten o'clock." Mass thundered as he brought his rifle up to zero in on the movement.

"What's going on down there, Mac? We need to keep moving." Rivers asked.

"A shattered shin and a gunshot wound to the same thigh."

"Is he conscious?"

"Yes, sir," replied the man. "The lieutenant kicked us off our ride before the SAM hit. I may have been the last one out."

A quick pop-pop from Mass, interrupted the wounded man. "One down." Mass said, but I may have just kicked over a hornet's nest."

"I see it, Mass." The shadows swarmed like ants now. "How many men am I looking for, Army?" Rivers asked the wounded man quickly.

"At least three others. I saw them go out. Oww! Careful!" The soldier sucked air in between clenched teeth.

388

Rivers smiled despite the circumstances. Mac was not known for his gentle touch when packing a bullet wound to stop the bleeding. "Mac, when you have him patched up, drag him to cover and give him your side arm. Then take up the rear. We are going to keep looking and draw the enemy away. What's your name, Army?"

"Jennings."

"Jennings," Rivers said. "Don't go to sleep. Don't even close your eyes for a minute. You copy?"

"I copy, sir."

"Hey, TOC, did you get all that?" Rivers asked into his open mic.

"Got it. Jennings, alive, wounded.

"Where's that MEDEVAC?"

"Crew is scrambling now. I'll get you an ETA as soon as they're airborne."

Rivers had been counting silently as the enemy streamed out of the building where Mass had taken out the first combatant. The guards moved both right and left. Some of them were going to circle around behind the Team. At two dozen, Rivers quit counting.

"Anybody have a grenade handy?" he asked. He wanted to stem the flow of the rapidly increasing odds against his small team.

Hayes pressed one into his open hand almost before he finished the question.

Rivers pulled the pin, waited one second, while his brain calculated the wind up and flight time for the 70-yard throw. He wasn't actually doing the math; it came as a gut feeling of *now!* Rivers reared back and released the grenade in perfect form and follow through. While at the Naval Academy on a daily practice

389

schedule, Rivers had once cockily placed a baseball on a spot the size of a folding chair at this distance. Today, he had the leeway of a couple of beach towels laid end to end to get the grenade into the entryway spilling out soldiers. Rivers didn't bother to watch the grenade's flight toward its mark.

With the other two immediately following him, Rivers advanced quickly in the same direction that Mac had been establishing. He kept his weapon at shoulder level with his finger loose on the trigger.

Rivers got off two shots, aiming just behind muzzle flashes in the shadows that were spitting steel in their direction, before the grenade exploded. He felt Mass take at least one more shot and saw Hayes' muzzle flash a few times toward their rear.

Mayhem broke loose then. Bullets whizzed, coming even through the flames in the middle of the street where everyone on both sides kept their distance by hugging the perimeter.

The rumble of tumbling rock and buckling concrete escalated quickly. Rivers traced it with his eyes in time to see the second story of the building that had received his hand grenade cave into a V at the entryway. The two stories on top of that buckled under the pressure and broke in half collapsing in giant hunks of concrete that piled on top of the rubble below. As the chunks hit the sharp rubble underneath, they cracked further, evidence of shoddy building materials.

Anyone left on the ground floor was pulverized or crushed and trapped in a tiny air pocket. But the troops had stopped mounting against them. The SEALs now had to take care of the ones already on the loose, and any reinforcements that showed up.

The string of vehicles parked along the road—for who knows how long because everything now carried an equal layer of dust and soot—provided a perfect cover to shoot from. Unfortunately, the cars parked with equal frequency on both sides of the firefight. Most of the windows sparkled in a billion pieces on the street while reflecting the red, orange, and yellow flames.

Rivers and Mass crouched behind a car with a massive trunk that was almost two decades old. Rivers definitely preferred more distance between himself and his target, but he would take what he could get. He and Mass crouched at a tire to help absorb any low shots. Hayes, behind them, kept the middle covered between their position and where Mac was stashing Jennings in an alley.

While exchanging near-deafening volleys of bullets, Rivers itched to get up the street. He knew from the layout of the street, helicopter, and where Jennings had been discovered, that searching for any Americans ahead of the chopper's path made no sense. They would be at the downed helo or along the path where they exited as they flew their route in.

Rivers cocked his head and sighed with delight. "Too easy." A string of four Republican Guards of nearly equal height lined themselves up perfectly for a simple shot for Rivers. He started with the one in the back and moved to the closest one. So they landed on top of one another in the same neat line they had been trying to advance in. Four bullets, four body drops. He even conserved ammunition.

A man straightened up from behind a car in the vicinity nearest the collapsed entryway. Rivers identified a live shoulder rocket. "I've got him." He told Mass. Rivers aimed for the center of the white tip on the rocket, rather than the man. Just in case, Rivers sent a double shot down the throat of the rocket launcher.

The rocket detonated before leaving the tube, taking with it the six men close to it in a fireball. No one would be reusing that launching tube again. That helped the SEALs' odds significantly.

Mass was picking off men one at a time. They kept following one another around a small transport truck, which must have been empty because it had multiple bullet pricks in its panel siding and it had not exploded yet. Mass waited until a soldier made it fully around the truck so that those behind him could not see the danger ahead. Then he sent a bullet to catch him. The pile of bodies was beginning to mount. Besides that spot, the forward group of Republican Guards was down. So Rivers left Mass to his game of cat and mouse to check on Mac and Hayes.

Hayes had two clips beside him on the ground and was reaching for his side arm as Mac scurried toward Hayes' position. Hayes seemed to be holding off the half of the enemy who had gone this direction pretty well on his own. More enemy combatants had to be seeping into the area from somewhere. The number of bodies littering the street should not have left as many people still firing at them as there were.

Rivers whistled, and Mac turned from his takedown shot with smoke still wisping from the barrel. Rivers tilted his head to let them know they were moving out. He took aim over their heads and fired one shot per second toward the flank until Mac and Hayes caught up with Mass.

"Are they going to find Jennings?" Rivers asked Mac. He hated to leave him behind.

"Never, Boss." I stuffed him in a trash bin and covered him with some pretty stinky stuff.

"I'm sure he'll thank you later." Rivers grimaced.

"While I was waiting for Hayes to clear me a spot to run and we still had a little daylight, I think I spotted another one of our guys." Mac was running at half height behind the line of vehicles and next to Rivers. He pointed up the road in the direction Rivers had determined to search next. "There's a silvery SUV with a very awkwardly dented roof. It's 'bout another block up from here."

"Lead on," Rivers positioned Mac in front again.

Sure enough, even in the darkness, lit only by the fire father than two blocks back, while they were still two cars away Rivers could see a body lying in a dented-in SUV roof.

There was no chest movement, so Rivers didn't hold a lot of hope. Mac reached up to feel for a pulse at the man's neck. Hayes turned back to cover Mac's movement with half a dozen rounds.

"Go easy on the ammo," Rivers warned. "We've got a long night ahead of us."

"No joy." Hayes said. "This was James Bevins, private first class." Hayes crouched low again as he tucked the man's dog tags in his breast pocket. They would not be able to take the body with them until a larger force arrived.

"That's three including the pilot." Rivers spoke into his throat mic. One live, two deceased."

Chapter Fifty One

Moe shouldered the straps of Liliya's empty green grocery bag and fingered the little fabric sack of coins and small bills tucked into his roomy robe pocket. Stepping into the quickly cooling evening air he looked up at the purple velvet sky. The stars weren't visible yet, but they would be soon. The constant background soundtrack of bullets being flung back and forth continued as it had for days, weeks even. Nothing too close though. A particularly large plume of black smoke danced into the heavens and disappeared against the darkness of the sky.

"Where am I going to find food enough for the both of us?" Moe wondered as he wandered. He felt a twinge of guilt at the tiniest pinch of relief he felt that he wasn't searching for food for five or six people, just two.

He walked by a local Arabic and Indian restaurant tightly padlocked behind a steel grate. It wasn't exactly located in a restaurant district, but they had cheap food and the owner, whose wife was Indian and the main cook, said they did pretty good with their take-out family meals. Moe wondered if they were ok. He had no idea where they lived, but it was probably close.

He passed an ATM that looked like it had been mauled by a pack of tigers. Then he turned to go up to the normal grocer that he and Liliya used when they were getting staple items that were not available in larger quantities at the local corner market where he normally picked up fresh pita and a vegetable or two every day.

Moe was glad to see that he was not the only one on the street after dark, but all his neighbors looked at their feet and walked with the weight of the world on their shoulders.

Grocery carts were chained together outside the establishment next to two men with guns across their chests. The older man held a shiny new AK-74 automatic rifle with a folding stock; the younger man, Moe thought he could be the older man's teenage son, nervously fidgeted with a wooden-stocked rifle that looked leftover from the Ottoman Empire. The new 74 was lowered to Moe's gut height, and he swallowed hard.

"Have you got money to pay?" the man asked.

"Yes, of course." Moe said raising his hands.

"Let me see it."

"I'm just going to reach into my right pocket slowly." Moe said. "Are you the owner?"

"Yes. But I'm tired of being robbed." The man's face softened when Moe loosened the strings of Liliya's fabric sack to show the man his ability to pay. "Very well. Take only what you can carry, so there is enough for everyone until the trucks start running again. My brother-in-law will check you out when you are ready."

"Thank you," Moe bowed slightly at the waist. "This is really good of you."

Moe squeezed through the space between the stacked concrete blocks that allowed the main door to open only eighteen inches or so. The store had more stock available than he expected. Even produce lay out in non-refrigerated cases, though the fruit looked to be in better shape than most of the green vegetables and lettuces.

He grabbed a few oranges for the vitamin C and some wilty spinach for iron. Just as he was about to head for canned goods, meat especially, that would not have to be cooked with electricity, Moe remembered a camp stove that he had bought and stored for a camping trip when the girls were little. He scurried over to find that fuel cells and matches were still available! He took eight days-worth of those little cans of fuel. No bread was left, but plenty of boxed cereal and one dozen eggs with only one broken egg in the container remained on the shelf. He hurried back to the produce section to find more vegetables, especially potatoes and onions to add to the canned chicken and fish. Now that he had a way to heat food, soup wouldn't be bad. Salt and garlic and one pound each of white sugar and white flour filled his quota. He slowed his trot to the cash register only long enough to pick up a bag of quick-cook pasta that he carried, confident it would fit once he repacked with the heavier items loaded on the bottom.

The older woman in front of him returned the flashlight she had borrowed and began to repack her bag. Moe laid his items on the counter. His heart was racing. He had felt such a hurry to get the stuff, make the best decisions for nutrition and taste, variety and ability to eat, he suddenly hoped Liliya had stashed away enough cash. He had not even considered the cost of the goods as he ran around the store.

Baghdad Intersection
Crash Site
1850 hours

Over an hour after the crash, the fire still threw smoke into the air over the neighborhood. Rivers and his Team were still searching every block and each alley for survivors and bodies of the three unaccounted for Army soldiers on the Black Hawk. It was difficult to see any distance in the dark since the sun had set and the fire had died down.

Rivers squinted against the dark. He thought he saw a lump in the street a block and a half ahead. Maybe his eyes were playing tricks on him. Then a definite figure scurried across the street.

Rivers stiffened.

"I saw it too, Boss," Hayes said behind him.

"Stay under the parked car cover and approach silently, 800 feet ahead. Mass and I will pop up on this side. Hayes, you and Mac continue two car lengths ahead of the action."

Just over ninety seconds later, with the four of them in place, Rivers stood to full height and walked between the parked cars. He had his sidearm drawn with the silencer screwed in place for this close-up work. Pointing the Glock at the back of a lump of a person dressed all in black he realized why he had had so much trouble distinguishing what was going on. The woman's black garb had absorbed the slight firelight instead of reflecting it. He could see lighter colored skin on the backs of her young hands. The woman was making quick work of rifling through the pockets of a U.S. Army serviceman. Rivers recognized the camo pattern on the one pant leg that stuck out behind the woman and stretched toward Rivers' position.

397

Rivers pinched his lips together and gave a little up-down whistle to get the woman's attention. She started so badly that she fell backward, landing on her rear end, and the watch in her hand fell to the street. But she managed to whip her neck around to the noise.

Her eyes widened like she was being attacked by a phantom. Her mouth gaped wide but no sound came out. Her open-mouth breathing came in three shallow gulps of air. But her gaze confused Rivers. She was looking not at him but about a foot or so above his head and behind him. Mass should have been still crouched behind the vehicle covering him toward their rear and across the street.

She scrambled over the body of the soldier in the street like a wounded animal. The woman's gaze never wavered though. Her hand disappeared into a fold of her clothing and then deposited respectfully a few white pieces of paper on the ground. When she finally broke her gaze and turned and ran, Rivers dared a glance behind him to see what had captivated her so radically. Only darkness.

"That was weird." Mass whispered.

Rivers had an idea of what she had seen; he had heard tales from other wars. But he would think about that later.

A light breeze skittered the papers across the rough road and Rivers stamped his boot to still two and stooped to pluck up the third. Family photos. Rivers shuffled them with thick fingers just as he heard the first light whup-whup-whup of a helo on approach about two miles out.

He pressed two fingers into the soldier's throat to check for a pulse. His flesh was still warm, but there was no vibration of life left in him.

"Set a flare and clear an LZ." Rivers ordered his men. "TOC, do you copy?"

"Copy, Navy."

"We found another one." Rivers freed the man's dog tags and shone his Maglite on their silvery surface. "Conner didn't make it either. The helo is a mile out. Setting flares and clearing the area for a safe descent."

"Thank you. That makes three deceased and one live. Two still M.I.A."

"Our counts agree." Rivers rose to his full height to help his men watch for any enemy movement that would threaten the helicopter's safe landing.

When the chopper was close enough for rotor wash to begin to stir up dust in the street, Rivers was facing the direction the first helo had gone down. The flash of automatic gun fire grabbed his attention from the corner of his left eye. "Take cover." Rivers warned as he ducked behind the rear tire of another vehicle.

As a shooter it was nice to include tracer bullets in your ammo clip for being able to accurately adjust aim at night. As a chaser, tracer bullets were just as helpful to draw a path directly back to the spot the barrage was coming from. A third-story window with the curtain half open. Rivers took three neat shots, centering his rifle's crosshairs across the window's width at four inches higher than the tracer bullets were originating.

The tracer bullets then sewed a harmless row of stitches of light from the ground all the way into the night sky before silencing all together.

Rivers heard one of his men also take out a threat.

The helo buzzed the Team and the red flare, kicking up a whirlwind. Rivers closed his eyes into slits to keep the dust out but still maintain a watchful look out.

The chopper flew right past without stopping. It banked right to circle around.

Rivers lifted his eyes to the building tops. The pilot was probably looking for a wider place to set the chopper down. A place that offered a little more margin for error than a few feet either direction as this narrow street with its three- and four-story buildings had.

As the rotor noise and wind died down, a choppy whistle pierced the night. Short-short-short long-long-long. Rivers recognized it as the beginning of a Morse code S-O-S before the whistler even got to the second S. Rivers zeroed in on the rooftop where it originated. Another 2 blocks away.

They had another live one!

Rivers blasted away a two-fingers-to-the-mouth whistle worthy of a stadium and took off running toward the soldier. He slapped Mass on the shoulder as he passed by to get him to follow.

"We found another one alive, TOC." Rivers updated the man on the other end of his mic. "Rooftop about two more blocks south."

"Excellent!" The man said. Rivers heard him repeat the information to someone on his end before he came back to him. "That will either be Vinchenzo or Spencer."

"Copy that." Rivers said as he and Mass ran.

"Your MEDEVAC called back that they see you and are looking for a LZ. They will radio coordinates a-sap."

"Copy that." Rivers said. "Mass and I are at the residence where the soldier signaled from. Going radio silent as we breach and until we know what we're up against."

"Good luck, Navy."

"We don't deal in luck, kid. We're SEALs." Rivers retorted. But even as he reached for the door that he thought should offer a way to the roof, his mind flashed to the woman in the street who was more scared of his shadow than the handgun he had pointed at her.

Chapter Fifty Two

Moe hiked the green grocery bag up on his shoulder for the fiftieth time or more and looked both ways before hauling himself up the break in the dilapidated staircase to his home.

He thought of the place he had brought Takita into through her eyes. He closed his eyes in shame. He and Liliya had provided a happy home for their children before all this destroyed even the walls that kept out dirt and noise. His heart gripped onto the name. Liliya.

With every step he climbed, Moe forced himself to unwrap his thought tentacles that clung to the joyful picture of her face as she turned to look at him in his mind. For survival, for Takita, for finding Liliya, their daughters and little son, he had to shove the longing for her into a little treasure box that sat in the shadows of his heart. He turned a key in the lock and placed the key in his pocket. No, he changed the thought. Moe managed a small smile, as in his mind he hung the key to his thought-box around his neck, so it could lie next to his heart.

Breathless, Moe leaned against the cool stairwell wall on his landing. He walked everywhere in Baghdad most of the time, but those stairs with an extra twenty-plus pounds of groceries, made his heart and lungs really work.

A crack of candlelight shined through the seam at the door to his flat.

Through breaks in the muted gun battle taking place in the neighborhood he heard a man's voice. Coming from inside his apartment. With Takita.

Moe dropped the green bag of food and pushed open the door forcefully. "What's the meaning of this?" he roared.

Takita shrank back, eyes wide. The man whose back was to the door turned toward him, and Moe's hands went to his hips indignantly. He took up the entire doorway as the door slapped loudly against the wall.

Moe deflated just as quickly.

"I apologize," Moe recognized his neighbor, Jamali al Baghdadi. He had spoken to Jamali's wife day before yesterday while Jamali had been asleep. "Takita, thank you for showing our guest hospitality. It's okay," Moe gestured her to resume her place at the kitchen counter where she had prepared tea. "Please rejoin us."

Takita took a shy step back to her teacup, but jumped back again as Moe gasped and whirled around. "Oh the food!" He pictured cabbages rolling down the stairs, even though he didn't buy any cabbages.

Moe had to move out of the candlelight to see around his own shadow. Only a few of the potatoes that he had placed loosely into the bag around the boxes and other vegetables had spilled out onto the landing. Moe grimaced as he turned the bag right-side up and saw the egg carton. Maybe he could salvage the broken ones if he hurried.

As Moe straightened up and hitched the bag over his shoulder, it hit him. He looked up at Takita. "You made tea? Wait. How did you make tea?"

He didn't know what his face looked like, but it must have been pretty funny because the girl who had been through so much in the last months broke into a wide grin that showcased even white teeth. "Come look." she said.

Moe glanced at Jamali. He was smiling broadly, but did not interrupt.

"We didn't wait for it to actually boil the water." Takita said. Moe slid the groceries onto the counter, his eyes now fixed on the stovetop. "Maybe we should have, in case there is a break in any of the waterlines from all the bombs. But next time we will. See, I used these little candles I found in the drawer. I put three here in the well." She pointed to the burner area of Moe's electric stove where she had removed the eye and set it on the back burner. "Then I put these two wooden spoons down, so the flame could still get oxygen." She pointed to two long-handled cooking spoons. "Then I balanced the skillet with a lid on top of them."

Moe looked at the set up. "And you used the skillet instead of a pan because?" He could see the intelligence of it, but he wanted to let her tell it.

"Because the skillet's surface area distribution of heat would heat the water faster." She might as well have added "of course" but she didn't. She just shrugged.

"I can't wait to get my wife to try this." Jamali said.

"There is still tea. Do you want some?" Takita asked pointing to the teapot she had wrapped in a bath towel.

As Moe nodded Jamali peered into the green bag. "Where did you get food? Everywhere I've been has been ransacked or is closed up tight."

While stirring his tea, Moe explained how to get to the store and what his neighbor should expect. No sugar or milk, it was his habit to stir tea.

"I guess you're wondering why I'm here." Jamali said when the conversation lulled from the normal pleasantries. Even the shooting seemed to take a breath to refresh at that moment.

"You are welcome anytime, my brother." Moe shook his head, but he noted the dread that had moved into his stomach cavity with his neighbor's words. He braced himself.

Jamali looked all around the kitchen and living area not able to let his eyes rest anywhere.

"Go ahead." It was Takita that finally broke the tension. "It is better to know." She spoke as if she already knew. And perhaps Jamali had already told her.

"Do not fear, my brother." Moe touched the man's shoulder.

Jamali sniffed and found a spot on the tile floor to inspect while he recited his story. "Sarina, my wife, told me only an hour ago that you had come by to ask questions about your wife, Liliya."

"Yes, and the children." Moe nodded. Jamali didn't seem to notice the interruption.

"I am sorry. I didn't know you didn't know until she told me today. I would have come sooner."

He seemed to be begging for forgiveness. "It is okay, my friend. What do you know?"

Jamali still stared at the floor. "I saw them taken from this apartment by the SRG. It was almost week ago."

"You're sure?"

"You know I have a good view of your front stairs from my living room. I saw the truck and their red triangle insignia from there." Jamali finally looked up, but his gaze settled somewhere beyond Moe's shoulder.

"No, I mean the day. What day did you see them come for Liliya and the children?" Moe's mind spun with possibilities, probabilities, and grief. The Special Republican Guard were six battalions—of 1200 to 1500 men each—of super-soldiers spoken of in hushed tones. They were charged with protecting the Husseins, the palaces, and everything related to the president. When the SRG came for someone, they were not generally alive a week later. *But maybe*, Moe's mind grasped at a bubble of hope, *maybe it was the Americans disguised as the SRG.*

"Um," Jamali's eyes rolled left and back to the floor without daring to look at Moe. "Well, it was right after I had brought the kids' bicycles in from the balcony. You know after the air raids started. So it must have been...last Thursday. Maybe it was Friday." Jamali finally looked up, though he still avoided Moe's eyes. "I missed going to prayer at the mosque on Friday and it threw off the calendar in my head."

Moe took a moment to think. What day had he and Liliya concocted the plan for him to go to the Americans? It was after work on Tuesday, March 25. He had gone to work like normal on Wednesday and kissed his girls and his son goodnight, sending them to bed early so he could go over the plan once more with Liliya after dark. Then he had struck out in his truck going south, hugging the edge of town. So many of the helicopters flying over the neighborhood had come from that direction. Liliya had agreed that was the direction to take.

He remembered turning off the engine and leaving the key under the seat where the stuffing was falling out. He wondered briefly if the truck was still there on the side of the road in the last neighborhood on the south edge of Baghdad with the other vehicles, less than three kilometers from the American base where Missy Judah lived.

He had quickly walked those three kilometers with the taste of freedom snapping at his heels. He asked the first soldier he had come to for asylum in the United States because of the religious persecution he and his family were suffering. Of course, it was not as bad as other people had faced, but he and Liliya had not told many people of their Christian conversion either. After the conversation with his mom, they had decided to wait. The waiting had turned into years of avoiding talking about the topic that was most dear to them. What had happened? What had he and Liliya done in teaching their older girls about sharing Isa's love? Where were they now? How had the SRG made the connection? He had spoken to no one until he arrived at the base around midnight between Wednesday and Thursday. He knew Liliya had said nothing.

Liliya had told Aroosh and Rohi that he had left for work early before they woke up on Thursday. They wouldn't have had an opportunity to tell any of their friends because they didn't know he was missing until Thursday night when he didn't come home from work. There was no school on Friday or Saturday.

But Jamali said they were taken on Thursday or Friday. It had to have been Friday afternoon. The SRG was always more active on Fridays after afternoon prayers. But the only ones who knew he was gone on Friday afternoon were the Americans.

Moe schooled his features realizing he had taken too long to respond. "Thank you for coming all this way to tell me about Liliya and the children."

He needed to think. Why? How?

Jamali must have either sensed he needed to be alone with his thoughts, or he was anxious to depart after spilling his bad news, because he made for the door without finishing his tea.

Moe bolted the door after his friend and put the groceries away by rote. Three broken eggs went into the skillet to start their long cooking process over the tiny candles. Takita stood at his elbow to watch. Two words ran on a carousel in his mind. Why? How? Why? How?

Baghdad Crash Site
1955 hours

Mass took the stairs behind Rivers in silence. Standing five feet below the landing on a pitted-concrete stairwell, Rivers clenched his fist in signal to Mass. They both stopped short. Quietly waiting for the next volley of fire or helo pass to provide some cover noise, they watched.

A pair of kids sat on the dusty concrete floor moving pieces on some sort of board game in a patch of moonlight shining through a common window at the end of the hall thirty feet away. It was probably fine, but Rivers wouldn't take chances.

The boy was probably six or seven and the girl maybe eight. They took turns nicely, but hardly spoke to each other. The whirring helo advanced toward the area again, getting louder as it got closer. No response from the children; they just played their game.

Rivers held his elbows away from his body and pressed heavy hands against his rifle slung across his chest to keep the dangling weapon from tapping against snaps or zippers and making noise. He and Mass stole silently up the next flight of stairs while the helicopter was about a half-mile out circling for an LZ.

They passed the fourth-floor landing cleanly and continued to the roof-access level. If Rivers had figured correctly, the man who had signaled them should be through that door and thirty to forty feet further down the side.

The door used a common metal crash bar to access it from inside. Rivers crouched down and eased it open after Mass was in place above him with his rifle nosing through the crack at the doorjamb first. They attracted no immediate fire. Rivers pushed the door open all the way.

The moon lit the ghosty roof-scape from their left. Fluttering, flapping, levitating figures twisted like an army of wide apparitions before them. It was a full two seconds before Rivers brain was able to identify laundry hanging to dry—lots of laundry, factory-level laundry. It flapped in the wind of the helicopter fly-by while light-colored robes, dresses, scarves, and sheets reflected the moonlight.

Rivers let his breath go and it came out in a funny little wheeze.

Mass gave a nose-chuckle too.

They hustled side by side toward the far-right edge of the rooftop.

A little whistle drew Rivers' attention. He shifted the business end of his gun toward the sound. A figure in white began moving toward him from one of the lines of sheets. "It's just me." The apparition said in a mid-western twang of English.

"Take off the sheet and show us some ID." Mass said.

"Sorry about that." The figure appeared to bunch up from the bottom and then float to the ground from a height of about six feet.

Rivers lowered his weapon as the man in U.S. Army fatigues reached toward his collar and pulled out his dog tags.

"Corporal Alex Vinchenzo, U.S. Army, at your service. And boy am I glad to see you!" As he stepped closer, Rivers picked out freckled farm-boy features that matched his accent.

"What's with playing ghost, Vinnie?" Mass asked.

"Vinchenzo." The young corporal corrected as if he'd done it a thousand times a week. "I had a run in with a couple of kids who wanted to play up here about an hour ago. I donned the sheet and scared them off. Couldn't have them telling anybody I was up here or running into Spencer."

"Spencer is here too?" Rivers asked glancing around for him.

"Yes." Vinchenzo hesitated. "But he didn't survive the fall." The man turned and began walking toward the far corner of the rooftop.

Rivers saw the shape of a body draped with a sheet lying in the corner of the rooftop. He tapped into his mic again. "Navy to Army TOC. Come in. We've got the last two."

"What was that, Navy? I didn't copy."

"We found Vinchenzo and Spencer. One dead, one live. Do we have pick-up coordinates yet?"

"Still working on that. Thanks for the update. Is that all men accounted for?"

"Yes, by my count."

"Thank you. It is pretty crazy here, and I lost my tally sheet."

Rivers rolled his eyes. "Well don't lose *us*, kid. We are still waiting for the MEDEVAC to set down. Out."

Rivers peeled the sheet back to check Spencer in case the corporal had missed anything. "What happened?" he asked Vinchenzo as he dug two fingers into Spencer's neck to check for a pulse. The skin had already cooled considerably in the night air.

We had incoming small arms fire. Then Havilland, the pilot, picked up the vapor trail of a SAM. He told us to bail immediately. Spencer and I got out first since we were sitting by the doors in the back. We both just rolled right out." He slowed the story to look around.

"I twisted and turned in the air so much and then all of a sudden I slowed down, and bounced back up a little then started heading down again. It was the clothes lines." He pointed, and Rivers stood to get a clear view of two aluminum poles bent into an arch. "I don't know how I got so lucky. I landed flat across three lines and when I touched down on them the second time the end poles just kind of bowed over and deposited me on my butt. I don't even have a scratch." He held out uniformed sleeves as if Rivers could see underneath the cloth.

Vinchenzo stared at Spencer's face until Rivers reached back down and covered him up. "And him?"

"He wasn't so lucky." Vinchenzo's features squeezed together. "I guess the width of the Black Hawk was the difference between life and death. He came down back-first, same as me, but he landed on the half wall there."

"You're both lucky you didn't end up impaled on one of these laundry poles." Mass said.

Rivers grimaced. It would have been grizzly work recovering Spencer's body from that.

"It was bad enough the way his body was contorted and balanced on that wall." Vinchenzo looked down. "I got sick twice before I could finally get him down."

Rivers reached out a hand to squeeze the young man's shoulder in support. Vinchenzo was about the same age as his younger brother, Sam. "It's ok. I got sick my first time too." Rivers admitted.

"Really?" The young man glanced up to hold Rivers' eyes, his face aching for hope.

"I think it is because we are never supposed to see things like that. Our mortality. Man was not created to taste or see death."

Chapter Fifty Three

Judah replaced the last curtain rod that held the sheer white panels of fabric on the pergola, once so beautiful in their swaying, now tattered by 39mm-bullet holes. She dropped the last panel into the three-foot heap and jumped down from the chair she had dragged over to reach the pole.

She took her next quarter-hourly stroll around the perimeter of the rooftop, looking down on all the streets for any sign of the SAR operation coming to get her. Judah had lost count of the number of laps she had made around the disastrous Eden. In the darkness she had lost the smoke of the downed Black Hawk. Though she could easily pick out lights shining in most areas of Baghdad except the one in which she stood.

If I just had a phone, she wished again. She had been considering trying to make her way to the crash site and catching a ride out of town with the medical responders. Surely someone was coming. There or here. Just sitting still grated against every "do-something" cell in her body, even post giving up control. It had been hours since her contact with the base. What was taking so long?

She could not tamp down the urgency she felt to get off the rooftop. But she dragged four seat cushions over to her hiding place with the discarded pottery anyway.

"Lord, should I go ahead and leave?" She prayed as she traipsed back over to the heap of sixteen tattered curtains that fairly glowed in the moon-lit night. "I could find a phone on the way or call in to cancel the search when I get to the crash site."

Just sit still. She frowned as the quiet voice resounded in her spirit.

Judah dropped the armload of fabric next to the cushions laid out end to end as a sleeping pallet that she hoped she would not have to use. But doing anything was better than doing nothing.

Her belly rumbled a complaint then. "Lord, I'm hungry and thirsty." She sighed when she heard her own voice. "And obviously irritable. I'm sorry." Judah threw herself into the pile of curtains as if it was a pile of raked leaves. She let her neck drop back into the softness. She laid still and looked at the stars that were able to break through the light pollution and moonlight.

Butter purred to be brought into the pile. Wakefield rolled over and scooped him up and flopped back to her back. "You decided to wake up, huh?" She stroked the soft fur, thankful for the company. She closed her eyes for a moment just identifying the sounds she could hear. They faded further and further into the darkness as she sank deeper into the pile of fluff.

Rivers doubled the sheet long-ways that Vinchenzo had used for his costume. "The three of us are going to carry him out."

"Down to the ground?" Vinchenzo's eyes bugged out. Spencer was not a little man.

"All the way to the LZ, if we have to," Rivers said as he laid the sturdy sheet flat on the rooftop adjacent to the body. "This is what no man left behind looks like."

Vinchenzo nodded.

Mass said, "I'll take his head." He squatted and shoved meaty fists under Spencer's armpits while Rivers maneuvered around to his feet. They laid him gently on the folded sheet while Vinchenzo watched closely.

Rivers saw the young man's emotional state. "You tuck him in," he said and showed him how to push the sheet that covered the body underneath its weight all the way around so it would not catch on anything or fall off.

"Good work," Rivers nodded. "Now you stand here next to me and we will split the weight of his feet and take him behind us." Rivers showed him how to stand hip to hip with him, then squat, grab the corner of the sheet in both hands, and bring it around to the front of his waist. "Mass will take his head, and be right behind us." Rivers had found it helpful over the years in dealing with newbies to never refer to the person by name, nor by the term *body*, if at all possible.

"Forward." Rivers ordered already thinking about the kids playing two floors down. He pulled the door open, and the procession carrying about 225 extra pounds divided by three began down the five flights. Rivers cringed. Both his and Mass's weapons clicked against their vests with every step.

Rivers slowed them just before the kids would be able to see their feet descending the stairwell. He didn't hear anything, so they proceeded. The patch of moonlight still shone on the floor, but every game piece had been picked up. "Guess we scared them off."

At ground level, the door hinges were on Vinchenzo's side and it opened out. Rivers maneuvered them around so that he could unlatch the door with his left hand and push it open far enough for Vinchenzo to push it all the way open. They shuffled out letting the body droop in the middle so Vinchenzo could keep the door ajar. Then they continued back two blocks to where Mac and Hayes waited.

Mac and Hayes had set up on a little stoop with an overhanging vinyl roof and were leaning comfortably against the wall with feet stretched out in front of them, identically crossed right ankle over left. Hayes had obviously been rubbing at his eyes as his grease paint, which had been in tidy streaks when Rivers and Mass took off, was now a smudgy mess.

"You guys comfortable?" Rivers asked.

Mac jumped to his feet a fraction of a second before Hayes. "Sorry, Boss." Haven't seen anybody in at least ten minutes. Except that blasted chopper boring holes in the sky."

Rivers closed one eye and cocked his head as his cheek curled into a half smile. "I think the phrase 'boring holes in the sky' refers to firing missiles but not hitting anything," he said. "Not circling to find an LZ."

Hayes frowned. "Oh." He shook his head. "How did I miss that?"

"Asleep in SEAL school, again." Mac shook a school-teacher finger at him in laughter.

"Coordinates came in on our way over," Rivers said. "We've got a little way to hike. And we will end up further away from the package we are supposed to pick up. I asked them to hold up our helo for the mission until we can drop these boys off and high-tail it back to the palace district."

Vinchenzo's head darted back and forth between the two pair of men. His eyes rounded. "You guys are SEALs? And you're on a mission?" He wiped his mouth as if he'd been eating. Rivers had seen other men do it too as if psychologically they were trying to clean themselves up, to better themselves because of the caliber of men they were around. "And you interrupted your mission to come get me?" Vinchenzo's face registered guilt first then his chest swelled with pride. Rivers chuckled; farm boy was as easy to read as a chunky, toddler's first-reader book.

"Not just you." Hayes said as he gestured to the body they had laid on the narrow sidewalk. He and Mac came down the stairs.

"We went ahead and prepared Bevins and Conner for travel." Mac said. The two bodies were laid side by side with their eyes closed at ground level next to the building.

Vinchenzo shivered and loosed a little mewling sound. Apparently, he had not seen his teammates in the shadows.

"Deep breaths." Rivers gave him a whack on the back to distract the young man and give him a moment to compose himself.

"Anybody else see a problem?" Mass asked. "We've got five walkers and five non-walkers. One of whom is too hot to move."

"Nobody else made it?" Vinchenzo's hands moved toward his face. He was not slow at math.

417

"Jennings made it, but he took a bullet and broke his leg." Rivers reassured him.

"At least it is the same leg." Mac shrugged.

"Where is he?" Vinchenzo's head looked like it was on a lazy susan.

"He's ok. A couple of blocks back," Mac said. "You want to go with me to help carry?"

"It is quiet." Rivers said shaking his head and searching all the dark windows. "But I don't trust it."

"I think the grenade is what did the trick." Hayes said.

Rivers ignored what he was sure Hayes meant as a compliment, but he was too young to realize it wasn't really. "Why don't you go with them as a rear guard, Hayes? Mass and I will stay here for a breather and keep Bevins, Spencer, and Conner company."

The three took off quickly to retrieve Jennings, but not before Rivers heard Vinchenzo begin to chatter. "My whole life I wanted to be in the Special Forces. I was gonna go Rangers, you know being Army and all. But SEALs were a close second in my book. And looking better all the time."

"One of the first things we learn at BUD/S," Rivers could barely hear Mac say, "is that quietness is paramount. Slither like a snake and pounce like a panther."

"Yes, sir."

"Slither like a snake and pounce like a panther?" Mass snorted. "I don't remember learning that in BUD/S. What is he, like 22 or 23 years old?" Mass asked Rivers with a grin.

"Don't knock it." Rivers chuckled. "Do you even have 10 years on him?"

"Well, nine." Mass admitted. "But I've been on the Teams for all nine of them. That tends to age you."

"I thought you were out for a year." Rivers led him. He had read his service record and after-action reports and knew everything.

"Eleven months. Rehab after the incident."

Rivers pictured the incident to which Mass was referring that had been painted in the report. The one that had gotten his partner killed so severely there was nothing left to bring back home, and so badly injured two other SEALs that they had been "promoted home." It was the incident the rest of the SEALs in their mass meeting refused to partner with him over. "But I was still a SEAL. Otherwise I would not have made it back. Rehab was harder than BUD/S. That grit and you are the reasons I'm here today."

Rivers shrugged. "You were a good bet."

"I'm just trying to say thanks."

"You earn the trident every day. Just like the rest of us."

"Ooh-rah, sir!"

"Ooh-rah."

Rivers stared at the embers still glowing at the crash site blocks away. They would have to send someone else back for the pilot. What had Vinchenzo called him? Havilland. It was still too hot to get him out. But the U.S. would not have to worry about their tech being stolen and used against them as in some chopper crashes. There was going to be nothing to salvage but Havilland's charred corpse on this one.

The four men reappeared in under five minutes. "He is about to pass out again, boss." Mac said as they scurried up carrying Jennings between them in a makeshift armchair. Jennings' elbows crooked around Vinchenzo's and Mac's necks loosely, with Mac's pistol barely still clutched in his right hand.

Rivers met them and took the gun from his fingers before it clattered to the pavement. "I thought I told you not to go to sleep?" Rivers said gently as the two tried to stand him on his feet. Jennings knees buckled and the two carriers caught him under his arms where they were still wrapped around their necks. Rivers checked the bullet wound on Jennings' thigh. No fresh flow. But that break looked nasty. "How's the tightness of the tourniquet on this leg?" He asked Jennings.

"Can't feel a thing, sir."

"That is probably good." Rivers grimaced as he stood back to full height. "You did good soldier. You can take that nap now."

Jennings seemed to have been waiting for permission, because his eyes rolled up in his head as his lids closed. His whole body went limp but Mac and Vinchenzo braced against it.

"Mass, you take Jennings, fireman carry." Mass was the biggest among them and was no slouch in the weight room. He could probably carry the injured man with the least jostling. "Each of the rest of us will take a body. Vinchenzo, I want you in the middle, armed. Just don't shoot anybody on our side, okay?"

"Yes, Boss." Farm boy was grinning from ear to ear as he took Mac's Glock from Rivers.

He sighed inwardly. This story was going to go far and wide and would probably grow like a fish story.

Mac and Vinchenzo helped place the passed-out Jennings on Mass's wide left shoulder. He barely moved at the extra 190 pounds. Mass secured Jennings' legs at the knees, and the soldier moaned unconsciously as Mass touched his broken leg.

Rivers pointed to the two bodies lying side by side and motioned for Vinchenzo to help Mac and Hayes each take one body to their left shoulder. Rivers kept an eye on the street and windows for threats. Each SEAL adjusted his rifle on its sling around their chest and neck to free it for an easy firing position, if necessary.

As the Team lined safely into the alleyway he had pointed out, Rivers hoisted Spencer's body in an identical fireman's carry. He passed his men to take point, praying that the GPS in his head was accurate as he threaded his Team though alleys and streets for almost a kilometer to the abandoned soccer field that the Army TOC man in his ear had described. Their direction also matched the last direction from which Rivers had heard the helicopter.

Chapter Fifty Four

Rivers caught a glimpse of trees through the side street and could tell there was a field-sized gap between buildings that lined the streets.

"One more block to the left here," he said.

It had been a fairly quiet hustle to the LZ. He had motioned one family back inside with the rifle around his neck. They had peaceably disappeared. A lone overly brave man had screamed from a second-story window before opening fire on the group. It had cost him his life, courtesy of Vinchenzo. And only one of his stream of bullets had caught any of them. Spencer's body had taken one in the butt, saving Rivers' left shoulder and heart from any damage.

Rivers slowed the group with a raised fist. They halted immediately behind him, using the building as cover. Rivers stretched his neck cautiously around the corner to check the four-lane road for threats before they started across it in order to enter the soccer field.

There was the SAR helo sitting comfortably on the green winter grass. Understandably, it had been a little while since the grass had been trimmed. "We have a helo for these Army boys."

Rivers grinned as he spoke. I want to go back around one more block that way." He pointed to his right. "It will put us more in direct line with the chopper." Otherwise they would be crossing a four-lane highway and the majority of a soccer field with absolutely no cover whatsoever. Mac, who was covering the rear about-faced and led the line back one block the way they had come, and around one block further.

Six highly alert guards with big guns surrounded the helicopter with still rotors. They had been there a while.

Rivers whistled to get someone's attention. One of the beefy Army guards found him immediately. Rivers waved and then drew a horizontal circle in the air with his first finger to get the helicopter warming up so they could take off as soon as they got everyone inside.

With well-practiced precision the men on the field began moving to cover Rivers' Team while they huddled together quickly crossing the highway. The Black Hawk rotors began to spin within seconds of Rivers' whistle.

The wind picked up significantly as Rivers stepped from the street onto the grass that depressed under his boots. In the same tight formation, they dashed across the field as one unit.

The rotating wing of the Sikorsky UH-60 Q sent a wash of heavy current over them that hunched them all over in a crouch as they approached. Good thing it was a big bird. While still five steps away the side of the aircraft slid open. A white-helmeted man with his visor pitched back to reveal a grinning dark face with fat eyebrows greeted them with arms ready to relieve Rivers of his burden.

Rivers shook his head and motioned Mass forward first. "Here's our live one. Broken tibia and gunshot wound to the thigh. He's been under a tourniquet for almost two hours." Rivers recited to the medic.

The medic checked the tourniquet but did not remove it and started an IV line while Mass jumped aboard and received the bodies from the rest of the SEALs.

Rivers passed Spencer up last and then turned to shake Vinchenzo's hand before he boarded. "You did good, kid. Don't let anybody tell you anything different, especially any survivors' guilt." Rivers stared at the farm boy until he finally looked up. He swallowed hard and nodded. The unfounded shame of survival had already begun to descend on the young man. "I'll take that weapon back now. Mass might need it and you're in good hands." Rivers held out his left hand, and Vinchenzo plunked it down.

Rivers cuffed him on the shoulder. "You're going to do just fine. Get out of here." The guards were lining up to board as they had switched places with Rivers' men one at a time.

While Mass pulled Vinchenzo up into the Black Hawk MEDEVAC, the first medic called out over the rush of the propellers, "Hey, Navy!"

Rivers turned back to see the bushy-eyed fellow bend to pull out a weighty plastic bag from the lowest stretcher.

"Armstrong from TOC said to tell you dinner is on him next time you're in town, and here is a down payment."

Rivers took the plastic bag from the Army medic and looked inside as the other soldiers boarded to fill the aircraft to capacity. Rivers looked up with a smile. "I might just take him up on that."

Rivers moved about twenty feet from the door, set the package between his feet and took an offensive posture while the last two guards entered the DUSTOFF and closed it up tight.

Spooling up to full power the MEDEVAC was airborne less than ten seconds later. The SEALs provided a circle of ground cover until the helicopter was a hundred feet above the treetops and moving west again. Rivers assessed that they would be following the route out of Baghdad via the boulevard to the airport that had been cleared—or mostly cleared—by the morning's invasion.

At the first clear spot to hunker down under cover once they were back in the dark city streets, Rivers untied the plastic bag and passed out four of the five bottles of water with wrapped chocolate protein bars taped to their sides.

Rivers tapped his mic to ON once more. "Thanks for the chow, Army. Much appreciated."

"Thank you for the escort, Navy. That offer for dinner is good for the whole team and your girl, Commander."

"I really appreciate that." Rivers breathed deeply and tried to stuff the mind-picture of his beautiful blond wife in her wedding veil waving good-bye to him from the window of Marine One on the White House lawn back into the box labeled "package." It wasn't working so well. "Over and out." He choked out.

Rivers cleared his throat as the sounds of the helo disappeared altogether. "Stuff it down the hatch, ladies. We've got a mission to finish."

He drained his bottle of water and stuffed the last bite of the bar into his cheek. He shoved the water and bar the man had sent for Wakefield into his back pocket.

425

Rooftop by Iraqi National Museum
2200 hours

Wakefield pushed her scratchy eyelids open. The night was black and still. Judah couldn't determine if it had been seconds or hours that her eyes had been closed, nor where she was lying.

She sat up from the pile of fabric and listened for what had awakened her as she pushed her mind from 0 to 60 in seconds while the day—or two days rather—rushed back into her consciousness.

She squished her toes in her combat boots that now had more than a little real-world-combat experience and wished for clean socks. Setting Butter aside to continue his nap in peace, Wakefield unwound her rifle sling from around her back and walked to the edge of the rooftop to check her perimeter.

The road where Saddam had escaped was empty of movement, though that vehicle's shape and every rust spot was fixed in her mind as clearly as if it still sat there belching exhaust.

At her 1 o'clock she saw movement at ground level across the main street through the Iraqi Museum's metal fence posts. From their profile presentation, the men were definitely armed and slinking out of a doorway much like the one at the base of her apartment building. The door practically disappeared into the building until it was opened, and then it looked completely obvious, and she wondered how she had not noticed it before.

Wakefield watched as the fourth man shut the door behind them, and the group moved in a disciplined diamond formation up the street, away from her position. She felt her cheeks tug upward as she pulled her AR-15 scope to her eye for a closer look.

She clicked the focus to 210 yards, and let herself breathe fully for the first time in days as a familiar face filled her scope.

Unfolding her rifle stock to its full extension, Wakefield fitted it into the well of her shoulder. Fixing her crosshairs on her target, Wakefield fired her silenced rifle with a pft.

The diamond broke apart as the men in her scope dove for cover. The concrete a full four feet in front of the man walking backward in the diamond-shaped team had a divot chunked out of it by her .223 Remington bullet.

She gave the Team about three seconds to settle out of her way. Three of them were no longer visible in her scope. One man had mis-determined the trajectory of her first shot and sat with his back in full range. As Wakefield laid down a pattern with seven more silenced shots in four seconds, she saw the man scamper out of her view, presumably to join the rest of his Team low against the museum fence wall.

Wakefield dashed back to her sleeping space and grabbed up one of the curtains. Returning to where she had fired from, she saw the single lump of a head pop up like a gofer game even without the aid of her scope. She thought she saw the quickest silhouette of a rifle too.

Twisting the moon-reflecting color of her bedding around the end of her weapon, she lifted the whole thing into the air and waved it back and forth three times and then brought it down and unwrapped the white fabric.

The sound of another helicopter reached her ears. *It has to be for me. Oh! it is all finally coming together,* Judah thought.

Then she remembered the men who had been stationed at the ground floor. Were they still there? It had been quiet for what felt like hours, but then again, she had been asleep. As she gazed over the edge of the building to the ground below, she couldn't see anything in the shadowy area at the ground level. The moon was high in the night sky, but still the building cast a shadow that shrouded its entry.

Wakefield's mind slammed into overdrive as she processed ways to meet the SEAL Team on the ground. There was a rather rickety looking fire escape that ran from the fourth floor to the first floor. There were also all the sheets. She could tie together the 16 she had collected and easily reach the ground.

What was the best way? The most efficient way? The safest way? Her old need to control her situation reared in her belly which managed to growl about the same time. Judah gripped the edge of the roof molding with her left hand and smoothed her hair back with her right. *Be still* was the last instruction she had heard in her spirit.

What if she just followed that small instruction and let the SEALs come rescue her? Her spine actually stiffened with the thought, and she rolled her eyes at her own stubborn will. "Judah Amberly Wakefield, you calm down!" she told herself.

She pulled her hand back from the wall and glanced down to see the four-man diamond retrace the corner she had turned from the main street onto the side street where she was. "You do not have to be in control of every single thing nor do you have to be right all the time." Wakefield's eyes widened and she backed away from the wall. "In fact, you didn't even get your own name right, Judah Amberly Rivers. Or is it Wakefield-Rivers?" She shook her head with dislike. Way too long. "We'll figure that out later."

Judah went over to the grouping of two lounge chairs nearest the door and sat down. Was it still being in control if she was practicing the self-control of letting someone else lead?

Butter wandered over then and sprang lightly into her lap.

The whup-whup-whup of the chopper was getting nearer all the time. She twisted her neck around from facing the door to check the progress of the helo. It was still on a straight trajectory for her location. "I bet it sets down on the lawn of the museum. And I know the perfect hole in the fence to sneak onto the grounds in with the fewest steps from here," she whispered to Butter. At least being a witness to Saddam's escape was worth something.

She groaned inwardly. How was she going to word that in her report? She let her head bounce against the back of the chair. And just like that, Wakefield began to transition in her mind from being a combat soldier on the loose on her own in a hostile city to being a pencil-pusher riding a desk and profiling interview subjects.

Butter clawed up her uniform to hide in the crook of her neck as the Black Hawk skimmed only 100 feet over her head in a beeline for the museum. Every hair Judah had just slicked into place became a riotous mess. "Don't worry, they're here to rescue us." She plucked Butter off her BDU jacket and plopped him back in her lap to wait.

A spray of gunfire burst through the noise of the helicopter as it moved away from her, and Judah bolted upright in her chair. Then a second and third burst resounded. It was definitely coming from the ground floor. Wouldn't the SEALs be moving with silenced weapons? They would still produce a little pop, but she would barely be able to hear it from the roof, even if a chopper was not landing a couple hundred yards away.

"Hi honey, I'm home." Rivers filled the doorway.

Judah giggled as the moon reflected off his teeth in the widest grin she had ever seen on his face. "Welcome home. How was your day?" She asked as she walked closer to him much more calmly than she felt. The helicopter sounds diminished. But the gunfire reports increased greatly.

"Pretty average." Rivers cocked his head. "Yours?"

"Mine was kind of long." Judah sighed. "I didn't have time to make dinner. So we're going to have to go out tonight." She shrugged. Just three feet from coming home to his arms.

Rivers' arm sneaked behind his back, and he tucked his rifle to his side. "Actually," he brought his arm back around to the front. "I brought take out."

Judah broke eye contact to look at his hand. A semi-crushed bottle of water with a crinkled lump attached to one side, but it looked like a Thanksgiving feast to her.

She received it from him as she slipped into his embrace. She felt him bend forward to pull her tighter to his frame. "Thank you for coming for me," she whispered. "Where's the rest of your Team?" she asked.

"I left them downstairs."

She pulled back from his hug and kissed him then. This had been a perfect surprise worth waiting for, worth giving up control over. "I suppose I'm never going to live this down?" Judah said as they broke apart to catch their breath. Her heart raced and it had nothing to do with the increase in volume of rounds being fired from multiple directions.

"Probably not." Rivers cupped her jaw in his hand. "Right now, it is the best day of my life. I have my wife back." He pulled her into his chest again. The strong inflation of his lungs under her cheek may have been the most comforting feeling she ever felt, never mind that the Kevlar was scratchy on her cheek and so was his chin on her forehead.

A whistle pierced the air from the doorway behind Rivers.

"I think that's our cue to go." Rivers said. "Grab your helmet. Do you need to get anything else?" He looked around the rooftop.

Butter rubbed his small yellow head against her ankle, and she reached down to grab him under his belly. "I wish I could have shown you this place before the men did all the damage. It was like Eden."

"Wait!" Rivers pushed her back a foot from him with his hands on both shoulders and looked her up and down and then spun her to the back while asking, "Are you all right? I didn't even ask?"

"Careful. I'm fine." She widened her stance to regain her balance and pushed her rifle back into the most comfortable position on her shoulder. "Do you mind?" She held up Butter.

"What are you going to do with him?" Rivers eyes narrowed a little.

"Take him back to the base with me. The ladies would love him. And I'm sure he'll grow up to be a great mouser."

"Why not?" Rivers shrugged. "Let's get out of here. Our exfil will not wait forever." He looked over at the museum.

She followed his gaze and squinted as she looked all over the lawn for the helo. "Where did it go?" She asked as Rivers took Butter from her hand and opened a thigh pocket pouch. He dropped the kitten inside and helped him turn right-end-up before tamping down the Velcro seal.

"Take a look at the roof."

Judah caught a glimpse of the lights in the helo's interior as it opened in the middle of the museum's roof. A few men piled out and she saw tracer fire coming to that point from a couple of directions on the street and the lawn surrounding the base of the museum.

Rivers' hand to her back guided her into the stairwell. Holding the metal railing Judah traipsed down the flights of stairs in the dark for the last time, but blew out her breath in a huff. The night was still not over.

When she hit the final landing, Judah unscrewed the top of the water bottle with a crackle and took a big swig. Swishing the warm water through her teeth felt refreshing. She wanted to swallow the whole bottle, and then another bottle, in one air-less gulp, but she knew she should take it easy. Putting the lid back on the bottle, Judah wiggled the big melty protein bar from its wrapper as she continued walking over to meet Rivers' Team.

"Hi guys!" She smiled brightly. "Nice of you to drop in. Sorry about the neighbors. They are having kind of a rough night."

Chapter Fifty Five

A boom awakened Ellie from her light sleep, and she turned over on her cot with a standard-issue squeak to listen. It had been close and it had been big. The sound of foot traffic and hurried speech rose in number and decibel. Then a pitchy siren undulated as it wailed.

"Too little, too late." Ellie sat up with another screech of metal and shook her head. Three other women in the tent began to move around in the dark. "Might as well flip on the light." Ellie suggested. "That sounded like an all-hands-on-deck call."

Just as someone clicked on a pair of bald overhead lightbulbs, another officer, in logistics if Ellie remembered right, stuck just her head into the tent flap, pulling the canvas around her neck for privacy in case any of the women was disrobed. "We had another mom-bomb," she announced. "Only this time, we didn't get to her in time."

The room came alive with movement then. Ellie began to pull on her uniform pants at the same time as shoving her feet into her boots. "Casualties?" she asked with an inward groan.

"I'm sure. It happened at the front gate," the woman said and then closed the tent flap and disappeared.

Used to dealing with both attacks and diversion attacks, Ellie decided it would be most useful to head to Intel House to check on the detainees. The increase in foot traffic right past their front door would make it easier to break someone out of holding and disappear into the chaos.

In fact it might be interesting to measure some of the detainees' responses to the news of a successful attack. "Oh, Judah, would you hurry back!" Ellie whispered.

Pushing back the tent flap, Ellie watched the stream of people sluicing past her. It was mostly orderly, with a few hot pockets of people stopping and others having to flow around them like rocks in the stream, and two guys running with an orange hard-shell stretcher with legs pumping as if they rode a tandem bicycle on the far edge of the crowd.

Ellie forked her fingers into her dark curls to fluff them off her scalp, then timed her first step into the fray that would take her to Intel House while everyone else continued on to help at the front gate.

Along the route, she began to pray for her new friend. "Lord, there are still so many conversations we have left to share. Please give her wisdom and keep her safe and bring her home quickly. Help her endure..." She trailed off in her mind as possible scenarios flashed before her. None of them good. "...whatever she is in the middle of. Blind the eyes of anyone who would want to hurt her."

And with that, she shoved open the door at Intel House. A very quiet Intel House. The guard with an almost-bald head and a dark thatch of hair on top that was only slightly longer stood from his metal-chair post in the stairwell before she had completely crossed the threshold.

Stiff as a board, he looked more like a Queen's Guard at Buckingham Palace with his weapon muzzle on his shoulder and his gaze more distant than the back wall. He filled the entire doorway.

"How is everything going here?" Ellie shut the door against the noise behind in the street of the village, if you could still call it that. "Any visitors or anything unusual going on with our guests?"

"Ma'am."

She sensed his uneasiness before she had finished her first question and so walked over to the far end of the room, away from him, and began making a pot of coffee. But she watched him in the reflection on the glass carafe.

His head did turn slightly toward her with her back turned. He was trying to get a read on her. She kept her arm movements slower than normal and moved to an angle so that her hands were visible most of the time. Hundreds of hours of guard-duty experience during a time of pressure told her what he was looking for to assess a threat. And saying "I'm not a threat," was not one of them.

So Ellie kept showing him she was not here to break anyone out or further the disturbance. Reaching under the table to retrieve several bottles of water from the pallet that had been unloaded there just a day ago, Ellie plunked each one up on the counter next to the coffee pot. By the time she had unscrew the little white lid from the last bottle and let it glug into the back of the machine, the guard's shoulders had visibly relaxed in the reflection.

She hit the on-switch which glowed orange. "You going to want some?" She asked turning toward him—still using slow movements. She reached for a cup for herself, even though she

435

really didn't feel like coffee. She felt like an interrogation with the full gamut of video-taping and a full-court press with Judah Wakefield asking questions and her assessing language and facial expression.

"Definitely, ma'am." The marine spoke again, but his voice was half as tense as his previous single word. "But not until CAPT George gets back."

Ellie's head snapped up. "George was here?"

The soldier's features tightened at the jaw and eyes and then relaxed, but he did not look at her. "Yes, ma'am. Just after the explosion. Gave orders, nobody in, nobody out."

Ellie felt her eyebrows peak. *Good for him*, she thought. *Although it will cut down on my fun.* "Do the upstairs people know?" she asked now that she had him talking.

The coffee hissed its first drips.

"I told them after he left."

"Not the prisoners though—I mean detainees—right?"

"Of course not, ma'am." He made eye contact for the first time. Bewilderment etched his face as if to ask why would he do such a thing.

"Good. You are all right, Marine. Okay, I will wait right here until he returns." The drips had become a dark brown trickle and the aroma had already reached her nose.

The guard's white-finger grip relaxed on his weapon's stock. One easy way to build rapport was to tell them you trusted them. It was human nature to want to trust someone who trusted you. Ellie smiled and turned her eyes back to the coffee pot. Good thing she wasn't actually here to break anyone out.

Chapter Fifty Six

Hayes stood in the hallway and stared as David and Judah walked to the entry together. Rivers reached up and pushed up on the jaw of the youngest and newest member of the Team to close his mouth. "Did you think I'd marry a wuss?" David asked.

He turned back to Judah, "This guy with his jaw slightly unhinged is Hayes. We are working on his manners. Usually our pick-up packages don't walk out under their own power." Rivers shrugged and threw his wife a flirty smile. "They also don't usually look like you and carry an AR-15 with the skill to use it."

Judah cocked a single trim eyebrow at him in reply. She pushed back her hair in a gesture so familiar to him that it made his stomach drop as he thought *what if I had lost her?*

She fastened her helmet in place as he turned back to introduce the rest of his Team. "The big guy is CPO Masterson, Mass, my buddy. And this is Mac."

"Nice to meet you all." Wakefield leaned forward to shake each man's hand. "Sorry to get you out like this. But I sure appreciate you coming for me."

437

Rivers walked over to survey the path to the exfiltration plan while he checked in with Jackson at the original TOC on his headset. "We have the package, and she is in good spirits," Rivers reported with a smile. "The helo's arrival stirred up some unfriendlies. They don't sound like the Republican Guard that we've been dealing with all day." Rivers squinted into the night. Mostly it was the undisciplined and non-rhythmic shot patterns that gave him that impression. Why waste ammo shooting from the ground to the roof without a line of sight or hope of hitting anything but the windows of the museum?

"Copy, that. Any idea who it is?"

"There are so many factions of factions in this city it could be anybody. Shia or Sunni Islamic Militias or the Ba'athists." Rivers loosened his helmet and pushed it back an inch to rub his forehead. He felt a hand on his bicep.

"It could also be Kurds, Turks, Assyrians or any number of insurgent groups, based on the interviews I've been conducting." It was Judah at his sleeve.

Rivers covered the microphone with his fingers in a fist. "It could be the neighborhood watch, for all we know."

"I've been watching the area for hours. I believe it is a new group being formed called Al-Awda, which means 'the struggle.' They're the opposition party being stirred up in this area by a guy living safely in Lebanon, or maybe Syria, from what I've been able to piece together from a couple of interviews. I saw an unusual flag fall out of a guy's jeans pocket before the sun went down."

"Hold on." Rivers spoke into his mic and covered it again. "What do they want?" he asked Judah's upturned face that reflected a couple of muzzle flashes every second.

"Well, they're secular, not fanatical Islamists. As he was wearing Western jeans."

"Small comfort when they are angry and have automatic weapons." Rivers looked at the firestorm outside. Wakefield was staring outside too when he looked back at her. "Are you doing that reading-your-notes thing again?"

A small smile lifted her lips as she kept searching her memory. "Saddam." She burst out a moment later. "They want Saddam to stay in power. At least that is what the one we caught said in an interview about three days ago, maybe four. He was easily forthcoming with that information though, so they probably want more than that."

Rivers frowned. "Well, we're not going to be welcome at their party then. Suggestions for getting to the rooftop LZ?" He included everyone in his glance.

The guys kicked around a few ideas, none of which would work. "We need air support. Even if we get there and make it onto the roof, that helo can't take off with all those rounds in the air. I can't even tell how many bodies are out there firing."

"But it is a lot." Hayes chimed in.

Judah had been quiet during the whole exchange. "Let me run this by you. It is a bit radical," she said. Her face looked strange. It was an expression he had never seen.

"Lay it out," Mass encouraged. "We like radical. And we've got nothing else at the moment."

"Ok. What if this group has spread out here because they think Saddam is here? Or they are supposed to meet him here?"

"What? Why would they think that?"

Judah hesitated. Rivers didn't remember her ever hesitating. "Because he *was* here." She bit the side of her bottom lip. "I saw

439

him, by chance, disguised, come out from looting the museum just before noon."

The room exploded with questions hurled at her.

"How do you know it was him in disguise?"

"Where did he go?"

"Is he still alive?"

"Why didn't you take him out?'

She held up an authoritative hand to bring quiet. "He was with a driver and one bodyguard. They hid him in the trunk of an old car and drove off that way." She pointed away from the main street. "I was not in a position to take him out, and if I had tried, I most certainly would not have survived the encounter, and probably wouldn't have been successful anyway."

Rivers watched his wife's jaw muscle flex and relax several times as she replayed the scene in her mind before she met his eyes and gave a decisive nod. That was the Judah he knew. She had come to a decision.

"If we are not going to receive air support, what do you say we move the 'party'" she pointed outside, "to another location?" She began nodding and almost smiling now.

"Hayes, was it?" She made eye contact with the one who had accused her of not killing Saddam when she had the chance. "Can you run over by that sofa," she pointed into the darkness near where the stairwell began, "and grab the black tablecloth and the small pillow from the floor, please?"

"How come you never say please, Boss?" Hayes asked as he moved.

"Probably that last little four-letter word you used." Rivers called after him. "Boss."

"What are you thinking?" Mass asked.

"If these people are who I think they are, they have *some* of the information from their group, but not all of it. A common communication breakdown when any organization is growing. I think *they* think they are here to protect the escape of a king who has already pulled an Elvis and left the building." Wakefield's eyes were alive as they reflected the muzzle flashes from the open doorway.

"Here you go." Hayes handed over a shiny pillow and long cloth to Judah. She leaned over and placed them on the floor to take another swig of her water.

"So what is it for?" Rivers asked. An idea that he didn't like was forming in his mind with the black cloth as he remembered her get-up in the desert of Afghanistan when they'd first partnered together to retrieve the nuclear weapons from Filasek.

"I want to update their information for them." Judah delivered the plan matter-of-factly. "I saw the vehicle in which they took Saddam out of here. Perhaps someone will recognize it." She shrugged, even as she unclasped her helmet. "Then they can make some mobile-phone calls to verify my information. Once they realize he is not here, they should move on. They will want to support their cause in a way that is useful. They will want to move to where Saddam is in order to protect him."

"Don't they realize that the more people around him, the easier it is for us to spot him?"

"Probably not. These guys are low-level, follow-orders grunts." Judah shrugged.

"How, ma'am? The Wad-people are trying to prevent us from finding him. What makes you think they won't shoot an American uniform on sight?"

"Al-Awda," she corrected.

"Because she won't be American." Rivers pursed his lips. As much as he hated to put her at risk, moving the group away from the site and the helo was the only way this was going to work without air support, which Jackson had passed on the edict of "impossible until morning" in his ear.

"Go ahead and show them." Rivers picked up the black cloth and handed it to her. "But I want you to stay in the street where we can cover you."

"How do I do that? They are all inside under cover." She took the cloth from him and put it between her knees as she bent down to grab the pillow.

"I don't know, but I'm sure you'll think of something." He did not allow his voice to waver. He did not like coming all this way to get her out only to send her immediately into harm's way again.

She unclipped her rifle from the sling and handed the weapon to him. She took the pillow and bunched it up on her shoulder and looped the canvas sling around the pillow and one shoulder and fastened it on its smallest setting. She wiggled back and forth a little to test its hold. Hardly a jiggle at all.

Wakefield bent to retrieve the tablecloth from her knee-hold and started at her chin, wrapping the long cloth over her head and then over her nose and then around her shoulders, letting it drape over the pillow and her uniform. She wound it once around her body and held it in place by tucking a section into her belt and letting the remaining fabric fall toward the ground.

The place was silent—except the gunfire that continued outside—as she continued her transformation by leaning slightly at the waist and shuffling forward slowly.

"Have you got any more of that grease paint?" she asked. "I hope I won't have to get close enough, but you never know."

Rivers watched Mac and Hayes shove little round containers at her simultaneously.

"Any toothpicks or small wires?" She looked around at the floor.

"What for? I have some det cord." Rivers said, "Or we could rip out some electrical wire from the wall. How long do you need?"

"Just an inch or so. The detonation cord will do."

"How about the plastic part of a shoelace?" Mass asked.

"Much better." Judah replied. "I didn't relish putting on grease paint with explosive material."

Mass flicked open his utility knife and sliced off part of his shoelace and handed it to her.

Judah dipped the tightly wrapped plastic end into the can of face paint. After a dozen or so movements between the tin and her face, she looked up. "What do you think?"

She had aged forty or fifty years. Bags puffed under her eyes and deep wrinkles etched the skin around her eyes and mouth. "I can't do anything about the blue eyes this time." She shrugged and pulled the black cloth back up over her nose.

"How did you do that without a mirror?" Rivers stared at her in disbelief.

"I've been putting make-up on this same face since I was 13, Commander." He could see she was smiling. "Nothing seems to move."

"Well, don't smile like that, it doesn't match your character's look, and you might want to add some wrinkles and liver spots to the back of your hands." Rivers couldn't stop shaking his head at the transformation.

"What about the boots?" Mass asked. "They show a little bit."

"I'm a combat granny." Wakefield shrugged. "I can't do anything about them, and I am not going barefoot.

A few twists of the shoelace casing later, Wakefield's head came up. "I'm ready."

Mass held up his right hand in a stop motion as he pressed his left hand into his earpiece. "Are you getting this, Boss?"

Rivers stared at the floor as he absorbed the information Jackson was relaying into his ear. A suicide bomber had penetrated one of the forward operating bases, and the detonation had killed four and injured ten more. All the FOBs were at heightened security measures now. "Does not shift our focus." He gave Mass a sharp look. "Let's get this party moved to the next location so we can get home for some decent chow. You are a go, lieutenant commander." He nodded to Judah who turned at the doorway before stepping out and winked at him.

"Second floor." He ordered Mac. "Don't let her out of your sight."

Rivers gave Judah a 30-second head start and then tapped Mass to follow him in slinking out the door. They melted into the deep shadows next to the doorway and Rivers went down to a prone position and followed through his scope his wife's progress down the road in the direction she had pointed out that Saddam had left the neighborhood. Mass sat Indian style at his feet and constantly moved his distance finder from window to window, checking for anyone aiming at the old lady shuffling up the street.

"Why didn't you say anything to her?" Mass whispered.

"I didn't think she needed to know that we had been attacked on not only one of our own bases, but on the base where she is stationed." Rivers huffed. "It is likely that she knows someone who was killed or injured. She didn't need anything else to think about while she is executing the performance of a lifetime in front of an al Qaeda offshoot."

Chapter Fifty Seven

*C*halk another one up for the Arabic culture that honors their elders, thought Wakefield as she turned away from the man whose eyes made him appear in his late forties. She didn't need to pretend she had an age-related palsy, just letting her nerves rattle freely through her body and voice created an equal effect.

She could hear him on the phone behind her in the street speaking animatedly, to whom Wakefield could only guess was the man over him in the organization. "I've got sixty guys out here with an American bird pinned to the roof of the National Museum, and you're telling me you left without us?" There was a pause and Wakefield tempered her desire to run. "Well not *you* then, but you *knew*, and we've been just sitting here shooting at shadows and playing peek-a-boo with the Infidel invaders."

A strongly worded diatribe followed but faded from Wakefield's hearing as she stepped from the street into the alley one block beyond her building. She still didn't dare run, but oh, she wanted to.

Weaving her way, one shuffling foot in front of the other, around the block to approach the small space between buildings

446

from the back, Wakefield found a window that was low enough for her to climb in with ease, even in her costume.

From the rooftop, she had heard the Al Awda men who were now dead, clear the lower floors, so she knew she wouldn't be surprising some family when she entered.

"Give Rivers your peace when he hears this and can't see me," Wakefield whispered a prayer before breaking the glass. The tinkling sounded louder than the surrounding gunshots she'd been hearing all day.

"I'm all good." Rivers' low-register whisper at her back made her nearly jump out of her skin.

She whipped her head around to see him and Mass about eight feet behind her. "Where did you come from! Did you follow me? What if they had seen you?" It all came out in a rush.

"I wasn't going to let you out of my sight." Rivers shrugged. "You want a leg up?" he asked coming closer and leaning down to create a step with his hand about eighteen inches off the ground.

Wakefield willed her heart rate to return to normal. This one was going to take a minute. She knocked the remaining glass inward with her elbow in two strikes, and placed one hand on either side of the window jambs. Stepping into Rivers' palm she put her second boot onto the bottom sill. Shards of glass crackled under her weight.

She transferred her weight to the sill and balanced as she quickly pulled up her foot. Setting it down just momentarily, she went ahead and thrust it blindly into the space inside.

Not running into any objects or furniture, she moved one hand from the window and checked the airspace in front of her to keep from hitting her head on anything, then she executed a two-footed hop down to the carpeted floor.

It looked like she had landed in a living room. She turned around and stuck her head back into the walk-space between the buildings, leaning her elbows casually on the sill and frowned. "You're quiet, I'll give you that." She said to Rivers.

"And that was the most lady-like B & E I have ever seen."

Judah rolled forward on her elbows and pecked him on the lips. "Thank you. I think." The surprise on Rivers' face was priceless. "You guys coming or not?" She couldn't keep from smiling.

"Newlyweds." Wakefield could practically hear Mass's eyes rolling.

The two SEALs made short work of climbing in the window after her, rifles, packs and all.

"Coming in." Rivers said as he reached for the main apartment door with one hand a moment later and reached for his ear with the other. "Yes. We have her."

Wakefield assumed he was speaking to the rest of his Team through coms gear as she stood between the two men waiting to leave the apartment.

A few feet back into the lobby area the four men formed their suffocating diamond around her and pelted her with questions. Wakefield held up a hand. "Give me some space." They each took exactly one step back. Funny. "We should give them a few minutes to leave the area. It sounded like they might have some sort of phone-tree communication standard set up, because they didn't appear to have walkies."

"What did they say, ma'am?" It was young Hayes.

"Well, they have a force of 60 men, or more, that's what he said on his cell-phone to his boss as I was leaving. So I am glad we didn't try to take them, and it might take a few minutes for word to get passed from person to person. He was really mad that he had not been informed that Saddam had already left the premises." Wakefield raised her eyebrows. "I haven't heard language like that for quite some time."

"What did he say?" Hayes asked again.

Wakefield cut her eyes to the left to look at the young man with his thin facial scruff and slightly round cheeks. Even his SEAL leanness had not elongated his face yet. She put him at age 22, possibly 23. Normally, by that age an enlisted Navy man right out of high school could achieve an E-4 rating. Hayes was a SEAL, meaning above average, *and* Rivers had chosen him for the mission to get her out of Baghdad. Despite his evident over-eagerness, he did have an air about him that suggested competence. She would guess E-6. "Petty Officer First Class, do you speak Arabic?"

"No, ma'am." He looked away from her gaze to find Rivers. "How'd she do that?"

"What?" Rivers asked.

"Know my rank? Did you tell her? I was only promoted last week."

Wakefield smiled inwardly. "I could tell you, but then I'd have to kill you." she deadpanned. "Naval Intel." She explained away her informed—but very lucky—guess.

"Not to interrupt all your fun," said Mac who had repositioned so he could see out into the street, "but we have movement out here."

The five crowded toward the single window, but stayed in the darkness, out of view from the outside.

"That's a lot of fire power." Rivers commented softly. "But not a lot of organization." Rivers began to relay his view into the microphone and then asked whoever was on the other end to update their ride for him.

Wakefield agreed with his assessment. Her view from several feet back and over his shoulder showed a retreat that looked more like a bunch of farmers going home from the fields carrying hoes or pick-axes on their shoulders and wearing bandanas over their noses than soldiers toting the serious weapons that were actually on their shoulders.

The shooting in the immediate vicinity around the museum and grounds had stopped altogether.

"See that space in the parked cars over there to our right, along the fence and between the grey car and the black car?" Wakefield asked them without pointing it out.

"Sure."

"There's a break in the fence over there, we can exploit."

"That would offer a lot lower exposure time than going back around to the front or going over the fencing." Rivers said. "Is the fence just cut there or what?"

"It looked like it was about eighteen to twenty inches wide and just pulled outward toward the street. Like an emergency exit door without a frame or a secret exit or something."

"The parked cars will offer some cover." Mac stated.

"We will give them another five minutes to clear out and then cover each other to go two at a time." Rivers glanced at his watch.

FOB Beta Intel House
9 April 2003
0115 hours

Ellie began to fidget with the peeling paint on the staff door-table after almost an hour. She had drained half the pot of coffee and still the office was empty. The sounds outside had shifted.

Ellie was glancing past the marine guarding the stairwell to the detainees when the door rattled. The marine never had returned to the metal folding chair after she arrived, but he had returned to his silent watch, albeit less stiff than when she had walked in the door. She saw him stiffen and glance quickly at her as the front door opened.

CAPT George stepped into the room with Blackstone and his interpreter Hakim Bousaid in tow. He seemed to take in the whole room at once. Nodding once at the marine while speaking to her. "I'm glad you're here. And very glad for the coffee." His gaze stopped on the pot.

Ellie stood and pushed her chair back with her knees. It scraped the concrete. "Probably going to need another pot," she glanced at Blackstone. "I promised one of those cups to your guard." Without waiting for permission, Ellie walked to the coffee station, pulled another Styrofoam cup off the top of the stack and splashed the Vienna-roast up to the rim.

As George trooped to the coffee, Ellie vacated the station and headed straight for the guard. "Here you go. Black, right?" She pushed the warm cup into his capable two-handed grip and stepped past him into the hallway. Thinking better, she leaned just her head back into the main room, and asked quickly, "Did you have a preference, Captain? Or shall I pick the one who looks most uncomfortable?"

George put the sugar shaker down with his left hand while stirring with their shared group spoon with his right. He looked up at her slowly.

She rocked backward one step into the room when her neck began to ache at his delay in answering. "Are you not here to interview the detainees, Captain?" Come to think of it, she had not seen him conduct a single detainee interrogation. He

451

reviewed the tapes and watched through the glass and directed the others, but did not interact directly with the detainees. "Come on, it'll be fun," she goaded.

A ghost of a smile flickered on his face and he followed her past the marine who slurped his coffee with closed eyes.

Once they were out of the others' hearing Ellie turned to George. Blackstone was asking Bousaid to make another pot of coffee to which Bousaid replied "This, this machine is not how we make coffee."

"Sir, I can help you out if you need it. I know it's been a while since you were in the interrogation room."

George fixed her with a stare as he tasted his coffee. "I didn't get this job because of my leadership skill set. I prefer the interrogation desk to the paperwork desk. Let's go." He was now smiling and tossed his head to indicate that she should take the stairs up to the next floor.

So up she went. This might be more interesting and fun than she thought.

Chapter Fifty Eight

"Want to join me?" Rivers asked, crouched down beside Judah next to the mature tree nearest the opening in the fence that she had managed to open seconds after they had crossed the road. "Or are you just going to let that -15 rot there at your side?"

She gave a chesty harrumph and retorted, "How about if I cover your six this direction while you cover the guys as they cross?" He glanced away from watching the windows for threats to see that his wife was indeed in a back-to-the-street posture, and had her AR-15 balanced on one knee while she sat flat on the other ankle. She was methodically searching the direction they would be going and all the grounds in sight through her scope.

Rivers turned back to watch the windows and doors. "That will do." Mac and Hayes scurried across the silent street and slipped in the opening in the fence, leap-frogging past him and Judah to the next tree with a trunk large enough to conceal them, just as they had planned. *Plan the dive, dive the plan.* The old SCUBA phrase ran through his mind.

Twenty seconds after Mac and Hayes passed him, Mass jogged across the street by himself and continued past him as well.

"I've got movement at the front door." Judah whispered.

Rivers checked the last window on this grid cycle. Empty. He swiveled around to see what she was seeing.

"No threat." She assessed aloud even as he was still focusing his scope to clarify the subject at the correct range. She gave a little chuckle.

"What?" he asked. "Oh." The movement at the door was a pair of bare-faced young men with arms loaded down who stood at the door trying to close it behind them. Their hands were too full for either of them to get the door to latch. One of them began down the front steps and called back to the other to leave it and hurry up. The other didn't want to, but after looking around the grounds like a prairie dog, he took off after his friend, leaving the unlatched heavy wooden door of the museum to swing outward.

A single bullet thunked as it hit the trunk next to David and sent a chunk of bark sliding across his cheek. "Down." Rivers pushed Judah over to the ground and dove to cover her body with his.

Her weapon twisted in the air as she rolled to the ground. She collapsed under his weight with a whoosh and a groan when the air was pushed out of her lungs.

A silenced weapon. He had not heard the shot on the quiet street. Or even seen the muzzle flash. He examined the bullet's trajectory in his mind's eye based on his known position, the burning sensation of the scratch on his face and the sound the bullet made entering the tree trunk. And the fact that the shooter had missed.

Judah began to push at his chest from underneath. "You're lucky I wasn't taking a shot," she muttered. "I might have hit you when you tackled me. Now scoot off. I can't breathe."

Rivers slowly reversed his momentum and rolled off Judah to put himself between her and the shooter's probable location while continuing to look for the shooter. A displeased mewling filled the air and razor claws pierced his lower quad. The cat!

Rivers spun his body on the ground to give the kitten some room in his pocket while still protecting Judah from the shooter and looking for the threat at the same time.

"Boss?" a very confused sounding Mac whisper-called out.

"Shooter from the west, south-west." Rivers called out to his Team. He heard the rustle of fabric as the three turned to help.

Nothing for thirty seconds.

"When I say go," he said to Judah, "I want you to sprint for the ladder the exfil team dropped from the roof. Tug on it twice to let them know you're coming up and high tail it up the ladder. Don't stop no matter what goes on down here. You got it? You see the ladder?"

"Yes." He heard the nylon rifle sling drop onto the shoulder of her BDU so that she would be able to climb the ladder with both hands free. "I've got it. I trust you."

"Good." He inhaled as on the street a second-floor curtain parted in the slightest bit while he was looking at it. "Go." Rivers spit. The highly polished barrel of a rifle sneaked out in profile against the side of the building flashing a reflection. Judah was up and running.

Rivers pulled the trigger.

The muzzle flashed with a barely discernable tunk-sound on the other end before his bullet found its mark. He kept his rifle

455

trained on the light-less rectangle of the window for five more seconds, then turned to find Judah.

FOB Beta Intel House
9 April 2003
0205 hours

Ellie kept her features frozen as the marine led the man away clipped tightly in his chains. When the door clicked shut, she released her smile. "Gotcha!" she jumped to her feet and turned to face CAPT George. "Did you—"

George cut her off, "I saw it this time!" He looked pleased with himself. "I see exactly what you mean. That was amazing." The officer was practically dancing around the room, touching the table and then the walls. "So now to use it to our advantage."

"And find the leak." Ellie felt her eyes go wide. Surely that was the more important item.

"Yes," George nodded from the mirrored glass, "so we can use the weakness to exploit the enemy and then cuff the responsible party, haul him off to Leavenworth, and throw away the key."

"I believe the penalty for treason in the time of war in your country is death." Ellie knocked on the door to be let out while watching George continue touching everything in the room. He would just lightly run his fingers across the surfaces. From the window he walked back to the table and chair on the interviewee side. Must be a tactile learner, she decided. She grimaced though. Maybe it helped him process the micro-facial reading techniques she had worked with him on after each of the last four interviews.

"Might want to wash your hands before you eat, sir." Ellie shot him a twisted-mouth frown. "We've had more than a couple of people spitting on stuff in here."

Ellie walked out of Interview Room D and shoved her head around the corner into the hub area. "Hey, Wilson," she called, "you get all that?"

"Of course, Israel, I get everything." He waved his left hand at her without turning around and pushed the headset closer to his right ear. Then cocked his head slightly and he reached forward to adjust some knob or the other.

"Hello?" Ellie heard Brady Grady's voice wend its way down the stairs.

"Coming right up," Ellie called out. Then she turned back to George. He was now back at the mirrored glass. "Base C.O.'s here," she said, "or did you want to take another lap?"

George looked up from where he had been giving the floor the 1000-yard stare. Ellie had time to put a sweet smile on her lips so he wouldn't feel offended as George's eyes came back into focus on the noise in the doorway and process what she had said.

He gave a little smile at being caught so far away in thought. "That was really fantastic. I can see how you and Wakefield have such success." He was already making his way toward her. His simple "I'm coming" was unnecessary.

**Iraqi Museum Lawn
9 April 2003
0123 hours**

Rivers felt like his head was on a swivel. Where is Judah? He scanned the lawn left to right and back again at near distance, then at mid distance. He dared to hope for far-distance which included the mammoth building that housed so many Iraqi and even Babylonian treasures.

The dark thread of the climbing ladder split the building into two sections and offered Rivers some perspective since he was very familiar with its size. From the rope ladder he traced a direct line back toward himself. He stood to check if she was lying in any low spots in the grass that needed a good mow.

He leaned back into the tree that provide a little bit of cover from at least one direction as he took his gaze all the way to his feet, in case she had not moved when he told her to run. Nothing except her impression matted into the grass.

Following drilled protocol he retraced his gaze back in a straight line all the way to the rope ladder.

There she was! Six feet up and scrambling ever higher up the ladder, hand over hand. He breathed again. Then forced his heart's pumping back into a normal firing pattern between 60 and 70 bpm. There are two ways to climb a ladder. Two and a half. Some people reach one hand at a time on every other rung, pulling up one leg at a time after them. They let go of the ladder one hand at a time. Others, led with their legs charging up the rungs and either slid their hands up the supporting sides as they went, or let go with both hands to catch the side at a higher level while their legs churned away. He had watched hundreds of SEAL candidates climb rope ladders. The ones who let go with both hands caused rope ladders to jerk worse and worse, especially long ones. By the time they reached to top of their first long climb, they either learned to hold their grip lightly and slide it up the swinging rope, or they eventually rang the bell. Never failed. Judah fell into the first category. Rivers had instinctively slid his hands up with churning legs on his first climb.

She made it to the first spreader, the wider stabilizing rung that kept the long ropes from twisting against the building as she shifted her weight from side to side. Then Rivers gave a low whistle that carried easily on the thin air. When he saw Mass who was the next closest to the ladder break away from his hiding place toward the hedge under the ladder, Rivers turned to continue inspecting for threats to his men from hundreds of windows and doorways and rooftops that overlooked the green space surrounding the museum.

By the time he was exposed on the ladder, Mass and Mac would be in place on the roof edge, along with any sentries that had accompanied the Black Hawk SAR pick up team. They would cover the buildings that he had been watching. Rivers broke away from his cover tree and darted through the grass.

Within two vertical steps on the rubber coated rungs, the rotors began spooling above him. His hands sliding up the ropes as they had thousands of climbs before, Rivers only let go to move over the stabilizers every nine steps. Nineteen seconds later he tossed his right leg over the side of the flat roof's lip. Then twisted his body over the four-foot ledge and began to haul the ladder up after him even as his feet landed. No point in leaving equipment behind when no one was shooting at them.

The wind from the helicopter niggled its way under his collar as he brought up the rope ladder. As the final rung popped over the ledge, he felt a tap on his shoulder. Turning just his head, Rivers saw a man who was every inch his equal in size with unmistakably Asian features. "We've got this, Commander. Go ahead and join your people."

"Good man, Chun-Louis." Rivers read the man's embroidered name badge and smiled his thanks as he took off, bent at the waist to approach the open hatch in the side of the helo. He could see Judah already strapped in on the far side and arching back to drain the last of a water bottle.

He stopped at the door to let Mass climb aboard first as he took a final look at the city of Baghdad from this advantage, standing on the skid of the helo. Heavy artillery lit up only one portion of the city in the direction of the airport. It looked like lightning strikes coming from within. But it would have been strangely beautiful if he had not known the destruction that accompanied every single flash of light.

Chun-Louis and his partner had made short work of rolling up the rope ladder and were carrying it to the chopper between them when Rivers shifted his focus back to them. A lukewarm water bottle was pressed into his palm, and he said thanks as he twisted the top off and gulped it down.

The interior of the helo was dark so as not to attract attention, but in the moonlight, it was easy to distinguish that his men and the medics aboard had left one seat empty next to Judah. He buckled himself into it as she watched him and opened the plastic pouch of another food bar.

She handed it to him and reached for another in her lap. Her battle helmet had held most of her blond hair back, but face-framing strands floated around her features like a halo that she had to squint against.

Judah bit the wrapping of the second protein bar open as the last two men climbed aboard and slammed the door shut. The sound didn't lessen. But the wind died abruptly. Judah ran a practiced hooked finger along both sides of her face to loosen the wild hair that had blown into her mouth when trying to take a bite of chocolate-covered protein.

Rivers switched his bar to the other hand and reached for her hand before she could resettle it into her lap. She turned her eyes to him and even though he couldn't distinguish their sea blue in the dark, he could in his memory, and refreshing began to flow back into his bones.

They began the assent.

The co-pilot twisted in his seat. "Where to?" He yelled back. When Rivers glanced up, the man was looking to him for a route with his fist covering the microphone in front of his lips.

Rivers glanced at Judah quickly and shouted back, "FOB Beta."

The co-pilot's black mono-brow rose to a peek in the middle. "But, sir!"

"I know," Rivers said. "But that's where we need to go."

The co-pilot twisted back in his seat, and Rivers watched the pilot's shoulders stiffen as he received their destination. But the man steered them south, and they roared over the city after climbing to the helo's operational ceiling.

"High and fast, it's the only way to fly." Rivers said to Judah as he squeezed her fingers. He checked on each of his men. They displayed a variety pack of expressions from a smile to a smirk. But they were all pleased with their performance. As they should be.

The rescue flight crew not so much. Worry etched their features.

Chapter Fifty Nine

Ellie pushed herself up the last tread of the stairs to find Commander Brady Grady pacing and three of his puppy-dog aides huddled and whispering among themselves on the far side of the Intel staff's door-table.

"George is right behind me." Ellie said strolling into the room. "Coffee anyone?" Someone had started a new pot in the last ten minutes or so because the sucking sound of an empty water reservoir started to gurgle just as she entered the room.

"I loath the stuff." Grady sneered as if it had offended him deeply in some distant past. The three aides gave a small head shake in triplicate. One of them happened to be staring longingly at the coffeepot as he did it though.

Ellie tried to stifle an eye roll. *Have your own mind, man*, she thought but refrained from saying it aloud. She just sauntered over to the pot and poured a fresh cup.

"Actually, it is you I came to see, *Seren* Dayan, but George should hear this too." Grady nodded to the captain whom Ellie heard enter the room behind her.

"Oh yeah?" She cupped her hand around the steaming cup and turned her body into the center of the room.

"We implemented the new protocols you suggested at the airfield. And there is now a backlog of people. Officers are complaining about the time it takes to get on the base." He spoke the accusation in a tone that suggested some reluctance mixed with a pinch of hope that maybe she had a suggestion.

Ellie placed her coffee on the table and straightened back up. It had been his decision to use her suggestion. "Has there been any other explosion?"

Grady's brow lowered. "Of course not. You would have heard it being this close."

"Well then, frankly, I'd tell my officers to stuff it." Ellie shrugged and reached for her steaming beverage again. "These protocols will keep what happened at the front gate from happening again. The extensive and repeated questions will help catch lies and deceptions, the length of time will make any perpetrator start sweating. We designed these protocols for our airline, El Al, and have implemented them all over the world. No one has ever blown up or hijacked an El Al flight since the day they went into practice." Ellie shrugged once more and swigged her coffee. "We do things differently in Israel. The whole world is against us. Well, the Muslim world. *You* guys are pretty generous." She smiled. "We know what works, but it's your base."

Ellie watched one of the aides practically hyperventilating. *Those guys,* she thought, *would any of them ever express an original thought? Even if their nation's security depended on it?*

Grady received her information with disappointment scrawled in his forehead lines.

"There are no shortcuts if that is what you were hoping. By its design, the protocol's lengthy inspection is what makes it work."

"Okay," he resigned. "Also," Grady directed his next statement to the captain. "Wakefield is on her way back. The SEAL Team found her and the SAR helo will be delivering her shortly. You can meet her if you want to."

"I think a hearty 'welcome home' would be appropriate." CAPT George nodded.

"That's what I was hoping. She was out there a while…" Grady trailed off. One of the triplets cleared his throat quietly.

"Is she ok?" Ellie finally burst out when no well-being report was coming forward.

"Didn't say." Grady shrugged. "But she walked to the pick-up LZ under her own steam."

"That sounds like our Judah." George said. "Even with a broken bone, she'd want to do it on her own if she possibly could."

Grady chuckled and glanced at his watch. "ETA about 15 minutes now." Then he started toward the door, his little ducklings arranging themselves into a pecking order line to follow him.

George quickly began unrolling his BDU sleeves that he would need against the night air as he moved closer to his cover on the table.

"We will have at least an hour past that ETA." Ellie reminded him. "New arrival protocols."

George re-rolled his left desert camo sleeve and said, "What do you say we tackle another one downstairs?"

The last of Grady's little underlings closed the door behind them.

"Why don't you pick our next one?" Ellie offered. She had picked the previous four at a 75% success rate. Three had been hiding something, one was clean. She frowned as she considered those odds spread across all the detainees. But, she acquiesced, she had chosen the three men most likely to be involved in nefarious dealings as per earlier interviews, so the numbers were definitely skewed in her favor. She hoped the numbers were skewed. George mounted the stairs to the holding cells.

Airspace over Baghdad
9 April 2003
0229 hours

Wakefield looked at each man in the aircraft. The aircrew were nervous. The men on Rivers' Team were happy. "*What* do you know?" She double squeezed David's hand and tugged so that he would look at her. He did turn, and she could see he was holding something back.

To his credit, and as she knew he would, he began speaking to her immediately. "There was an incident at your billet a couple hours ago."

Her breath caught in her chest. "Just on the base or in the female officers' quarters?" she asked struggling to keep pictures of a shredded, blackened tent with bodies burned beyond recognition being carried out of the curling smoke from forming in her mind. It wasn't working well.

"At the front gate." Rivers' words redirected her fears to the newly installed gate system. The little shed-house with the bench. The drive-on option and the walk-up station. It had all appeared while she was at the airport, taking care of business.

465

She closed her eyes to re-read in her memory the man's name badge who had cleared her through with the other men dressed in their ghilli suits not so many hours ago. Carter. "Did PFC Carter make it?" she asked.

"I don't have any details, except that they are calling it a second mom-bomb attempt. Apparently, one was thwarted earlier in the day. Security is going to be through the roof on the tarmac when we land."

"If I know W-2, we won't be touching down." The young man across from them called out speaking mostly to Rivers.

Wakefield leaned forward and tucked the last bite of her dry protein bar into her cheek. "What do you mean?" she asked. That didn't sound good.

"W-2?" She heard Rivers as at the same time.

The man jerked his head toward the front. "Chief Warrant Officer 2 Paisley, the pilot, call sign W-2. I'm not sure what he's gonna do if he ever gets a promotion."

The man shrugged deeply as a duck-bill-shaped frown deepened on his lips. It appeared to indicate to Wakefield that he had given it considerable thought. Weird, she assessed. "He doesn't like delays much."

Rivers snorted next to her, and she looked at him. "W-2 is going to hover a few inches off the ground so he is not subjected to the delay of the entry protocols."

"If she's lucky." The young man shrugged again. Judah threw him a questioning look. "He may make it a few feet just to make a point."

"Lovely." Wakefield sighed. Then the implications began to sink in. That meant that Rivers would not be coming with her. She sighed again. She had not really had a chance to picture what coming home would look like, but with her second sigh she knew her heart had assumed Rivers would be by her side during the debrief and inquiry.

She leaned in a fraction closer to his shoulder and held his hand a little more snuggly.

She tried to identify his scent above the oil, metal, and disinfectant of the aircraft and the cordite and sweat that clung to them all, but couldn't find it.

They circled the landing strip where Judah had first arrived at the FOB in a full tour. It had changed significantly from the dusty little place the COD had dropped her off less than two weeks earlier.

As they hovered in place and then began a slow descent, Wakefield unbuckled. Leaning into Rivers to provide a semblance of privacy she said over the sound of the engines and rotors, "I'm really trying to be grateful that I got to see you at all, but it's not working very well."

Chen-Louis slid open the hatch and a whirlwind eddied into the cabin.

"I'll pray for you. You'll do fine." He smiled and kissed his first finger and placed it on her nose. Then he nodded at the door.

She shuffled forward so she didn't step on anyone's big booted feet in the non-existent walkway to the opening. They each in turn awkwardly rearranged their feet and offered her a hand past them.

In the hatchway, she saw two men in white vests and anonymous goggles and helmets reaching up to help her down. Apparently the ground crew at FOB Beta was aware of W-2's ways around protocols too.

She gave a slow blink to clear back water stinging her eyes and nose. She would only consider the wind as a source of the wetness. Stepping onto the rail, she motioned the ground crew to wait a moment. Turning to the interior again. She looked each man in the eye, even the flight crew. *Heroes all*, she let show through her eyes, but said, "Thanks very much."

Hopping down to terra firma once more seemed like a stretching of the cord between her and her husband. She knew it wasn't, but still, it felt like more than a physical separation.

When the ground crew hurried her toward a newly built shack with a hand to her shoulder, the helo began to ascend. She heard it in the whine of the beating rotors. She turned back to watch. About the time the skids hit the height of the roof of the tiny air traffic control hut, she felt that bond between her and David snap.

She snuffled back a drip in her sinuses. And kept stepping forward.

A door on the front of the building opened and half an army of men and women waited for her inside the little hut. "ID, please," said the man who had opened the door and stepped in front of her view.

She reached into her collar to loop a finger around the beaded necklace of her dog tags. "How did you all fit in here?" She asked wide eyed. The man stepped forward to snap a photo of her ID with a funny little camera. He didn't answer but said, "Right thumb for printing, please."

She brought her forearm up to the height of the scanner from her elbow and pressed her thumb into the spongy 1x1 square on the funny camera scanner thing.

"While this processes, the lieutenant will ask you some questions."

A camera flashed in her face and she squinted and turned away.

Twenty minutes passed like twenty years as details of her service record and military service protocols were put to her in the form of questions from a series of two young officers and two enlisted personnel. The same questions were repeated no less than three times. Sometimes the same person was asking, sometimes someone different.

Who had come up with this rigorous detail? She wanted to scream.

Just when she was about to lose her cool and demand to see Brady or at the very least get another bottle of water, the very first man's little camera computer thingy dinged, and she could see a green glow reflect off his face.

"You're free to go, Lieutenant Commander Wakefield. Thank you for your cooperation."

She didn't reply. Turning on her heel, she took off at a fast trot for space where she was more comfortable. The Intel House, Commander Brady's HQ, a shower, the chow line, her cot. She didn't have a decision made yet. Just away. Exhaustion oozed from her bones.

"Dang it!" she whispered as she rounded the corner of the little hut. "I forgot to get Butter from David."

Chapter Sixty

FOB Beta Airfield
9 April 2003
0345 hours

"Judah! Judah, over here!" Ellie waved her arms overhead. Never mind the dozen stiff workmates lumped beside her.

Wakefield lifted her head wearily. Ellie watched her reinforce her strength with a deep breath.

Her friend's steps didn't exactly spring with joy at being home, but her pace did increase a bit as her eyes took in their small band of people gathered to welcome her back. George had rousted all of his staff who were not working front gate clean up to meet Judah at the edge of the airfield—after she cleared security, of course.

"Hi everybody." Judah put on a smile that couldn't quite reach her eyes. "Thanks for being here in the middle of the night."

"Old George wouldn't let us sleep anyway." LT John Miller shrugged. Everybody nervously chuckled.

Wakefield thrust out her hand to Miller. "Well, thanks, anyway." A smattering of titters made its way through the crowd.

"Marlow, Al Zikiwi, Anderson, Jamal, Meyer-Smith" Wakefield greeted each man by name as she shook hands with each one in the circle around her.

Ellie could wait no longer. As Wakefield released Meyer-Smith's hand Ellie shoved her arms into their space and wrapped them around Judah's neck. "I'm so glad you made it back!" She squeezed tighter and pulled Judah a little lower as she came down off her tip-toes. "Are you okay?"

When Ellie felt the woman nod slightly in her embrace, it seemed to open up a dam of questioning from the others.

"What was it like?"

"How did you get lost, I mean separated?"

"Are you hungry?"

"Did you kill anybody?"

"How did you get evac'ed?"

"Is it true the SEALs came in after you?"

"Can we help you in any way?"

Ellie felt Wakefield draw back upright and release her.

"Hold up, everybody." Judah held up both hands to quiet the melee. "First, I'm okay." She clicked her tongue in her cheek and held up her fingers to indicate O.K. "Second, I think Grady here gets the first crack at me. Thanks for coming, sir. Could we possibly wait until I've had a moment to sleep and collect my thoughts?"

The C.O. nodded once quickly. "I'll clear my schedule for ten-hundred hours." He extended his hand toward Judah, and Ellie sidestepped out of the way so the two could shake hands.

"I'll be there." Judah promised. "What time is it now?"

"Almost zero four hundred," someone said.

471

"Goodness. You all get out of here," Wakefield shoed them away by flinging her wrists gently. "We'll talk more after I debrief. Thanks for coming down."

Ellie saw the woman's eyes glisten. She recognized sheer exhaustion. She had experienced it all too often.

The crowd began to disperse. Sort of. They were all going the same general direction, away from the airfield and toward the village or the main street of the base for a few more Zs.

"Hold up." Ellie felt a hand pull her sleeve. Judah slowed to give the rest of the guys a chance to move away. The captain looked back, but Judah waved a hand as if to say, "Go ahead; I'll catch up soon."

"What is it?" Ellie whispered.

"Can you do that thing with the showers you did last time?"

Ellie grinned. "I'd be happy to. But it probably won't take much bullying at this hour."

Wakefield exhaled deeply. "It *is* late. But, walk with me to the gate? I need to see the attack before it's all cleaned up."

"Follow me." Ellie threaded her arm through Judah's much the same way that Wakefield had at their first encounter. She led her up the dusty street. "By the way, we have a leak." Ellie updated her after they had passed Intel House. Blackstone and Bousaid were the last pair working that night. The others had disappeared into the two-story building or were getting ready to crawl back into their bunks.

"I know." Wakefield slowed. "How do you know?"

"How do *you* know? George and I just discovered it tonight in interviewing detainees after the second mom-bomb was successful."

"Grady asked me to look into it days ago, and I wasn't able to get to it. For obvious reasons." Wakefield sighed. "What do you mean *second* mom-bomb?" She slowed their gait.

"We have a lot of catching up to do," Ellie promised. "But let's go take a look at the gate and then get you showered. You smell terrible!"

Wakefield burst out laughing. The laughing turned to crying within three chuckles.

"Yep." Ellie patted Wakefield's arm and kept leading her forward. "That's a pretty normal let-down. Just keep putting one foot in front of the other."

Wakefield sucked in a few breaths of dusty moist early-morning air and wiped the backs of her hands across her eyes. "Oh no." she blew out the breath she had just regained.

"What is it?" Ellie slowed them this time to check Judah's face for trauma.

"My very brand-new husband was leading the SEAL Team that extracted me. Last time I saw him I was in my wedding gown. And now I stink." Judah began to giggle again.

Shaking her head, Ellie resumed walking a quarter-step ahead of her friend, lightly pulling her along. "If he's a SEAL, I'm sure he has smelled worse. And besides, you look about 90 years old in that grease paint. Gotta be a story there."

FOB Liberty North
9 April 2003
0503 hours

Rivers cleaned his weapons at a table with his Team quietly. By rote he dismantled first his pistol piece by piece. He laid the hunks of metal on the felt cloth while he stared at the fake-wood grain of the tabletop. So many things should be different. The protocols he had lived by for years were not enough.

Hayes sniffed again, and Rivers realized he must have heard it a dozen times already in his subconscious.

"What is it, Hayes?" He asked without looking up.

"Did that house-to-house search bother anybody else?"

Rivers looked at him then. For a newbie he was able to articulate—no not *articulate* exactly—*pinpoint* the underlying uncomfortable item in their whole long mission for getting Judah out.

The room was silent except the clunks of metal being polished with gun oil and set on the table. "Well, is that normal?" Hayes pushed. "I mean, I know we train to identify tangos versus women and children, and we assess threats by body movement and unhappy little lumps under clothing, but…" He trailed off.

Hayes' eyes flited among Rivers, Mass, and Mac. But Mass' and Mac's eyes were fixed on him through their lashes because the angle of their heads was on their guns. Their experience on the Teams had taught them to seal their lips on things like this. And Rivers wasn't even sure what "this" was yet.

"No," Rivers was surprised himself at the extremely low register his voice came out. "That was *not* normal." He caught Hayes' eye. "And yes. It bothered me." He decided right then and there, "And," Rivers emphasized, "we are going to do something about it."

That seemed to break the stony silence of the other two. "Don't get me wrong," Mass leaned forward on his elbows with one Popeye-forearm lying in front of the other across the oily felt. "I'm glad we got your girl and all, Boss, but I don't ever want to have to make decisions like that again."

"I think we got it right in the end." Rivers was glad his voice had returned to normal pitch. He nodded and resumed the methodical cleaning inside his field-striped barrel rifling until the paper showed no dark residue. "I think each of them were only defending their families."

"We did show up in the middle of the night, unannounced."

"It's war. It should be *unannounced.*"

"That one girl...her brother saved her life."

"She was crazy, man. If she had taken one more step at us...I would have shot her."

"The old man in the house before that is the one that got me. He couldn't understand us. I know that now."

"That was my bad," Rivers owned up in the swirl of conversation. "I should have made sure we had at least two local dialects available on our Team."

As the comments continued to eddy around him, Rivers mind went into a sluggish overdrive, like a monster truck that has too much power but can't switch gears.

He reassembled his Glock and laid it flat on the felt and pulled back his hands like he might in a competition. "Hot chow line is open," he announced, cutting into the conversation and metal clunks. "This is going to be a problem for all of the Teams, so all of us will put our heads together to solve it." Rivers stood. "But not right now." He paused. "Get some food and lots of water. Take a siesta. We will debrief at fourteen hundred. The following morning we will begin discussing the problems, implications, and solutions. I will bring in the full Teams just as we did in Virginia to bring out all the problems, then our strategy guys will tackle it."

Rivers secured his weapons in his locker, snapped both locks closed and walked heavily toward the sausage links and reconstituted scrambled eggs. Maybe oatmeal would be in order today. The list of problems without solutions grew lengthy in his mind. He would have to write it down before he would be able to sleep.

In the doorway of the chow tent he turned back to the guys behind him. "Do I need to say that this is all classified? Nothing outside our group of four until we get to the big meeting later. I'm sure others are experiencing the same thing right now. But right now, this is for our ears only."

Three heads nodded up and down before Rivers cleared them to pass him. He brought up the rear to attack the steaming silver dishes piled high with food.

Chapter Sixty One

Judah Wakefield slid her tray of breakfast onto the table. Dressed in a crispy clean uniform, washed hair wound tightly into a regulation bun, a little bit of make-up, and about five hours of deep sleep, she felt like a new woman. The fuel on her tray, along with coffee, would complete her readiness to sort through everything that had happened since last time she was on base.

The list of to-do items stretched in her mind. *Check on Moe* and *Find the leak* topped the list. Ellie plunked a plate of cheese and toast and a glass of juice on the table across from her and then pulled a green apple from her pocket. "Thought I might find you here. It is time for my second breakfast."

Wakefield grinned as her friend sat down. "Did you even sleep last night?"

"Nah." After I chased that Italian lady from the showers, I went back to the interview room. "We still have a lot of catching up to do."

Wakefield nodded and kept swallowing spoonsful of oatmeal with raisins until she forced herself to slow down.

Ellie made a face. "I don't know how you can eat that watery mush."

"If you put milk on it, you can't really tell it is watery."

"If you say so." Ellie was unconvinced. "I'll stick to food I recognize." She bit off a hunk of bread and tucked it into the hollow of her cheek. "Even if it is white-paste bread."

Wakefield took a bite of her own buttery toast. "So, the explosion at the gate didn't look as bad as I had expected."

"Yeah. Me either."

"Was it worse in the beginning?"

Ellie shrugged. "That was my first look at it. I went directly to interviewing."

Wakefield frowned and nodded. She wasn't sure she could have done that, but she supposed Ellie had seen a lot more messy suicide-bomber scenes than she had.

"I sure put my angel guards through their paces yesterday." Judah shook her head. "I can't tell the story yet, but man!" She widened her eyes in a way she hoped Ellie would be able to grasp the implications. "It was really wild."

Ellie's thin nose wrinkled." So you earned that stench yesterday?"

Judah looked at the remains of her breakfast and chuckled. "Yes, I did! But I hope I smell better today."

Ellie spun her apple core on her empty plate. "Definitely."

"Have we heard anything from Moe?" Judah asked searching for a topic they could talk about as she folded her last bite of toast into her mouth.

Ellie inclined her head and pressed her lips together briefly. "Probably better if we wait on that one."

"Okay," Wakefield said, "then tell me one of those Israeli military miracle stories you were so matter-of-fact about earlier."

Ellie grinned and straightened her posture as she leaned forward. "You said you had not heard about the rescue at Entebbe?"[1]

Wakefield shook her head and continued eating her eggs and oatmeal in alternating bites now that she had slowed down.

Ellie's animated face told the story as well as her words as she painted a picture of a tiny nation with low self-esteem. "We had just lost 11 athletes at the Olympic games in Munich in 1972 and then so many men and women in Yom Kippur War of 1973. After we won at great expense, the Palestinians, with the help of the Arab world, began to rewrite history and somehow the world was buying into their propaganda stories." Ellie shook her head as if she actually remembered reading the headlines that would have run just before she was born. "Then 4 July 1976 a commercial Air France flight from Tel Aviv to Paris was hijacked right after its stopover in Athens where German hijackers boarded."

Ellie detailed the story as if she had been a passenger, scared to death and wondering where the flight would finally come to rest after hours and hours of flying. "Days later all the non-Jews had been released and sent home, save the flight crew who choose to stay with their Jewish passengers. Ninety-four Jews, some of them not even Israelis, and the flight crew of 12 remained for a week! When suddenly on the night before Deadline Day dawned, out of the blackest night, a group of 200 Israeli Elite Commandos arrived.

---

[1] Movie of this story *7 Days in Entebbe* released 16 March 2018 in the U.S. Find a written account on line
https://www.theguardian.com/world/2016/jun/25/entebbe-raid-40-years-on-israel-palestine-binyamin-netanyahu-jonathan-freedland

"They had gotten ahold of the building plans of the hangar where the hostages were being held because an Israeli architect had designed the building back when Idi Amin was friendly toward us. They took off in Israel on Shabbat and flew below the radar for eight hours, sometimes as low as 35 feet! Soldiers were puking their guts up from the turbulence." Ellie's mouth turned from a great smile downward into a grimace.

"Idi Amin was out of Uganda, where the hostages were being held that weekend, and the Israeli commandos had a car that looked just like his car in the back of one of the aircraft they flew into the country. They pulled it out and for a while the Ugandans thought it was Amin returning early. So the commandos were able to get fairly close, but then there was an incident. A few Israelis started firing when one of the Ugandan soldiers recognized it was not Amin's entourage." Judah leaned into her friend's recounting.

"One commando was shot in that exchange, but did not die until later. The commandos rescued the hostages, including some children and hustled them onto the plane waiting to take them home. By way of Nairobi first. Probably needed to get some fuel."

Judah could see the action in her mind's eye. She had stopped eating, fork still in hand.

"So the miracles that surround the Entebbe rescue are that the hijackers landed the plane to let a woman hostage off who faked that she was having a miscarriage—she wasn't even pregnant! They didn't just shoot her. She was able to give information to the Israelis who would be going in. This whole crazy plan to just fly into their turf—who even thinks in bold moves like that?" Ellie shook her head with a huge grin. "They found a car that matched Amin's. He drove this really rare

480

Mercedes limo. They flew four huge transporter planes and two Boeing 707s as support planes 2,500 miles undetected by so many nations that hate us. We landed on an unlit runway. The whole airport had been shut down that Saturday night. We had to stop our approach early in the plan, but still managed to get into the correct hangar and release the hostages. The building happened to have been designed by an Israeli, who happened to still have the plans! Things like this don't happen by chance once, much less six, eight, ten times in a row!

"Only four Israelis died in the whole rescue. Three of the 103 hostages didn't make it out and one elite soldier who had been shot early in the raid. The commando Yonatan Netanyahu died. Jonathan in English. But everybody calls him Yoni."

"Why does that name sound familiar?" Judah searched the books of her memory, but Ellie beat her to finding the answer.

"Yoni was the older brother to Benyamin Netanyahu, our Prime Minister from 1996 to 1999 and who currently serves as our Minister of Foreign Affairs."

"What! So he is like your boss?"

"Well, in a very round-about way, I suppose. It was his idea to send a few of us over here to participate in this action to build Israel's reputation among the Coalition Forces."

"I think it is working." A lieutenant sitting immediately to Ellie's left broke into their conversation.

It startled Wakefield out of the story enough to check the time as the young man continued speaking directly to Ellie. 0953 hours.

"I'm sorry to interrupt, ma'am. I recognized the uniform and sat here on purpose. I wanted to say thank you, but I've been so engrossed with your story. Do you remember the soldiers working the escort service from gate yesterday morning?"

Ellie nodded slowly and cut her eyes to Wakefield and back to the young man.

"Well, PFC John Astor is my little brother. He was there."

"I remember."

"Well, you probably saved his life and countless others by recognizing that first mom-bomb near the gate. He told me all about it." Wakefield placed his accent as being from Wisconsin, Michigan, or Minnesota even as she absorbed the information he was sharing.

"Is everybody calling it a mom-bomb now?" Ellie shook her head. "That's kind of weird, since neither woman was actually carrying a baby, you know."

"It just stuck," Corporal Astor shrugged. "But anyway. Thank you for saving my brother's life. If you need anything while you're here, you just ask. You can find me in the logistics office. Right across the street from you at Intel House."

Wakefield could feel her jaw loosely hanging as she put the pieces together.

"Way to bury the lead!" she finally found her tongue. "You were the one who stopped the first bomber?" She stared at her friend. "You're sitting her telling me this miracle story of what happened three decades ago, when all the time, *you* were involved in a miracle *yesterday*?"

"Not just involved," Astor emphasized. "She recognized the problem. And redirected the group to a wide-open space and then grabbed the baby-bomb right out of the terrorist's arms!"

"Ellie!" Wakefield sat leaning into the table.

"It wasn't exactly a miracle." Ellie shuffled her arms under the table and looked back and forth between them and lifted her shoulders. "The 'baby' should have smelled like a dirty diaper and it didn't. Someone else would have caught it eventually."

"Well, you were the one who did," praised Astor.

"And who gave you the nose to sniff these things out?" Wakefield asked. "God did." She answered her own question. "I still say it is a miracle. And I can't believe you didn't say anything."

"You're a hero all over the base, ma'am. Everybody is talking about the woman who stopped the first bomber."

Ellie was blushing full-on now, but managed to say, "Well, let's make Netanyahu happy and make sure you tell them I'm from Israel, hmm?"

"Sure thing, Dayan." The young man stood and stepped backward over the bench to get out. It reminded Judah she was going to be late to Grady's debrief. She smiled. It was totally worth it to hear Ellie's story like this, right after the Entebbe story.

"I have to go too," she said, standing. And pulling her tray after her. "I am so proud of you and pleased to call you my friend." Judah nodded.

"Go on now," Ellie shoed her away. "You're embarrassing me. You're going to be late. I'll get your tray."

"You're a dear. I'll see you at the office when I'm done. We are going to celebrate your hero status after work tonight!" she promised.

Chapter Sixty Two

Wakefield strolled through the threshold of Intel House feeling taller than she had in days. Meyer-Smith and Goldberg sat at the far end of the door-table near the coffee pot explaining some detail to the administrator, LT Marlow. Only Dov looked up, so she waved and kept walking. At the stairway, she headed down to see what everyone was doing. The whole building was unusually quiet. Was it always? Or had her normal-meter shifted in the racket of the last few days?

Noiselessly, she nodded to two of the Marines stationed outside the interrogation room doors and entered the circle of observation windows that surrounded Wilson's sound equipment. He had reoriented his desk to face outward since she had last been there, and sat typing away with his headphones in place. When he reached to make a knob adjustment, he saw her standing there watching him and jerked his arms back like the knob was on fire.

Pushing back one side of his earphones and then placing that hand on his heart, he said, "Sorry, ma'am. I didn't hear anyone come in. You startled me."

"I'm just here to observe until the next round." Wakefield smiled at his obvious embarrassment. Red was mottling his neck all the way up to his ears.

Judah looked in on each of the interviews and settled in front of the window to watch Ellie. CAPT George was in there with her conducting the interview with a new detainee she didn't recognize from before. That was an interesting development.

Forty-three minutes later a Marine escorted the detainee back to third-floor holding. Judah poked her head around the corner just as the captain and Ellie exited the room chatting away like best buds.

"Hey guys," Judah called to get their attention.

They stopped short and turned to her. "Hi." Ellie smiled. CAPT George looked at Ellie. Some sort of expression Judah didn't understand passed between them.

"Welcome back officially." George nodded to her, but it looked stiff and forced. What was going on?

"Let's take a walk. You can tell me how your debrief went." Ellie said nodding toward the stairs. "Can you record those last observations, Captain?" she asked.

"No problem." George said as he made for the stairs.

Really, what was going on? Judah felt an uncomfortable fear creep into her belly. Junior officers don't ask senior officers to do their paperwork, and if they do, well, the senior officer certainly doesn't say yes!

Dread increased with each step up toward the main floor she took behind Ellie. Wakefield couldn't put a finger on what the dread related to, but it felt like a big-ship anchor.

They were fifteen steps outside the front door before Ellie slowed down and let her catch up to her side. "Why are we going this way?" It was the first question that popped out of Judah's mouth, though certainly not the one pressing on her mind the hardest.

"It seemed secure from electronic or prying ears."

"Electronic ears?" Wakefield choked high in her throat. "What in the world?"

"Exactly." Ellie pursed her lips into a frown that made her lips disappear altogether. "And the field next to the runway seemed like it would be pretty ELD-free."

"What about those directional microphones? They're pretty good these days."

Ellie sighed. "Well, I can't guard against everything. We will just have to whisper."

Dropping her voice, Judah asked, "What are we whispering about?" At the same moment the pilot of one of the CODs on the ground revved his engine so Ellie didn't even hear her. "That's obviously not going to work," Wakefield said at a higher-than-normal volume. "What is going on?"

"The captain and I have been working on our little project under the radar. The problem is too many raids have been unsuccessful, by just minutes." Ellie emphasized. "Food still on the table, beds still warm. Once an open window. That kind of thing."

"And it can't be explained away?" Wakefield's face dropped. She was thinking of Grady's request for an investigation before she had been interrupted. Twice.

"We wouldn't be here if it could."

Wakefield nodded slowly. "What is the common denominator?"

"Us." said Ellie flatly. "All of the intel on the raids that were compromised were generated from FOB Beta."

"No outliers?" Wakefield asked to be sure, because that would be unusual.

"There was one, but according to an after-action interview with the neighbors, they were just messy housekeepers, and it was not unusual for them to leave on a vacation or a weekend away with junk on their balcony, dishes, clothes, toys. So the family could have just happened to leave some time before the raid, and it just appeared to be in a panicked hurry because of the TV trays with dishes still on them and the dirty diaper on the living room floor."

"Oh classy," interrupted Wakefield. She had been picturing Ellie's description in her mind in order to perform her own analysis, and abruptly stopped at the diaper. "How many have there been?"

"At least five. Not counting the outlier."

"That certainly seems like a legit problem."

"Thank God there have not been any ambushes. It seems the people-of-interest have either been told, or have decided on their own, to vacate the premises instead of trying to defend their location with force."

"But that might not remain the case." Wakefield felt her mind spinning with how to narrow down where the information was leaking from, and the processes by which it was being transmitted to the people of interest. Someone was awfully connected. Had anyone in their office been in Iraq before? Was someone under duress? Was someone compromised? Was it more than one person? Could a team accomplish this level of treason and keep it under wraps?

487

"Takita, dinner is ready." Moe called the young woman. She sat staring at the floor, still wrapped in her own memories as tightly as she had wrapped herself in the quilt from his daughter's bed.

Moe frowned; he should have let her cook the meal. She seemed to come back to life when her hands had something to do.

"Takita?" He called again when she didn't move.

She mumbled, "I'm not hungry." At least that's what he thought she said.

"No matter. You need to eat anyway."

She couldn't seem to break free from the trance. Moe looked around the kitchen, and his eye settled on a metal thermos set back against the wall near the sink. Perfect. He moved it to the edge of the countertop, then casually brushed it with the back of his fingers as he turned toward Takita again.

It rocked once, clattered flat onto the counter, and then crashed onto the tile floor as it went spinning across the floor.

Takita shot out of her chair. Her doe eyes and alert stance looked ready to bolt in any direction as she fixed her eyes on the source of the noise that had shaken her.

"Sorry." Moe said. He really was, too. He had wanted to startle her out of the blank stupor, not scare her to death. "It's okay." He used a soft voice. "Come get some of this vegetable soup. I worked hard on it." Moe smiled at her when she finally took her eyes off the offending thermos to look at him. "And it is your turn to clean up the kitchen, whether you eat or not," he shrugged.

A defiant, teenage expression he had often seen on his own daughters' faces when they thought something he said was unfair briefly crossed Takita's face.

Moe dunked a spoon into his bowl and carefully balanced his walk to the small table to eat. Although it was with limp posture, Takita did move to the bowl he had left steaming on the counter next to their camping stove for her. It worked, and he grinned. He pulled out a chair for her and waited for her to shuffle over. And then shuffle back to the counter because she had forgotten a spoon, and finally back to the table.

She was a few spoonsful in when she spoke and startled Moe perhaps as much as the thermos had startled her. "I'll cook next time," she said with more energy than he had observed all day. "Your wife did all the cooking before, didn't she?"

"Yes, how did you know?" Moe looked up.

"This," her spoon made a tinging noise against the rim of the glass bowl, "is terrible. Don't you have any salt?"

"Oh sure." Moe retrieved it from the pantry. When she was done he gave it a trio of shakes over his bowl and dug in again. It was better.

"We need to talk about the future." Moe said.

"What future?" the girl's face looked so old.

"Well, the fighting sounds like it has settled down around here, but the battle over this city has just begun. It will continue for a long while. Do you have any relatives outside the city we could look up and let them know you are all right? Perhaps you could stay with them while this continues."

The girl's frown deepened. She kept lifting the spoon though. "I have two uncles and my grandmother—my mom's mother—that live away from Baghdad."

Moe watched her face as she described between bites. "One of my uncles, I'm pretty sure he is crazy with hate. I could never stay with him. He is probably in the city anyway, because if there is a fight, he will find it. My other uncle is ok." She shrugged. "My mom's mother though, she lives in a village called Fallujah." She shook her head. "I haven't been out there since I was 12 or 13. There was nothing to do."

"A village sounds like a great place." Moe said.

Takita looked up at him again. If possible, her face fell further.

"Do you know her address or how to get there?"

"Really? Why can't we just stay here? I can help you look for your family."

"It is not safe here. This building is falling down around us. And the fighting will get worse before it gets better." He went back to eating.

"I could probably find it on a map. It is about two hours from here by car." Takita finally relented when Moe quit talking.

"Would you prefer your other uncle?"

"No." Takita shook her head. "My grandma's may be boring, but at my uncle's place I'd have to help take care of his six kids. He could probably use the help, but I am just empty of energy. Even lifting this spoon, seems to take so much effort." She glared at the spoon as if it was its fault.

"That will lessen up as time passes." Moe said softly. "If you let it. Forgiveness will go a long way toward lifting that feeling that is trying to smother you too."

"Whom do you suggest I forgive?" her eyes narrowed, piercing him, before she returned to her bowl.

It was the first time he had seen any emotion reach her eyes. He was only a mechanic, not a psychologist, but Moe thought

490

that even difficult feelings were a step up from the vacant stare of the past two days. He tossed his head back and forth slightly even though she was no longer looking at him. No way was he going to point out names of people she needed to forgive. The Holy Spirit could do that, all by Himself.

Chapter Sixty Three

Spring blue had turned to orange, and even that was vanishing from the sky every minute. A chill had already begun to set into her arms and legs with the night breeze. Wakefield stomped a little harder with each step she paced beside Ellie in the grasses that ran the perimeter of the landing strip that was becoming more of an Army heliport than a mini-airport, since the Baghdad airport was now under U.S. control.

"Lemme make sure I have everything straight." Wakefield stared into the fading-from-peach-to-navy-blue streaks on the horizon over the barely discernable rise of the western hills. Her mind collated the information Ellie had laid out about their investigation and outcome from memory over the past ninety minutes. "You've narrowed the focus to our office. I mean it has to be one of the translators, right?"

Ellie frowned and then shrugged. "You'd probably like to think so. They have connections, speak the language."

"But you're suggesting we don't rule anyone out, just because they are American." Judah sighed. She didn't want to think that any serviceman who had experienced 9/11 could betray his country's trust, but you just never know about people's inner motivations. "So, the 12 of us plus the growing level of support staff. It feels like there are a lot more people floating around the office than when we left to interview that guy's 'uncle' and saw Moe. You don't think it is Moe do you?"

"Probably not. The timing of the first problem makes it highly unlikely, but not impossible. However, we *can* eliminate anyone who arrived to work with us after the first botched raid."

"Of course. I was just commenting. But you and CAPT George are sure it is none of the pencil pushers Grady brought with him? Half of that entourage he walks around with feels fishy to me."

"I think that look is fear." Ellie said. "Those boys are scared out of their wits and trying desperately not to show it."

Wakefield gave a begrudging shrug. They would have to get over it or they would go mad with the anxiety while stationed over here.

"Do you guys have notes or anything? Maybe something different will stand out to new eyes."

Ellie sighed as they finished another lap of the landing strip. "Let's go eat." She stepped out of their pattern and into the path that had been worn between the airfield and the little tent city of FOB Beta. Wakefield twisted her next step to keep up. "The problem George and I ran into is that we didn't want anything electronic for anyone to find, and we couldn't leave anything displayed on paper for people to find."

"What did you do?"

"We've been working exclusively at night on connections, and working the questions that come up there into interviews and conversations during the day. We have a story board but only on little bits of paper, and George locks it away every night before catching a few winks. Thus the purple circles under my eyes." Ellie tapped the top of her cheeks with both first fingers. "I am ready for some good sleep."

"Where does he lock it up?" Judah wondered as they rounded the corner and the ever-present guard challenged them for their ID.

The guard ran a flashlight across the photo card. Wakefield squinted and turned away as he turned the powerful light into her eyes to compare her face. She pushed the flashlight beam toward the ground. "Indirect light, soldier. You don't want to blind the whole base."

"Sorry, ma'am." He tried again. With the light trained on the ID hanging from her neck, he checked the photo against her face.

"That's better," she said, and he waved them through.

When they were alone again, Ellie said lowly, "George takes the information back to secure it in his footlocker overnight and he carries it with him during the day. We seal it and unseal it together every night with top-secret tape. I've never observed any tampering."

"Well, it's not fool proof, but it would definitely take some effort and courage to break into a captain's footlocker while he was sleeping right there."

"Keep thinking," Ellie invited. "You can join us in the dungeon at midnight."

"Are you kidding me? You're calling it the dungeon?"

Ellie shrugged an exaggerated shrug at the entrance to the chow hall tent. "It seems more mysterious that way. Especially at the zero-hour."

Wakefield shook her head. As if it needed any help. Then she stepped into the din of prime-time dinner hour on an Army FOB behind her friend.

Camp Liberty North
10 April 2003
1300 hours

Rivers looked at his dive watch as he climbed the three stairs into the new temporary housing for the SEAL team meeting he had secured. "Thirteen hundred on the dot." He twisted the doorknob and halted as he pulled the door open.

The room was packed out.

Whispered conversations ceased as he took a step into the room while removing his cover. "I think I'll just talk from here." He grinned at the great group that had responded to the invitation. "Thanks for coming. It's not our space at The Facility, is it?"

The guys made noises of agreement as they shifted around toward what had been a desk that occupied the front of the room. Two of them sat on the desktop at the same moment. "We are definitely going to need more room." Rivers said as he moved to the center of the space made by shuffling bodies.

"This is a time when I want all of us to put our heads together. I don't think this campaign is going to be a short one. Unfortunately.

"I know each Team has already debriefed on your own, and none of the team leaders have had a chance to read through all the reports yet, so we want to give everyone as full a picture of the landscape as we can. What are our Teams really facing over here?" He cast the vision for the meeting to the crowd of warriors. "We ran into some issues on the palaces raid—we are still calling it a successful mission except for missing our main target who had already skipped—but I'd like to hear what went well and not-so-well for your Teams. Mass, would you mind scribing for us? He looked at his partner who had chosen to stand in the back of the room that was now the reoriented front. "And you too, LCDR Jonesy."

"We will gather the chess players again," Rivers continued, "to work out plans for improvements, and if you have suggestions or ideas, please write them up and submit them to me in the next three days. But today will be a review of the problems."

"Got it, boss." It was Hayes with enthusiasm spilling into his eyes from the side of the room.

For the next two hours while the air conditioner failed to keep up, ninety men began to sweat through their uniforms as they laid everything on the table. "Thank you for your honesty." Rivers commended them. "And keeping even tempers," he chuckled. "I know those were some hard criticisms. Jonesy and Mass, you guys confer and then report to us the things that stand out the most from your notes." Rivers instructed.

"How long will we have?" Mass asked.

"Three minutes should do it." Rivers cocked an eyebrow at him. "We were all in the room, we just need a recap with the stand-out items. Jonesy has been leading SEAL Teams in this environment for years," Rivers looked at him directly, "And you may provide any insight that comes to mind as we go along."

Mass lowered his head and leaned toward LCDR Jonesy, apparently not willing to waste a second in argument.

"Before we move on, sir, my Echo Company put this in our report, and I've been told it has been put up the chain to CENTCOM (central command) and General Franks."

Rivers nodded at LT Wimpfheimer and cut his eyes quickly toward Mass and LCDR Jonesy who were huddled in their bubble with pens pointing to different sections of notes on their papers. "Go ahead, Wimple."

"We breached the Republican Palace from underneath, same as your company. Only we found some bodies in the tunnels."

Rivers looked up sharply. The blond-haired man with a tough jaw had his full attention now.

"It was more than 'some bodies'" another voice chimed in and disappeared before Rivers could get a fix on him visually, so he turned back to Wimple who was nodding.

"It was hundreds of bodies. Maybe more. We left them in place, because of the cooler temperature underground. It seemed better than unearthing them, so to speak. Like was mentioned earlier, we really needed some way to make a record of those deaths. Families need to claim their bodies and put them to rest. We don't want to be blamed for their deaths either. I can see some journo getting wind of this and saying we were the ones who killed them. That's why we've kept so quiet about it. But it was horrible. Just horrible, Commander. Never seen anything like it. Bodies on top of bodies curled in agony."

The room had gone silent. Even Mass and Jonesy had stopped their whisper conference. Wimple's chin quivered with suppressed emotion.

Rivers felt righteous indignation rise up within him. Not for his men's reputation, though that was a side thought. All the families suffering without knowing what had happened to their loved ones. Even evil men had mothers. But knowing Saddam as he did from studying reports, Rivers was pretty confident that the men the SEALs had discovered would have been considered law-abiding citizens if they had been born in a different time or under a different ruler.

"Somebody get me General Franks on the horn."

"I'm acquainted with one of his secretaries." A deep voice spoke. Rivers identified Smithers, one of the guys sitting on the desk on the far side of the room. Rivers pulled his SatFone from his back pocket and tossed it over the heads in the center of the room to Smithers. He caught it one handed as he planted both feet on the floor and then began to weave his way to the door on the far end.

"Give me a shout when you get him on the phone." Rivers said before the man shut the back door. The man nodded, already punching in numbers.

Rivers looked at Wimple. "We are going to make this right, if I have to move the whole of the U.S. Armed Forces to do it." Rivers promised him.

Rivers took a deep breath and turned back to Mass and Jonesy. "You guys ready."

Mass shoved his papers into Jonesy's hands with a slim smile. Jonesy snorted and stood up to address the men.

"Besides that hiccup Wimple's team just mentioned which is probably about to occupy the rest of our week, most of what we need is can be solved with equipment and new procedures or protocols. We heard several times that a few weeks or even months of work in this region is not going to make a dent in the mess of the myriad of political alignments and deep-seated hate for one another. Add in the radical element and Saddam or Bin Laden giving orders to their factions from hiding in exile. It is going to take a lot of sorting."

Jonesy flipped Mass's page in front then. "We need some sort of real time support. Whether spotters on hillsides, drones in the skies or people monitoring button-hole cameras. Both for our accountability or safety if we are accused of something we didn't do, and to give us quick access to information and second opinions—intelligent and informed second opinions—and from people not in the heat of the moment—we need to know whether someone is a combatant or innocent bystander without having to haul whole families in. I agree with whoever called that impractical." Jonesy nodded. "Mass does too; he has it circled and starred."

The room gave a chuckle and Mass tipped his head forward in a bow.

Wimple stuck his head back in the door then. "Franks will be with you momentarily, sir."

Wimple tossed the phone back over people's heads and Rivers said. "You guys take 20 and we will reconvene. The room emptied out as if a drain had been installed.

Rivers put the phone to his ear to listen to international static until Franks picked up.

Chapter Sixty Four

J udah dragged herself to the door for the senior staff morning meeting. These midnight investigations were already starting to wear her down, and she'd only been to two so far. She didn't feel free to talk to any of her colleagues anymore. But the investigation was not opening up. Her mind still churned with the ups and downs on her colleagues' service records, family history, and, as of last night, now their medical records.

She took a fortifying breath and tucked behind her ear a hair that floated in the light morning breeze before pushing open the door. Everyone was already in place around the door-table. Her eyes fell on the only empty chair, the one with a bent-short leg that tended to dump the unsuspecting sitter on the floor. The unwritten rule of the table had been to leave it for the last person to arrive and most everyone had taken a turn or run into a last-to-arrive situation. Early on, she had sat there herself, but not today.

"Lieutenant Marlow, run downstairs and swap this chair for one of the ones in interrogation, better yet, exchange it at the logistics office, and while you're there ask why we don't have a normal table yet."

"Yes, ma'am." Marlow jumped up to follow orders setting his administrative pen and paper for taking notes down on the door-table and vacating his chair.

The rest of the group waited a beat in silence, but CAPT George broke it by ribbing her, "Too good to sit in a broken chair, Commander?" he shook his head and tsk'ed his tongue.

"There is no reason we should have broken down furniture at this stage." Wakefield shook her head as she slid into Marlow's empty chair.

When the others' teasing died down it got quiet for a minute. "What are we waiting for?" she asked.

"Marlow's not back to take notes. We can't start without him." Anderson said from next to her as he took a loud slurp of his coffee.

"Oh for Pete's sake!" she snapped. Then regulated down her voice as she looked up at CAPT George. "Start the meeting. I'll take notes until he returns." She slid the notepad into her lap and pressed her fingers around the pen expectantly.

Thirty minutes of conversation later her fingers were beginning to cramp with trying to keep up, and her penmanship was starting to deteriorate. She looked longingly at her cold coffee cup sitting still full in front of her. Where was that guy? She couldn't even think to participate in the meeting while recording everything that was being said. Something was niggling at the back of her mind too.

"Is that everything?" George had already pushed back from the table, clearly ready to get on with his day.

Marlow stepped through the door just then, the folding chair held by its back preceding him, and a triumphant smile decorating his cheeks. "The new table is right behind me." he announced. "I may have tossed around a few of your names to get some action out of the logistics staff." He shrugged. "But I'd say getting rid of a bomb should be worth a table and a chair. Easy."

Bodies began jostling in the room to clear space for the logistical men who were entering the room behind Marlow.

As Judah stretched her neck muscles side to side, suddenly the thing her mind had been trying to push into her conscious thoughts since yesterday jumped into focus and out of her mouth. "Moe."

"What *about* Moe?" Ellie asked.

"We've seen no actionable intelligence out of that one." George said as he also stood.

"Nothing?" Judah frowned. She had felt so confident about him and his story.

"There was a message. One. He let us know during the attempt to get Saddam that the raid was going on and that Saddam was leaving with his body doubles." George said. "Real helpful. What about his tracker?"

"What did we do with his wife and kids?" Judah asked, stilling herself as the chaos of the furniture exchange flowed around her.

George shrugged and shook his head in a tiny gesture. Ellie shrugged.

"Are you telling me we haven't picked them up yet? Judah asked leaning forward to quell the sick feeling heaving in her stomach. "Like we *promised* him?"

The door-table skidded across the sawhorses a few inches before a man each took a corner to pick it up. The four of them set the heavy door upright to lean against the wall.

Judah pointed outside and jutted her jaw toward Ellie, inclining her head toward the captain. She wished she could order him outside too.

Going against the flow of intelligence officers making their way to the lower level to await delivery of their first interviewees of the day, the three midnight-investigators reconvened in the small outdoor space between the corner of Intel House and the ramshackle concrete-block shop next door.

"Don't get upset," the captain warned. "It has only been a few days. And." His forehead wrinkled. "I wasn't thoroughly convinced of his character and leanings in the first place."

"I was." Judah and Ellie spoke together.

Ellie continued, turning to Judah. "Honestly, with you going missing and all the other interviews and the mom-bombs, I just forgot about him."

"So we have not collected his family and we have not heard from him. Plus, we have this steady leak of information coming from our facility." Wakefield shook her head. "This is not good. Perhaps there is a *reason* we have not heard from Moe, and the reason is, he opened his mouth here." She jerked her thumb over her shoulder to indicate the Intel House.

The other two were quiet, but their faces showed Judah they were leaning toward her assessment.

"Sir, permission to go find him?" she asked while she had his favor.

"How are you going to find one man, even a family of five, in a city of eight million people? Many of whom are angry with the people who wear your flag on their uniform."

"We have his home address." Wakefield remembered writing it down in Moe's file and quoted it to him.

"And we know where he works. Worked." Ellie added. "I'm going too."

One of Grady's pencil pushers walked up to their circle of three. "Sir," he held out a sealed envelope. "Message for you." When George reached for it, the messenger turned and walked back across the dusty street with the empty-handed logistics boys.

Slitting the tape, the mouth of the envelope yawned open when George pushed on its creased sides. Scanning the contents he said, "That little search party is going to have to wait. We all have a humanitarian mission to attend to first. Turns out that little tunnel horror-legend that has come up in our interviews so many times since we got here is true. And Hussein got to them before he disappeared." George handed Wakefield the missive and turned his back to them. He pounded his fist once against the Intel House wall as he let out a single curse. Then he walked away.

Judah quickly scanned the document and held it at an angle so Ellie could read it at the same time.

"Hundreds of bodies piled atop one another." Wakefield whispered the number aloud. Anger filled her belly.

"I will go. I will be a witness." Ellie stood with her eyes closed as she whispered the words from a place of inner strength.

Wakefield was quiet for a moment pondering Ellie's strange reaction. When the woman's eyes flicked open Judah was still staring at her.

"When was the last time you remember seeing photos of bodies stacked like cord wood?" Ellie asked.

Then it dawned on Judah. "Germany. 1945."

"And Poland and Denmark and Austria and Czechoslovakia and Lithuania, Latvia, France, Italy." Ellie trailed off. "I know what this feels like. I will be a witness to this atrocity. To this pain."

Judah didn't know what to say as she saw the pain of generations lost cross her friend's face, so she just placed a hand on her shoulder and gently squeezed.

**FOB Beta
Convoy Gathering Space A
11 April 2003
1502 hours**

Ellie refused lunch, but did take a full canteen of water. When the first caravan of Army grunts left FOB Beta by the repaired front gate three hours later, Ellie sat in the front seat of the second vehicle. Judah wanted to wave goodbye as her Jewish friend disappeared. But she just watched and counted 14 trucks of men plus Ellie as they went through the gate toward Baghdad. She knew the dead of the terror prisons would be treated respectfully with Ellie keeping watch.

Wakefield returned to Interrogation Room D, heaviness weighing on her.

Chapter Sixty Five

Rivers dragged the last box of body bags from the transport truck and handed it to a young soldier in fatigues. "We are going to need to order some more of those." Rivers gestured to the Army private, one among thousands crawling unheeded over the palace lawn and exploring the tunnels where once only the highest echelons of Iraqi royalty or servants were allowed to walk.

"Got it." Another young soldier, PFC Hanson, marked Rivers' order on a clipboard that seemed attached to his arm. Rivers had not seen him separated from it since they had arrived mid-day, day before yesterday. The PFC whipped out a SatFone identical to Rivers' and placed the order while Rivers scanned the ordered chaos of the lawn.

"My guy said the fans and ice the Israeli chic ordered are already en route." Hanson spoke up from behind Rivers. "Do you want to turn them back to wait for the body bags?"

Rivers didn't turn to speak to the young man, but kept watching the lawn movement. "That is 'Israeli officer' to you. She could kill you with one hand tied behind her back, and probably wouldn't appreciate being called a chic. No. Don't turn the fans back. Have your guys send another truck once the bags are ready."

Rivers was more than ready for the fans. They should help get fresher air into the tunnels. It was bad down there. The smell of death eked its way through masks and many of the men had tied a bandana over their medical mask to filter out more of the odor.

Rivers walked across the spongy grass, back to the entrance of the little shed where he had watched the Teams storm the palace days before. He thought he remembered seeing some great coils of rope in there with all the lawn equipment.

His briefing with General Tommy Franks had turned into a special project for him to lead. The general had 'suggested' a joint operation for the 90 SEALs who had shown up at that debriefing meeting and 1000-plus enlisted U.S. Army soldiers from the FOBs springing up to surround Baghdad, a couple hundred men from each base, and all of the international community represented among those bases who wanted to come.

"Keep it out of the press, as much as possible," Franks had warned, "but record it for posterity."

Rivers had met men and women from Australia, Great Britain, Israel, Spain, and Poland. It offered him fresh hope to see the nations coming together against the evil this regime had poured out on its own people. Even if they were uniting over body bags, it was a start.

Rivers took a last look around the perimeter and adjusted the rifle slung across his chest. Everything looked in order, so he descended the stone and earthen stairs and entered the dark shed area, avoiding the staircase leading into the tunnels deep below.

The Israeli had offered him a perfect solution for organizing the display of victims to get as many people in and out as quickly as possible. For one so young, she had spoken up with confidence. Not the boldness of some officers trying to make a name for themselves. "This is how you do it," she had said and then laid it out simply in lightly accented English. Experience, he finally identified the root of her confidence. And she was right about the timing too.

Urgency quickened his steps as he ducked into the doorway. There was a lot to be done, and the announcement of the time to help identify the bodies was already in printing at several of the FOBs. One hundred thousand leaflets would be dropped over the whole city beginning at 1400 hours.

Power had been restored to most of the city that had lost it during the initial days of bombardment, so Rivers lightly rubbed the wall at the doorway to feel for a light switch. Nothing at American light-switch height, but just lower than his shoulder he found it.

Dim light from a single bare bulb shooed darkness from the middle of the room into the corners, where it lurked like a live thing behind push mowers and other yard-keeping implements.

"Where did I see that rope?" He asked himself glancing around. The place felt so much lighter than his first trip.

He didn't see any rope from this angle. He walked around the stairway and descended about half a flight, turned and began to come back up, in order to duplicate his route and angle of entry so that if the rope was around, he might be able to find it.

Yes. "There you are." Second shelf from the top. Nearer to him now than when he had come in from the door. A box of oily junk parts sat in front of it hiding it from the other angle. Rivers shone the flashlight's beam over it, the nylon rope gleamed white and clean. "Perfect."

Ascending to the main floor again, Rivers scooted another box of used spare parts out of his way with his boot. He shoved a lawnmower forward out of his path. He stretched around the greasy parts and touched the rope, but he would not be able to grasp the spool of rope with any kind of leverage at this distance. So he pushed against the wooden shelf unit to stand upright again. Then popping the flashlight into his back pocket to shine upward, he stooped to lift a pair of five-gallon jerry cans out of his way.

Something shiny caught his eye as he stood to move them. He plunked the cans down closer to the doorway and out of his egress path. Returning, Rivers pulled the flashlight from his pocket and directed the beam under the shelf where he had seen a little flash.

Light reflected from a small brass lock in the side of a well-used brown leather briefcase thick enough to hold several laptops.

"What do we have here?" Rivers noted there was no dust on the case. Its flopped-forward handle boasted a molded grip, not pre-molded plastic or even leather, but molded from the fingers that had carried it.

Rivers shone the light around as far as he could get to the back without moving it. It was unlikely to be booby-trapped with explosives. Its location and orientation felt to Rivers as if the case had been stashed in haste. Hidden behind gas cans and a lawn mower. Still, better to be safe than sorry. He checked the left side. No wires, no fishing line, no lasers that he would interrupt by moving the case. He picked up the handle, raised the case out of its little cubby hole, and listened for tell-tale clicks or beeps of activation of timing devices, Rivers brought it fully into the light and began to walk toward the full light of day.

It felt heavy, but it was more paper-weight than laptop-weight. Still, he decided as he set it in the sunlight, he would call a bomb-squad guy over to open it.

Rivers hustled back inside and pulled the spool of half-inch nylon cord toward him. He hoisted it onto his shoulder and walked it over to where he had last seen the Israeli, leaving the brown leather bag on a grassy patch of sunshine.

**Republican Palace
13 April 2003
8:05 AM local time**

Ellie leaned against the open front doorway of the palace. Both large doors hung open as if airing the place out of the resident evil, or bad fumes. Whichever. The SEAL who had been assigned to lead this mission seemed to really understand it. That was a nice change from other American higher-up officers she had interacted with in the past. Most of them didn't know how to take her.

Ellie took a slug of water from her canteen. The men were definitely making progress. She calculated how many bodies she had seen. Each took a toll from her, but the math portion of her brain was still working fine, and for that she was grateful.

The two enlisted U.S. soldiers LCDR Rivers had assigned to tail her stood, one inside and one outside the palace, on her right and in her left.

She saw Rivers trucking in her direction across the lawn with his arm threaded through a coil of rope on his shoulder. He stopped a pair of soldiers said something to them, one went back toward the white tent that had become an HQ of sorts, and the other jogged back in the direction of the little shed where Rivers had been coming from.

She checked out the rope as he approached. Perhaps a little bit thicker would have been better, but the clean whiteness would be helpful to keep the line visible.

"What was that all about?" she asked as the SEAL mounted the bottom stair.

"I found your rope." He grinned and hoisted it off his shoulder, continued up the stairs, and dropped it into the arms of the outside soldier he had assigned to her. "I also found a bag, I asked the bomb squad to take a look at before I open it."

"Hmm," Ellie grunted, already moving to finger the spool of rope. "This will do nicely, Commander."

"How do you want to work it?"

"Tie a knot in the end, to keep it from curling up or unraveling," the woman began.

"You guys paying attention?" the SEAL called to the men he had assigned to her.

The one who had been inside moved closer and nodded. Ellie stepped back so his view was clear. "I want you to cut 70 meter lengths and knot each end securely. Then lay it straight on the lawn. Repeat the procedure laying the next line parallel to it with about five to five and a half meters between them.

"The bodies will be moved, in the body bags after the sun starts going down. We will all need to help with that. There are so many people down there. Each body bag will need to have the face section unzipped once it is laid on the line. The heads should all be touching the rope, on each side. Leave about a meter between each body so a family member can move in closer if needed."

511

Ellie looked the young soldiers in the eye. "You don't want more than five and a half meters between the lines because the people need space to move past, but not enough to pile up the people. You understand, yes?"

Both men nodded.

Rivers spoke up again, "Can you guys convert meters to feet?"

"Multiply by three." The soldier's reply was short and close enough for government work.

"You look like you're covered here." Rivers told her. She could see he was itching to get back to the bag mystery from his backing down the stairs.

"Sure," she shrugged. "We will be needing more rope, if you find any." There were so many bodies down there.

"On it." He nodded. "And the metal detector and ice and fans are en route as we speak. I'll let you handle that set up as well."

"Go on." She waved him off. "We've got this."

As the man turned around to continue off the stairs, she saw a pair of white puffer-suited men following another soldier out of the HQ tent toward the little shed. "That should be interesting." Ellie kind of wished she could follow him over and see what was in the bag.

Chapter Sixty Six

Rivers jogged over to intercept the bomb-squad and then slowed to walk to the bag with them as he described where he had found it and the condition.

"I don't think it is an IED, but—"

"Better safe than sorry with this many folks running around." The hollow sound of one of the bomb tech's voices interrupted.

"My thoughts exactly. How are your lock-picking skills?"

"I brought a kit." The other bomb technician held up a little clear plastic case.

As they arrived, the soldier guarding the bag smiled nervously. "No ticking, sir. Do you mind if I get out of here before they start working?"

Rivers chuckled. The man was already inching away from the bag. "Thanks for keeping an eye on it. As you were." The man he had commandeered took off double time across the green grass.

Rivers smiled at the two men dressed in white Michelin-man attire. "I'm just going to back a ways over here too, while you guys work."

513

"That's all we're waiting for, Commander."

Rivers frowned at his impertinence, but it would just take longer for him to see into the bag if he took the time to dress him down.

As it was, inside three minutes the bomb tech with sass had laid down his lock-pick set and the pair were on either side of the bag, using two-foot-long poles with hand-claws to turn the bag and slowly pull it open centimeter by centimeter, one of them checking for trip wires or electronic sensors with each centimeter.

"All clear, Commander Rivers. It just looks like paperwork, and it is all in Arabic scrawl." It was the same speaker as before.

"I'll thank you to keep your opinions to yourself, Michelin-man."

"Never heard that one before, sir." The man did everything but roll his eyes.

Rivers stood to his full height, which was a solid six inches beyond the other man's insolent frame if he had stretched to his tip-toes. "Don't be like that." Rivers said simply. "Dismissed."

Rivers went to his knees to take his first look at the contents of the leather case as he tuned out Michelin-man's two berating buddies. They returned to the tent on the far side of the lawn near the shade trees. Rivers had been in those pads enough times to know how steaming they got in the sun, despite their reflective white fabric.

Rivers removed an inch-thick handful of paper and flipped through one sheet at a time. The man was correct that they were written in scrolling Arabic lettering, but it was not a scrawl. Some of it was hand-drawn documents. Most of it was laser-printed documents. Almost every page contained either a black or red inked date or raised imprint seal. Very official looking.

He couldn't read a word. He tidied the papers back into a stack and slid them back into the bag. "I know somebody who *can* read them though." A smile pulled at his cheeks and he stood. He would courier the bag to Judah now, and then as soon as the ID viewing event was completed, he would make a little visit to FOB Beta and get a first-hand account of the translations. And bring her little Butter kitty back to her.

Until then, he would have a couple of people take apart the entire shed and floor for anything else that might be hidden. "I'll send them downstairs too." He adjusted his rifle upon standing. "If someone important enough to carry this many papers with official seals was comfortable enough to hide those papers, not defend them with his life, came through here, he probably came from the palace through the tunnels. There could also be physical clues to say who it might have been, in addition to the content of the official documents."

He felt a smack to the center of his back. "Not good, a SEAL talking to himself."

Rivers turned to find Mass's big grin in his face, and snorted. "Maybe it is time I retire then."

"Naw. Boss, you're too good to retire. I'll just follow you around so people won't notice you talking to yourself." Rivers chuckled. Mass *would* too. "Whatcha got there in your supersized briefcase?"

"Not quite sure yet. But I am pretty sure it will become a new work assignment."

"Is there a Commander Judah Wakefield in the office?"

Wakefield looked up from the coffee-pot end of the new table where she was comparing impressions with CAPT George from the long interview they had just concluded where she got to play the translator. "That's me." She did not recognize his long oval face as he moved from lurking in the doorway.

"I have a courier delivery. Gotta sign for the chain of custody." He set a large clear plastic bag on the floor and shoved a clipboard and a pen toward her. She walked over and glanced backward through the printed names and signature lines as she signed her name on the fourth line. There at the top sat her favorite name: David Rivers.

"Thank you," she said to the young Army grunt with the long round jaw. He disappeared as quietly as he had appeared.

Wakefield hefted the plastic evidence bag by the rolled down and sealed top and set it on the table for a better view. A well-used, high-quality, leather briefcase. It did not seem personal. "Come take a look," she invited George over as she turned the bag around to see the back side of the leather case.

The captain scraped his chair against the floor. He leaned over and pressed the clear plastic against the brass locking mechanism to view it more clearly.

"Curious." He glanced up and caught her eye.

Wakefield knew by now that they both had a thing for a good mystery. "Shall we?" she asked, more than a little curious herself. "Is there any kind of a note or instructions or anything? Where did that delivery kid go?"

516

Wakefield walked over to the door to look for him just as it was opening again. "Sorry," the young man's face was longer than before. "I forgot to give you this. I had stowed it in my back pocket and, people are always telling me—"

Wakefield cut him off. "It's okay. I'll take it now. Thank you." The small envelope had her name on the front in Rivers' all caps writing. The white envelope was a little rumpled, but the lick and press seal held fast.

Wakefield watched the young man amble back toward the gate with his hands in his pockets. Where had he come from? Maybe Rivers' envelope would provide more information.

The crackle of plastic drew her back to the room. George had the case lying on its side and was smoothing the plastic with wide fingers to see better. "We could open it, sir." Wakefield gave a half smile at his eagerness.

He bellowed loud then, "Lieutenant Marlow."

"Sir?" Marlow hurried into the room.

"Do we have any evidence gloves?"

"Um, no, sir?" Confusion wrinkled his face until he caught sight of the bag on the table.

"Go commandeer us a box. And get some of that sealing tape you put a signature on."

"You think logistics will have it, sir?" He was already reaching for his cover.

"Best bet." George said, his back still to her and Marlow.

After Marlow closed the door. Wakefield strolled back to examine the case. "We have evidence tape." She reminded him as she slit open the envelope.

"But *why* do we have that tape?" George asked breaking his gaze at the briefcase to lift a single eyebrow in her direction.

"Oh. Right." Wakefield put it together. "No explaining that way." They had ordered the tape to seal the edges of the leak investigation every night. It was on file in the logistics office and could be found if anyone knew to look for it. But no one outside their group of three would know to look.

She pulled the folded yellow sticky note out of the envelope. "Not very wordy." She commented as she pushed open the envelope to look for anything she had missed. "This is it."

Judah pulled open the gummy side and read in masculine all caps: CAN YOU TRANSLATE THESE FOR ME ASAP? I'LL BE BY AS SOON AS THE BURIAL IS COMPLETE AND BRING A YELLOW SURPRISE WITH ME.

"Where are we in the body identification and burial process?" she asked George.

He frowned. "Probably a couple of days." He shrugged. "Your guy is involved in that, right?"

Judah couldn't keep a small smile of pride from her lips. "I believe he and his SEAL Team are leading the organization, sir."

George nodded once and turned back to the briefcase. Judah shrugged. Well, David getting to lead the work was a big honor to her. "There must be some documents or recordings of some kind inside the case. He wants a translation."

"Does he say whose it is?"

"He'll be here as soon as the burial is over. You can ask him then, if it is not evident in the translation."

George wiped his palms on the seat of his uniform and turned the bag around for the fourth time. "Hurry up, Marlow." He growled under his breath.

It was another three minutes before Marlow opened the door. He walked in holding out a pair of large-size latex gloves toward the captain and wearing a little grin. Wakefield gave a tiny shake of her head as she smiled. Marlow had come to recognize the captain's enthusiasm to move quickly in the few weeks they had been serving together. Marlow held out the open box toward her, and Wakefield saw the tape roll on Marlow's wrist like a bracelet.

"Thanks," Wakefield said automatically as she pulled two gloves out of the box like tissues one after the other and slid her fingers into them with a snap.

George was already breaking the seal and unrolling the evidence bag by the time she was gloved up, and Marlow placed the box and tape on the table and stood to watch.

"Uh, this need to know." Wakefield prompted Marlow to return to his duties. The lieutenant's face fell. "Sorry. At least for now," she added.

"I sure hope so," Marlow muttered in disappointment, pushing his cover into his belt as he turned away.

"Oh my goodness." George had the briefcase standing open on the table with the plastic bag shoved behind it. His right fist was full of paper of varying hews. Some were a crispy white, others had yellowed with age. George's left hand shuffled through the pages like he was reading a magazine from back to front. "You've got your work cut out for you, Wakefield."

Wakefield felt her eyes widen further and further as the pages flicked by. There were hundreds of documents there.

"You going to want some help?"

"Let's see what we have first." She leaned toward George and tugged a random page from the already-viewed side.

She silently read the header and then the body of the document, her lips moving as she mothed the Arabic words.

"Oh boy." She looked up to find George staring. "I'd better do this all myself." She looked at the ceiling. "If one of the factions here in Baghdad had found the equivalent documents on our letterhead, the information contained would have been designated at least super-secret." She tried to impress the importance of what Rivers had sent without revealing any of the information contained in an unsecured environment.

That leak had to be plugged soon! She sighed. It was getting really old not to be able to speak freely to her boss and coworkers.

"I'm going to need a quiet, secure space to work, and a computer that is disconnected from the Internet."

"Why don't you take Interrogation D, and set up facing the glass. There is no Web connection cord in the rooms down there. There's no reflective surfaces on the walls so no one could see anything on the screen."

Wakefield frowned as her eyes couldn't help wandering back to the page. "We will have to make sure the recording mics are turned off. Better yet, I'll remove them. Sometimes I have to speak out loud to get a feel for author's intention when I'm working."

George nodded and stuffed his half-ream of papers back into the bag and snapped it shut. He headed down the stairs to the dungeon carrying the bag in front of him like a baby.

She wasn't supposed to let it out of her sight for the chain of evidence custody she had signed for.

Wakefield gathered up the plastic evidence bag, tucked the box of gloves under her arm, and threaded her arm through the roll of tape as Marlow had conveniently carried it too. Then saw their interview notes they had been working on spread across the table at the coffee pot end. She shuffled those together too and put a finger between the Arabic document and their notes to keep them separate.

She could hear George's weight descending the stairs now, but she couldn't see him anymore. She left their cups of coffee and half-full bottles of water and hurried after him. She shook her head. It wasn't going to do him any good to get there ahead of her; George couldn't read Arabic.

At the foot of the stairs, Judah quickly looked to the captain who was talking to Wilson, but holding the bag in the exact position as when he had left upstairs. Both his hands were occupied with the weight and position of the bag, so Judah felt satisfied with the chain of custody. He could not have removed a piece of evidence in the seconds the case had been out of her sight.

She shook her head. Custody was so engrained in her she couldn't even trust her boss.

Normally the marine guarding Interrogation Room D, which she had adopted as her own, was a step ahead of her, but he had been looking at the assortment of items in her gloved hands and arms. "Can you get that door?" she asked him.

"Ma'am." He opened the door and walked in ahead of her, gave it a once over and stepped back out, though it had been less than ten minutes since she and George had left it.

Wakefield unloaded her arms on the floor in the corner, holding onto the papers, separating the two contents once more. As George entered Room D, Judah stuck her head out the door. "Hey Marlow, can you grab something to sanitize this table for me?"

"Right away, ma'am." He had wiped his earlier disappointment from his features.

While Marlow went to the supply stash, Judah Wakefield scampered to the tabletop, and planted her boots right in the middle with a thunk. She reached over her head and unscrewed the microphone head from the light that hung above the table, leaving an empty plug-in dangling from a black wire. She stuffed the tiny foam-covered microphone into her hip pocket. Hopping to the chair then the concrete floor, Wakefield moved toward the one-way glass. "The video feed is already off," she said. "But why don't you redirect the lens, just in case?"

George walked around the corner as Marlow returned and wiped the table down.

When George returned, he still held the case like a kid holding a dog that was just a little bit too big to carry, with both arms underneath. The video recorder was hanging from his palm precariously. He paced the room as the men disappeared. Then set the camcorder on the table beaded with cleaner.

Wakefield studied her C.O.'s face as he dried the table with his sleeve and finally set the case down. He was overly excited about this.

"You know this is going to take weeks to unravel, right?"

"I know. What can I do to help?"

Wakefield sighed. So much for a quiet space on her own. "First, let's sort them for priority."

His grin was infectious though, and Judah found herself smiling back at his enthusiasm. "Three piles. One for completely hand-written papers, or stuff that looks like notes. Another for stuff that looks like official papers at a national or state level.

"And the third?" George asked.

Wakefield took the first document and laid it on the far end of the table from where they stood across from one another. "That pile is the what-in-the-heck-is-this pile."

"Most of these have some sort of date stamped or written." George said a few minutes later. "As soon as you start the first translation page, I'll organize each pile by reverse date."

Wakefield glanced up, she had not placed anything in a pile for at least a minute as a familiar name sent heat flashing through her body, freezing her somehow in place.

Arafeh Filesek.

"What is it?" George asked.

"I know this man. I mean knew him." Judah looked up to find a very concerned C.O. coming around the table toward her.

"I'm ok." She held up a hand. "Sorry. It was just a surprise. Filesek is the one who gave me this lovely reminder of how hateful people can be." Judah traced the scar on her cheek with two fingers.

"I had wondered about that. It is above my paygrade in your file."

"Really?" Wakefield cocked her head. With her clearance level, she didn't see many personnel files that were redacted, especially to a C.O. whose clearance should have been higher than hers. Interesting that George had dug into her file. "You could have asked." She shrugged as her body temperature came back down to normal.

"Well?" he asked.

"I used to get loaned out to the CIA," she began and gave him the short version.

"Are you kidding me? That's crazy!" Captain George stood there engrossed with papers still in his hands.

"Oh, that's just the highlights," Judah sniffed. "I am glad I can laugh about it now. Almost." She placed the Filesek paper on top of the what-the-heck pile and left it there, to reach for another page.

Chapter Sixty Seven

Moe sat up cross-legged on the bed that he should be sharing with Liliya. He could not power down from the day's thoughts. He had tried lying down, reading scripture by the limited candle light they had remaining, praying. But his legs and his heart were restless. He stared into the darkness around him. Then he squinted and blinked and squinted harder. Much of the smoky cover that had hidden the sky for almost two weeks had cleared in the last few days.

The shadows seemed to shift with their own life, but Moe didn't trust his own eyesight by starlight. He could almost perceive people trickling out of the alleys. Mostly singles, but a couple here and there. He rubbed his eyes and forced himself to focus more sharply on one spot that was a little lighter than the others in the faint light of the new moon plus two days.

It was people. And not just a few. All the movement he could see was heading in the same direction too. Toward the city center. He had not seen so many people out since the day Saddam Hussein was torn from his pedestal in the square and dragged through the streets, if only in statue form.

Moe stood and slowly crouch-walked to the unstable, open-edge of his bedroom to conceal himself behind a low and jagged remaining right-side wall to peer down at street level.

Dozens of people streamed at a slow steady pace, oblivious to the distant gunfire still echoing through the city and the dusk curfew announced by American papers that fell from the sky. Knowledge dawned all at once. Moe felt both hope and dread equally in the atmosphere.

And he knew he needed to join them. He would leave Takita a note. She shouldn't have to revisit the place of her horrors anyway. Those American papers had also announced that beginning at 10 AM the people of Baghdad could come and help identify people who had been found in Saddam's tunnels of terror. Well, the flier had not called it that, but Moe did.

It appeared that his city would line up to wait through the night. A silent solidarity of shared grief and loss. He should be there. "Lord, would you come and walk among us. Be with this city as she sees the truth of what President Hussein and his sons have done. Help us to grieve well and not allow hate to rise in our hearts."

So Moe pushed against the floor to get up. His knees protested with cracks and pops. He draped his outer robe around his shoulders and traipsed back down his ramshackle stairs—with the last two stairs missing altogether—for the first time in two days. He joined the foot traffic streaming toward the city center. He had a strange feeling of hoping against hope. He wanted somehow for Missy Judah to find him there among the mourners and tell him his family was safe. That there was no abduction; that his neighbor had seen some other family taken by the Special Republican Guard visit.

"Wouldn't that be good, Father?" Moe suggested in prayer as he let the idea have some freedom in his heart.

Republican Palace
Allied Troops HQ Tents
13 April 2003
1300 hours

Rivers walked back under the awning of the tent the whole force was working from. He looked back at the line of Iraqis stretched further back than he could see. In some places before they reached the rope funnel toward the metal detectors, the line was more of a mass. He guessed that, at minimum, half of them were armed.

If they had wanted to rise up and make a stand, this was the time they should do it. But it had been more than 12 hours since the line had begun to form. All the bodies had not even been lined up at that point. A new tunnel had been uncovered and the 10 AM start time had come and gone.

"Lieutenant Commander?" an Army Specialist pushed her helmet back to wipe sweat from her dark brow. "We are going to need more water for this line. Can I get your signature to order another couple of trucks?"

Rivers stuck his head back into the tent where the first two truck-loads of water bottles had been unloaded. Each semi-truck carried 30 pallets, 51,000 bottles of water. Heat had accumulated inside without the benefit of the light breeze that came through every few minutes outside. The ice-and-fans swamp cooler provided a little relief from the raging Baghdad sun outside, but that was only available near the bodies, once people had stood in line for six to ten hours.

"Where is—" he stopped as she handed him the requisition form on a clipboard and a pen. As he handed it back, he offered her his hand. "That was really well done on the timing." He nodded at the pallets along the back wall that were still stacked high and uniformed men and women from around the world were grabbing a case at a time to pass out bottles down the long line.

"Thank you, sir." She smiled through the stress and heat and stood a little straighter as she walked away to get the order filled.

Rivers walked around observing. Was 2200 soldiers and aid workers enough to serve the hundreds of thousands of people who had come?

As he passed the soldier check-in station, he heard a New-England-accented grumble as a soldier joined a que 12 people long. "This is such a waste of time. We need to be back out there."

Rivers wheeled up and stood practically on the man's heels. The enlisted man turned around with his elbows extended, but quickly tucked them back in as his eyes roved over Rivers' rating insignia and designation. "Do you have a better suggestion for the way I might keep track of 2200 men and women under my command who are spread out over a mile, coming and going in enemy territory on their own? Do you suppose the two minutes you stand here will make any life-or-death difference out there? Would you like to volunteer to forego anyone even knowing you are missing until morning muster if you get lost or are kidnapped? Oh look, it is your turn."

"Sorry, sir." He had the decency to look down sheepishly. "Won't happen again." He strode to the woman checking off names in the hour-by-hour chart. "Germaine," he told her quietly.

When Germaine was out of earshot, Rivers noticed that the line held up a pretty steady pace of 10-15 people. So, he held up the line himself. "Sergeant," he addressed the woman checking names off in their boxes. "Why don't you set those papers on the pallet stack you're sitting on and let people check off their own names. They will recognize their own names faster, and you can come back every hour, on the hour, and make sure no box is left unticked for that hour."

The woman was already on her feet and setting the list on the pile of empty pallets. "I'll just add my name to the end, and get out there, sir."

"Just make sure you're back here on the hour to check the list." Rivers turned to the next person in line, an older man in an Australian officer's uniform—he wasn't sure what his rank was called, but he looked reliable—so he said. "You're her back up. I want you checking this list every hour on the hour too."

"Aye, Mate." He nodded and closed his eyes in a brief secondary affirmation.

Rivers addressed the rest of the line which had grown to 25 by then. "Keep passing the word as new people join the line, how to check yourself off the list."

After seeing nods all around, especially he was watching the last man in line, Rivers went to check on the third metal detector being set up to help move the security line a little faster. If even one in every eight people came to look for loved ones in a city of over 8 million people, he did the math in his head using a 6-second delay for a security pat down. It would take 34 days for a million people to move through with just the two metal detectors. Was that correct? His eyes widened. "I should have done the math earlier. This will not work."

Republican Palace Grounds
13 April 2003
4 PM

Just like all those ahead of him, Moe endured the rough pat-down by two Americans one after the other, and was finally pointed toward one of five metal detectors. He was glad to have finally made it to the front of the line. Albeit the pace had picked up suddenly to a steady walk a few hours ago. The soldiers had passed out water all day to everyone in line in the full sun. As the angle of the sun was only inches from dropping below the cityscape high-rises, the soldiers were now at work running electrical cords, generators and large lights around the perimeter and throughout the lines of corpses lying under white body bags. So many bags it looked like snow had fallen on Baghdad.

For the hordes of people in the area, it was quiet. The normal rustle of people moving was there, but words were whispered, save the occasional wail of identifying a family member among the orderly cord of people weaving back and forth among the grid of thousands of people laid nearly shoulder to shoulder, with only faces exposed above white shrouds.

It felt fitting to Moe, as he dared look upon each face, to be helping trample a path into the grass of the beautiful front lawn of the ousted, run-away king. The lawn where they had never been allowed to trod before. Even as a palace employee his ID had not allowed him inside the palace perimeter. Now, Presidential Palace mechanic and peasant alike filled the palace yard, while the palace was filled with American soldiers, not Iraqi tyrants.

Moe found himself looking as far ahead in the line as he could accurately identify as too-big-to-be-my-son, or a face as

529

not-his-wife's or not-his-daughters' faces. He pressed his fingers tightly into the little paper cards he had received at the metal detector. He turned the second corner with at least eight more lengthy rows to go by his count with none of his family in sight. The soldier had said the cards should be placed on the chest of the body with the person's full name and date of birth, and a contact name and address when a body was identified. Moe could still hear the instruction being repeated at the entry way. "If you know the approximate date of the last time the person was seen, please include that as well." The woman soldier had a way of speaking that imparted empathy and command presence at the same time. She repeated those same phrases in English and in Arabic over and over.

The repetition comforted somehow. Moe didn't feel he needed to use up the space in his mind to remember the instructions. He kept hoping he would not need them.

The lights snapped on and the buzzing of the lights and the generator overcame the woman's voice over an hour later. There were only three rows and he would be done. He hoped Takita had found his note and was okay by herself. He had not expected it to take so long.

Then there she was. Liliya's beauty still took his breath away.

He couldn't inhale. He opened his jaw wide to suck in breath, but it felt like a straw-sized opening in his chest. As he forced himself to lean over, all the air in his lungs was pushed out and a low moan accompanied them. Sorrow settled over him as their dreams of life as an old couple shattered before his eyes. He stepped out of line as he had seen so many others do, to place an identification card on a chest. He crouched between his Liliya's body and the stranger lying next to her.

He kissed his fingertips and smoothed her hair one last time. He would not be allowed to linger, he knew.

He penned her name slowly and left the card on her still chest. So still. "Good-bye, my love."

Moe pushed his fingers into the grass beside her to push himself up off the ground. The line of hopeful, dejected mourners opened up to receive him back to their ranks.

Numbness threatened his vision as he lumbered forward in the trench worn by thousands of feet in front of him. Thirty seconds later when familiar features snapped his head around on auto rotate, he realized he had not even been watching the faces of the dead. There was his firstborn.

He dropped his three remaining cards as he gasped and went to her. A hand squeezed his shoulder lightly and whispered a comfort in Arabic as she handed him his cards. Moe looked up. It was the kind watery eyes of the old woman who had let him back into the line moments earlier.

She stepped back into the line and disappeared while her words were still tangled in his mind. He couldn't seem to untangle anything.

The cards in his hand were not right. He shuffled the cards and dropped them again. It was a pen he needed. He patted his pockets. Aroosh. The name he and Liliya had argued over and chosen with care for the little girl who had made them parents, who had taught them what love really was, who had introduced them to the fullness of the love of their heavenly Father.

"You made me proud, my baby girl, every year of your life." He said as he laid the card now printed with her name on her body with the same care they had chosen her name. Aroosh had been found.

The grass was beginning to dew up. The cards felt thicker now and more flexible with the increase in evening humidity and the fans blowing over the ice added to it.

As Moe rose this time, he felt years older. He looked across Aroosh's body to see his middle child lying next to her sister in death. "Thank you, Lord, that she did not die alone." Such a crazy outpouring of thankfulness bubbled up in his heart. He swiped at the streams of tears flowing down his cheeks unashamedly.

He did not rejoin the line, but stepped across Aroosh's body to place the card with Rohi's name on her 13-year-old body. She had been afraid of the dark so much longer than either of the other two. But even the darkness of death had left no shadow of fear on her face. That fear had disappeared overnight when she asked Jesus to come into her heart when she was nine.

Moe turned and stretched his right knuckles back to graze Aroosh's cheek while cupping Rohi's chin in his left hand. "My daughters, Aroosh and Rohi, I release you once more back into the arms of Jesus for his safe keeping forevermore."

Moe touched each smooth nose one last time, then pushed his hands against his knees to stand and could not tell which was quivering more, his hands or his knees. The line absorbed him again so he could find his son.

Chapter Sixty Eight

Judah Wakefield jumped at the unexpected knock on the door and quick opening. Habit snapped the laptop lid closed immediately. Blinking several times to refocus her distance vision, CAPT George finally materialized.

She leaned against the chair back, yawning. "Haven't seen you in a little while."

"You haven't seen anybody in a little while. Days." George's mouth twisted down momentarily. "But I came to let you know, *Seren* Dayan is on her way back."

Wakefield reopened the lid, saved her place in the documents she had been translating. "It is about time. The third group has already come back, but never her."

"It is completed. They can't keep the bodies outside any longer. Apparently, it was getting pretty bad. They had removed identified bodies each night. I don't know if there was a mass grave or they released the bodies to the families or what. I didn't hear. But the clean-up is all that is left now. So she felt like her job was completed."

Wakefield stilled her hands. "She is going to be exhausted."

"Yeah. I thought you'd want to meet her as soon as she gets off the convoy."

533

"Of course," Wakefield scraped her chair back. Then she tossed her head in a little jerk toward the door.

George stepped all the way into the room and closed the door behind himself. "What have you found now?" He practically danced over the table.

"I really think this guy was insane." She shook her head and stood to gather her accumulated things. "It has to be Hussein's satchel. No one else would have access to such a range of information and official papers. The industries and ministries, ancient and brand-new papers. Some of those papers," she pointed to the large safe-cage in the corner that had been brought in to secure the evidence, "were printed the very day the SEALs took the Republican and Al Faw Palaces."

George wandered over and ran his fingers over the coated wire cage.

Judah rubbed her eyes and smoothed back her light hair. "Remember those drawings we put in the what-the-heck pile?"

She waited until George nodded and turned back to her. "They were land surveyor reports. Several different surveyors over the last three decades. And there were detailed archeologists' reports, going back even further." She waited a beat to deliver the location. "Hussein has been digging up ancient Babylon down to its foundations in order to rebuild it. He has poured billions of his oil-riches into it."

George's eyes and forehead wrinkled. "What? Why?"

"It is just a guess," Judah tucked her cover under her arm and picked up her laptop bag, "but I think, based on those genealogy lists going back ages and ages, Hussein thinks his family is a modern branch from King Nebuchadnezzar who once ruled ancient Babylon."

The captain scoffed. "What did he do? Contact ancestory.com?"

"It much more detailed than that, sir. He has DNA reports with some set of markers circled on about eight different reports, and he has a family tree. Well, it was a backward family tree that started with him at the top." She rolled her eyes.

George shook his head. "As he would."

"You ready to go?" she asked.

"Yeah, yeah. I'll walk with you." George followed her up the stairs and out the door toward the front gate where the next convoy drop off would be made.

As soon as they were out of Intel House and under the cloudy night sky, George began to ruminate more questions. "Where is anybody going to get a DNA sample from thousands of years ago to compare to?" He shook his head. "That's ludicrous."

"As I said," Judah agreed, "the guy is clearly obsessed with this place and this topic. I don't know how it has not been in our preliminary material that we used for his profile. He has kept it under wraps pretty well, so maybe insane was not the correct assessment. Because he is clearly in control."

"But what good is it?"

"Think about it. It'll come together." Judah gave him a moment, but then couldn't wait any longer. She could see the convoy headlights on the road. "An obsession this deep-seated and for this length of time—those surveys go back decades—he's not going to be able to control his need to go back, to revisit the place. In his exile, he will eventually try to sneak back to the site of ancient Babylon." Wakefield couldn't help but grin. "And we know exactly where it is and where its ancient boundaries are located."

George was still nodding, and his fingers tapped together as his brain processed, assessed, and began to formulate, when the first truckload of soldiers disembarked.

Ellie's exhausted face and disheveled hair were among them. All officers in the first load.

Minutes later she walked through the gate. Judah greeted her with a hug. "Welcome home."

Ellie sighed big. "Thanks. I think I'm really ready for home."

"You'll be happy to note that we updated your entry protocols while you were away."

They walked side by side, this time Judah leading a quarter step ahead, toward the female officers' quarters.

"I wondered about that. But not enough to care right now."

Wakefield patted her friend's shoulder. "The front gate team has been updated to include some officers that have the authority to point out people they recognize by face *and* name, not just face, and allow them entry with their valid IDs. It cut down the time tremendously for everyone, even those not ID'd had shorter lines to contend with."

Ellie just bobbed her head twice slowly as they plodded on.

At their billet, Wakefield threw the flap back and said, you grab some clothes and toiletries, I'm going ahead to clear the showers for you.

"Thanks, Judah." Ellie said. "But I think I'd rather just collapse right now. I'll shower in the morning." She trudged into the tent without looking back and began to unbutton her uniform on the way to her cot.

"Oh. All right." Judah shrugged. "I'm going to see if I can still get some dinner. Sleep well, my friend. I'm glad you're home."

Chapter Sixty Nine

Moe slammed the door on his truck. Everything was packed and secured now except their last-minute suitcases. He had walked out the three miles to where he had abandoned his vehicle when he walked to surrender himself to the American Army troops.

It was not too much worse for having been through a few weeks of war. A few more dents than he remembered. A lot more dust. He noticed it mostly around the door handles where his fingers had removed the thick layer of cement dust.

Back up the broken stairwell, skipping those missing stairs with a giant step and help from the bannister, for the last time to unlock the door to the home he had shared with his beloved. Even if he returned from this trip, eventually this building would be torn down. If there had been an intact government to regulate these things, it should have been condemned the first night. Every other family had moved out.

"Takita," he called out, "are you ready?" The girl came out of Aroosh and Rohi's bedroom wearing some of their western clothes. She hoisted Aroosh's backpack to her shoulder. Moe could see the seams straining from across the room. He smiled. He was glad that she could use some of the girls' clothes.

"Don't worry," she spoke before he could ask. "I have two more traditional sets of clothes with me," She gestured to the backpack. "And half a dozen scarfs too. I just don't relish being hot while we drive if I don't have to."

Moe frowned, but didn't press it. He hoped he would have time to see any trouble coming in time for her to put those more traditional clothes on in the truck as they traveled.

"Any calls?" he asked.

She shook her head and handed the small tiny-screened Nokia phone back to him. "It's charged."

He pressed a button to take him to the incoming calls list. Nothing since he had bought it from the guy hawking them outside the market on his second trip to stock up before they went to find Takita's family. He was pretty sure the guy had stolen it or picked it off a dead body in the street somewhere. But it wasn't like he could replace his phone legitimately. He shrugged and powered it down to conserve the battery before sliding it into the side pocket of his own backpack on the kitchen counter.

What to do about Missy Judah? Why had she not ever called him back for five days?

He slid open the drawer where Liliya kept paper and pens. He didn't know what he would say until the pen hit the paper, and he began to scratch out his tale of the last week in brief and his general plans for next. He signed his name and added his phone number. The heaviness on his heart lifted just the slightest bit as he reread his own pain on the paper all in one place. "No wonder I feel so exhausted all the time." He blew out his breath, wiped at his ever-tearful left eye, and folded the two sheets of paper in half, and wrote MISSY JUDAH on the front.

"Can you grab this last bottle of water too?" He handed it toward the girl who seemed to be handling the death of her family much better than he was handling his grief.

"Sure, should I fill it all the way up?" She walked toward the faucet.

"I've already turned the water and gas to the building off."

She tucked the two-liter bottle with four inches of missing liquid against her hip and kept walking toward the door.

Moe put the pen back in the drawer and swiped a dishrag over the countertop one last time. He tossed it in the sink and set the note up like a peak-y mountain on the clean counter.

Takita was on the landing one floor below as he pulled the door closed one last time. He took the key with him, but there was no point in locking the door. He would not be back.

"Good-bye, little home. Lord, lead on." He pressed his forehead into the door and his words washed back over him. Then he straightened up and trotted down the four stories to the ground.

FOB Beta
16 April 2003
1510 hours

At fifteen hundred hours, the next day Wakefield finally pushed away from her translation desk for a late lunch. She stopped by the tent to check on Ellie to see if she wanted to join her fieldtrip into Baghdad again after lunch. Ellie was still lightly snoring away, but Judah could see her brow furrowed and eyes tight in her dreams even from the doorway. "Lord, bless her with restorative sleep," Judah whispered.

Wakefield walked straight through the chow line with no line and no waiting. She swallowed hard as she saw the offerings: white-bread hot ham and cheese—not because it was grilled or steamed, but because it had been sitting at room temperature and the temperature was hot. Chips, wilty lettuce, and bug juice.

In the hall, she took the first seat she came to and choked down the sticky white-bread sandwich. "Note to self," she said as the bread stuck in her front teeth like glue, "don't work so long you miss cooked lunch again."

Half an hour later, after another quick stop at her quarters, Judah opened the Intel Office door in her full gear with Kevlar, CAPT George stood up from the table. "Where's Ellie?" he asked.

"She needs the sleep." Wakefield shrugged. "Look, I'm not worried. The address we have on Moe is on the edge of the Amil District, the Army cleared it days ago. The three-Humvee convoy will be fine. I'll get a couple of the soldiers to go in with me to check on him."

"Don't you get yourself lost again, Wakefield. I'll have to take one of your stripes for the inconvenience you cause me."

"It is not like I did it on purpose."

"Exactly. So no extra-curricular trips, Commander. None. You go straight there and straight back. I expect you back in three hours, with or without the man's family. Or a very good excuse which had better involve explosions or bullets. Do you get me?"

Wakefield had thought he was kidding at first, but the longer the captain talked the straighter her posture became. He was not kidding. "I will toe the line, sir."

"Dismissed."

It was the first time she remembered him addressing her formally. She would not disappoint him.

Chapter Seventy

H e could not stop rubbing the eight-day old stubble on his scalp. It itched like crazy. His insides itched too. He rubbed his ears and then his chest.

Saddam had watched the valley for most of the day longing for signs of life from his nation. He hated the close company he had to keep and all the noise they made. The second day on the run, Yazeen had connected up with Uday and Qusay and their wives and security details. It had almost been fun for those first two days. Saddam frowned. He also hated being exposed to the Kurdish people's hatred of him up here. Posters with his face marred with paint had been up in three different Kurdish villages they had passed through.

Not that their hatred was without cause, but, it was Qusay who had done all the recent damage to their population. That boy had no finesse. No thought toward hiding his vile nature, and it would be his undoing. If not for the Americans, or the Kurds, he might take him out himself.

Saddam whirled around from the south-facing doorway of the moldy hut where they had stopped for the day. He held his hands over his ears. It was still hours until it was finally time to move on again. He couldn't wait to get away from these boys even if his escape was a shockingly horrible old rattletrap car. "Shut up!" He bellowed and swore. "Just shut your idiot mouths and quit your arguing. You're both drunken fools who don't know anything." He crossed the small cabin in about ten steps which he stomped out menacingly.

The three women shrank back in the ratty sofas, but the boys still emphatically gestured in loud, slurred voices. Food stains adorned their fancy robes.

He lashed out with the heel of his right hand and punched the closer boy in the side of the head. "I said, shut your fool mouths. I can't stand the sound of you any longer."

"Hey!" It was Uday who had taken the brunt of his anger in the head and keeled over into the woman next to him on the sofa. But he did quiet down.

"Hey, nothing. If you two don't straighten up. I'll feed you to the Kurds myself."

Qusay sneered. "You are powerless up here. You have no army, no guards. Your own people hate you. You will never be king again." The elder prince's speech became less slurred as distain took the lead. "When a Hussein retakes the throne, it will be me who is ruling. I will see to that."

His son's eyes were little black slits.

"You and who else?" He challenged. "Who pays for your women, your security, your army?" Saddam threw an arm to gesture to the dozen armed inside-guardsmen standing as if ringed around a campfire, with them as the hot flame in the center. "Which of these men do you think will continue to follow your orders if the one who signs their paycheck gives an opposite order?"

When Saddam saw a fleck of fear cross Qusay's face he turned to the men. "Who do you work for?" He demanded of the bulky black-haired man standing closest to him.

"You, sir. I work for you first." He spit out nervously, staring beyond the back wall.

Technically Qusay did have his own business income and oil income from sources outside the palace. Saddam knew it; Qusay knew it. Which is why his face registered confusion. But Saddam had spent a lifetime convincing his people, his army, his nation that he was their supreme ruler. He was the one providing for them, and he was the one who offered them life or death when they followed his wishes.

"But. But." Qusay sputtered. "These men are mine. You men are mine."

"No." Saddam hissed. "No one will help you. You will be abandoned and alone. You both will have to live like rats in a hole in the ground until you die."

Saddam could feel power flicker out in his words as he cursed his sons. "One more outburst, one more argument, and I will leave you behind too."

It was very quiet then. Even the mountain wildlife had stopped their songs and run away. Saddam returned to the doorway. He leaned on the doorjamb and gazed toward the south, where his beloved Babylon lay just waiting for him to come back to the throne.

If it was the last thing he did, he would return to where he belonged.

Amil District of Baghdad
16 April 2003
1650 hours

"You ready?" Wakefield double checked her Kevlar's tightness while standing watchfully outside the middle Humvee. No incidents on the way into the city, made her more watchful now.

"Yes, ma'am." The convoy leader, U.S. Army Captain Chavers gave one last look at the perimeter guard posted around the convoy.

If all went according to plan, there was a seat in the convoy for each of Moe's family members back to the base. They would have to spread among the vehicles of course, but they would be safe.

Wakefield let her eyes drift up to the upper floors of the building at the address Moe had offered her. It had taken a glancing hit in the past few weeks. It was dark and several of the walls and windows, and lots of personal items were piled around the edges of the building where they had fallen after the missile strike. It did not look promising.

Wakefield swallowed and walked in formation with the five men who would accompany her inside. They each took the wide step one at a time where the stairs were missing.

"Is this place stable?" Wakefield heard one of the soldiers ask warily.

"Don't be such a worry wart, Campbell," someone else answered.

"We're going to the top floor." Wakefield reminded them. "If it collapses, at least we'll come down on top."

One of the soldiers chuckled. CPT Chavers shushed them all.

By the time they had climbed the four staircases, they had not seen or heard any human movement. "Is this the one, ma'am?" Chavers held up the paper he had with the address to compare it by Maglite to the handwritten apartment number on the doorbell.

"I believe so," Wakefield looked around in disappointment. This place felt long-ago abandoned. They couldn't be here. "Wait!" she touched the shoulder of one of the soldiers who had reversed his rifle to butt-first and was swinging it back to pound the door open at the handle level. "I have an invitation to be here. How about we try knocking first?" she asked.

The young man let out his breath as he lowered his makeshift battering ram.

Wakefield shouldered past him and rapped on the door. Ten seconds later she tried again and called out in Arabic, "Muhommad? Are you there?"

No answer, so she reached down and tried the knob. It twisted easily under her fingers and the door swung open.

"Now see, wasn't that better?" she asked.

The young man's head tilted. "Probably. But not as fun." He gave a half-frown half-smile.

CPT Chavers ordered, "Clear the flat."

Everyone entered the house and within twenty seconds all had reported "clear" and gathered back in the main room.

Wakefield stood in the circle with them, her arms bent to rest on her rifle barrel and stock, facing the small kitchen counter across the left wall as they had entered. That was when she saw it.

An A-3 sized sheet of paper tent-folded like a place-setting marker at a formal meal. Just larger. Her name was printed across the front.

"Get your guys out in case it is rigged to blow," she called out and dashed over to retrieve the paper. The Army escort obeyed her order without it being reiterated by their own chain of command.

It was probably fine, but seeing her name staring back at her reminded her that she really did not know Moe as well as she thought, and perhaps the whole relationship had been a set up.

She unfolded the paper to find a hand-written note that practically dissolved into the darkness as the last flashlight-bearing soldier left the room. She decided it would be better read it outside anyway.

Wakefield refolded the letter and traipsed down the stairwell after the clomping of heavy boots on concrete.

She leapt over the missing section of stairs and joined the convoy in the street. One of Moe's neighbors crossed the street calmly in front of them by half a block while she unfolded the letter again. The soldiers kept an eye on him, but he just looked back at them and continued on his way.

"Can you read that in the vehicle, ma'am?" Chavers asked.

Wakefield said, "You can go ahead and load them up," as held up her first finger while she scanned for any address without actually reading the content.

"No forwarding address," she said and looked up at Chavers. "Back to the base."

Disappointment weighed heavily on her. Had she been wrong about him? Where was he? Where was his wife and the children he had spoken of so fondly?

As soon as they reached the main highway and ring road back to their base, it was smooth enough and the threat seemed less, so she flicked on a borrowed Maglite and laid the letter on her lap to read it while shielding her hand over the front of the flashlight to keep it from interfering with the driver's sight.

The handwriting was a large hurried scrawl. And in English. That was nice of him to consider her when he was fleeing for his life.

> *Dear Missy Judah,*
>
> *I have called the number you gave several times. I hear not from you. I try to help by phoning information, but still I hear nothing. I wonder if I do not call right number, if I mix a number.*
>
> *My family is gone. The Special Republican Guard came two days after I was gone and took them away. I found their bodies with the others from the terror tunnels, but their souls are with Isa now. I am going away too. It is not your fault. I release you from your promise because it was made after my family was captured and probably dead.*
>
> *I found a young girl just about my girls' age who I can help, and we are going to see if any of her family is still alive. They live outside the city.*
>
> *I probably not see you again before heaven. So goodbye. Be gentle with my city that needs to know Isa's love.*
>
> *God bless you,*
> *Moses*

Judah pressed the button to extinguish the light, and refolded the letter and then folded it into a small rectangle that would fit into her pocket. She could feel his grief, his disappointment. She had let him down, and now his family was dead. She felt the tightness around her nose and stinging in her cheeks as tears welled up.

Yet something niggled at the back of her mind.

Chapter Seventy One

"Hello?" Judah Wakefield waved her hand in front of her face. She could see that Ellie had exited their conversation and was watching something over near the door of the chow tent.

Ellie glanced at her and then her eyes went back to whatever it was, this time over her left shoulder.

"What is so interesting?" Judah began to slowly twist around.

"The man who led the body-identification mission just walked in." Ellie whispered. "He actually listened to me."

Judah turned and Ellie's voice faded into the background as her eyes locked on David's. She fluttered her fingers at him and left her lunch on the table to go to him.

She walked straight into his arms and kissed him. "Am I ever glad to see you!" She smiled widely.

"I can tell." Rivers smiled and winked at her amid a few cat-calls and hooting from the lunch crowd.

She felt her face heating as she turned around. Ellie stood directly behind her. "Oh Ellie, I want you to meet David Rivers. He's my husband."

Ellie laughed. "Yeah, I got that sometime between the table and the kiss."

Judah tried to stop her blush and her grin, but could do neither. She looked back at her husband. "David, this is my friend, Ellie Dayan."

"We've met." He nodded and reached around her to shake Ellie's offered hand.

"You did a great job out there with the organization and the crowds," Ellie told him.

"I could not have done it without your help. I appreciated your experience and suggestions. And the way you helped comfort and calm people in line," David nodded as if he had been deeply moved. "It was beautiful for people who were in deep pain."

"Thank you, Commander. That is kind of you to say."

A group of men entered then and filtered around their little trio. "What do you say we move this little mutual admiration society out of the path?" Wakefield chuckled at the two of them. "Can you get some lunch and join us?"

"I am here for the rest of the day," he announced. "I've got a 1500 hours meeting with your base C.O., Brady Grady." He pointed at her. "But other than that, I'm yours. I'll come find you. Go eat while it is hot." He leaned in to peck her lips before jutting his chin toward her food tray and taking a step toward the chow line. "Go on."

Judah took her first deep breath in days. She stood watching him move up in the line until Ellie pushed her shoulder forward. "Get it together, girl. He's gonna think you like him or something." She laughed. "Come on, let's eat."

Judah tittered too as she followed her friend back to their table and sat back down on the bench while Ellie went around to her side of the table.

"I can't even remember what we were talking about," Judah admitted. "I feel so fluttery. What a girl!" She rolled her eyes at her own feminine response to David's unexpected presence.

Ellie smiled at her and fluffed up her dark curls with both hands before picking up her fork again. "We were talking about Moe's sudden departure. What was it that had you going on about his note?"

"Oh, I think it was the beginning where he talked about calling so many times. Where is the record? The messages?"

"Well, he couldn't have had the wrong number. Because we did get that one message about the look-alikes. It was a little late, but it proves he memorized the correct number."

Wakefield saw Ellie shrug and take a bite. Out of the corner of her eye Judah kept tabs on David's progress through the line. Now getting his drink. He would get water, she knew. It didn't matter what was available, he always preferred water.

"Do you think it could be related to the other investigation?" She heard Ellie ask.

"I suppose."

"Do you think you could be any more distracted?"

"I don't suppose." Wakefield closed her mouth in a teasing smile and glanced over at her friend. "I am listening, but my heart is over there walking toward us." She forced herself to concentrate on Ellie's question. "Here is what is kind of stirring up in me since Moe's letter," she said, thinking there were probably better places to put her thoughts to air. "I think we have stumbled into something pretty big, well, maybe smaller than big, but bigger than we thought with our midnight investigation of a—" she stopped and mouthed the word *leak*. "I think we are at the very beginning of something here, not the end. And I plan to see it through. And I hope you'll be around to help me."

Ellie nodded slowly, assessing. "My assignment rotation is almost over. But I will see what I can do. I know Dov is heading back to Tel Aviv in three days, and I am scheduled for two days after that, just as soon as our replacements arrive. I don't mind sticking around, but I'll have to run it up the chain."

Rivers slid his tray down next to hers and squeezed her shoulders, so tight under the thick uniform. But she felt the warmth and weight of his hands on her skin. "What do you have to run up the chain?" he asked, easily jumping into the conversation.

Ellie shot her a quick look for permission, and she gave the quickest of nods. "I want to stick around here for a little while after my initial assignment is complete."

Rivers nodded and squeezed the nape of Judah's neck sending a chill up her back. "I'd be happy to write a letter or something if you need support. I was going to write to your C.O., or country or something—okay, I hadn't gotten as far as an address yet in my thinking—anyway, I wanted to say what a help you were over the last almost week."

Ellie smiled, and Judah thought she detected a hint of a blush in her olive features. "I'll get you the address," was all she said.

Then she heard something. Judah squinted her eyes and leaned toward the tabletop to hear better. Rivers wiggled on the bench next to her. A meowing was getting loud enough for Ellie to ask, "Where is that coming from?"

Rivers pinched off a piece of his fish lunch, and Wakefield heard the trsschht of his Velcro pocket opening. "That is Judah's present in my pocket." He put a fishy finger to his pursed lips to let her in on their secret and grimaced as he inhaled. "Now I'm probably going to smell like fish for the rest of the day."

"I like fish." Judah smiled and reached under the table to scratch Butter under his chin with her forearm resting on Rivers' knee.

Intel House
17 April 2003
1616 hours

Rivers stuck his head in the front door of the Intelligence House where his wife worked and said, "Is this the knocking kind of door?"

"Nah. We let just about anybody come wandering in." A man with Navy captain's oak leaves on his shoulders stood behind a mound of paperwork he was passing over to a lieutenant (j.g.) one signature at a time. "I'm Captain George, what can we do for you, Lieutenant Commander?"

"I'm Wakefield's husband. I came to see if I can have her a few hours early today."

"Oh, Rivers. It is nice to meet you." George looked at his yeoman and said, "We'll finish up later." He walked over with his hand outstretched.

Rivers clasped hands to a firm grip.

"I don't see why that couldn't happen. She is in the middle of an interview right now." The captain glanced at his watch. "Be about another 12, 13 minutes. That woman is like clockwork. Well, except when she got herself lost. Heard you were the one to bring her back to us. Thank you."

Rivers made a sound in the back of his throat. "I think that was more for my benefit than yours. But you're welcome."

"You want to come down and watch her work-over a suspect? It is a work of art, those two."

"Sure," Rivers shrugged. "I've have never actually watched her in a formal setting. Strange," he said as he followed George past a pair of Army guards and down some stairs. "You've just married, right?" George asked still moving forward.

"Yes, sir."

"You're the one who went on his honeymoon alone?"

Rivers groaned. "That story has spread across the entire Navy now? It may have started as a honeymoon, but it was just a diving trip when the bride flew out. Did they mention that she made the front page of the *Washington Post*?"

"No. Still not worth the trade off in my opinion."

"Mine either. But we live to serve." Rivers shrugged. There were parts of Navy life that could not be controlled.

"Well, you'll be discovering new things and first times for years. And then she'll go and change things up, and it will be fresh discoveries all over again." George turned when he got to the landing in a low-ceilinged semi-dark basement. "After 23 years of marriage I still find myself amazed at how much I don't know about who my wife is and how she thinks."

"Sounds exciting, sir." Rivers smiled while looking past George at the interview room's one-way glass set up with recording equipment in a central hub.

"Come on, she is set up in Interrogation D."

Rivers stooped his shoulders a bit in the short basement. A guy wearing a headset surrounded by stacks of black boxy equipment and bathed in a blue computer-screen glow nodded a quick acknowledgment of his presence.

David stood near the sound man's table and looked in at Judah in her element. It was much brighter in the interrogation rooms he noticed. The light glinted off Judah's hair giving it a golden ball appearance in the tight, low bun she wore today.

He watched the way she moved, the way she interacted with Ellie, the way she watched the man while Ellie relayed the translation he knew she didn't need. From the angle at which she sat at the table, he could see she had a pen on her clipboard, but she never reached for it, never fiddled with the paper. He stretched left to glimpse her list of questions over her shoulder only to find the paper was blank. She was slow and methodical, her posture only expressing boredom.

"Better make sure she never has to interrogate you, Commander." George whispered in the uncannily quiet room for all the interviewing going on around them.

"Top priority, sir." Rivers nodded. Judah had stood to her feet, and Rivers heard her knock on the door for the guard to open it.

After the man had been cuffed and led away, the two ladies conferred for another minute behind a closed door. Ellie walked out first. Rivers moved around the corner to meet them. When Ellie saw him, she stepped to the side, out of Judah's line of sight, and cleared her throat.

Judah looked up, and he knew exactly the moment she saw him, for her face lit up. He hoped he could always put that expression on her features.

"I'll take care of the write-up." Ellie said as she took the blank clipboard and pen from Judah. "I think your prince has come to sweep you away."

"Want to go for a walk?" he asked.

To her credit, she looked at her C.O. for permission before nodding and taking his arm. George was crooking his pointer finger for Ellie to come back when he nodded to Judah.

"The airfield is the only place to get any privacy around here," she announced as if she had needed that space before. It reminded him that they had so much catching up to do. But he had other priorities today.

They walked in contented silence, holding hands, as she led him toward the airfield access point behind the little village street where she worked. He wondered what had happened to the former villagers.

"You are so good at your job," he broke the silence first. "George let me watch your interrogation for the last quarter hour or so."

"You really think so?" Her voice sounded unlike her normal self-assured timbre. "I've had so many second thoughts about my abilities here, under these pressures and conditions, especially the sleep deprivation." She was shaking her head when he looked over at her.

He slipped his hand out of hers and pulled her into his side as they walked. "I am very sure. I assess situations for a living, and you are doing well. George depends on you, too. He could probably be convinced that you hung the moon."

She laughed a little at that.

"How is your alone-time going?" he asked.

She just shook her head. "This is as close to it as I've seen since I left the wedding. Well, except for when I was waiting on the rooftop for a ride back to base. Oh, and when I was still on the ship, I found a supply closet every once in a while. Oh my!" She gasped. "I never got to tell you about the captain, the X.O., and that huge investigation right after I deployed. It was crazy."

He pulled her close again and kissed the top of her head. "Tell me all about it when we get home."

He felt her sigh as they completed their first lap and began around again. "When do you suppose that will be?" she asked.

"It is going to be a long war."

"Yeah. I've talked to too many people and seen too many things to think anything less either."

"Well, that's one of the things I wanted to talk about," he said. He felt her look up at him expectantly.

"The Teams are seeing the longevity of the coming war too. The politics, the religion, the pure stubbornness of this region." He shook his head. "We are going to be leaving a large team in place on the ground here. We will be asking for more funding for assets on the ground and equipment and personnel with data assessment, electronic skills, and we are hoping for drones too. But the dollar signs stuff is above my pay grade.

"However, the training and enacting protocols that will keep our guys safe, that is what I do."

"It is what you were made for." Judah agreed. She squeezed his waist tightly.

"I had it in the back of my mind to recruit you for the back-seat assessment team, but now," he sighed, "I see how good you are at what you are doing. And you are so needed here."

"Well, maybe someday."

He stopped and she pulled ahead of him as she kept walking at pace. "You'd consider it?" he asked.

She turned back to him. "Sure. Why not? It sounds intriguing. I'd get a front row seat to watch ops and offer real time help in assessing targets and locations."

"That is exactly why I'd want you on my team. You knew what was involved without me even spelling out the details." He was quiet a minute while he decided what to tell her. "We've had some issues identifying who were terrorists and who were civilians in some of our forced entries."

"I can see how that would be difficult. And worrisome." She tucked herself back into his side as if she had always been there, and they continued walking together.

"It is." He felt a weight lift at sharing the burden.

"We have a pretty bad intelligence leak somewhere in our office," she admitted. "Ellie, George, and I are investigating from midnight to four AM most nights and still have not been able to narrow the pool of suspects decently."

"Oh." That was bad. "I'll make sure not to send anything through this base for the time being. I'm glad we didn't have any of our Teams working through here the Saddam round up night. We didn't get him, but it was not due to leaked intel. At least I don't think it was."

"I'm pretty sure the thousand sorties flown per day for two weeks kind of gave it away that you were coming," she teased.

He laughed with her, though most of those had been finished by the time he and the SEAL Teams had arrived. "So, I am going to take the first shift in country. I am planning to set up our tours in three-month rotations. Three months in the field, and six to nine months at home on other duty."

"So you'll be home before me? That would work well. As long as we have some time together outside this pressure cooker of Iraq."

"It will probably be late July. Our three months won't start with time served, but after I get the plan approved. You still ship home September 8th?"

"As far as I've heard, I'm still on a six-month deployment even though I have changed locations." She slowed their pace and stopped him giving him a knowing look. "I want this to be a real marriage."

"You don't know how much I want a real marriage." He pulled her to him and let his kiss speak for itself.

When he pulled back, her smile was sweet and her face serene with her eyes closed. "We'll get there." She leaned her forehead into his shoulder. "There are a couple of things our nation needs us for. God, I ask that you strengthen our focus on you and the jobs we need to accomplish over here."

He loved how she just dropped into prayer. "Give us wisdom as we lead others and search out the truth, and an easy adjustment when we get home," he added. When they finished praying for each other the sunset was well over, and they had probably trapesed ten miles in laps around the airfield.

"I have to catch a ride back now," he hated the words.

She sighed. "I figured it was coming soon." She sounded tired.

A figure appeared around the edge of airfield shack. He recognized the waving-arm mannerism as *Seren* Dayan.

"It's Ellie." Judah flinched in his hold. "I wonder what's wrong now."

Ellie was motioning them closer now, even as she headed toward them at a quick clip.

When they were only 15 feet apart, Rivers caught a little smirk in Ellie's cheeks as she repeated toward Judah the same little come-here gesture CAPT George had made earlier in the basement, and then she began a series of long whispered comments in Judah's ear.

Unfortunately, the two women stood so David could not see his wife's face, just the slight stoop in her posture to reach to Ellie's height.

Judah stifled a high sound in her throat that was a cross between an affirmation and a giggle. Ellie pressed a SatFone into her hand which she dropped into her BDU's thigh pocket.

The two heads separated, and Ellie gave a little good-bye wave without a single word to him.

Then the little come-here gesture was pointed at him. Judah was grinning, and she took off at a trot.

What was she playing at? He was going to miss his ground transport at the front gate back to Liberty FOB in a few minutes.

When she disappeared around the corner without even looking back, Rivers sighed with a smile, "that woman!" and chased after her.

Judah heard the familiar tread of her husband's heavy footfalls behind her and picked up speed. This was going to be fun.

She could hear David calling her name behind her, but she just swung her right arm in a forward windmill to keep him following her.

The newest load of temporary housing trailers was stacked in the south side of the FOB just as Ellie had described, three across and five deep. Judah continued jogging down the length of the trailers and slowed to make a sharp left on the last row.

"Where in the world are you going, Judah? Come on, I've got to get back to my men."

"Just a little further," she turned to throw him a smile. She could now see the paper on the second of the three doors that Ellie had said would be the identifying marker to look for.

A set of wooden-plank stairs had been placed in front of the temporary barracks door, and Judah mounted them and turned to face her husband her breath coming in little huffs. Her heart beating fast.

As she looked at his confused face from above, while her body blocked the sign from his view, she reached out for his hand and he grasped her fingers with such familiarity. "I'm sorry Judah, I really am going to have to run to make it back to the gate before they leave without me."

"You really think the petty officer is going to leave without the lieutenant commander SEAL he was sent to drive?" Judah teased him while tugging on his fingers with her left hand and drawing him to step up on the first step.

She bent at the waist and kissed his lips while her right hand slipped beneath his stiff uniform collar and circled his warm neck.

"Actually the transport left without you about half an hour ago, according to Ellie."

"What? Why would they do that?"

"Apparently, you have been assigned TAD to FOB Beta tonight. My C.O. cleared it with your base commander, O'Reilly, I believe Ellie said."

"I don't understand." David said slowly in the darkening shadows between the rows of housing yet to be delivered to their resting places in the main tent city.

"She sent the SatFone in case of an emergency for either of us, but you can feel free to verify your orders." Judah shrugged. She could feel a smile tugging at her cheeks as she pulled away to reach for the phone, wondering how long it would take an astute SEAL to recognize they were being set up.

And she, for one, didn't care one bit at her colleagues' intrusion into her personal life. She'd been waiting for this day an eternity, even if it was making an appearance with no notice.

As Judah pulled the phone from her thigh pocket to hand to her husband, she stepped away from the hand-written sign on the trailer door.

MARRIED OFFICERS' QUARTERS

She watched his eyes tighten and then widen, and she knew he had read it.

"You still need to call O'Reilly?" Judah asked, cupping his stubbled jaw in her palm. She could see an unfamiliar indecision in his eyes as he stood mute and blood throbbed through his throat visibly.

She released his fingers and reached behind her to twist open the knob.

"I—but what about my men?" David whispered. "I have not even let them call their wives since we deployed." His head swiveled back and forth, even as he leaned toward her with his whole being. "How—um, how can I?"

Judah stepped backward from the step and over the threshold. "How can you what?" she whispered just as softly.

"Enjoy you like this?"

"What's the hold up? What are you thinking?"

David's eyes closed. "Every time I have deployed, I've cut off contact with whomever I was dating, and now with you too, because I hear the scripture circling around in my brain, 'It was the time of year when kings go to war.' You know from the time when David stayed home and ended up with Bathsheba because he was in the wrong place and the wrong time and then ended up murdering someone."

Judah could see her husband's breathlessness as duty versus desire raged.

"You may be my white knight, but you are not King David. No matter how strong your leadership gifting and having the

561

same name, dear husband. And you *are* at war. You are here. I am here, in this war zone. We are not neglecting our duty. And we have the SatFone for an emergency." Judah took another backward step into the room. "It's time," she said simply, and blinked slowly to steady her breath. It was past time.

When she allowed her eyes to flutter open, David stood on the top step reaching toward her.

"I *have* heard that the best advice is to listen to your wife's advice," he said. "And in that case," his hands caressed her shoulders to her wrists before grasping both hands and tugging her back across the threshold toward the top step, "we are going to do this right."

Judah's balance had been shifting between feet when he pulled her toward him, and she stumbled into his chest. "Hmm?" she asked as he kissed her to breathlessness and then pulled away.

Suddenly, Judah gasped, and her eyes flew open as one of David's arms came fully around her shoulders and the other scooped under her knees and she was no longer vertical.

A bubble of delight rose from below her stomach to her throat as she dangled in her husband's strength, and she laughed out loud.

David carried her inside, where a half dozen flashlights lined the walls and were turned up to reflect off the white ceiling. "Not quite the candlelight and canopy bed you planned in the Caymans, but it the nicest bunkhouse I've seen in a warzone.

"I can't see." Judah wiggled in David's hold, trying to turn around. He held her tighter against the squirming. "Why don't you get the door instead, wife? We'll have plenty of time to explore new surroundings in a minute." He pulled her head closer to his to kiss her again.

Judah maneuvered the door with her feet, and gave a nice kick. The door thumped closed and she heard the metal handle engage.

FOB Beta Baghdad
Married Officers' "Housing"
18 April 2003
0525

David rolled over in the small bed that had been set up for them. Ellie had put a lot of fast effort into transforming their little hideaway.

"It's not time for you to go is it?" Judah mumbled. "Just a few more minutes, surely."

"I have a 0630 meeting set up for my guys. I can't miss it." He sighed and pulled her into his warmth. "But I really don't want to go. I've only been married for a couple of hours," David said, "and now I stink at being single."

Judah pulled up their twisted wrists and mass of fingers to find her watch. "I'd say we are at almost 12 hours of married face-time now."

"I don't know how the next 12 will come about, but I'm sure they will be worth the wait."

To be continued...